TICKLING T

Ruth Brandon is the author of a number of innovative and highly acclaimed biographies, including *The Spiritualists, The New Women and the Old Men, Being Divine: A Biography of Sarah Bernhardt* and *The Life and Many Deaths of Harry Houdini.* She has also written four detective stories. *Tickling the Dragon* is her first mainstream novel.

BY RUTH BRANDON

Non-Fiction

Singer And The Sewing Machine: A Capitalist Romance
The Dollar Princesses
The Spiritualists
The Burning Question
The New Women And The Old Men
Being Divine: A Biography Of Sarah Bernhardt
The Life And Many Deaths Of Harry Houdini

Fiction

Left, Right And Centre
Out Of Body, Out Of Mind
Mind Out
The Gorgon's Smile
Tickling The Dragon

Ruth Brandon

TICKLING THE DRAGON

VINTAGE

Published by Vintage 1996

2 4 6 8 10 9 7 5 3 1

Copyright © Ruth Brandon 1995

The right of Ruth Brandon to be identified as the author
of this work has been asserted by her in accordance with
the Copyright, Designs and Patents Act, 1988

First published in Great Britain by
Jonathan Cape Ltd, 1995

Vintage
Random House, 20 Vauxhall Bridge Road,
London SW1V 2SA

Random House Australia (Pty) Limited
20 Alfred Street, Milsons Point, Sydney
New South Wales 2061, Australia

Random House New Zealand Limited
18 Poland Road, Glenfield,
Auckland 10, New Zealand

Random House South Africa (Pty) Limited
PO Box 2263, Rosebank 2121, South Africa

Random House UK Limited Reg. No. 954009

A CIP catalogue record for this book
is available from the British Library

ISBN 0 09 959311 4

Papers used by Random House UK Ltd are natural,
recyclable products made from wood grown in sustain-
able forests. The manufacturing processes conform to the
environmental regulations of the country of origin

Printed and bound in Great Britain by
Cox & Wyman, Reading, Berkshire

in fond memory of Diana Vincent-Daviss
1943–1993

AUTHOR'S NOTE

In order to construct the atomic bomb, it was necessary to find how much uranium was needed to produce a self-sustaining chain reaction. The metal was available in small cubes. Time was short at Los Alamos, and corners were cut. The experimenters assembled near-critical masses by hand, adding cube after cube. The geiger counter's ticking warned when criticality approached.

These experiments were known as 'tickling the dragon's tail'. One false move – one cube too many, one slip of the hand – could be fatal. Inevitably, accidents happened. In the course of these experiments, two men died.

I have received a great deal of help with this book. I should especially like to thank: Catherine Storr and Dr Gabor Levy for light on Martian history; Richard Norton-Taylor for insights into the workings of the Freedom of Information Act; Mike MccGwire for directions in the strategic studies maze; Prof. Joseph Rotblat; Nick Humphrey and Philip Steadman for Peace Movement materials and bibliographic contributions; Jan Marsh, Anna Benson Gyles, and, perhaps more than anyone, my ever-patient agent, Caradoc King, without whose constant encouragement I should never have attempted this.

Extracts from Lawrence Badash, Joseph O. Hirschfelder and Herbert P. Broida (eds), *Reminiscences of Los Alamos* (Reidel, Dordrecht & Boston, 1980), are reprinted by permission of Kluwer Academic Publishers.

CONTENTS

1 Memorial   1
2 Budapest   25
3 Bettina   41
4 Fission   70
5 The City on the Hill   89
6 6 August 1945   112
7 Snapshots 1946–1954   126
8 We All Sit Down   149
9 Relations   177
10 Boys and Their Toys   214
11 Potlatch   246
12 I'll Show You if You Show Me   273

CHAPTER I   MEMORIAL

WHEN I DIE, I want to be scattered. Bonemeal, dried blood, hoof and horn. No clergy, no tombstone, no platitudes. But this is not my funeral. Uncle Zigi has beaten me to it. A grand old man, a public figure. Dead or alive, not one to shun recognition. Zigi is not a candidate for scattering.

Even a funeral is not enough. Who's going to come all the way to Bushey? Only family and perhaps a few close friends. His wider public has demanded a memorial service. But where? His favourite restaurant? Too expensive. The House of Commons crypt? But he never made it to the Commons (can one imagine him being polite to selection committees?). Nor was he ever elevated to the Lords. Lord von Fischer: the name doesn't exactly trip off the tongue. But nor do a number of others that come to mind. Unfortunately he never caught the prime ministerial eye, or not in the right way. So that's out. Churches, cathedrals, chapels, mosques, all excluded on religious grounds. Synagogues, ditto. In Zigi's view, religion – any religion, all religion – was the root of all evil. Thinking with the gut, he called it. – You'd better think with my gut or I shit on you. So what are brains for? I'll tell you, my dear Miriam. Religion comes in, brains march out the door. Never trust a religious man. And I never have.

That only left one place: Conway Hall, home of lost causes and the South Place Ethical Society. I like Conway Hall. It embodies the immoderation of rationalism. Last time I was here, an Indian sage was giving a magic show. He was demonstrating tricks used by soi-disant prophets of the subcontinent to prove their prophethood and thus collect mountains of rupees from eager followers. He had a long white beard. He set fire to it, and when the flames were extinguished remained as bearded as before – just a little yellow around the edges. He told us how to do it but I never tried, and now I've forgotten. Bang goes a fortune.

No one else has arrived yet. It's only three o'clock, and the party doesn't start till four. Nothing but rows of chairs, dust, and painstakingly worked commemorative plaques in the arts and crafts style favoured by late nineteenth-century rationalists. I see they've got the piano up on the stage as I requested. I've had to organise all this. Fania's getting on now – eighty-three this year – and she feels she has a right to make the most of the time remaining to her. So she chose the programme, and then got back to her painting while I dealt with the boring details – booking the hall, arranging readers.

At least the music was no problem. Susanna, my eldest daughter, is a cellist. She and some of her friends will play for us. Zigi's musical taste tended to the Austria-Hungary of his youth. Schubert's Death and the Maiden quartet: the variations from the second movement. Part of the Beethoven cello and piano sonata Susanna and Zigi used to play together. And send them out cheerful with more Schubert: the rondo from the Gipsy trio. Fine. But what to put in between?

Fania insisted on starting with chapter 6 of Revelation, the one where the Lamb opens the seven seals and the Four Horsemen of the Apocalypse are revealed.

You can't do it, I said.

And why not? she said. What was Zigi's life about? The apocalypse. From beginning to end. So it's the wrong religion. For Zigi, what religion was the right religion, may I ask? That funeral, for instance? You know why we had that funeral?

Because Uncle Harry made the arrangements.

She shrugged. – Why always be fighting with the family? We disagree. But they're family, after all. At my age you need all the family you can get. They won't come to this anyway, so they won't be there to be offended.

The last family funeral I went to was my parents'. This one only showed how much time had passed since then.

At my parents' funeral, we had a full turnout of aunts,

uncles and cousins. The aunts and uncles were that age which they assume at the day of one's birth, remaining there, unchanging, for the next thirty years. No longer. Of that generation, only Bessie, Rivvy and Harry made it to Zigi's. And they were old. Wrinkled, shrivelled, shrunken. The rest, presumably, are dead. It was my parents who used to keep me abreast of these things. Only Uncle Harry looked the same in his bowler and well-cut lawyer's coat. Otherwise, rust and moth. Why was I shocked? It was only to be expected. I shouldn't have been surprised. What was I then – nineteen? Rose's age, I was going to say, but she's already twenty-two. And I'm forty-seven. An aunt's age. I look in the mirror, and what do I see? A familiar face. My mother's. Why are people so bothered about life after death when the proof of immortality is there, dancing in front of our noses, every day of our lives? This isn't the first time I have met my mother since her death. She was constantly with me when I was feeding Susanna. There, at my breast, gently snuffling – my mother. Could I mistake that line of the cheekbone, that set of the eye?

So the generations come and go. Funerals, however, are unchanging. Into the earth, and on with the next. The rabbi still wore wellingtons. And the box. At my parents' funeral I couldn't take my eyes off the two boxes, lying there. Inside there? My *parents*? I wanted to rip off the lids to make sure. Uncle Zigi's was bigger. He was a big man, six foot two and broad. When he got old he stooped a bit, but not much. The rabbi mumbled a few prayers, alternating Hebrew and English. My uncles and cousins bowed and muttered. We trooped out and paddled towards the grave. The rabbi in his wellingtons surged ahead. When we got there, uncles and cousins began shovelling in the clayey mud, passing the spade from man to man. None of your prissy symbolic handfuls of earth in a Jewish funeral. Spadeful after spadeful thudded down. It was drizzling. I held an umbrella, my stupid little red umbrella, over my shrunken Aunty Bessie. Men age better than women, in my family at least.

Except Fania, that is. In this as in everything else, she breaks the rule. Here she is now. She always favoured a dramatic presentation, and today is no exception. She is wearing a long black cape lined with red satin, a black cashmere dress, red cossack boots. Comfort with style. A black fur hat perched on her chignon. Fania likes hats: they give her a few more inches. Her hair was always black; as her fifties led into her sixties, it got blacker and blacker. Now she has relaxed back into iron grey, which suits her better. Scarlet lipstick meticulously applied. No smudging for Fania, no inadvertently scarlet old lady's teeth. We hug each other. She looks me up and down. I am wearing my non-vegetarian curly lamb coat. Dark brown curls to match my hair. I eat the inside, so why not wear the outside? It's my favourite coat. But I shall never have Fania's style. Even at eighty-three she can kill most other women stone dead.

Darling, it was so kind of you to get all this organised. Do you know who's coming?

Who isn't?

They're starting to arrive now. Fania is soon surrounded. Her red lipstick wears thin, deposited on cheeks around the room. A couple of Zigi's old friends from Hungary, André Harkanyi and George Frenkl, sit her down firmly between them. André is an economist, George a writer. They address each other, as always, in English. George's writing, unlike his voice, has no trace of accent. Zigi's friends' gatherings were always a buzz of strongly accented English. Only in extremis would a speaker lapse into German or Hungarian. Never Yiddish. That was the language of Fania's clan. Not only did they not speak it, they actively resisted it: they disliked its mode. Gallows humour, sly underdog wit, was not their style. (And yet, were they so far removed from it? Yiddish contains not a single term that refers to active sports, but twenty words for different types of fool. It's as good a summary as any of their approach to life.)

Susanna and her friends arrive with their various instruments. Just in time: it's already ten to four. Susanna was shaken by Zigi's death. They were very close – closer than you might have expected, given the difference in age. In some ways, especially in the last few years, she seemed to feel easier

4

with him than with either Tony or me. They sought each other out, took pleasure in each other's company. Tony didn't like it all that much: he and Zigi never really got on. He kept saying: She'll tire him. Or: Off to Zigi's again? What on earth d'you find to do there all the time? – Stop nagging me, she said. I'm grown up now, remember? What d'you think we do? I enjoy his company. He's an interesting man.

They played a lot of music, of course. That was a great bond. And she gave him some secretarial help – not that Susanna's secretarial skills are anything to write home about. Perhaps he was telling her the story of his life – the unedited version. I didn't ask.

Fania is surrounded. Susanna says: Maybe we'd better just get set up. I'll say hello to her later. The relief is evident. Susanna has never felt easy with Fania, the way she did with Zigi. She doesn't think Fania likes her. I tell her this is nonsense. But there is no denying a certain constraint. Rose, on the other hand, my younger daughter, quite simply adores her. Fania is the grandmother she would otherwise have been denied. There were Tony's parents, of course, but when did we ever see them? Rose used to visit them in Shropshire, but Susanna never liked it there – she's allergic to dogs, or so she said – and the visits tailed off. Rose always rather hero-worshipped Susanna, and in the end even the prospect of ponies wasn't enough to tempt her into going to Shropshire by herself. They were disappointed, naturally. Another black mark in our copybook. Rose won't be coming today. She's up in Edinburgh, in her last year at the university, and her life is filled with pressing engagements.

There are five of them on the platform: two violins, a viola, cello and pianist. They tune up, then the string players launch into Death and the Maiden. The buzz of chatter ceases. Suddenly Zigi's death becomes real to me. I hope to God my mascara is waterproof. Never wear mascara on occasions of this sort. I find the sight of Susanna up there almost unbearable. I fumble for a tissue. Tony, who is sitting beside me, squeezes my hand. As so often these days, we are more at ease when not alone together. I feel close to him today, closer than for a long time. This makes me cry even harder.

The music finishes. Eddie Angell, one of Zigi's colleagues, is to read the piece from Revelation. I notice a pair of cousins exchanging significant glances. They are the family's sole representatives today, and they are no doubt congratulating themselves on dissuading their mother (my Aunty Bessie) from attending. One is an accountant, one is a solicitor. I can never remember which is which. When I was in my teens they were gay dogs, or so it seemed to me then. Now they have three-piece suits and little paunches. They live in Stanmore and vote Conservative. I sometimes consult them profession-ally. They are rather inefficient. Each time I tell myself: next time, I must find someone else. But they are kind, and I don't.

Eddie puts on his half-moon spectacles and finds his place. His sweet, intelligent face is uncharacteristically grave. He and Zigi were colleagues for thirty years. Eddie Angell was one of the few people Zigi really loved. He is describing how the captains and the kings begged the rocks to fall on them and hide them from the wrath of the Lamb. I think about how Dr T. would enjoy this occasion. He won, at least in a way: he can dance on Zigi's grave. Each fighting to nullify the other's work. Should we have invited him? Hardly practical. Who would come all the way from California for an occasion such as this? Anyhow, what need is there for his actual physical presence? Dr T. is with us in spirit. What does this chapter of Revelation describe if not the work to which he has been devoting himself for the past half-century? *And the heaven departed as a scroll when it is rolled together; and every mountain and island were moved out of their places.*

Eddie gives a beatific smile over his glasses and steps down. George Frenkl takes his place. He is to talk about Zigi, whom he has known all his life. They were at school together – that school which produced half the physicists, economists, movers and shakers of the Western world, or so it sometimes seems. Including, of course, Dr T. As George unfurls his anecdotes, I try and picture them all there. A classroom full of boys climbing on desks and throwing ink pellets. The difference between them and every other classroom full of boys being that, in fifty years' time, this lot will be running the world – everywhere *except* Budapest. Trying to keep it together or (in Dr T.'s case) to blow it to bits.

George stops, and Susanna and the pianist begin the Beethoven. I watch my daughter's face. She is intent, enclosed in her cocoon of music. Music is her refuge. Susanna does not find life simple, she does not take it easily. Not like Rose, who waltzes through without a care. People find this surprising, this difference. Susanna's had all Rose's advantages, hasn't she? And more. Nature has showered her with gifts. She's more talented than Rose, better-looking. What more does she want? I shrug, I raise my eyes to heaven – What can one do? Children are so different. I'm lying of course. I know exactly what she wants. But I can't give it to her, because it's still not mine to give. She senses this holding-back, naturally; and resents it. It's always there, lurking between us.

Secrets, secrets. I sometimes feel that secrets will tear me in two. I look around my friends and family, sometimes, and wonder. Is it just me? Everyone seems so normal, so controlled, so exactly as they always are. Don't they have secrets? Are they as they seem or are they like me, thinking: If you only knew? If you only *knew*.

Glancing around, I notice Bella in a seat near the back. Bella! What's she doing here? Wasn't that husband of hers promoted to the Cabinet the other day? She ought to be careful. Surely it wouldn't do him any good if his wife was known to keep this sort of company? Uncle Zigi was seriously hated by Bella's husband. She told me herself, that time I met her in Peter Jones, in 1983, was it? Zigi knew, of course. There was that odd complicity between them: they were in hate, as some people are in love. Why? I could never really make it out. What had Zigi ever done to Michael? Not that I cared, as far as he was concerned. But I minded being estranged from Bella. I said to Tony: If I never set eyes on him again life will only be improved. But Bella's my oldest friend! Why can't we meet without him? – Friendships come to an end, said Tony. Marriages are more important than friends. You'll just have to accept it. I envy him sometimes. He is much more self-contained than I am.

7

That was the last time we met. Ten years ago. And now all of a sudden here she is. Looking her age, I have to say. That fine, fair skin doesn't wear well. It gets crêpey and brittle. She's wearing a big black wide-brimmed hat that is causing intense annoyance to the man behind her. Beside her, concentrating on the music, is Derry McCulloch. I catch his eye and wave discreetly. He nudges Bella. She smiles and waves back as though we last met yesterday, but I can see her cheeks redden. Still blushes when she's nervous. Derry, meanwhile, has sunk back into Beethoven. As he gets older and his eyebrows grow shaggier he looks more and more like a gorilla. A silverback. His hair hasn't thinned, just grizzled. He is getting bulkier, and his long arms dangle as he walks in a menacing way. In fact he is as mild and dreamy as any gorilla. They shamble about their patch of jungle plucking fruits and shoots and pulling down branches to make their nests. He patrols the literary jungle in the same way, ruminating new projects, chewing over potential bestsellers. Meanwhile, all around him, the trees are falling. But somehow he prowls on.

The music finishes. Tony gets up and goes to the platform. He is going to read Dylan Thomas's rage against the acceptance of death, 'Do not go gentle into that good night'. Among the gathered eccentrics he looks sensible and reassuring. Tony is in business. He runs a science publishing company which produces publications for agencies such as the FAO. He plunges into the poem. *Rage, rage against the dying of the light.*

I wasn't sure about including this. In one way, of course, it was obvious. What else did the peace movement do? – and Zigi, out there in front, louder and more eloquently than any of us. But on a personal level I felt it was wrong. It is not merely that, at the age of eighty-five, a person has a right to accept death. And who would not wish for a death like his? – perfect health and then, bam! a heart attack and out.

But there's more to it than the merely personal. Surely he must have felt his era had come to an end? For forty-five years the world was dominated by the questions arising from the events of 6 August 1945. The day Hiroshima was bombed. The day I was born.

These questions all boiled down to one question. Was the stand-off between Harry Truman and Uncle Joe, between Kennedy and Khrushchev, between Ronald Reagan and the Evil Empire, going to end in the destruction of civilisation?

There's nothing like a clear picture of Hell to put the fear of God into people. In the medieval cathedrals, Hell is far more particular than Heaven. Heaven is filled with vacuous ranks of souls doing nothing much. But Hell! The devils, flames, cauldrons, monsters, the defenceless naked bodies, the terror, the terror! We all have our vision of Hell, but some detail helps. My generation had the inestimable advantage of knowing exactly what it would be like. We'd been given a preview. *The appearance of people was ... well, they all had skin blackened by burns. They had no hair because their hair was burned, and at a glance you couldn't tell whether you were looking at them from in front or in back. They held their arms bent like this ... and their skin – not only their hands, but on their faces and bodies too – hung down ... Wherever I walked I met these people. Many of them died along the road – I can still picture them in my mind – like walking ghosts. They didn't look like people of this world. They had a special way of walking – very slowly ... I myself was one of them.*

For Dr T., Hell was the Russians spreading their grey sameness and their gulags across the whole of the world. For Uncle Zigi, it lay in the weapons Dr T. spent his life devising in order to ward off the Russians. You took your pick: one or the other. Medieval absolutes ruled. In committee-rooms at Washington and Westminster, in conference-rooms in Geneva and Reykjavik, in seminar-rooms at Livermore and Chelyabinsk, battle was joined.

Then the walls came tumbling down. The devil – *that* devil – disintegrated. And what were Dr T. and Uncle Zigi to do then? The bomb was their life. Now different Hells beckon. Time to go. Why rage?

Tony shuffles back beside me. – Was I OK? – Fine, I say. Fine.

Ieuan Davies has taken his place. Round, rosy face, fair-haired, bright-eyed. An unlikely candidate for specialisms in Hell. He looks like a rugby scrum-half. In fact he lectures in peace studies and was one of Zigi's lieutenants during the Eighties. He is reading an extract from that description Zigi wrote of the strange limbo he entered after quitting Los Alamos, before Hiroshima showed the world they'd done it after all. – Then I knew, he ends. They did it. And they used it.

Ieuan puts down his book and remains at the podium. He is to talk about what Zigi meant to our generation. Our frustration, our feeling of disenfranchisement. How his was a voice which could not be ignored however hard his adversaries tried to do so. The authority conferred by his personal history. Not many people – two, actually – quit the Manhattan Project, that fascinating intellectual magnet, on principle, before the problem was solved. They joined because they were terrified the Germans would get there first: but when it became clear that would not happen, most people made their excuses and stayed. Not Zigi: he turned from death to life, quit nuclear physics and turned to biology. – He was a great man and my good friend, Ieuan concludes. He sighs, and after a moment quits the podium, visibly moved.

Susanna, the viola player and the pianist launch into the rondo. The dotted rhythms dance around the room. I'm choking again. Even Tony is red in the face, a sure sign of emotion. As the music proceeds I regain control of myself. It ends. The audience (I nearly said congregation, but Conway Hall is no place for congregations) sits for a minute, then shuffles and clatters to its feet. I look round for Bella. After ten years I can't let her slip away, as I'm sure she'll try to do. Yes, there she is, almost at the door. Probably terrified that a journalist will spot her, or, perish the thought, a photographer. Nice little bit of fodder for gossip columnists there. I catch her as she emerges into Red Lion Square. She looks embarrassed. – Oh, hello, Miriam.

Bella, I say firmly. For ten years we don't meet and then – *here* of all places. Hello hardly does it.

Sorry, she says, and laughs. I was a bit nervous, actually. Not just you. You know – Michael's just got this job –

Don't worry, I can imagine. What brought you? I wouldn't have thought –

Now it's her turn to look surprised. – Zigi's death. It's hardly something I could just ignore, is it? Then, as I continue to look uncomprehending, You mean you never guessed? About Zigi and me?

You and Zigi – ? I stare at her. Of course. Now that she says it, it's so obvious. How could I have missed it? Only because I shut my eyes. I feel chagrined. Why does Bella always have this effect on me? Since we were seven years old, the same thing. She steals my thunder, and – I forgive her. Why? Because I want us to be friends. And why is that? Because we have always been friends. Because she's the nearest thing I have to a sister. Because we grew up together. They were very alike, of course. My mother always used to talk about 'kindred spirits', a phrase which marked her down as belonging to a particular generation of novel-readers. If kindred spirits ever existed, they were Zigi and Bella.

Bella says: He may have been your uncle, but he jolly well wasn't mine.

Indeed not. Pieces of my life rearrange themselves and fall into new patterns, unsettling but not altogether unexpected. – I somehow thought you knew, Bella says.

I suppose I did, sort of.

We laugh. The ice disappears as though it never existed. I should just leave it there, but I can't. Now that I know, I have to know a little more. Just to be sure –

When was this, anyway? I hear myself say, detached, amused.

Oh, years ago. Centuries. Before I got married.

Yes. Before she got married. I know when, exactly.

She shrugs. – I was hardly unique. He was famous for it.

Of course, Bella is right: he was famous for it. One of the many things he was famous for. And most of his lady friends, to judge by the number of attractive women here today, remember him fondly. – I often wonder how Fania coped,

11

says Bella. She never struck me as particularly saintly. She must have realised.

Of course she realised. If you married Zigi, I guess that was just part of what you were marrying. She gritted her teeth.

Did she ever talk to you about it?

Not in so many words.

Fania is not of a generation that believes in getting everything out into the open. What is not said may be ignored. But ignoring does not necessarily imply ignorance.

Bella says: Did she pay him back in kind? I always wondered. She must have been a beauty. Of course, when I knew her she was getting on a bit.

Our age.

We laugh, ruefully.

Oh, I suspect she had her friends. She certainly didn't discuss them with me, though. Or with anyone else, I shouldn't think. Girls from her background didn't. That kind of thing wasn't done.

But I thought she was a communist?

Was! Still is. The last remaining Stalinist. But that doesn't mean she felt happy being unfaithful.

I must go, says Bella. We're going to the opera.

And I'm going to have to get back to Fania's. She's got some baked meats laid on. I don't suppose you'd come?

No time, says Bella, trying to sound regretful. Anyhow, it'd hardly be suitable.

You've got to hand it to Fania, suitability was never her criterion. I'll give you a ring. You still at the same place?

We kiss each other. It feels good. Now I can admit to myself how much I hated not seeing her. There aren't many friends I've had since I was seven.

Bella hurries off. I turn back towards the hall. People are milling about. Susanna is talking to Tony, shaking her head. She is tall, the same height as he is, and very vehement. Her tawny-brown hair flails behind her, making her point in duplicate. I expect he's trying to get her to come back to Fania's, but pigs will fly first. This afternoon's performance was entirely for Zigi (and Tony's attendance, entirely for

Fania). I go over and tell her she and her friends were terrific. I'd like to thank them, but they seem to have disappeared. A cheque will say it better than I could, anyhow.

We've got a rehearsal. I must fly.

My cousins hurry by. It is clear they can't wait to get out. They don't know anyone here. The place is full of people they consider misguided fools if not actual traitors. It's a rollcall of Sixties liberals and Eighties bogeymen. Faces that launched a thousand campaigns. What are they doing in this sort of company? They came for Fania, of course, but she, surrounded by old friends, has barely noticed them. Funerals they can understand, but all this artsy-fartsy stuff leaves them cold.

Miriam, we were looking for you. Nice to see you. How's the family?

As you see. Rose is in Edinburgh. Are you coming back to Fania's?

No, can you give our apologies to Aunty Fan? We tried to get to her but she was surrounded. Got to get away.

I'll tell her.

Derry comes up. – Who were those two respectable gents?

My cousins. When I was fourteen I was in love with one of them.

He raises an eyebrow disbelievingly. Do gorillas have eyebrows? He hooks a long arm around my shoulder. – Listen, I want to talk to you about something.

Do you know Bella and I have just made it up after twenty years?

Hoped you might. Where can we have a word? He looks around. Everywhere, acquaintances loom. The pubs are not yet open. – Time for a little walk before you go on to Fania's? He cocks an inviting eyebrow at the chilly April afternoon.

Aren't you going?

I hadn't –

Why don't you? Then you can give me a lift and we can talk in the car.

I know Derry's car will be somewhere nearby. It always is. How can he bear to drive around central London? And how does he always find a parking space? He can; and he does. He is not one of those expatriate Scots who forever yearns after his native blasted heath. Derry is Metropolitan Man. He belongs to the Garrick and the Groucho. That's a Paul Smith suit draped around his King Kong frame. He's come on since first we met.

We walk towards the car. I enjoy being with Derry. It makes me feel very secure. After Bella, he is my oldest friend. Ours is an ideal sibling relationship, with just a whiff of incest to give it an edge.

So what's all the mystery?

How about doing me a biography of your Uncle Zigi?

I can feel my head snap round. – Me?

We have reached the car. Derry is unlocking it. He opens the passenger door. – Why not? You knew him as well as anyone. Don't you think it would be a good idea? Surely it must have crossed your mind?

It never has. Why not? Derry is right – it's an obvious idea and I'm an obvious candidate. Perhaps it's because Zigi was alive until so recently. Biography, to my mind, is something you do about the dead.

Are you busy at the moment? I thought you were rather between projects.

Thinking about another detective story, actually.

Well then, here's a real-life one to be going on with. What have detective stories got that biographies haven't? You're the detective, that's all. We could offer you a certain amount. Not enormous, but it'd keep you going for a bit.

I think about it. I can see a few problems looming, but nothing insurmountable. I feel intrigued by the idea. Zigi's life is not something from which my generation can feel detached. It profoundly affected what we did and thought and feared. But – but. But if I don't, presumably someone else will. Would I prefer that? I say: Maybe.

Great. Why not speak to Fania about it this afternoon?

Goodness! What's the hurry?

We're not going to be the only people in the world with the idea. You've got to get in first.

He manoeuvres through the traffic. We're driving up Farringdon Street towards King's Cross. Fania lives in north-west London – West Hampstead, to be precise, in a tall red-brick Edwardian terraced house. She has lived there ever since she came back to London with Zigi in 1946. It is a very large house. When first I used to visit it there were always lodgers on the top floor. I always enjoyed those visits. It was like glimpsing another country. The rest of my family lived in houses more or less identically arranged. Built during the 1920s or 30s, detached or semi-detached, gardens front and back. Front room and back knocked through and the wall replaced with pimpled glass doors. Shiny kitchens filled with units and appliances, bedrooms with fitted cupboards. The overall effect was pale beige, soundless, thickly carpeted.

Fania's wasn't like that at all. She and Zigi lived on only two of the three floors, but these comprised six large rooms as well as a kitchen and bathroom. There should have been more than enough space, seeing that they had no children. Nevertheless, they filled their rooms to overflowing. The largest, with french windows on to a small garden, contained a grand piano and books from floor to ceiling. This was Zigi's study. On the first floor, Fania had her studio. There was a complete absence of vertical wall-space, since books and pictures covered every available inch. Everything was always very dusty, because Fania hated housework (the question of Zigi doing any simply never arose) and couldn't afford, in those days, to buy in any help. (Later, it remained dusty, but for ideological rather than financial reasons.) This alone differentiated it sharply from all my other aunts' houses, which were clinically dustless. Even my mother, who also hated housework, never contemplated simply not doing it. This disregard for priorities seemingly graven in stone, the lack of domesticity combined with all the books, made Fania's place extraordinarily attractive to me. It represented a sort of freedom my mother had failed to achieve.

Insofar as I thought about it, I always assumed Fania and Zigi's childlessness resulted from their having married when Fania's childbearing years were past. But of course this was not the case. Fania can only have been in her mid-thirties when they met. She'd been married before but it hadn't worked. Her first husband was a communist organiser in the East End where she grew up. – He was so handsome, she explained and very magnetic. I was bowled over, and in those days, if you wanted to go to bed with someone, you got married. But I quite soon got bored with the slogans. They drifted apart, and he was killed early in the war. – Luckily for me, she always said. – Isn't that rather bloodthirsty of you, Aunty Fan? I would say. Couldn't you have got divorced? –Women of my generation, she said, did not get divorced. If you were unhappily married you were unhappily married. That was all there was to it. Do you think your grandmother was so happy with your grandfather? A brilliant woman married to a fool. – But they were religious. I thought communism was supposed to free you from all that? – Supposed to, maybe, she said darkly. Anyhow, the war solved the problem for me. What a monster I am. We're all monsters, darling. Some of us hide it better than others, that's all.

Maybe she couldn't have children. Or perhaps it was just never the right moment. For a child such facts as the existence or nonexistence of other children are simply part of the landscape, and when I grew older, especially after I had children of my own, this was not a question it was easy to ask. Fania is my great-aunt, although very little older than my mother. And contraception, abortion and fertility are not matters to discuss with your great-aunt, even a great-aunt like Fania. Was infertility such a tragedy for an independent-minded woman? My mother and father each had six siblings. Were their mothers' lives happier than Fania's? Large families held no folksy glamour for her. My great-grandmother was in her mid-forties when she gave birth to Fania; the family had not long arrived in England from the Ukraine. At least there were no pogroms in London. She died soon afterwards, no doubt with relief, and my grandmother, her eldest daughter, took the baby and brought her up along with her own children. My grandmother, like her mother before her, had married at sixteen. What was one mouth more among so many? Jewish cooking is poor people's cooking. Stuffed neck, chopped herring, solid dumplings to eke out the chicken soup – the expenditure is all of time, not money. Peasant economies such as housekeeping do not count time as a chargeable commodity.

It was Fania who taught her elder sister, my grandmother, to read English. They soon moved on from primers to more interesting literature provided by the local communists and anarchists. The Russian revolution promised to transform the Tsar's prison-house – and why not the squalor of the sweat-shop where my grandfather worked as a presser? But my grandparents were too busy, too poor, too tired, to take much active part in politics. They never talked about such things, at least when I knew them. I remember their house – by the time I was born they had graduated to a small Tudorbethan semi in Hendon. My grandmother seems always to have been in the kitchen cooking, or handing round cakes fresh from the oven. My grandfather sat in the dark dining-room, which smelled of the musty volumes – the Talmud, the Torah, the Midrash – over which he muttered and swayed all day. There was a picture on the wall which I liked to look at; it was a distraction during the long boredom of family visits. It showed a neatly bearded man in a peaked cap standing on some sort of platform and gesticulating at a large, enthusiastic crowd. Thinking about my grandparents the other day I remembered that picture, and realised for the first time that it was Lenin, haranguing the masses about revolution and electrification: not what one would have expected to find in that apparently unworldly household.

I don't know whether Vladimir Ilyich retained my grand-mother's active sympathies. Perhaps she just kept the picture because any picture is better than no picture. Maybe she chose not to talk about these things because her children were by then beginning their steady drift to the right, and who needs to look for an argument? But there was no such equivocation about Fania, then or ever. A communist she was and a communist she remained. My mother, who took to the *Daily Telegraph* during the last years of her life, used to mutter darkly about divided loyalties. By then she and Fania saw less of each other. But as soon as I was able to travel about London by myself, Fania's house, which was an easy tube-ride from where we lived, became a magnet to me. She represented every species of anti-authoritarian delight. I idolised her, just as my mother had once done; and she took me to her not very maternal heart. There was always a packet of biscuits for me to eat while I watched her paint (the experience of her sister's symbiotic relationship with the oven had put her off home baking) or listened to Zigi work off his day's frustrations on the piano.

Zigi and Fania met during the war. She did various jobs at that time: went over to America escorting evacuee children, returned because she couldn't bear to be away from England and her family, ended up as a nurse somewhere near Liverpool. Zigi was attached to the university there. By then he had renounced nuclear physics along with the bomb, and embarked upon the immunological research which occupied him for the rest of his life. The legacy of guilt.

Even Derry has his work cut out finding a space to park near Fania's house today. It's not usually so crowded, there must be a lot of people there. When we walk in the door the noise hits us like a brick. Waitresses are squeezing through the throng with trays of wineglasses and asparagus rolls. Tony and I insisted on hiring (and paying for) a caterer. A long life has not domesticated Fania. Neither has it left her rich. Once again, there are lodgers on the top floor.

I locate Tony in the room that used to be Zigi's. His piano, his books – everything is still in place: who is going to change it? There is even a book of Schubert sonatas still open on the piano. Only Zigi is absent. But wasn't he always essentially absent? His body has only followed his spirit. All these people knew him. They worked with him in different capacities, slept with him, marched beside him. But how much of him was ever really there? I often wondered. I, for one, never felt I knew him. And yet I have known him, supposedly intimately, all my life. Intimately? Used in connection with Zigi, the word is a contradiction in terms. Perhaps this is a condition of exile. You are forcibly separated from parts of your life, and parts of yourself as well.

I must be going, says Tony. Will you stay and help Fania? I'm afraid it'll be a bit of a let-down when everyone goes. Tony has become very fond of Fania over the years. I suspect he was always attracted to my family as much as to me. They were so eccentric, so noisy, so argumentative – so different from his own taciturn, sporting, animal-obsessed clan. I say, my family: what that came down to was Zigi and Fania. He never met my parents – we hardly knew each other when they died – and we've never seen much of the rest of them. But Tony and Fania hit it off from the start. I think she rather fancied him – she always was attracted to tall, blond men: Zigi, for example. As for him, I've more than once had the feeling that if he had to choose between us, he'd pick Fania. He admires qualities that she possesses and I lack – elegance, bravery, steely principle.

Of course I shall stay. What else would I do?

The house empties. The caterers are clearing up. The place smells of smoke and wine. Fania is sitting in an armchair by the window. She looks exhausted. She seems suddenly to have shrunk, to have acquired the brittle frailty of the very old. I pull up a chair and sit beside her. – Feeling depressed?

She shrugs. – Naturally.

Shall I make a cup of tea?

No, no, there's been enough eating and drinking.

Do you miss Zigi a lot?

Of course. Not that he spent much time at home, or that we got on so very well all the time. She is silent for a minute. – But I knew he'd always be back. And he filled the house whether he was here or not. What shall I do in this place without him?

You could sell it, and buy somewhere smaller. It might be a good idea. It'd give you some spare cash to live on.

I've thought about that, she says firmly. I don't want to do it. How long have I lived here? Forty-six, forty-seven years? A lifetime. I'm not going to start moving now.

He seems awfully present in this room still.

Yes, I sit here a lot. You know, after he died I went to his wardrobe and got some of his clothes and just crept into them and went to bed. And went to sleep. Unfortunately, I woke up.

What could be more natural? But Fania has always seemed so controlled. She does not readily admit to emotion. She has her painting, her politics, her many friends. And, as she says, her life and Zigi's were largely separate. Evidently not so separate as they seemed.

Fan, how would you feel if I wrote a book about him?

What? She turns to me in apparent amazement.

A biography. You know. Is it so surprising?

She shakes her head firmly. – Out of the question.

Now it's my turn to be amazed. – Whyever not?

He left instructions. In his will. No biography. All his private papers to be burned after his death. As she snaps out these sentences she seems to regain something of her old solidity. She is once again corporeal and intimidating.

And have they been?

Yes. I did it at once. Before anyone could come along and persuade me not to. So there you are. Nothing to be done. She sounds defiant and pleased, like a naughty girl.

But how could you do it? Didn't you want anything to remember him by?

I don't need dusty old papers for that.

I drop the subject. What would be the point of pursuing it? I shall tell Derry, not without relief. Let off the hook. I suggest to Fania that she might like to come and spend a few days with us. She thanks me politely and declines. Yes, she will come to dinner tomorrow. But now she feels rather tired. I mustn't worry about her. She's used to being by herself. We agree that Tony or I shall come by for her tomorrow at six. I hug her. She feels, once again, very insubstantial.

As I walk down West End Lane, my mind is whirling. I can't believe it. *Zigi*? That publicist, forever on a platform, organising, politicking, giving his opinions asked or unasked? That author of countless articles, pamphlets, memoirs? At home in four languages, voluble in all of them. – For us, it's not optional, he used to say. Who speaks Hungarian? It has its uses, but only as a code. He liked to tell how Hungarian physicists in America, when the atom bomb was first mooted, always used their native language when discussing secret matters on the telephone, to the intense frustration of the FBI, which habitually tapped their lines but could not make out a word. At this point Zigi would chuckle and say something incomprehensible in Hungarian.

In short, Zigi was not reticent about his life. It was there to be used as the basis for the message he proclaimed. He knew the immorality of the bomb because he had been one of its architects. He knew the speciousness of the weaponeers' arguments because he had let himself be convinced by them – for a while. And then rejected them.

Home at last. The house is empty. Like Fania, Tony and I have moved down to the lower floors: the top floor and the attic have been made over into a flat, with its own access. The girls use it, when they don't have any other living arrangements. It's not a bad setup, marred (for us) only by the rhythmic creaking of passionate bedsprings over our heads when we're trying to sink into a staid marital doze. As Tony says, it isn't one's daughters' sex-lives that one objects to, it's having to experience them oneself. We're thinking of moving our bedroom down a floor, but we'll have to devise a tactful explanation.

I wander into my study. Zigi's works take up a good two feet of shelf space. Most of them are collections of articles, but there's also his wartime diary and his *Letters to Susie*, a collection of letters he wrote, supposedly or really, to his 'adoptive granddaughter' Susanna as the 1980s took their terrifying course. I open it at random. He is writing from Washington in 1986, as the Reagan administration gears itself up to meet Gorbachev in Reykjavik. *Today I ran into my old classmate, Edward T. He is terrified that Reagan will forget his lines and talk his new weapons program out of existence. I meanwhile am busy trying to obliterate Edward's lines from the President's autocue. Sometimes I think it is not the bomb that is the devil, it is Edward. How else can one describe a man who spends his life planning new ways to destroy civilisation?* A charming man, he used to say. The best company you can imagine.

The phone rings. I shut the book and pick it up. It is Derry.

Did you speak to her?

And what did she say?

I tell Derry what she said.

I can't believe it, he says. Whatever Zigi was or wasn't he was never reticent.

I agree. But what can we do?

I think you should go ahead and do it anyway.

How on earth could I?

There must be stuff of his all over the place. Fania may have burned what she's got. Or she may not. But she can't burn what he's published, or what he wrote to other people.

I still couldn't do it. If he didn't want to he didn't want to. He had his reasons, I expect.

Did Fania give you any idea what they were?

No. Why are you so keen on this all of a sudden? It isn't as though it'll be a runaway bestseller.

Where's your detective spirit? Didn't I hear you referred to the other day as the queen of convoluted psychology? Why's he suddenly acting out of character like this? You should feel challenged!

Well I don't.

There's lots of people would jump at this.

Why not get one of them to do it, then?

Because you'd be better.

Let me think about it.

Later, Tony comes back full of some contract he's hoping to get. He's going to Rome next week to finalise it. Would I like to come? It's some time since he last included me in one of these jaunts. Zigi's death seems to have brought us closer together. I'd like to go, but I don't like the thought of leaving Fania all on her own.

That's ridiculous, he says, there are a thousand people who could keep an eye on her.

But they won't. We're the only ones who are really close to her. And now even I am thinking of betraying her. I tell Tony about Derry's suggestions. I assume that he will take Fania's side. Tony is a man of principle. It's both terrifying and reassuring.

He does not disappoint me. – Of course you can't do it, he says. No question. I'm surprised at Derry.

Just what I said myself. But now that it's Tony saying it, not me, I find myself automatically taking the opposite side.

But maybe Derry's right. If I don't do it someone else will, and probably not so well.

Tony gets up, stacks the plates and puts the kettle on for some coffee. – I can hardly believe we're having this argument. You say he specifically forbade it.

That's what Fania says.

Don't you believe her? Why should she make up something like that?

Why, indeed? I've been asking myself the same thing all evening, and I can't think of an answer.

Presumably he knew what he was doing, says Tony. Why should Zigi's life automatically become public property just because some publisher thinks he might make a few bucks out of it? And if you still aren't convinced, you might consider Fania. You go on about how much she means to you. If she doesn't want it, I think you should accept that. Does it matter why not? Perhaps she feels she's had enough of being married to a public figure. Perhaps she's looking forward to getting out from under Zigi's shadow in her old age.

He's right of course. Any rational person can see that. So why aren't I convinced?

What are we talking about, in the end? Property interests in the deceased? The ownership of rights to a life?

I think about Zigi. Even before my parents died, he and Fania were my other family. And afterwards, during that ghastly time after the crash, they got me through. In some ways I was the child they never had. Not quite the same, of course. With people who aren't your parents it's both easier and more difficult. As I found out. Oh, yes: the fact is that I, too, have my rights. I have my reasons to feel curious about Zigi. Perhaps I am not merely the best person for this job. Perhaps I am the only one.

The more I think about it, the more inclined I feel to try this book. It's creeping up on me, taking me over. Like Oscar, I

can resist anything but temptation. And what greater temptation than the prospect of satisfying one's curiosity – tracking
facts – hidden facts – to their lair? Perhaps this was simply the
last of Zigi's little tricks. He didn't intend to risk any slide into
posthumous obscurity. He knew, the adroit old manipulator,
that his instruction would absolutely ensure a biography,
would make it irresistible. What's he got to hide? they'd ask.
Satan wasn't the only one to know forbidden fruit is the
sweetest.

I can see it now. Zsygmond von Fischer: our life and times.
Next morning, I tell Derry I'll do it.

CHAPTER 2   BUDAPEST

I

FINE WORDS, FINE words. But I shall need something more solid if I am to construct this book. It seems I'm going to do it, in spite of my nearest and dearest. It seems I can't resist it. Quite the reverse: I'm apparently prepared to put all my life on the line for it. The mere pursuit of this project sets me against Fania, Tony, Susanna – the people who constitute that life. And once I've got all the stuff – *if* I get any, if there is anything to be got – then what? Do I publish? Cut myself off from them forever? Is that what I want? Presumably. Why undertake a book, sign the contract, take the money, put in all that work and thought, if the intention is not in the end to publish?

So what's the big attraction? In a word: power. A new, an intoxicating prospect. The one irresistible thing. Zigi has dominated my life. Sophisticate, national figure, glamorous outsider, thrilling object of family gossip. In at the birth of that thing which changed the world, overshadowed our existence, informed and shaped the politics of a generation. Orchestrator of our efforts to control it: personification of our conscience. For me personally, the rescuing father-figure – and all those other things which I shall describe in due course, should I decide to proceed. The *I decide* – that's the key.

For within this all-embracing, inescapable relationship, the balance of power has never been in question. Zigi held all the cards. He was older, he was cleverer, he had seen life. Who was I to compete? How was I to compete? I couldn't and I didn't. Competition never entered my mind. The notion was irrelevant. He affected me: I didn't affect him. That went without saying. But now the tables are turned. Zigi is dead, and what survives – what will survive – is his memory. His reputation. And Derry, my good fairy as always, has made me a present of it, wrapped it with a pink bow and laid it in my open hands.

What, after all, is biography? The story of a life: an accumulation of evidence. It sounds so objective. Facts are facts – who can gainsay them? Things happened or they didn't. But of course it's not like that at all. Biography is as subjective as any other form of literature. It isn't just about the subject: it's about the author. There are ways and ways of presenting, of selecting, suppressing, juxtaposing, of storytelling, of emphasising, of choosing one context, one comment, rather than another. Zigi is at my mercy: what I choose to make him. In the long run, what's the difference between a fictional character and one who really existed? Between a character in a biography and one in a novel? Isn't Anna Karenina, in the long run, more real than Tolstoy? Far, far more real than run-of-the-mill walking, talking, solid beings like you or I. And it's the long run that matters, from the literary point of view. In the long run we're all dead and in the hands of our biographers.

But where am I to begin?

Of course I know how you set about a biography. It's straightforward. You follow the spoor, you collect the evidence, you collate, you consider, you try, as far as possible, to get inside the skin. But what evidence will be available to me, if Fania stands by her ukase? The real meat of biography is letters and memories. No doubt there were boxes of correspondence, photographs – all kinds of stuff. Presumably that is what Fania burned. Even if she didn't, she isn't going to let me see it. And who will give me the goods if it becomes known that Zigi expressly forbade it? The people who knew him best were his Hungarian cronies. But if this prohibition was Zigi's idea they'll be aware of it; and if it was Fania's, they're sure to discuss any approach with her. They're her friends as much as they were ever Zigi's. More, perhaps.

There are other colleagues, lots of them, political and

professional. But nobody close. They can only help with the official life. In which case, one of them might as well write it.

There's plenty of published stuff, of course. All those books, papers, articles. Such as I don't possess I have borrowed from various libraries. Colloquia, festschriften, abstruse papers on nuclear physics and microbiology. Collected polemics.

I open one of the books at random. A festschrift on his retirement from the Medical Research Council in 1973. (The retirement was purely theoretical: he returned to work next day on a pension and an emeritus chair. It simply meant there was more time for politics.) Zsygmond von Fischer, born Budapest, 1908.

Well, that's one possibility. Begin at the beginning. Let us start by getting away from words. A little action. Budapest, unlike so many of its former inhabitants, is still where it always was. I shall visit the scenes of Zigi's boyhood.

And what exactly do you imagine you'll do once you're there? says Tony. Wander around? Drink in atmosphere? I told him I was going ahead, and of course he was furious. We didn't have a stand-up row – that isn't our style. Rows make me feel physically sick. I know some people enjoy them, but I can't imagine how. Tony and I generally skirt around potential rows, and quite often they simply evanesce. He goes off on one of his trips, and when he returns the slate is wiped clean. No chance of that here, however. This is one we shall have to live with. Tony is continually confronted with it in some unavoidable way – such as when I tell him what dates I'm going to be absent, and where I'm going. He retreats into silence and monosyllables.

I think only part of this hostility is based on his reluctance to upset Fania. This business forces him to confront what for him are my most unsettling tendencies. He's never been happy with my kneejerk inclination to disobey. He considers it juvenile and irresponsible. Tony instinctively respects authorities, boundaries, permissions, while I – like Zigi, like Fania – have always held such things in contempt. If he's told he can't do something, he tends not to do it. He certainly doesn't like deception on this sort of scale. I suppose I could have tried to talk Fania round, but I know her too well. Even if the time had been less inapposite, it wouldn't have worked. She's as pig-headed as I am, and once she's stated her position, nothing will budge her from it. So I shall go my own way, just as she would in similar circumstances. Does she suspect this? Probably. An undeniable strain has crept into our relationship. I don't feel comfortable around her, and nor does Tony – he, in fact, even less than me. When he is with her he is under a continual temptation to spill the beans, warn her – as though she needed warning – of the viper in her midst. So Zigi spreads unease in death, just as he used to in life.

How do I know what I'll do there? Once I get there I expect I'll find out.

What could be easier, these days, than to go to Budapest? Just get on a plane and there you are. It's only Europe, after all. Just four hours' ride downriver from Vienna. But it's as if this part of Europe has only just resumed existence after fifty years' blanketing in fog. All my life it's been unimaginable, attainable only via obscure communist-front travel agencies with names like Millennium Tours. Now here it is, back on the map. A European city. Its castle on the hill, its steep medieval streets, its tree-lined bourgeois boulevards. The graceful bridges between Buda and Pest; the Danube running down the middle.

A city like any other; and yet unlike. In London or Paris or New York, there is a sense of continuous process in one direction or another. Change, whatever the pace, is organic. The bomb-sites I remember from my childhood could hardly be guessed at now, any more than the quite recent solid respectability of some parts of Harlem and the Bronx. What was, is obliterated.

But this is not true here. The city is a palimpsest of violence. The century's wounds have been preserved, or simply gone unrepaired. Bullet-marks – from 1944? from 1956? – still scar the walls. In the heart of the city, buildings decay. Where there is no private property, what value have prime sites? What does the state care about repairing the plasterwork or giving rotting windowframes a new coat of paint?

Presumably all this is about to change. Late capitalism is the most recent of this century's seismic shocks. In the Buda hills, new villas burgeon. On the Pest waterfront, some buildings are finally being renovated. Japanese computer firms scrabble for advertising space. Television dishes sprout everywhere. The streets are filled with cars old and new. Taxi-drivers are young and well-educated – the sign of a troubled economy. The one sure thing, these days, is tourism.

Walking the streets, I search for the city of Zigi's boyhood. It is not hard to find. The wealthy and exuberant Budapest in which he grew up was never destroyed: it was simply left to rot. Enter any *porte-cochère* in Pest and there it all is, literally untouched. Elaborate, rusty, wrought-iron finials decorate graceful, crumbling staircases which spiral upwards to dusty heights and skylights opaque with grime. Elaborate plaster-work vaulting, unpainted these fifty years, arches flowery swags over tall, unwashed windows. Inside the stairwells run lifts encased in wrought-iron tracery, dating from the early days of the elevator: still, just, in use. A sight to break Zigi's mother's bourgeois, silk-encased heart. Not far away, the synagogue no doubt frequented by his father is in a similar state. It is enormous, an elaborate Jugendstil façade, carved Hebrew letters along the cornice, Venetian gothic windows, huge arched doorway with broken fanlight, massive decorated bronze doors still keeping the mob at bay. Self-evidently not destroyed: but shut, blackened, broken, decayed, abandoned.

In the days when this was built by that wealthy cousinage of bankers, lawyers, businessmen and professors from which Zigi sprang, Budapest was as much a hub-city as I feel it to be today. Today it is delicately balanced on the frontier of a recently separate world: upriver, the elegant prosperity of Vienna; downriver, Belgrade, teetering on the brink of civil war. Then, too, it was a frontier town: the eastern end of the Austro-Hungarian axis. Engaged, as now, in its own frantic growth and development; creating its own new culture in its own impenetrable language, facing eastward to the plains and the Carpathians while Vienna turned its face resolutely westwards and northwards. It was the very edge of Western Europe. And to it streamed the Jews.

Where they came from, there was no escape from the ghetto imposed from without by the authorities and from within by the community. But in Hungary, after 1867, there was no ghetto. The Jews were emancipated and granted full citizenship in the Habsburg territories. They couldn't believe their luck. Back in the shtetls where they were born, their fathers, sisters, cousins, still lived in that medieval, inturned, mystical world where intellects were sharpened discussing commentaries on commentaries, where rabbis held court amid mud and weeds and poverty. But some – the enterprising, the despairing – escaped.

Fania's family – my family – did not take this route. They originated – that is to say, had lived for some generations – not so far from here: near Czernowitz, in the Bukovina, that disputed territory bordering Hungary, Romania and Ukraine. Zigi's people came from the same area. Zigi and Fania used to laugh about their common origins: two Czernowitzers, a match the *shadchan* might have dreamed of. His grandfather, Zalman Fischer, crossed over the Carpathians sometime during the nineteenth century, and after 1867, left with his young son, Zigi's father, for Budapest. Fania's grandfather stayed. Stuck in the mud, Zigi cried triumphantly, enjoying the idiom, to which his ineradicable accent gave a particular tang.

He did not stick for long. Where enterprise had been lacking, desperation lent resolve. The shtetl was just over the border, in the Tsar's lands. Thirty years after Zigi's grandfather made the move to Budapest, Fania's father fled to London, to escape the pogroms and the cruel fate of lifelong conscription in the despot's armies.

He fled; but he brought the shtetl with him in the shape of all those odd and illogical practices and prohibitions which so infuriated me when I was a child. Kosher meat only, that went without saying. No eating milk with meat – even the sets of crockery for these things had to be kept separate. No shellfish. No pork. A quite different set of crockery to be used only during the Passover, with its separate and special dietary rules (no leavened bread, nothing to be made with wheat flour). No fire or lamp to be lit during the Sabbath, between sunset on Friday and sunset on Saturday. No riding then, either: you had to go everywhere on foot.

These things could be got round: you lit the gas on Friday afternoon and put a special slow-cooking stew, *cholent*, to simmer all through the Sabbath, smelling wonderful and tasting (by the time you got round to eating it) of very little; you got a *shabbes goy* to light your lamps and fires. My parents ignored most of these rules. But there they lurked in the background, creating their own subconscious guilts. My mother once ate a dish of lobster in the belief that it was chicken; told the truth of the matter, she threw up on the spot.

I hated these rules. I could see no reason for them. My parents, when asked, could produce no satisfactory explanation. There were odd phrases in the Bible about not seething a kid in its mother's milk, and a truism to the effect that in hot countries it is not wise to eat pork. But generally speaking explanations were not in order. These were simply the rules that went with Jewishness, and what was the point of questioning them?

The point was that there was no point. The rules are at the centre of the old question, the Jewish Question. When the Jews were expelled from their ancient homeland, thenceforward to be landless, some means had to be devised of preserving their identity. These prohibitions were that means. Their purpose was to keep the community as separate as possible from its neighbours. These religious or quasi-religious practices were badges of nationality. They built a wall around the Jews, invisible, but as solid as anything devised by a Nazi. Not long ago, the Orthodox community in north-west London requested planning permission to erect an *eruv*. This is a construction of poles and string, a legal representation of a house, within which an orthodox Jew may, on the Sabbath, consider himself at home and go about such business as would normally be permitted, on that day, only within his own four walls. For me the *eruv* is the metaphorical epitome of this entire edifice of custom: a legalistic evasion of an illogical prohibition comprising an invisible wall within which – and only within which – the community may feel at home. What is a Jew? I discarded all religious practices. I married a goy. But if either of my daughters should decide to become a Christian, I would feel that she had committed treason. Let me confess: I should find it hard to bring myself to speak to her again.

At that time, Budapest was the fastest-expanding city in Europe. Between 1867 and 1914, it grew from the seventeenth- to the eighth-largest city on the continent. It became the largest flour-milling centre in the world after Minneapolis. It was the only eastern banking centre financially strong enough to reject foreign capital. The Jews were the most significant element in this expansion. They constituted the majority of bankers, businessmen, doctors and lawyers. Their aim was twofold: to become prosperous; and to become irrefutably Hungarian.

For men such as Zigi's grandfather there was a simple answer to the Jewish Question. He already had a nationality. Judaism was therefore simply a religion. And he was not a religious man. Orthodox practices played no part in his scheme of things. In pursuit of acceptance as true Hungarians, he and his friends went so far as to celebrate the Sabbath, like all other Hungarians, on Sunday rather than Saturday. Fania used to tease Zigi about this. Even Czernowitzers still knew Sabbath fell on Saturday. To this Zigi would reply that, at least, his immediate family did not convert. But among his cousins he counted both Catholics and Lutherans. Conversion was a matter of convenience. In Budapest at that time, it was a great social and political – and therefore commercial – advantage to be a nobleman; and ennoblement was much harder to achieve for a Jew than a convert. So they converted. Acceptance was worth a mass. Later, even unconverted Jews achieved ennoblement. This happened not to Zalman Fischer, but to his son, Gabor, who was by then a rich and successful banker. So that Uncle Zigi was von Fischer, not just plain Fischer.

Von und zu Fischer, Fania jeered. A lot of difference that made to plain Herr Hitler when the time came.

It is May. England, when I left, was shivering under a brisk nor'wester. But here it is hot: Budapest is already sweltering in the eighties. I am sitting up in the battlements near the castle, sipping a coffee beneath an umbrella. The city is pervaded by the scent of lime blossom: there is a huge tree just opposite my table. I am intoxicated by the perfume. *Kaffee mit Schlag*, the scent of limes: essence of Mitteleuropa.

What shall I do next? This is not just a holiday. I must make some sort of move. I did what preparation I could before the journey. Some history; a few addresses. For instance, the school Zigi attended.

And not only Zigi. A unique galaxy of talents emerged from this school during the early years of the century. It was the *Minta*, or model school, founded by Mor Karman, an eminent educationist. It was attached to the university and intended for an elite of clever boys. It produced Karman's son Theodore von Karman, Leo Szilard, Nicholas Kaldor, Thomas Balogh, George de Hevesy, Edward Teller. Has any comparable group of alumni had more effect on the history of countries not their own? From the same background but a different school – the Lutheran Gymnasium across the river in Buda – came Eugene Wigner and John von Neumann. Three Nobel laureates (Hevesy, Karman and Wigner), two of the most influential economists of the century (Kaldor and Balogh), one of the originators of the electronic computer (von Neumann), the driving force behind the A-bomb (Szilard, Wigner and Teller) and the H-bomb (who but Dr T. again?).

The group is hardly explicable in merely human terms. At Princeton, where Johnny von Neumann at twenty-nine became the youngest member of the recently established Institute for Advanced Study, it was said that, although he was indeed superhuman, he had made a thorough, detailed study of human beings and could imitate them perfectly. Many years later, when all the scientists had settled in America, the topic of possible visitors from outer space was under discussion. Szilard quipped that the visitors had already arrived and decided to pass themselves off as Hungarians: an excellent disguise, since no Hungarian can speak any language except his own without accent. The joke stuck. Fifty years on, chosen friends address Edward Teller as E.T.

The Minta still exists. It is situated in a dark, narrow street behind the university in Pest. By now the sky has clouded over and a few large drops of rain are falling. Clearly, I am not meant to remain on the street and get wet. I step inside and watch the heavens open.

It is four in the afternoon: the place is almost deserted. A friendly teacher offers to show me round. We scurry about shutting windows against the storm. What did I expect? The school is a school: classrooms full of desks. The smell of the laboratories – formaldehyde, acid – suddenly recalls my own schooldays. But they are hardly what I came to Budapest to find.

Outside, the rain is falling in sheets. All taxis are suddenly occupied. After ten minutes or so I capture one, and we ride out to my hotel in the Buda hills.

I shower and change. What now?

Friends have supplied me with telephone numbers of interesting acquaintances in Budapest. But I can't lapse into social life yet. Not before trying out my idea. Which is . . .

It had crossed my mind that Zigi might still have relatives living in Budapest. It's not inconceivable. Of course Hungary was on the German side in the war, but the Final Solution was not implemented here as thoroughly as in some other places. It was possible for Jews to survive. Many did, and remain here still.

I have no idea about Zigi's family. Did he have brothers or sisters? He never mentioned them, and I never thought of asking. He didn't much like talking about his early life, and he was not a man you could push into doing what he didn't want to. Relations had to be conducted on his terms. One didn't probe. People have their reasons, and, given Zigi's background, these might easily have to do with experiences best forgotten. Maybe Fania would know, but I can hardly ask her now.

34

On the other hand, a name is a name. Fischer. There must be Fischers in Budapest, and they will be in the phone book. I shall begin at the beginning, and only hope that there aren't too many of them. And that my German will stand the strain. It was never my best language.

Predictably, many of the Fischers I call are out. I make a mark beside their numbers: ones to try again. Some don't understand a word I say. They're unlikely to be my quarry: I find it hard to believe that any relative of Zigi's would be a Hungarian monoglot. Some put the phone down on me. Some explain politely that, no, the name of Zsygmond von Fischer means nothing to them.

I come to the end of the list. No joy. I shall have to try the marked numbers again in the morning. I feel unaccountably cast down. Stupid really. Why did I imagine it might be so easy?

I glance at my list of contacts. One is a man I once met in London: a peace activist who managed, somehow, to acquire a visa and emerge, briefly, for a conference in the early Eighties, when they, or we, were still the enemy; when, in our own countries, we, and he, were the enemy within. The risks he then ran were of course on an altogether different level from the kind of minor inconvenience we might experience. He was a brave man and I liked him; the two do not necessarily go together. Zigi was at the meeting. I remember him and Andras chatting together in Hungarian. (Did Zigi have a Martian accent in his mother-tongue? I must remember to ask. Not that Andras will understand.)

I dial the number. A woman answers. I ask, in German, whether Andras Lukacs lives there. Yes, he does. Here he is. I revert to English with relief. Introduce myself. Does he perhaps remember . . . ? He does. What am I doing? How long am I in Budapest? Why don't I come round now, at once?

It has stopped raining. I dash out to a flower-stand, buy a tasteful bunch, get the hotel to call me a cab. We set off downhill. The meter spins wildly. The address I have given is in Buda, near the castle – far nearer than the university in Pest, where I caught my previous cab. The fare is just double. The free enterprise spirit. I pay up, omitting a tip. The cabby is impassive.

I check the address again. Can this be right? The building looks severely war-damaged. Can people really be living here? I push open the door. In the hallway, the usual battery of letterboxes. Evidently there are inhabitants. A rusty, dusty, rickety stair winds into the gloom. Second floor, Andras said. Clutching my flowers, I trudge upwards. Ramshackle walkways encircle a courtyard. First floor. Second floor. I peer at the numbers. A brass nameplate: LUKACS.

The door opens. Inside, the apartment gleams with white paint and modern furniture. A lime tree, in full bloom outside an open window, pours its scent into the room. Who would have guessed? I can see that capitalism must herald the return of the concierge.

Andras is a short, stocky man with glasses and black hair cut en brosse. He introduces me to his wife, Marguerite, who speaks a little German but no English. We beam multilingual cordiality. They explain about the cab. The fiddle here is a relatively elaborate one: the meters are not (as one might expect) dispensed with: they are fixed to run too fast. The flowers are put in water. Wine is poured. Pasta is cooked. I explain what I am doing, or trying to do, over here.

Andras turns to Marguerite and says something in Hungarian. She nods, and replies enthusiastically. He says: We know a cousin of Zsygmond von Fischer. She lives in Buda, not very far from here.

I feel that tingle of pleasure familiar to every questing biographer. The trail is beginning to unfold.

II

Uncle Zigi's cousin is called Ester Konrad. Not Fischer at all: a nice idea, but wrong. Marguerite is a teacher; Mrs Konrad is the aunt of a friend of hers, a teacher in the same school. When Andras came to London that time, greetings were conveyed.

Were they returned? Was that what they were discussing in Hungarian? Probably, says Andras. Zsygmond didn't seem too interested, to tell you the truth. We didn't tell Tant Ester that, of course.

It's odd, I say. He didn't like talking about his early life. He never would. Perhaps he associated her with that.

Perhaps.

Perhaps she'll be able to tell us.

Tant Ester's address and telephone number are found and passed over. Shall we try her now? Andras suggests. Plainly he is dying to know what will happen next.

Why not?

He dials. We all wait. We can hear the ringing of the phone at the other end of the line. It rings several times. Maybe she's out. Or gone to bed: it's ten o'clock and she's an old lady. Or died in the night: every biographer's nightmare. Zigi's generation is on its way out. I must catch them while I can.

Suddenly, she answers. I can hear her voice: firm and clear. Doesn't sound as if she'll die immediately. Not before I've had a chance to see her.

Andras turns and hands me the phone. The penetrating voice says: Hello? You are a friend of my cousin?

His niece.

Niece? There is a pause.

That's to say, his wife is my aunt. Did Andras explain? I'm writing his biography. I'm trying to find out all I can about him. I wondered if I might possibly come and see you?

Yes, she says. You had better come.

We fix a time. I am to call on her at ten tomorrow morning.

At ten next morning it is already hot. The meter of the cab is less jet-propelled than last night's. We drive into a district of treelined streets and leafy villas set in walled gardens. I try the iron gate. It is not locked. A gravel path; stone steps; a tall, solid front door. The villa is stuccoed. A long time ago it was painted white, but now the paint is cracking. I ring the doorbell and peer through the panes. A polished floor; a window at the back; more green the other side. A figure appears, limping slightly. It is an elderly woman: presumably,

Tant Ester. Heavy, solid, with a round, brown face and grey hair pulled back in a bun. She opens the door.

Frau Konrad? I'm Miriam. Miriam Oliver. We spoke –

Yes, yes, she says. Come in.

Inside is pure art nouveau. White walls, tall ceilings, elaborate pierced wood screens. A few pieces of dark, carved furniture. Cylindrical metal light-fittings, ornately traceried. At the back, through tall windows, a wooden veranda overlooks a garden. On it, two wicker chairs and a table. Tant Ester gestures towards the veranda. It is shaded by an enormous horse chestnut. Tea? she says, and, waving away my offer of help, limps to a small kitchen where a tray containing a teapot, two cups and a small jug of lemon juice is already prepared. She carries this out to the veranda and sits on one of the chairs. I sit on the other. Tea is poured into shallow china cups. She sits and waits for me to begin.

It's very kind of you to see me, Frau Konrad.

Please call me Ester. She pronounces it Eshter, in the Martian manner. Every word, in this foreign language, is pronounced separately and with precision. She sips her tea and gazes at me over the top of her cup. She has reached the age where one can be oneself: no need to pretend more politeness than one feels. Her eyes are brown and bright. I see now that the brown complexion is composed largely of liver spots. She is wearing a smocklike dress of navy-blue cotton, perhaps homemade.

She says: You knew Zsygmond well?

Oh, very well. I've known him all my life. And I lived in the same house with him and Fania for quite a long time.

Fania?

My aunt. His wife.

His wife? Fania?

You didn't know he was married? But that was before I was born.

Oh yes. I knew he was married. I correspond with his wife. Her name is Bettina. The bright brown eyes rest unwaveringly on my face. You didn't know about her?

Dumbly I shake my head. Ester smiles.

Obviously not. A stupid question.

She sits back and sips her tea while I try and adjust the assumptions of a lifetime. What does all this mean? That Zigi was a bigamist? Did Fania know? Was this why he – or she – tried to head off this project? But why did he never mention it? What's there to be ashamed of in having been married before? Even as these questions whirl through my head I can hear Zigi's voice. And what's it to do with you, my dear Miriam? People's private lives are their private lives.

I am sorry, says Ester. I have upset you.

It's a surprise, I admit. And then, quickly, before I can think what a damn stupid irrelevant bourgeois detail it is – but how can I *not* ask it: Are they – were they – still married?

The brown eyes twinkle. It isn't hard to talk to Tant Ester. She knows exactly what's going on behind the façade. She has not lived a sheltered life. – No, they divorced. Bettina divorced him even before the end of the war. Nineteen forty-four? I think so. She pauses. We all grew up together. It was a very small world. Zsygmond's father was my mother's brother, and Bettina's father was a cousin of my father. A lawyer. They were both lawyers. We were at school together. We were very good friends. When he suggested marriage, Bettina said to me: Ester, shall I do it?

And what did you say?

What can one say? In these cases, people want to hear you say what they think. But – she shrugs. I didn't trust him. So I was not surprised that it ended. I correspond with her, but not with him. I didn't know about any other wife. So for me she doesn't exist. Just so, I never saw Bettina's new husband. Who is now also dead. For me Bettina is still Zsygmond's wife. What does it matter?

Did you always live here?

It was my husband's house. The communists put people to live with me here. But now – I am alone again. She gestures around at the space, the quiet green shade. The house is not as big as it feels: it has only one storey. But it is deep, and the rooms are very tall.

Is your husband alive?

He died in the war. My children are in America. But I preferred to stay here.

It is very hot. How strange life is, to have brought me to this quiet garden at the other end of Europe in order that the neat patterns of my existence should be so rudely disarranged.

But Ester has not finished yet. Her eyes, which turned inward at the thought of her vanished children and dead husband – and how did he die? Better not ask – are once again brightly fixed upon me. There is also a daughter, she says.

What?

A daughter. Bettina and Zsygmond had a daughter. Marianne. He never mentioned her? She shakes her head. No.

What does this feel like? It is as though Ester were, ever so gently and politely, throwing rocks at me. Thud. Thud. Of course it is not her intention to wound. Quite the contrary. Why shouldn't Zigi have a daughter?

He had no other children? With your aunt?

No.

So. And you knew him well?

I thought so. We were very close. I thought. He was – like a second father to me. In a way.

Always a qualification. Who knew him well? Not I.

So. You feel – displaced? Is that the word? It is difficult for you.

Silence. She has no more questions.

I try, once again, to collect myself. – Did they keep in touch? Zigi and –

Perhaps, Ester says. I don't know. You would have to ask them. I can give you Bettina's address.

She gets up slowly and limps into the house while I wait on the quiet veranda. I wish I had listened to Fania. I wish I had never started on all this. But now it's too late. Whatever I do, I can't leave it here. That would be unbearable: out of the question. I've begun it, and now I shall have to go on to the end.

CHAPTER 3   BETTINA

I

ESTER'S FRIEND BETTINA, the first Mrs von Fischer, has an address in San Diego. How we Czernowitzers get around! Or maybe she's not from Czernowitz, but from Poszony, or Arad, or Szeged; and before that from some mud-strewn shtetl in Galicia or Bohemia. Who's to say where we're from, or where we'll go to next?

Ester has given me a phone number and an address. I don't like phoning people I don't know. So when I get back to London I write to her. I post the letter, and wonder. Will she, won't she? Telling all: why should anybody want to do it? But then, why should they *not* want to? Some people want to spill their beans, some don't. Fania doesn't. Zigi didn't. I do. Will Bettina? And Marianne? I don't like to think too hard about Marianne. For some reason (jealousy? Am I suddenly displaced by a sibling?) the notion of her makes me uncomfortable. But she's more than a notion. I can't just disinvent her. No doubt we shall meet sooner or later. One thing at a time. I wait to hear from Bettina.

Her reply arrives sooner than I expected. It is typed: why should that surprise me? Anyhow, it's a relief: as well as being legible, it indicates a certain accessibility of mind. Yes, she will see me, if I should care to make the journey out to San Diego. – I have often wondered about Zsygmond, she writes. After we parted he did not stay in touch. Of course I heard of him from time to time, but never in a personal way. I am sorry to hear of his death. But after all, he was not young. I am not young myself. You had better not wait too long!

So here I am on the plane, using up some of Derry's none-too-generous advance. These days, with the girls grown up, I am a free agent. I still find the sensation intoxicating, even though it's some years now since Rose left home and there were no more meals to prepare. Until that moment, I was always responsible either to or for somebody. Now I'm on my own, and so are they.

Tony, since it has become clear that I am going ahead with this project, has simply refused to talk about it. It's my business; he doesn't want to know. He doesn't approve, and this overcomes even his natural curiosity. I started to tell him about Budapest and Ester. – Don't tell me, he said. That way, I don't have to hide anything. I want to be able to see Fania without having to force myself not to tell her all sorts of stuff you've found out. He wouldn't look at my photos of the blue Danube. He puts himself (he is put) in an impossible position. He knows I've found *something*: he is unaware only of the detail.

There's a certain selfconscious rectitude about Tony that I find infuriating, especially when I'm in the wrong. It's one of his most English qualities. – A nice English boy, Zigi said, when he heard we were planning to get married. Kind. I expect you'll be happy in a domestic way. – And what other way do you suggest? I said, handing a biscuit to Susie. She must have been about one and a half, that all-demanding, all-wrecking age. Naturally, Zigi ignored her. Babies bored him; he never pretended otherwise. In this he was unexceptional. Bella's mother put it in a nutshell, that time when she thought I needed money for an abortion. She phoned and said she wanted to see me, there was something she wanted to discuss. I went round for a drink. Her house was so familiar from my childhood that the very smell of the hallway, unsniffed for the past several years, almost reduced me to tears. What came to mind for some reason, perhaps because of the slight nausea I felt all the time during early pregnancy, was the Cruel Food competitions we used to have. We competed to see who could invent the most disgusting combination: Bella won, with sardines and chocolate spread. Nothing beats fish and chocolate in the disgusting stakes.

Mrs Brockenhurst didn't find it easy to get around to the point. She asked me how I was feeling, and poured me a soda-water. Finally it emerged: she was afraid I might be short of cash for an abortion. Should this be so, she would happily give me the money. – It's hard to put it tactfully, she said (she was drinking whisky, sans soda-water). All I mean is, you should feel free to choose. It shouldn't come down to a couple of hundred pounds.

I explained that this was not the, or a, problem.

Fine, she said. I just wanted to make sure. It'll be a hard slog, but I expect you realise that. Not that it would necessarily be so very different even if you were married. Hugh's been a wonderful father, since the girls went to college.

That was very much Zigi's approach to children: perhaps he would have stretched a point, down to sixth-formers. – I have no suggestions to make, he said. Don't forget, we're always here, Fania and I. But he is no longer here – only the echo of his words. And we have been happy, in a domestic way. Is there a better? Was Zigi happy, at any point? It is the act of an unhappy man, to try and wreck the happiness of others. I'm always here. To the grave and beyond.

It's a long flight. I have a book, but one can't spend ten or eleven hours solidly reading. There are the usual distractions. The movie is one I've already seen. The meals come and go. I used to knock myself out on flights like this with a mix of vodka and Marzine, but these days I find it hard to be so cavalier about such things. In my old age, the propaganda is getting to me.

In the next seat, a man with a wispy red beard is looking over a mathematical paper. Time for a little conversation. Is he an academic? I ask.

He tells me about himself eagerly enough. He goes into great detail. He is German, a physicist, on his way to a conference, then later to do a little work with a company he knows in Palo Alto. When we arrive he will be met by a friend. He will stay for ten days. Then he returns to Germany en route for Peking. Having come to the end of his programme, he returns to his paper.

I ponder this. It could hardly be called an exchange. I know all about him; he knows nothing about me. It never crossed his mind to ask. Perhaps I am invisible? No; I must have a certain visibility, since it was I who triggered this torrent of information. He even pointed out, in an access of educational zeal, small clouds marking the micro-climate around a power-station far below us. So he sees – somebody. What? Who? An insignificant individual. A slight woman of medium height, short dark hair sprinkled now with grey threads. Reading a novel: clearly not a serious person. No, that's wrong: my neighbour would never emerge far enough out of himself to register so intimate a detail. Perhaps the secret lies between my legs. All those stories and myths about the cap, or ring, or cloak of invisibility omit to state that middle-aged women carry the talisman around with them all the time. It's not always a disadvantage, but it can be disconcerting. Charm, the kind Zigi had in such abundance, consists in finding everyone visible. Charm consists in being – or appearing – genuinely interested in your interlocutor. Surprisingly, it can be combined with immense egotism. Zigi was living proof of that.

I wish someone was meeting me. I hate the business of arriving, half-dead, and then having to make all those big decisions about what to do next. Should I rent a car at once and try to find a reasonable motel away from the airport? Crash out in the perimeter Holiday Inn and hope that the person in the next room doesn't play the television too loud? I have a friend who loves Holiday Inns. – I love knowing that my room's always going to be exactly the same, she says. Wherever it is. Tucson or Timbuktu. But, wherever they are, I hate them. I hate all hotels. The feet in the corridor and over my head, the half-heard snores, other people's sex through the wall at three in the morning. I like the large facts about travelling alone – the anonymity, the sense that nobody knows where I am, that I've escaped, that I'm autonomous. But I hate the details. Decisions, decisions.

Tony and I came to San Diego once, when the girls were little. We were doing the great trip across America, coast to coast, while we still had the chance, before school holidays bound us hand and foot. We rented a camper van and off we went. We drove down the coast from San Francisco. All I can remember south of Big Sur is an endless coastal suburb. I don't suppose Bettina's building existed then. Twenty years is a long time in California.

Bettina is now Mrs Kustow. According to Ester, Mr Kustow is dead. Turning off the freeway into the northern suburbs, I arrive at a condo set in lushly landscaped grounds. There's money here somewhere. Mr Kustow's? A few people are walking around among the palm trees and oleanders. No one looks less than about eighty. The building is set around a patio and swimming-pool. Nobody is swimming. The penny drops: it's a retirement home, an old people's development. You realise you have escaped from childhood when you are no longer segregated with your age cohort. For a few years everyone mingles freely. Then the segregation begins again. No wonder death is on Bettina's mind.

She is standing at the open door of her apartment: the doorman warned her I was on my way up. There is a wide terrace, shaded with bougainvillaea. An electric barbecue stands in the corner. Nothing too good for Grandma, except company. I think of Ester's shabby veranda, her sombre, watchful figure sitting across the table. Bettina is not sombre. She is small and plump, her white hair is set in carefully styled curls. She wears a bright pink muu-muu. – Miriam? My dear, come in. Have you eaten?

She draws me into her home, like every aunt I ever knew. For aunts like Bettina, visitors mean food. – Isn't this a terrible place? But I'm too old to move again now. Still, at least it's possible to shut the door and be a little private. Yes: she wants to tell her story. She can't wait to tell her story. To speak, at length, to someone under seventy. Doesn't anyone ever come to see her here?

It's so kind of you to agree to see me.

Am I so busy? The American overlays, but can't conceal, the thick Hungarian accent. The stamp of the Martian. It chimes oddly with her idiomatic command of English. The familiar phrases, framed, studied, are presented for triumphant inspection. – Tell me about Ester. What I wouldn't give to see her. My oldest friend.

You could fly over.

I'm not sure I could stand such a long flight. And she's the same. We're old, darling. She has her hip, I have my heart. You're still young, you don't know what it's like. Don't get old, that's my advice. When did you arrive?

Yesterday.

So you're all upside-down still.

Not really.

What will you have? A coffee? Some salad? Some fruit? In Budapest I could have offered you a pastry, but here everyone wants to be healthy. Did you like the food there? Over here, I'm always looking for something a little bit smelly, but I can never find it.

It was delicious, I say. I know what she means. It was the opposite of American food: solid stuff, full of harsh flavour. Concentrated essence of food, and lots of it.

We sit on the terrace. A slight breeze rustles the bougainvillaea. – Do you miss Budapest?

I miss *my* Budapest. But that disappeared fifty years ago.

Is that when you left?

No, darling, I left long before that. In nineteen thirty-three. I was twenty-three. But you don't want to hear about that.

But that's exactly what I do want to hear about!

Down on the emerald-green lawn, two old ladies are strolling, immaculately hairdressed, wearing Bermuda shorts. What stories are locked inside them? In these apartments, so expensively assuaging their families' guilt, what tales could be told, if there were only someone to listen! A beehive, every cell packed with narrative. I remember, when Susanna was born, looking at her, a barely human lump of life, and wondering who might be locked up inside. Now, at the other end, the problem is the opposite. The people are here, fully formed. All they require is revelation.

I switch on my tape recorder.

Bettina takes me back to the Budapest I glimpsed beneath the grime of today's neglected city. In her Budapest, the paint was fresh in the hallways, intellectual adventure in the air. It was a sort of cosmopolitan village. As in a village, everyone knew or was related to everyone else. But there was none of the village sense that life is elsewhere. Bettina's Budapest was where life was taking place. And she was at the centre of the centre. Her mother, the wife of a prosperous banker, ran a sort of radical salon, so that her three daughters (Bettina was the youngest) grew up amid all the city's bright young thinkers.

As she speaks, I try to peel away the layers of the American matron – the white bubble-cut, the too-pink gown. Beneath here, somewhere, is the girl who married Zigi. What strange chance has led us to meet in this wholesome condominium? She grew up steeped in the essence of European subtlety. In her Budapest, there was always another gauze to be lifted, always another slightly shifted view. But in the harsh light of southern California, everything is simplified, one thing or the other, black or white, good or bad, sunlight or shadow. Who, meeting her now, would suspect that other world? And who, then, could have envisaged this? Only the biographer sees it all. Worlds are laid out before us, stories handed to us on a plate. If I were writing a novel, what would I make of Bettina? But I am not. The novelist embroiders – the finished book is a tapestry. But the biographer must resist that temptation. Biography must foster the illusion of fact.

Of course, Budapest did not constitute Hungary. At this period, just before and after the first war, Hungary was still in some ways a primitive country. Zigi liked to tell a story about a weekend he spent in the country with an aristocratic friend when he was eighteen or so. When they came back to the castle after a day's hunting, and Zigi finally reeled up to his bed, there along with the bolsters and pillows was a young girl: just another of his thoughtful host's amenities. To the Viennese, stories such as this summed up Hungary: it was medieval, male and cruel. But the habitués of Bettina's mother's salon –

poets like Endre Ady, musicians like Bela Bartok – were busy creating their own culture, to rival that of Vienna. – Have you heard of Ady? Bettina said to me. Of course not. He was doomed by the language. If a Hungarian wants an international reputation he mustn't be a writer – or not in Hungarian.

The group Bettina is describing is the group from which the Martians were drawn. They all lived within a few blocks of one another, in elaborate, solid apartment houses a few streets back from the river on the Pest side. Even today, those buildings speak of spacious bourgeois comfort. The von Neumanns lived down the street. The Schutzes lived across the big square: there were three boys, and a girl who married Edward Teller. The Fischers owned the building next door to where Bettina lived, on Liberty Square. Zigi's family had the top floor, there was an aunt on the floor below, and the old parents below that. Every evening the young people would meet, walk by the river, sit in the cafés, argue, discuss, dance.

When Bettina was eight, at the end of the Great War, there was a great upheaval: the end of the Habsburg regime. Her parents and Zigi's had grown up amid certainty and stability. Now all that ended. There was no more certainty.

In 1919 Bela Kun's communists took power. – All I remember, she said, is music and pictures. The Marseillaise and the Internationale. For three months – luckily it was the summer – there was nothing to eat but icecream, because the peasants wouldn't sell food for cash. You can't eat money, they said. I don't know where the icecream came from, but I liked it very much. The whole city was covered with wonderful posters. Those were my first associations with communism – icecream and music and wonderful art. But it didn't last. It was overturned by a fascist – Admiral Horthy, a horrible man.

Horthy was terribly antisemitic. Even so, not all Bettina's friends were dismayed when he took power. They were bankers and lawyers, and to them even Horthy seemed better than the Reds. He needed financing, just like anyone else, so they still held their old positions. But there was no future for

48

the young people in Hungary. A quota law was imposed at the university: students could only enter in numbers proportionate to their national grouping in the population. The effect, as intended, was to keep the Jews out. People began to find out who they really were in other people's eyes. It didn't matter if you were baptised or not – you were still Jewish. The one essential thing was to be cleverer than the rest. You had to be a genius. Then you could get to the university or, even better, go to a university elsewhere.

And how did you do in the genius stakes?

Her brown eyes twinkle. – Ah, genius, that was just for the boys. If you were a girl, you married one.

So there they all sit in the Minta school, all these budding geniuses, knowing that this isn't just some figure of speech, some over-the-top family exaggeration. Geniuses is what they've got to be. Innovate or die! There was a big annual mathematics prize for all the schools in Hungary. In Zigi's year, Edward Teller won it. They were in the same class, their birthdays a few weeks apart. – Edward always had the edge over him, said Bettina. Very single-minded, very serious, very ambitious. You know the type.

The young Edward would request that he not be addressed during meals so that he could go on thinking about his current problem. An instant target for school bullies, unpopular with teachers: dismissive of all subjects but mathematics, and so far ahead of the class in that subject that he became bored and apathetic. – So, you are a genius, his maths teacher remarked. Well, I don't like geniuses.

Zsygmond, Bettina comments, was never ambitious in quite that way. There was always a slight distraction, less than total concentration. Edward knew Mici from when he was at school, never looked at another woman. No diversions of that sort. But for Zsygmond, there were always diversions. He was always so devastating, and always so ready to devastate. Always planning conquests. Still when you knew him? That sort of thing doesn't change. Unfortunately, it takes the edge off the concentration. But physics fascinated him. He liked to say: It's where the big thinking is happening. So he kept on

49

with it, even though he knew he would never be quite as good as Edward.

For some reason, she continues, he and I generally went around together. I don't know why he liked me. You know how these things are. We were a group, we grew up together, certain patterns get established. I was never a great beauty. Better than what you see now, of course. I had a good figure – not too thin – with long, long black hair. And I could make him laugh. I made everybody laugh. But Zsygmond could have had anybody. Such a beautiful young man! Perhaps it was because I wasn't interested. A new experience for him. I liked him, but nothing special. I liked dancing, of course, and parties. I was very modern. And Zsygmond was a wonderful dancer. But so conceited. The only child – can you imagine? His mother worshipped him. Nothing was too good for Zsygmond. Too good – nothing was good *enough* for him. Certainly no girl.

By then, anyway, I'd decided I wasn't interested in marriage. The boys could escape into science. That world had no frontiers, if you were good enough. Things weren't so simple for the girls – we couldn't just go off on our own to study somewhere in Germany. But I wanted to be independent. So when I finished university, I opened my own school. It was a kindergarten, run on the most progressive lines. I was twenty-one.

I found my own land without frontiers. I became a communist. That was my escape route. Our parents tried to hope that everything could still go on in the same old comfortable way. But I knew I would have to leave. I just couldn't quite see how. And communism had very good associations for me. Music, and processions, and icecream. I didn't personally know many communists, but I knew it wasn't just a dream – there was a whole country right next door that was doing it.

Listening to Bettina, I reflected on the luck of those boys. To have been born in Budapest: the whole world open to them, anywhere but at home. They were exiled, it is true, but not suddenly, violently, unexpectedly, like their cousins in

Vienna and Berlin, where all life beckoned, where everything was on offer – until, abruptly, the shutters clanged down and the offer closed. For the Martians, there was no desperation, no compulsion. They just knew that when the time came, when they were ready, they would leave.

When Zsygmond left, says Bettina, his mother's life ended. Not literally – that was in Belsen – but emotionally. He was her life. What else did she have? But where else could she live? She could hardly follow him around the world. But she couldn't keep him in Budapest. He wanted to go. His father supported him. If Zsygmond was clever enough to find a place outside, that's what he should do. So he did.

Here we arrive at a junction where two trails meet. The path rejoins the well-known road. Zigi enjoyed discussing the phenomenal flowering of genius in the Hungarian émigrés of his generation. Many, though by no means all of them, were physicists. – The making of us Hungarian physicists, he would say, was that physics was not taught in Hungary. This sentence would be enough to drive Fania from the room. How many times had she heard the tale? Twenty? Forty? A thousand? But I always enjoyed it. Following that remarkable collection of young men, those bred-up geniuses, as they began their wanderings around the world. Von Karman, von Neumann, Wigner, Szilard, Teller. Balogh and Kaldor, the pillars of postwar British economics. Arthur Koestler. Alexander Korda the great film-maker . . .

The first to leave was Theodore von Karman, whose father was Mor Karman, the founder of Zigi's school, the Minta. He went to Göttingen early on, and after to the United States. By 1926 he was settled at Caltech, in Pasadena, where he became known for his brilliance in the new field of aeronautics, and for his exotic lifestyle. He imported his mother and sister, and together they established a salon, decked out with ottomans and oriental rugs, where intellectual discourse would continue until the early hours, kept going by whisky, black cigars, and generous helpings of goulash.

After him came – or went – Johnny von Neumann, the most brilliant mathematician of his generation. His travels led him first to Zurich, and thence to America, to Princeton. His father was a big banker, one of Horthy's financial backers. But Johnny didn't like Horthy, and Budapest wasn't big enough for him.

So by the time I left, Zigi would drawl, it was absolutely the normal thing to do. He went to Göttingen, to study with James Franck and Max Born. By the end of his time in Göttingen, things were starting to get nasty. Hitler had come to power, and Jews were being thrown out of state employment, which included all academic posts. If you weren't a German national you left, which is what Zigi did.

We kept in touch, says Bettina. He came back from time to time, and occasionally we wrote. Every time he came back his mother would hope he was home for good this time, and then when he left there'd be another nervous collapse. Scenes at the railroad station, the house more or less in mourning. Eventually he stopped coming back, but we still kept in touch.

There were a few obvious places for a young physicist to go outside Germany. The main ones were Cambridge, where Rutherford was, Manchester, where he had been, and with Niels Bohr in Copenhagen. Edward Teller went first to Manchester, and then came on later to Copenhagen to work with Bohr. But Zigi went straight to Copenhagen. Professionally, it was fine – Bohr was a great teacher and a great man. But Zigi felt terribly lonely there. So he wrote to Bettina. Why didn't she come and join him and they could get married? Then he could settle down and perhaps get a Rockefeller Foundation fellowship, and she could get out of Hungary, and they would see the world together.

This letter arrived quite unexpectedly, said Bettina. Her eyes have a faraway look: she is back in reality, back in Budapest, far from the misty improbabilities of a Californian third-age condo. We were having breakfast – just me and my parents, my sisters were both married with children already. It was the winter of 1933, it must have been December. It was very cold, snow was falling, there was that white light, everything white, the sky, the air, the ground. And here was this letter from Denmark. I knew who it was from, of course, but there was nothing special about that, we wrote to each other from time to time. I opened it and read it while I was drinking my last cup of coffee. I remember I burst out laughing, the whole thing seemed so ridiculous. My mother asked me what I was laughing about, and I said, Zsygmond Fischer wants me to marry him. And she said: Well, is that such a stupid idea? So I began to think about it seriously. I can truly say to you, it wasn't something that had ever crossed my mind before.

I put on my boots and my fur coat and on my way to the kindergarten – it wasn't a very long walk from our apartment – I thought and thought. I liked Zsygmond, and of course he was very attractive, but I hadn't any illusions about him even then. So I got to school, and there was Ester. She was my deputy at that time. And while we were waiting for the children I told her about this letter. I expected her to laugh like I had. But she said: Well, why not? I said: I don't love him. But you like him, she said. And you won't mind going to bed with him. Who would? It's as good a basis for marriage as most. You're always saying you want to leave. So it's sooner rather than later.

Then I started to think seriously. When you leave your country and your friends, the great fear is loneliness. But that didn't have to be true for me. My life didn't have frontiers any more than Zsygmond's. The big difference between our two worlds was that no one knew I was a communist. Science is open. You publish, you discuss, you collaborate, you move forward, you publish again. But my world was secret. The basis of communism, outside Russia of course, was secrecy. The Party was organised in cells, no one knew more than they absolutely had to. You had one contact, you didn't know their real name, who gave you small jobs to do from time to time. It was very thrilling and dramatic. You felt you were part of an inner circle that would change the world. I was a member of a cell; I had a contact at the university. I went to her after school was over and told her what had happened. She said: Do it. Get married. It might be useful. I'll give you a name in Copenhagen. So I thought some more. And then I wrote to Zsygmond and said, all right, I'd marry him.

Silence. Another tape ended. Once Bettina began to talk, why should she stop? There seemed no reason why I should not sit there for days, changing tapes every now and then, while she recounted her entire life. She wasn't tired. On the contrary, the telling gained in vivacity as it progressed. These memories were her reality: it was the present she couldn't believe. How had she arrived at this point? That, of course, was the story. We should get to the present in the end, if I had the time, the inclination, the tapes.

I'm playing them back now in my study in London. The house is empty: even I am barely present. I am with Niels Bohr's group in Copenhagen in that winter of sixty years ago. Bohr is a giant, philosophically and physically. He is quiet in manner and the more he is excited or in earnest the quieter he becomes. His voice drops to a whisper as he rehearses his thoughts, trying them out again and yet again in an effort to reach a formulation that will satisfy him. The joke goes that, whatever the size of the room or the gathering, he always pitches his voice just too low, so that the end result is invariably a straining, craning knot around the large, sombre figure of the whispering Master.

It is one of those moments when intellect and imagination must stretch themselves around concepts so new as to be, for most people, literally unthinkable. Copernicus realises the world circles the sun, and shatters the medieval universe. Newton watches the apple drop, and Newton's Laws result. Einstein shows that space and time are conjoined, that gravity may bend light, and that energy is part of the same equation. The implications of his findings are so bizarre that Einstein himself can't at first bring himself to take them all in. But the equations are there: it *must* be so.

Now it is the turn of Bohr and his colleagues. They are uncovering a universe as inconceivably microscopic as Einstein's is huge – and as strange and unthinkable in its implications. Their concern is with the structure and composition of the atom. For atoms are not – as their name indicates, as had always been thought – indivisible, the smallest particle of matter. In 1919 Ernest Rutherford published a paper describing how, when he bombarded nitrogen with alpha rays, he produced oxygen and protons. What are these protons? Evidently, they are among the building-blocks of atoms. What other such blocks are there? How are they arranged? What are the properties of this sub-atomic world?

Rutherford was not the first to envision this world. His great achievement was to demonstrate its existence empirically, by experiment. Before him, Hendrik Lorentz had realised that atoms were built of particles, which he called electrons, and that light shone from them as they oscillated. Max Planck devised a way of measuring this energy in quanta, or packages, of radiation. And in 1913 Bohr used Planck's constant to produce a new model of the atom, in which electrons could only move in certain orbits. When an electron absorbed a light quantum, it jumped to a higher orbit: the quantum leap.

Like Rutherford, Bohr visualised the sub-atomic world as a sort of miniature solar system of nuclei surrounded by orbiting particles. But by 1933, when Zigi came to Copenhagen, this was old stuff. Werner Heisenberg, one of the young giants of the new physics, wrote: My whole idea is to destroy without a trace the idea of orbits. His equations led to the terrifying conclusion that, at this level, momentum *and* position could not be simultaneously predicted.

All certainty vanished. De Broglie showed that electrons are neither particles nor waves, but may be either. An electron must embody all possibilities – all velocities, all positions, all properties – until observation pins it down.

Experimentalists gave solidity to the theorists' flickering models. In 1932 James Chadwick discovered a new atomic particle – the neutron. And in 1933, Irene and Frederic Joliot-Curie, the daughter and son-in-law of Marie Curie, who had first isolated radium, the most radioactive of natural elements, finally induced artificial radioactivity by chipping a proton from the aluminium atom and changing it into a radioactive form of silicon – that is to say, a form which is decaying naturally and giving off energy as it does so.

This, invisible, barely envisageable, but *there* and utterly absorbing, was Zigi's world. What mere religion, what man-made system of beliefs and principles, could compare with its beauty and fascination? The comparison is not otiose. The effect of these discoveries upon those privileged to comprehend them must have been not unlike a religious revelation. The initiate alone knows the truth of the way things are: the rest of the world is out in the cold, denied the transcendent vision. Such knowledge may induce humility or arrogance – in Zigi's case, undoubtedly the latter. I never knew a man more aware of his superiority to the mere run of mortals. But in either case, the consciousness of being set apart is more than delightful: it is irresistible. Mephisto is a master of psychology, or he is nothing.

These, then, were the questions discussed in laboratories and seminar-rooms, in Berlin and Copenhagen, Rome, Cambridge, Paris and Leipzig, by the close, argumentative and competitive community of initiates: those who understood. Youth was no barrier: Heisenberg was only twenty-six when he made his great discovery of the uncertainty principle. Intellectual power was the only thing that mattered – that, and the daring to follow an idea through to its conclusions. It was an almost entirely male world, its only significant female inhabitants being Irene Curie and Lise Meitner, the demure Viennese Jewess who was Otto Hahn's close colleague at the Kaiser-Wilhelm Institute in Berlin. And it was a world of pure knowledge, or so it seemed at the beginning. Rutherford joyfully proclaimed his discoveries to be of no practical use whatever. – Follow me, Mephisto croons. What harm can it possibly do?

What did politics matter, except insofar as it became easier or possible to work in one place, harder or impossible in another? All these people talked the language of the new physics: whether in English, German, Italian or French was incidental. – In the day-to-day politics I still was hardly interested, said Teller, except that I wanted to continue my work.

They didn't know their luck. They were going to stay alive

when otherwise they would probably have died. When I was in Budapest, walking along the Danube embankments, I couldn't help thinking about the groups of Jews who were marched down here every morning, every afternoon, every evening, every night, picked off the streets or out of buildings in the newly walled ghetto, and shot, their bodies falling into the river one after the other. If Zigi, Teller, and their friends Leo Szilard and Eugene Wigner were not among them, it was because they were programmed for export. Physics was their saviour.

I shall not forget my first introduction to this world. Zigi was my guide on that occasion. Every detail of it is imprinted on my memory.

This happened nearly thirty years ago now. Can it really be that long? I remember it so clearly. The end of my first year at Cambridge. Sitting in my room, while footsteps echo up and down those endless Girton corridors, passing my door, never stopping. I am sitting on my suitcase, waiting for my parents. They are coming to collect me. Their only daughter, the apple of their eye. They're not usually late. I can't imagine what's happened to them. I'm beginning to get rather annoyed. Outside, the sun is shining on the tennis courts. There's a party I could be going to. But it suited them better to come today. So – why aren't they here?

I open a book. I'm not good at waiting. Perhaps I'll go outside and leave a note for them. They should have been here an hour ago. Have they forgotten? I go to the phone at the end of the corridor and ring home. No reply. They must be on their way.

Someone stops at my door. I call: Come in. But the person standing there is not my mother. It is Miss King, my tutor. She looks terribly embarrassed. My legs, my stomach, are suddenly filled with lead. When she opens her mouth I know what she is going to say. Though of course, until she says it, it still might not be true. But the words are not to be stopped by mere wishing. – Miriam, she says. I've just had some bad news. Your parents were in an accident. A car crash. My dear, she says, very fast, to get it out while her strength lasts, I'm afraid they're both dead.

For a while we sit there. Miss King doesn't know what to say, and neither do I. It is an occasion beyond speech. I have a sense of being suspended in space and time. Finally she manages to whisper – Is there anyone you'd like to get in touch with? A relative?

Fania. My aunt.

Give me the number, Miss King says, relieved at having some tangible task to get her out of this appalling situation. Would you like someone to sit with you?

But most of my friends have already left, and eventually I accompany Miss King to her office while she makes her call.

Darling! Fania cries when, at last, the receiver is handed to me (for, luckily, she happened to be home, not out shopping or immersed in some art exhibition). I can't believe this. You must come straight here. We'll sort everything out. Just put your luggage into a taxi and get a train to London. And get a taxi the other end.

Shall I ever forget that journey? The last journey of my childhood. From now on, I am responsible for myself. Mixed with the terrible grief is an even more terrible – because guilt-filled – sense of freedom. But by the time I reach Fania's house, all ambivalence is swept aside. I collapse into her arms, and find myself finally able to cry. The problem now is to stop. All through the gruesome week that follows – of identifications, funeral arrangements, the funeral itself – Fania and I are a pair of perfect Niobes, setting each other off at a glance.

For a week – this privileged week – Zigi puts up with us, not to speak of the rest of my family. Families bore Zigi, and orthodoxy appals him – a regression to some savage irrationality he thought civilisation had left behind. My uncles and aunts, however, are not conscious of being in civilisation's backwash. They assume that we shall sit *shiva* – the seven days' ceremonial that follows a death, when the family congregates at the house of the mourner for prayers and company. What is more, they assume that we shall do this at Fania and Zigi's house, since this is where I, the chief mourner, am staying. For the duration, Zigi is denied access to his study and his piano, his room being the largest in the house, and the one nearest the kitchen. He decamps to his laboratory, putting in two or three brief appearances at the *shiva* for form's sake. It is assumed that, from now on, I shall be living, when not at college, with Zigi and Fania. It is some time since they have had a lodger: I can have the rooms at the top of the house.

At the end of the week Zigi reappears. The ceremony has had the effect it was no doubt designed for: the first awful week has been buried in company and sympathy. Now there is a mere lifetime to get through. I had thought I was going to Greece with some friends; but how can I do that? Yesterday I went through my belongings to see what I needed to bring to Fania's. I opened my mother's wardrobe, hoping, perhaps, to find that she had been hiding there all this time, that all the pantomime of the past few days was nothing but a terrible joke. The clothes, the shoes . . . I howled into my mother's underwear, smelling her particular scent for (so I imagined) the last time. (In fact, like her face, it will follow me through the years, an intermittent mirage – a whiff from an old handbag, a glove . . .) How can I just go away on some holiday with friends? What kind of company will I be?

When I get back to West Hampstead, Zigi is waiting. He opens the door of his room and beckons me inside. – Time for a talk, he says. Sit down. He points to an armchair, fetches the piano stool and sets himself down facing me. Placed, as is his wont, in a suitably superior situation. Not that this is necessary. I need no symbolism to recognise Zigi's effortless superiority. In his mid-fifties, he has lost none of his capacity to devastate. His hair is greying now, but still thick and wavy, and he has kept his figure: tall, well set up, perhaps a little bulkier than he was, but we are not speaking of an ascetic here. Zigi likes his food, and is an excellent cook. Distinguished in every way. While I – I –

If there is one characteristic that I associate with that period of my life, my late teens, it is lack of control. I cannot get on top of myself. There is too much of me, it is in the wrong places, it sweats, blushes, does not respond as I would wish.

My body gives no inkling of the sophisticate within. Who will ever delve beneath my unpromising surface to plumb my hidden depths? Not Zigi, that's for sure. I know the kind of young women Zigi likes. Slim, with perfectly applied makeup, unperturbable, cynical. Who wants a beautiful mind, at that age? I would trade mine for a beautiful body any day. And just now I am not at my best. Dusty, jeans slightly too tight, uncombed, tearstained.

Enough of all this, Zigi says. It's time to pull yourself together.

He is staring at me like a hypnotist, his eyes fixed upon mine. And all I can do is stare back. I feel thunderstruck. For the past week I have lived in a trance, cocooned in warm waves of sympathy. Aunts have hugged me to their bosoms and thrust cheesecake and strudel into my hands. They have confided, in tones worthy of a state secret, that they have left their chopped liver, chopped herring, chopped egg, in the fridge, and that when I need new supplies I must call upon them. They have clustered together in corners and fixed me with eyes full of horror and sympathy. They have discussed among themselves the wisdom or otherwise of confiding me to the doubtful care of Fania. She can't cook, and they've never much taken to Zigi (or vice versa). My uncles, meanwhile, have assured me that they will handle the business end of things – an offer I gratefully accept. I mustn't worry about money, they tell me. I don't; I never have, and why should I start now? My Uncle Harry, who is a wealthy solicitor with (so Fania assures me) highly dubious associates, has fixed an appointment for the coming week, when we shall discuss matters such as the sale of my parents' house, my allowance, and similar details. I am a victim, a miserable victim of unforeseen catastrophe. One does not attack a victim. But this, unmistakably, is what Zigi is now doing – or is preparing to do.

It's very sad, what has happened, he says now. No one is denying that. But it's not unique. Why go on as if it were? Since when is it unusual for a grown-up to lose her parents? All right, you might have expected them to live another twenty, thirty years. But you think that's the usual way of things? In the last century, this was normal. In this century even. In the shtetl where your grandparents lived, was it so unusual? As for my generation – what do you think was happening to us at your age? At nineteen I had left my home for ever. I knew it was for ever, and so did my parents. We could feel the storm coming, though of course we didn't know exactly what sort of storm it would be. Who could foresee Belsen? Thank God, nobody. But one thing we knew. We had to succeed so that we could get out. We knew it, we felt it. Everyone wonders why there are Hungarians at the centre of everything. Physics, economics, psychology, business. *That's* why. Can you think of a more compelling reason? I'll tell you an old joke: Only a man from Budapest enters a revolving door behind you and comes out in front. We had to! There was no option. *Most* of the people I knew as a young man died before I was forty. They were killed, or they killed themselves. The only way to survive was to have the courage to move on. My grandfather left his shtetl, which was of course wiped out, including all his family, by the Nazis. He came alone to Budapest. He made money milling flour and my father became a banker. My aunt's husband didn't do so well: my cousins weren't so clever; they stayed in Budapest when I left. Where are they? Dead, all dead. My parents died because they wouldn't believe they were really in danger. Your parents have died, but you have still a home. Here is your home. I had no home. Science had to become my home. Science was lasting, science was secure. Only science.

He has been speaking more and more quietly: now his voice peters out altogether. There is silence. I can think of nothing to say. I feel vaguely ashamed – of the lack of horrors lurking in my life, of my unworldliness, my inexperience. What is this tirade *for*? My nineteen-year-old self is quite unable to understand it. Why should my parents' death make me feel guilty or ashamed? And yet I am prepared to believe there must be some good reason behind all this. Uncle Zigi is my idol: I adore him. Amid the narrow, north-west London surburbanism of my family he is a breath of exotic air, a bridge to that life of intellect and politics which it is my aim to enter one day. But – what has all this got to do with me, now? Zigi, too, seems to sense this disjunction. There is a pause. He shifts his weight, but does not get up – the only act which would release me: that I should rise and quit him in mid-flow is unthinkable to both of us.

Look, he says. If all this hadn't happened, what would you be doing? You must have had some plans.

I explain that I was going to visit Greece with some friends. We were due to leave tomorrow. I haven't heard from them. Miss King was going to speak to them. Presumably they have been too intimidated to ring. They assume I won't be coming.

Why not? says Zigi. Why should your life stop? You must go. You must get on with things. What will you do here? Get in the way. Ring them. Go.

And I went.

Looking back, it seems clear that his conscious intentions were all contained in that last exchange. But Zigi could never have arrived directly at this wholly benign conclusion. True, my parents' death affected me; but it also affected *him*. On the crudest level, it meant that he was no longer the centre of attention in his own house. This was not only intolerable but unjust, since my sufferings in no way approximated to his. So that his was a speech of indignant self-justification. As for the brotherhood of science, this was my introduction to the other great refrain of his life. A haven in all countries and under all circumstances, carrying with it the certainty of friends, of like minds, of incomparable intellectual pleasures. A place of divine unworldliness, where politics should not enter. Not, unfortunately, open to all.

Copenhagen, said Bettina. What did I know of Copenhagen? I'd never even met a Dane. As I sat on the train I didn't know what had happened to me.

The Devil had happened to her. Needs must, when he drives. She was no longer in control of her life.

The Devil: a purely mental construct. Ugliness lies in the eye of the beholder. For Bettina and Ester and Zigi and all the rest of those unfortunates for whom the mere act of living where they had always lived now became fraught with mortal danger, his identity was clear. He had a black cow-lick and a ludicrous little moustache. For Hitler and his friends, he had a curved nose and no foreskin. The constant truths about the Devil are that he is always on the other side, and always appears in times of uncertainty. At those times, his counterpart, the Saviour of the Just, the Emperor of the Last Days, must of course also make his appearance. In the suffering which followed their defeat in the First World War, the Germans recognised this saviour in Hitler, who gave the Messiah's traditional promise: a paradisal Thousand-year Empire if they could only defeat Antichrist and his Jewish armies. In other words, the usual scenario. Ever since the First Crusade was initiated, in the hope of diverting the destructive energies of French robber barons from the surrounding countryside onto the Turks then holding Byzantium, the Chosen People, landless, separate, urban, has been a frequent target for such emperors. The next year, 1096, saw the first great massacre of German Jews in the overpopulated lands along the Rhine. The same old story: the same old players.

IV

Bettina was very happy during those early days in Copenhagen. She had always been fond of Zigi, and now she began to fall seriously in love with him. – Suddenly I was dazzled, she said, near the beginning of the new tape. You perhaps think this is a joke. You only knew him when he was an older man. Somewhere I have some photographs . . .

She goes to the other side of the room, where there is a wall of bookshelves, and pulls down an album. She hands it to me open at a page of black and white photographs, slightly yellowing now. From them smile a young couple. She is of medium height, with a sweet, round, intelligent face, dressed in a shirt and slacks, her hair cut fashionably short; the long braids came off when the schoolgirl metamorphosed into a

63

businesswoman. He is tall, broad, blond: gorgeous. – His grandmothers got raped by Russians somewhere along the line, I observe.

Yes, we all used to tease him about it.

She is gazing at him, but his thoughts are elsewhere. He is smiling slightly, but not at Bettina. He didn't change much: unmistakably, Zigi.

At first their life was like a delightful game. Copenhagen in the snow was a toy city. They had a tiny apartment where Bettina played at being a housewife. Living in Denmark was without tension. – Like being released from prison, she said. It was only when you came to a place like that that you realised all the undercurrents that were always there in Budapest. And then there was the sex. The revelation of sex. She said: I used to dream about it all day when he wasn't there. I couldn't believe my luck, to be married to a husband I loved so much and who loved me in return. Why else had he asked me to marry him?

As time went on, this question why began to worry her a little bit more. You can live on sex for just so long. A few months? Maximum. After that she began to realise some of the other things about being married to Zigi. Like how much he wasn't there, and how when he was there, he was often really somewhere else. Where? With Bohr, of course, talking about physics, thinking about physics, arguing about physics. Occasionally he'd ask some of his colleagues over to dinner and Bettina would cook a delicious meal and they'd eat and drink and then they'd all sit around for hours and hours talking about their work, which was what interested them more than anything else. In order for anything to compete for their attention it had to be exceptional. Teller had his music – he was a wonderful pianist. Or chess, which demanded the same sort of concentration. Or some physical release. A lot of them played ping-pong very intensely. Bohr liked to go sailing with his family. He was very attached to his wife and sons. They all lived in a big house in the middle of a park which had been built by the founder of the Carlsberg brewery. It was a house which was given as a mark of honour to the greatest man in Denmark: Bohr had recently moved into it. He was a very tall man, very deliberate. Very relaxed, not like all the young men around him. Not driven. Because of course he led a normal life. Where should he be but in Copenhagen with his wife and family?

Zigi and all his friends knew that they would never have that kind of life, not in the city or country where they were born or where they would have chosen naturally to live. So their anchor was their work. They were completely entranced by it. – It's the most wonderful game in the world, Zigi used to say to Bettina. We are trying to discover the secrets of the universe. They're all there, waiting. All we have to do is think, and be brave enough to follow our thoughts as far as they will lead us. He sometimes tried to explain what they were all thinking about. – It was all right while he was talking, she said, but when he stopped it became misty. I couldn't visualise those concepts. Their world had its own language, and I didn't speak it. And Zsygmond was not a good teacher. He hadn't the patience, and he didn't have that desire to communicate his thoughts to people outside. So why was I there? It seemed more and more not just as though he had no real need of me but that I was an actual nuisance, with my demands.

I ponder Bettina's question. Why, indeed, was she there? Why did Zigi suddenly feel this urge to matrimony? Perhaps even he was not as totally self-contained as he liked to appear. The Tellers had just got married then; and for Edward Teller, getting married solved the problem of life in exile. Mici was always the only girl for him, and when they got married, he was immediately at home. They created their own little world and took it around with them wherever they went. They became a sort of social magnet: a real home, where friends were always welcome. Perhaps Zigi saw that for the Tellers it worked, that clearly their personal situation was more satisfactory than his, and so he thought he would try it, and Bettina was the obvious choice. And then there was the question of long-standing competition. I never met a more competitive man than Zigi. Everything anyone did, he always had to do himself, at once and better. But for him, the problem was not solved. He wasn't capable of that sort of contentment. He could never lose himself in another person.

He'd never really had one girlfriend, Bettina muses. He always preferred variety, but I was as near as he'd got, and I was so suitable! But it became clear that, for us, it wasn't going to work in that way. He didn't feel contented – on the contrary, he had to deal with all these new demands. So he kept away.

Why didn't you just leave, then?

That was my first reaction. Just to go back to Budapest and my old life. I didn't know what I'd done wrong. At that age, everything has to be your own fault. If Zsygmond was losing interest in me, then that must be because I was getting dull. Here I was in that northern city, away from my friends, my family, my work, stuck in this tiny apartment, with no money and a husband who had lost interest in me. I was very unhappy.

I had a communist contact in Copenhagen. The Party in Budapest gave me a name. He was almost the only person I knew by myself, nothing to do with Zsygmond. So I talked to him about it. He was very definite. He said: Don't leave; bear it for a little while at least. In Budapest, what use are you to us? But here, who knows.

Did he know what your husband was doing?

Probably. What else did I have to talk about? But it meant as little to him as it did to me. By then, it was obvious that there would be a war. My friend explained that, in the case of war, it might be important to have a strong organisation in Denmark. And my parents felt that I should not come back to Budapest. My mother was not a woman to have illusions just because that might make life pleasanter. She said: I am too old to move again. What happens, will happen. But you are young, with your life before you. Of course, I am sorry you are so unhappy. Perhaps things will get better with Zsygmond, perhaps they won't. If not, you can leave him. But Hungary is no place for you. See how things work out. Give it a year. Say to yourself, in a year's time I will decide. So that is what I did.

Would Bettina's contact have been so innocent of what

Bohr's group's work might lead to? Probably. At this time, only a few people saw that these questions which so absorbed the physicists might eventually, and contrary to Rutherford's certainties, have practical applications. Leo Szilard went to Berlin when he left Budapest, and while he was there he read a book by H.G. Wells, *The World Set Free*, in which London and Paris are destroyed by atom bombs. It was written just after Rutherford first split the atom, but the German translation was published only in 1932.

Szilard liked to tell how he read the book at a time, in 1933, when he happened to have realised how a chain reaction might be achieved. He was immediately struck both by Wells's prophetic talents and also by the fact that Wells's war came about because the scientist who discovered how to release the power of the atom published his procedure. Szilard could see where things were leading in Germany. So he got out (the day before the frontier closed to Jews), went to London, and did not publish, but patented his procedure and assigned the patent to the British Navy, which made no use of it whatever. These things were in the air, but they were a long way from being common knowledge.

In the autumn of 1934, Zigi was offered a job. He was invited to the Soviet Union, to Kiev, where he would talk things over and see whether he wanted to stay. – Naturally, says Bettina, I was enthusiastic. But what we found there was a shock. People weren't just poor, they were frightened: there was an atmosphere of terror everywhere. Zsygmond had some old friends there, but they pretended not to know us. I know one was sent to a camp not long after we left. I didn't want to admit all this even to myself. I tried to make light of it. I could see no other hope for the world. But Zsygmond decided he didn't want to work there, and I have to say I didn't argue. We came back to Denmark, and almost immediately there was another possibility, in Switzerland, to go and work with Pauli in Zurich. And of course in Zurich people spoke German, so I made friends, and got a job, and life wasn't too bad. So I still stayed with Zsygmond.

Is that the front door opening? I listen, hand poised on the

OFF button. These days, Zigi's life seems more real than my own. It is the intervals when I am forced not to think about it that lack substance. This person I thought I knew better than almost anyone, was all the time someone I had no inkling of. If Zigi could conceal a wife and child, what else may not be lurking there, waiting for revelation? And all this is out of bounds – something I can't discuss either with my own husband or Zigi's widow. (How else am I to think of Fania?)

I don't know how long I can keep it up. The other day, for instance, Fania came to dinner. A perfectly usual event. I can hardly cut off communications just because of this. On the contrary: she needs us now more than ever. She's not looking too well. Time passes, and the reality of her solitude sinks in. Zigi was good company – better company than we are. We have told her time and again she must come round whenever she feels like it, but we all know that it will be up to us to arrange these occasions. Quite apart from pride and habit she doesn't have a car, public transport between her place and ours is unreliable, and she isn't rich enough to call a taxi just to drop in on the off-chance. No: she must be invited. Often. So she came, and we had a drink, and I made dinner, and Tony and Fania talked. – Is something wrong, Miriam? she suddenly said. You aren't usually so quiet.

No, I'm fine, I said. What should be wrong? But I wasn't convincing, and she wasn't convinced. What was wrong, of course, was this impossible topic, sitting on the table between us like an incubus. I couldn't see round it: I could think of nothing to say. I avoided it by getting up to make the coffee. The real conversation at the table was going on between Tony and me, though of course none of it was spoken out loud, and Fania kept catching its echoes. She probably imagines that it's somehow her fault – that we don't enjoy her company, that we ask her round as a chore. Which is not entirely untrue, but not for the reasons she thinks. Shall I tell her? Then relations really would be cut off, but at least she'd have her indignation to sustain her. I tentatively put this to Tony. He said: You can't. It's your problem and you're going to have to find your way round it. Guilt, guilt, it chokes us all. Luckily, he's away a lot at the moment on business. Setting up contracts, renewing contacts. But that won't last for ever.

False alarm. It's the next-door house. From my study I can hear their front door more clearly than my own.

Bettina let me have a photo of her and Zigi – the one she first showed me, taken in the days before things went sour. How hopeful they both look, how innocent – even the spoilt deceiver himself: whims hadn't had time to harden into habit yet.

Every mother's dream. Why can't Susanna find a boy like that?

And if she did, wouldn't we be delighted?

CHAPTER 4   FISSION

I

AT THE END of our time in Zurich, Bettina continues, I was pregnant.

This I suppose, is Marianne. My – cousin? No; we are not, strictly speaking, related. Zigi, who connects us, is not a blood relation. That, at least, was spared me.

We are into our second day now, Bettina and I. Today she's wearing a black kaftan with gold embroidery. Dressing up for guests. One of life's harmless pleasures. I, too, have secret binges of trying on various garments in combination. If I want to wear this necklace, then I shall have to do without that belt. It reassures me to think that I shall still indulge these pointless vanities forty years on. Shall I look as good then as Bettina does now? I have been considering the mystery of her appearance. Those bubble curls can't be all her own. They're too substantial. Old ladies have thinner hair. But why stop at white? Why not a green wig, or blue, or sequined? Shall I allow myself a sequined wig, at eighty-three?

She is anxious, maternal. How was the motel? She hopes I will lunch with her. She has prepared some special Hungarian dishes. At this rate, I shall not merely lunch with her, but dine, and lunch and dine tomorrow and for the rest of the week. I laid in some new spools of tape this morning.

Otherwise, she goes on, I think I would not have gone with Zsygmond to America. So you see, Marianne saved my life. In 1938 you still could see Budapest as a possible place to live. I don't know how the baby happened. It wasn't a sensible time to be having babies, and we were very careful. But there it was.

These things weren't as advanced as they are now. And I found I was very happy. It seemed a positive thing to be doing, amid all the terrible happenings. I was so happy that Zsygmond didn't dare suggest what I know he thought of first, which was of course that I should get rid of the baby. He was fond of me after all, and he was never a cruel man. All sorts of things, but not that. So there we were, chained together by this invisible person.

I can imagine. Oh, how well I can imagine! Suddenly I feel an almost irresistible urge to confide in Bettina – to tell all, to finally confess. What a luxury! What a relief, after all these years! What harm could it do? It isn't as if there'd be any danger of gossip. Zigi, our only point of contact, is dead. We live at opposite ends of the earth. We'll probably never meet again. And here, at last, is the one person who might understand.

I can feel my mouth opening. I can feel the words coming. Then I shut it again. What would be the point? It would only upset her, and why should I do that? Anyhow, it's not my soul I'm here to expose. Zigi's the one under the spotlight. And now Bettina is talking again. We're back in our appointed roles. She talks, I listen.

So where to go? We couldn't stay in Zurich. We were only allowed in on that understanding. It was a temporary place while something else was arranged. Russia was out of the question, that was clear even to me. That left America. Or Britain, but America was bigger, and Zsygmond had more contacts there. And we both felt that if we were to start a new life we would prefer it really new, outside Europe. Luckily Zsygmond was not a lawyer or doctor or historian. You could say he was a product designed for export. There was always some job for a good physicist in America. He found a post at Columbia, where Fermi, who was also a refugee, was working. The job had very little pay and no security, but it was a job. So we went.

When we landed I was seven months pregnant. One of our old Budapest friends, a musician, was already living in New York, and he had found an apartment for us. He met us off the

71

boat. He thought New York was the most wonderful city on earth. He introduced us to his favourite restaurant and apple pie with icecream. Then he took us to this apartment he had found near Columbia. I was shocked. In Zurich, everything was so neat and clean and full of light. But this! The windows hadn't been cleaned for ten years, and when I cleaned them, I could see the cockroaches. Still, it was heated, and there was a shower, and a stove and a refrigerator. We thanked Max very much and took it. I spent my first week in America painting it white. This was the spring of 1938.

Soon we got to know people. Zsygmond had met Robert Oppenheimer in Europe, and he introduced us to some interesting people. Musicans and artists as well as scientists. It was wonderful for me to meet people who were not physicists. To have general conversation in which I could join, not just wives' things among the wives. We drank to the confusion of our enemies. We thought we all knew who our enemies were. We were still young.

Quite soon I was approached by some people to join the Party. I suppose it was obvious I might sympathise. I was a little uncertain what to do. They were all very romantic still about Russia, and I had actually seen what was happening there. They didn't want to know about that. But they were such nice people – the best people I knew in New York. So I joined, or rejoined. I didn't talk about it with Zsygmond. I liked having my own secret again. He had his science. I really didn't want to spend my life just being the mother of this baby. I needed something of my own. Because Zsygmond was never there. He left the apartment every morning, and where did he go? Into another world. The door of the apartment would shut and leave me trapped. That was how it felt.

I used to wonder if he had another woman. My friends thought I was crazy. They said, what time can he have? Between you and the baby and his work? And in a way they were right. His work came before everything. His real wife was always his work. But there's always time. For Zsygmond, there was always time. All those days when he was working late at the laboratory, when he would leave in the morning and

I wouldn't see him until perhaps ten in the evening. There were times, even in Copenhagen when we were first married . . . I never found out. Perhaps I didn't ask because I didn't want to be told.

So he was always somewhere else, at a conference, visiting a laboratory. Wherever it was, he was at home, because his home, ever since he left Budapest, was never a particular place, but a group of people, a set of ideas. And nearly all these people of course were now in America. The Tellers were in Washington – Edward had a job at George Washington University. Everyone always used to meet there – they were a sort of social centre. Eugene Wigner was at Princeton. Leo Szilard was also at Columbia. They used to meet all the time, to talk about their work and what was going on. Because this was just when it was discovered that the chain reaction should be possible.

II

Here he is, then: Mephistopheles in person, the Great Satan who will dominate our lives for the next half-century. He has made his entry and immediately taken his rightful place at the centre of attention.

In December 1938, Otto Hahn, at the Kaiser-Wilhelm Institute in Berlin, discovers that when uranium is bombarded with neutrons, fission occurs. He communicates this discovery to his erstwhile colleague Lise Meitner, whose Jewish ancestry has condemned her to exile in Stockholm. She is from Vienna, but, since the Anschluss, Austrian nationality is no protection against German law. Meitner's nephew Otto Frisch is working in Copenhagen with Bohr. He visits his aunt that Christmas: they work out the mathematics of a possible chain reaction. The products of the original fission do not account for all the neutrons contained in the uranium nucleus. If the stray neutrons can be induced to produce more fissions in their turn, then the result will be a chain reaction. The energy of the atom – that energy described by Einstein – is now within reach. Almost. Not yet; not quite yet. But it is immediately obvious to anyone acquainted with the subject what this might mean to a world on the brink of war.

Frisch, back in Copenhagen, carries out some verification experiments. They work as he had hoped. He talks to his mentor Niels Bohr. They agree that discretion would be wise. They will refrain from publishing this finding. But Bohr is just off to America, to a conference in Washington. How can he not give this gathering of old friends and colleagues his exciting news? Bohr is a generous man. It is not in his nature to keep the whole apple to himself. Before the words are fairly out of his mouth, there is a rush for the doors, as physicists race to the phones to get their labs to set the experiment up. As the uranium atoms are bombarded with neutrons, they split into two nearly equal parts. These fissions may be watched: each tiny pulse of energy causes a jagged green peak of light to appear on the screen of the oscilloscope. Science has moved into a new era, and everybody knows it. – There is a chain-reaction mood in Washington, wrote Teller at this time. I only had to say 'uranium' and then could listen for two hours to their thoughts.

Where are the free neutrons, the neutrons Frisch and Meitner could not account for, the neutrons that will produce the chain reaction?

In March 1939, Edward Teller and a friend are playing a Mozart violin sonata together. The phone rings. It is Leo Szilard. He says (in Hungarian, naturally as between fellow Martians – but the listening security men assume he is speaking in cipher): I have found the neutrons. And Teller knows that the last doubts have vanished.

The era of innocent knowledge is over. For the second (or twenty-second, or two-thousandth) time, the gates of Eden clang shut.

Until then, said Teller, my work and my life had been simple and straightforward. I worked in science because doing so was the greatest reward I could imagine. All other meaningful activities seemed to require accepting contradictions and compromises.

Now, however, nothing is simple and straightforward. All the scientists know what this new discovery may lead to, though few care to discuss it openly. All are aware (who should be more aware than they?) of the impending war. The land of science, just like the rest of the world, is riven by the barriers which are everywhere being erected.

When Teller first left Hungary at the age of eighteen, he went to Leipzig to study with Werner Heisenberg. For Teller, Heisenberg was a brilliant physicist and a good man. A great rapport sprang up between them. A similar rapport existed between Heisenberg and his old friend and teacher Niels Bohr.

But how can friendships, even such friendships as these, survive the polarisation now going on in Europe? Heisenberg does not want to leave Germany. He is German through and through. Those many of his old friends who have had no choice but to emigrate press him to join them in America. An honoured position will be his for the asking. He refuses all entreaties. He is no enthusiast for National Socialism, but what will happen to Germany if all the decent Germans leave? And what about German science? Someone must remain to start it up again after the war is over. He feels this is his responsibility.

Staying, he cannot avoid the consequences of his learning. The German government is as aware as anyone of Hahn's and Meitner's discovery and its possible consequences. Heisenberg is asked to evaluate the time and effort necessary to construct a nuclear bomb.

German physicists are in a quandary. For is not the basis of any nuclear bomb that Einsteinian 'Jewish physics' so abhorred by the Führer? The work which led to nuclear fission is anathema to Hitler, even while his generals lust after its possible consequences. Heisenberg cannot accept this concept. Physics is physics: the structure of matter is not Jewish, not German – merely itself. But even he cannot say this too loudly if he wants to remain in Germany. The physicists will have to do their best under difficult circumstances. In November 1940, they hold a meeting in Munich to try and clarify their position. They conclude that the Special Theory of Relativity belongs to the experimentally verified facts of physics; that it does not necessarily lead to a general relativistic philosophy; and that, as yet, no one has succeeded in transcending the mathematical formalism of quantum theory to obtain a deeper understanding of the atomic structure. The bitter pill of necessarily accepting relativity is sweetened by the addendum that, before Einstein, Aryan scientists, like Lorentz, Hasenöhrl, Poincaré, created its foundations. Einstein merely built on what was already understood.

And how long might it take to construct a bomb on the basis of this ideologically corrected foundation? Now there's a question! And one only the scientists – led by Heisenberg – can answer. They ponder it for the first two years of the war, during which Germany is militarily so successful that nuclear weapons seem not only remote but unnecessary. But by the summer of 1942, when a high-level conference is held in Munich to discuss the subject, things have begun to swing the other way. However, Heisenberg can now report that a bomb will take a long time to build – at least three years, maybe ten. At any rate, there is no question of its being ready before the end of the war. The German Army therefore decides in 1942 not to go all-out for such a bomb. Instead the physicists are left to concentrate upon basic research: the construction of a chain reaction.

That summer, after this decision has been taken, Heisenberg crosses the border to visit his old friend and mentor Niels Bohr in Copenhagen. Denmark is under German occupation. In order to justify his visit, Heisenberg agrees to address the German Cultural Institute in Copenhagen. Bohr is invited to attend.

It goes without saying that the Germans have Bohr under surveillance. He is a Danish patriot, a notorious anti-fascist. He is half Jewish. He is horrified by Heisenberg's invitation. He will have no truck with Nazis or their front-organisations.

What does Heisenberg want of him? This can hardly be regarded as just a friendly visit. Nevertheless, he reluctantly agrees that they shall meet.

Afterwards, they could not even agree as to where their conversation took place. Was it in Bohr's study? Or during an after-dinner stroll in the town? So far were they from convergence that even so solid a point of fact could not provide them with common ground.

Bohr cannot imagine what Heisenberg is hoping for. In this situation, past friendship becomes irrelevant. Heisenberg has thrown in his lot with Hitler, offered his talents to the Nazis. How can he expect Bohr to forgive and forget such a thing, to behave as though the new situation does not exist? Even worse: he asks Bohr to agree that a German victory might be the best thing for Europe, since it would be the best defence against the threat from the East – Russia. By this time Bohr is almost speechless with fury.

Heisenberg persists none the less. As he sees it, this is the last chance. The bomb can still be stopped. The scientists, at least on his side, are still in control. He tries to tell Bohr that the chain reaction is now his only goal. No bomb. Hurriedly, he draws a primitive sketch of a reactor and passes it over. If everyone follows this line then a great evil may yet be averted.

But Bohr cannot see their conversation in these innocent and reassuring terms. He assumes that Heisenberg's sketch represents a bomb. It seems to him that Heisenberg is pumping him, to find out how much the Allies know and how far they have got. Relations between Bohr and Heisenberg, once the warmest of friends, will never recover from this conversation. Other old friends become equally distrustful. Two years later, when the Manhattan Project is at last seriously under way, another one-time collaborator of Heisenberg's, Victor Weisskopf, offers to kidnap his old friend during a visit to Switzerland. Oppenheimer takes the suggestion seriously enough to forward it to the military authorities. The machinery is set in motion. But, finally, the plan is not carried out.

Reading a book about this incident in the hope of finding

some useful reference, I notice Zigi's name among the list of cited sources. The author refers to an interview conducted in 1989, four years before he died. It's hardly surprising. Zigi knew Heisenberg well, was part of that Copenhagen circle. Not much is quoted – a sentence here and there. I wonder what else he said? That very afternoon, I write to the author. I am researching a biography of Zsygmond von Fischer. Was his interview taped? If so, does he still have the tape, or a transcript? Might I have a copy? Naturally, I'd be happy to pay.

Time passes. I sent my letter to America, care of the publishers. Who knows how many forwardings it may have undergone? Then, when I'd almost forgotten about it, a package arrives. It's the tape.

I shut myself in my study, slide it into my machine. Zigi's voice fills the room.

Copenhagen, he says. It was another world.

There is a long pause – so long that I begin to wonder whether the rest may have been inadvertently wiped. But no, here he is again. Evidently, he was lost in thought.

I never hope to be so happy again, he says. The richness of that time – it is more than I can convey.

What is he going to say? Will he describe that fusion of all pleasures – intellectual, emotional, sexual – which must then have been his? Will Bettina, in this unguarded moment, far from home, be permitted to emerge into the light? But no – she is not mentioned. The pleasures to which he refers are pleasures only of the mind. – I have had a long life, he says. A lot of experiences. And I can tell you, the intellect is what endures. Nothing else can compare.

Nothing? says the interviewer. You have quite a reputation as a connoisseur of life's pleasures, Dr von Fischer!

So you can believe me, says Zigi. I know what I am talking about! No, no. There is no comparison.

A little later he is asked: Did you know Heisenberg well?

Quite well. Perhaps not so closely as some.

Were you surprised when he stayed in Germany? When he refused to consider coming to America?

A pause. In my mind's eye, I can see Zigi shrug his shoulders, raise an eyebrow. – He was German. It was his choice.

Do you believe his account of the meeting with Bohr?

I was not present. How can I know what was said? In my experience, Heisenberg was not an untruthful person. But neither was Bohr.

But after the war ended, you would not meet Heisenberg.

Why should I? He was a physicist. I became a biologist.

He was your friend.

Sir, my mother and father died in Belsen. For many years it was hard for me to consider as my friend a German who willingly offered his services to Hitler. I did not seek a meeting with Heisenberg. There was no reason to do so.

The words 'my mother and father' strike me like a hammer. In all the years I knew Zigi, I never heard him refer to his parents' fate other than obliquely. For some reason, this unlooked-for sentence affects me disproportionately. Of course, the immediate picture in my mind is of *my own* mother and father undergoing those unspeakable torments – not so far-fetched a notion, after all. How could one bear the pain of such knowledge? How could one bear to survive? Perhaps he could not. Perhaps the reason he never particularised was because it was not bearable. Perhaps the reason he would never speak of those years was because the then Zigi was someone he felt should have been annihilated, like his mother and father? Thinking about this, I am struck by how little of his inner life, his personal life, Zigi ever revealed, even to those who might have thought themselves his intimates. Women, especially, found that irresistible. Each felt she would be the one, the unique and only one, to penetrate the mystery, to receive the secrets of Zigi's soul. But no one, to my knowledge, ever did. Not Bettina, certainly. Fania, maybe? Did that wall of showmanship ever break down? The sophisticate, the cynic, the dazzling intellectual, the political operator, the idealist, the lover – all parts he played to perfection, sometimes several of them at once. Did he ever allow *himself* – let alone anyone else – to peer behind them?

When the émigré scientists met Heisenberg again after the war had ended, they were shocked to see how the five years had aged him. Before, life had seemed to him a straightforward, happy affair. Now, as Victor Weisskopf put it, he 'visibly carried a load'. Nevertheless, many, like Zigi, could not bring themselves to let bygones be bygones, to take up where they had left off in 1939. Heisenberg and the other German scientists were treated with suspicion – almost ostracised – for many years. Almost alone, Edward Teller was prepared to offer the hand of friendship. Teller was a humane and tender-hearted man: the notion of ostracism horrified him.

Heisenberg could not understand these rebuffs, any more than he understood why Bohr reacted to him with such fury in 1942. This brilliant man was a psychological innocent. *He* lived the life of the mind. Physics was his world to the exclusion of almost all else. It was his refuge and his anchor. Was this also Zigi's case, is that what he meant? But without a feel for politics, for delicate relations, which of the Martians could have survived? No: Zigi lived in the world, all right. No wonder his interviewer was puzzled. But in a way I think he was telling the truth. Zigi did not like the world and its complications. He was not in sympathy with them, never really part of them. They remained essentially something that had to be coped with. Unlike Heisenberg, the allure of knowledge did not blind him to reality. But it was perhaps only there, amid the intricacies of science, that he could find relief from those base mundanities which must be cultivated if he was to conquer, as conquer he must.

III

The atom bomb was, from the start, a Martian affair. It was Teller, Szilard and Wigner who bullied Einstein into signing the letter that finally, ever so slowly, led Roosevelt to set the ball rolling. Seen objectively, the President's lack of urgency was understandable. In the summer of 1939, war, though imminent, had not yet been declared. Since there were no combatants, the United States was not even a non-combatant.

But for Europeans, such considerations were mere niceties. For them, the final battle was under way. The Emperor of the Last Days was already busy eliminating the forces of Beelzebub. Those who had made good their escape could only watch in horror. Armed with the safety of an American passport, the photographer Roman Vishniac set out, in 1938, for the ghettos and shtetls of Central and Eastern Europe, to record what he knew were the ultimate moments of the ancient Jewish culture in those parts. Doomed old men read their Yiddish newspapers, set out their rails of second-hand clothes. Young girls smile from windows. Porters tote their loads. Horses are bought and sold. All is as it has been for the past five hundred years, and as it will forever cease to be in the five years to come.

The Martian physicists, rushing from conference to laboratory, thought of their families and thought, too, of their erstwhile colleagues still in Germany and of the weapon they might put into the Emperor's hand.

So they set out to find Einstein, the greatest name in science, a man even the President must listen to. They went in Teller's old Plymouth: Szilard could not drive, and Wigner was no initiator, although he was happy to go along.

Zigi was not one of the party. This has never surprised me. I have always assumed that, like some others, he had no wish to see three centuries of physics culminate in a weapon of mass destruction. And if it was going to, wished no part of it.

Bettina says: Did he tell you that?

I think back. Did he? In so many words? Or did I simply take it for granted? People are consistent. Zigi did not become famous on account of his enthusiasm for the bomb. Not that the three plotters should be seen as the Three Weaponeers. Their motivation was twofold: one, their fear of Hitler; two, a hope that such a weapon as they envisaged might finally, by forcing world control, put an end to war altogether.

He had pneumonia, she says. He always hated the

American climate. It made him ill. You know what terrible asthma he sometimes had. I always thought he would die one of those awful nights. Sitting up in bed, gasping and moaning. I got so cross, I thought I would never again in my life be able to go to sleep. Between him and the baby. That summer it was very bad. You know how damp New York can be in summer, and dusty as well. And then he caught a cold and it went to his chest. That was always the danger. He was very ill: it was before antibiotics. And when Szilard called to tell him of the Einstein plan, he still wasn't recovered. He was furious. They weren't going to wait upon him, and I wouldn't let him get up. His place in history gone for ever.

She doesn't strike me as a cynical woman. Nor – to all appearances – as one who is taking the opportunity to repay a long-held grudge. Perhaps, after all these years, things are starting to get a little muddled. Not that there weren't plenty of one-time eager beavers who later repented. These things are rarely cut and dried. But we all know about Zigi. Vain, maybe; insufferable, often. But a man of undeviating principle. That was always part of the charm. So many of those who brandish their principles are also prigs and bores. Zigi, never.

You don't believe me? What did he tell you?

I can hear his voice. – History is history. The trouble with the British is that they are dominated by the past. But our concern, my dear Miriam, is the present and the future.

He didn't talk about the past much.

All right. You don't want to believe me for some reason. I can't make you. But I can't alter facts. He was ill, so he didn't go to see Einstein. But the work, the work! He was fascinated by it. They all were. It was the big question – could this be done? And because of the political situation, it became even bigger. To turn away from it, one would have to be very strong. And these were not necessarily strong men. They were clever, but that is not at all the same thing. They struggled, some of them.

Did Zigi struggle?

She shrugs. – He was not looking for an excuse *not* to do it. What he wanted was a justification for doing it. He wanted to know. That was stronger than anything. And was that so wrong? We all thought Hitler was going to win. We all thought only a miracle could stop him. And here was the possibility of a miracle that was *almost* pure science. Why does science develop in one direction rather than another? Accidents of history. What great scientist wants to devote his life to working on weapons? But here was the war. I suppose the atom bomb was inevitable, says Bettina.

Inevitable? Am I to believe this? A philosopher I knew once tried to explain determinism to me. He gave one of those useless intellectual philosophical illustrations, about matches in a box I think it was – the sort that render philosophy wonderfully remote from life. But I got the idea – that my fate is not mine to decide – and I loathe it. Determinism, as far as I'm concerned, is just another of Mephisto's notions. The atomic bomb was inevitable only because some people found it irresistible.

I remember, Bettina goes on, the day Hitler invaded Belgium. I heard the news on the radio, and of course Zsygmond wasn't there. The radio kept me sane. Most of the time I had no other company. And here was this news, and who could I talk to about it? Marianne? How I remember that smell of milk and nappies! Zsygmond was in Washington. There was a big scientific meeting there and Roosevelt was to address it.

Teller was going to that meeting, and Zigi went with him. Roosevelt spoke about the search for truth. It was a great adventure, but in other parts of the world – he meant Hitler, of course – scholars were not permitted that search. Teller and Zigi knew all about that. Why else were they in America? Roosevelt went on to talk about the scientists' responsibility. People would be holding them responsible for what was going on, blaming them for their discoveries. But it wasn't their fault. No one could be held responsible because peaceful discoveries were being misused.

The two Martians felt as if Roosevelt was talking to them personally, although of course they had never met him. In that whole room, only they knew about the Einstein letter. And if others were misusing work they might have done, it was up to them to use it correctly. The future of the world depended on their efforts.

Zigi had a slight stoop. It was a result of that asthma. Asthmatics hunch their shoulders in a characteristic way. King Henry VII of England had the same stoop – you can see it in that famous portrait. I always used to tease Zigi about it. Carrying the world's cares upon his shoulders. He alone responsible for its salvation. Only the greatest of destinies for him – who but a Martian should save the planet? This teasing always annoyed him. For one thing, he never liked being reminded of physical defects, however slight; for another, his life's work was no laughing matter. Zigi never managed to acquire the trick of laughing at himself. It was one of the many ways in which he never became really British.

How did you feel about it? I asked Bettina.

I? She sits back in her chair. I felt terrible. In my whole life, I don't think I ever felt worse. She holds up a hand and counts the points off on her fingers. One, my family, all our families, were going through who knows what? Now we know. Then, we could only guess. Luckily, we never guessed anything as bad as the truth, or how could we have borne to survive? Two, I didn't know exactly what Zsygmond was working on, it wasn't a thing he discussed with the family. But I knew enough to know I wouldn't like it. And the Nazi-Soviet pact didn't make me feel better. Three, I could see less and less point in being married to Zsygmond. But in a strange country, and with a baby, what alternative was there? So we carried on, and Marianne grew bigger and the apartment grew smaller.

But I was very lucky in one way. We stayed in one place, which meant that I could make a life of my own and friends of my own. It wasn't always so easy. People went where the jobs were, naturally. The Tellers began by thinking they would settle in London, and they found an apartment there. Then Edward was offered another job in Washington, so they went there. Then he moved to New York to work with Fermi at Columbia, so they moved again. Fermi went to Chicago to construct his atomic pile: the Tellers moved with him. And then they moved on to Los Alamos. If you are married to a great scientist, you follow behind and you don't complain. What have you got to offer the world by comparison? But in New York I found I could make a real life of my own, something I hadn't had since Budapest. There were several of us young women in the same position, trapped with our babies. We would all have liked to find work – none of us was rich; Zsygmond and I were really very poor. But where could we leave the babies? So I suggested we start a nursery. It was something I knew about – I'd done it before. Everyone was very keen to help. We found a couple of rooms. There was a lawyer in our group, a very nice man called Abe Kustow. He generally specialised in labour law, but he helped us through the various regulations, what we needed to comply with before we could get started. He had a couple of kids of his own who were going to come. So eventually we opened our nursery. Marianne was eighteen months old – it was not long after war was declared.

Kustow, I say. The man you eventually married? I'm sure I know that name.

Probably. Later, when the McCarthy witch-hunts started, he helped defend people. You're too young to remember that, perhaps. But he was also very active in the Seventies.

Defending the draft-dodgers. Of course, that's what it was. In my mind's eye I see again that famous photograph, the hairy, bearded anti-war protesters and their calm, smiling lawyers. Yet another of the lost worlds through which I have lived. What need have we of dinosaurs when one-time Weathermen are still among us?

So, says Bettina, returning us to New York. I began to make friends. My kindergarten went well. And I began to see that there might be life outside this marriage I was in. Abe's wife died, and he was left with a couple of kids. He and I started to get fond of each other. Quite soon it seemed I saw more of him than of Zsygmond. And then America entered the war, and of course the day came when Zsygmond announced that he was going off to do an important job and would we come with him. I said: Where is this job? He said: I can't tell you, but it's a long way from New York. And I realised I didn't want to leave this new life I was making. So I said: No, I don't think I shall come.

Was he upset?

He was hurt. When had anyone ever said no to him? We had terrible arguments. We shouted and shouted, poor little Marianne got quite upset. Both her parents in the same place for once, and what happens? I scolded him for debasing science. I didn't know what this important job was, but I'm not a fool, and I knew what was the work he'd been doing, and I'd heard all those discussions about the possibilities of atomic energy. He said to me, all this idealism is very fine, but what's the good of it without a world to be idealistic in? Marianne will need something more than idealism if she is to grow up. This is a war, he said. We are living here. If I am asked to do work, I do it, I don't complain about insults to my conscience. Hitler insults my conscience. This way, I can do something.

You could fight, I said. This way you can do what you want to do anyway and it makes you feel good.

This way, he said, I might be able to save a few lives. Anyone can fight. And so on and on we went. And finally he said: Am I the only one who is doing what they want? What you want is to stay right here with your friend Abe. Do you think I'm blind or stupid or something? He could fight. I don't notice him rushing off to fight. What could I say? In fact Abe was over the age limit, but of course that wasn't the point. Have you noticed how rarely arguments are about the subject which seems to be under discussion? So off he went. A few days later, a security officer came to the apartment and asked if I knew where Zsygmond had gone. Checking on our discretion, I suppose. From the official point of view, we were still enemy aliens. I could truthfully say I didn't know. And quite soon I moved in with Abe.

Did you get divorced? (Has Aunty Fan been living in sin all these years?)

We divorced in 1944. Abe and I got married then.

And did you keep in touch?

No. But that hardly describes it, Bettina says. I never saw

him again. A few letters, then nothing. Out of the house and out of our lives.

IV

I switch off the tape. It's always the same. You start something – talking to someone, working in a library – and it seems that the time available will never be enough. The first day is spent in panic. Everything at top speed, nothing can happen fast enough. And then suddenly – the end. No more, and days in hand. All those spools of empty tape.

She was sorry to see me go. – Does anyone come to see you here? I said. Marianne? – Not very often, she said. She lives in Washington. My son teaches at the university near here. I see him sometimes. You mustn't be sorry for me. I have had a good life. An active life. I have done what I could.

She walked me to my car, across those lush lawns, past the swimming-pool where a few elderly heads bobbed up and down. – Come and see me when you're next around here, she said. Get in touch if you need to know anything more. I promised I would. I felt terrible as I drove off, leaving her there in her luxurious segregation.

I am nonplussed by several aspects of Bettina's story. Zigi's enthusiastic approach to bomb-building is certainly not what I expected. But most puzzling of all is the very end. The abrupt and total disappearance. The deletion from his life of Bettina and Marianne. Divorce is one thing, distance, separation. But this? His childhood friend, his wife and companion throughout the dark days in Europe, and their child. Never to be contacted, never to be mentioned. What could explain such total obliteration?

Did Zigi ever talk to you about his life before the war? I ask Fania casually one day. We are in my kitchen. I am preparing some soup; she is reading the paper. Tony is not yet home.

No. What is to be read on her face? Evasiveness? Does a shutter (as spy stories phrase it) come down over her eyes?

Not visibly. She looks up briefly from the paper, shakes her head. – Why?

I just wondered. I was thinking about him. How that part of his life is a sort of blank.

What does it matter?

Aren't you curious?

No, says Fania resolutely. No, I am not. She shakes her head again, returns emphatically to her paper. The conversation is closed.

Fania is not normally an incurious person. She doesn't pry, but she is interested in other people. She is not one of those solipsists who goes through life only answering questions, never asking. She isn't lonely, she doesn't, as Bettina does, have a compulsive need to talk, to tell, to keep on talking. But this taciturnity is deeply uncharacteristic. Frankness is Fania's mode. No unnecessary mystification. If she knew, she would tell.

But how can she be satisfied – how, for more than forty years, can she have been satisfied – with this blank? She can't, is the answer. It defies possibility.

What can have happened at Los Alamos?

88

CHAPTER 5   THE CITY ON THE HILL

I

LOS ALAMOS: THE all-American – that is to say, totally cosmopolitan – city on the hill. Shining – with radioactivity. Cradle of the atomic age. How many acres of paper, how many gallons of ink, have been devoted to it! Our very own Labour of Hercules. Puny man against the forces of nature. The race against time. The Forces of Good massed against Satan, who has once again changed masks. Now it is Hitler who leads the massed legions of the Devil, while the Emperor of the Last Days is a Jew. The fragile figure of J. Robert Oppenheimer is leading his troops in the race to Armageddon. Jewish science, kicked out of Germany, is pitting itself against the pure Aryan breed. And the notion that these may be the Last Days is not entirely fanciful. No one can be quite sure that the machine they are battling to construct will not, should they ever get it to work, ignite the atmosphere. The chance is remote, but it is there. It cannot be dismissed out of hand.

On 2 December 1942, Fermi and his team produced a chain reaction – the world's first – in a graphite pile. On 28 December, President Roosevelt authorised an expenditure of four hundred million dollars for the Manhattan Engineer District, the name assigned to the atomic bomb project. He thought that should cover it. The actual expenditure, between then and 1946, was $2.2 billion. The project was entrusted to the Army Corps of Engineers, under General Leslie R. Groves, a man with strict notions of military discipline. He drove the scientists to distraction; they returned the compliment.

The Los Alamos site was selected in January 1943; the first conference was scheduled for April. Los Alamos was a remote mesa thirty-five miles from Santa Fe, empty except for a small boys' school. One criterion for the site was that it be remote enough to ensure secrecy. Another: it must have a good winter climate, so that people whose skills were in demand elsewhere should not be unnecessarily put off. Possibly at odds with these priorities was the need for excellent and advanced laboratories. These would have to be built and equipped from scratch. Access was by dirt road, up which all the delicate and sometimes massive equipment was to be hauled. The only telephone was a hand-cranked Forest Service line. Later, another was added. One in Oppenheimer's office, one in Groves's.

There was also the small question of housing. Oppenheimer's first estimate was that the job could be done by six scientists. This was quickly revised upward to one hundred. By May 1945, the population of the mesa was 1,100 civilians (scientists and their families) and 1,000 Army technical staff.

At Los Alamos, that scientific commonwealth which Hitler had destroyed blossomed once more. The magic land of Science had moved from Leipzig, Göttingen, Copenhagen and Cambridge to a remote hilltop in New Mexico. For some of the European scientists, the wire-ringed hilltop was too stark a reminder of the concentration camps: they had to leave. But for most, although they had never been here before (the exception was Oppenheimer, who owned a ranch nearby), Los Alamos represented a homecoming.

There was, of course, one essential distinction between Los Alamos and the lost domains of prewar physics. There could be no more pretence that this was pure intellect, disinterested inquiry. The end product – should they succeed – would be fearful. But the pleasure of arriving at it pushed this awareness to one side.

The allure of knowledge! Prometheus, bound to his rock, endures endless torture on its account. Adam and Eve, unable to resist it, are cast out of Eden forever. Johnny von Neumann (the Martians were gathering) advised a young graduate student, Richard Feynman, that irresponsibility was essential to science. – A scientist, he said, is not responsible for the whole world.

There is, of course, a distinction between curiosity and actual eagerness. Fermi was curious, but could not bring himself to be actively enthusiastic. – I believe your people actually *want* to make a bomb, he remarked to Oppenheimer in surprise.

Dr T. certainly did. For him the temptation was such that all reservations vanished. – I have no hope of clearing my conscience, he wrote. The things we are working on are so terrible that no amount of protesting or fiddling with politics will save our souls. I worked because the problem interested me and I should have felt it a great restraint not to go ahead. I cannot claim that I simply worked to do my duty.

He was already a captive: in thrall to the bomb. Not just this bomb and the next, but all their successors.

In the spring of 1942, just before Heisenberg's group effectively abandoned their bomb project, Oppenheimer invited a small group of theoretical physicists to Berkeley, where he taught. They were to discuss the problems connected with the explosion of an atomic weapon. The discussions were brilliant and productive. Led by Teller, they took a form that had not been anticipated. In his view, the fission bomb was now a sure thing. He said that what they should really be thinking about was the possibility of igniting deuterium by a fission weapon – the hydrogen bomb.

This idea had first been mooted by Fermi the previous September. Walking back from a pleasant lunch with Teller at the Columbia University Club, Fermi wondered aloud – out of the blue, as Dr T. remarked – whether one might be able to use an atomic bomb to heat a mass of deuterium sufficiently to start a thermonuclear explosion. This possibility filled Teller with excitement.

Teller put the distant but absorbing question of whether deuterium could be exploded firmly before the Berkeley seminar. He presented a rough proof of what could be done and how. His theories were strongly criticised, but with the new difficulties new solutions emerged. The discussions became fascinating and intense. Facts were questioned, and the questions answered by still more facts. One day the job would look hopeless; the next day someone would have a bright idea that made everything seem easy. By the end, they were all convinced that they could engineer a thermonuclear explosion – and that it would not be too difficult. This new bomb was called, by all of them, the Super.

So this was Dr T.'s project when he arrived at Los Alamos that April of 1943, accompanied by his wife Mici, their two-month-old baby Paul, a Steinway grand and a Bendix washing machine. The atom bomb held no more real interest for him. In his mind, it was already a foregone conclusion. Particular problems might interest him for a while, but essentially he was there to work on the Super. He claimed that exploration of the thermonuclear problem was one of the laboratory's objectives, and that several of the most gifted scientists recruited to work at Los Alamos came only because they were intrigued by the thermonuclear possibilities.

In fact the bomb was far from being a *fait accompli*, and Teller, with his concentration on the Super, was not helpful. He was assigned first of all to the Theoretical Division, led by Hans Bethe. But he was soon transferred to the Problem Division, whose head was Fermi. This division solved problems opaque to other divisions, and also provided a home for problem children. Dr T., with his insistence on the Super, was one of these. Bethe complained that it was necessary to bring in new scientists, since the Theoretical Division was very shorthanded.

That was one reason why a team from Britain was eventually invited to Los Alamos. It included Klaus Fuchs, the 'atom spy', who became Bethe's deputy. So subtly works Mephistopheles: Dr T.'s thermonuclear obsession ensured that the Russians would be kept abreast of all developments, which in turn ensured that the end of the war need see no abatement of Mephisto's thermonuclear concerns.

I asked Zigi once if he had known Fuchs. – Of course, he said. He worked in the next office. A strange man. – And did you suspect anything? Zigi shrugged. – Naturally not. If I would have suspected, I would not have been alone, and then how could he operate? Nobody suspected. If you ask, was I surprised – no, not entirely. In something like that, how could there not be spies? His only importance, said Zigi dismissively, was domestic. He helped McCarthy more than he helped the Russians. They had their own people. Kapitza, Kurchatov, Sakharov. They didn't need Fuchs.

This, of course, was only Zigi's view.

Zigi, too, worked in the Theoretical Division. This much he allowed to emerge, although he did not like talking, much less writing, about his time in Los Alamos. In this he was atypical. For many – perhaps most – of the scientists, this was the high point of their lives. What intensity, what company, what a challenge, what resources! – The fascination of our work took hold of our minds, wrote Victor Weisskopf, an ex-Austrian who worked in the Theoretical Division. Never before had my colleagues and I lived through a period of so much learning.

The question was not just whether it could be done, but how soon. Before the Germans got to it first? Before the end of the war? Bohr had commented that the thing might be achieved – if a country were prepared to turn itself into one huge factory. This, or something not far off it, was what actually occurred in the Manhattan Project. What scientist could bear to tear himself away before the end?

That, however, is exactly what Zigi did.

II

As the Allies advanced into Germany during 1944, Heisenberg and his colleagues were evacuated from Berlin to a small town called Hechingen. They were discovered there that December by an American mission code-named Alsos (Greek for Grove), which had been sent to find out the state of the German atomic effort and the whereabouts of the scientists involved. It then became clear that the Germans had never got past the stage of academic research. The threat of a German bomb had anyway been receding for some time. As Germany collapsed and the scale of industrial effort necessary to manufacture the bomb became clearer, it was plain that fear of Hitler was no longer the mainspring driving the machine.

The war in the Pacific of course continued. Might the bomb, should one successfully be made before rather than after a Japanese surrender, now be dropped on Japan? Six possible locations – military targets closely surrounded by workers' housing was the specified ideal – were selected. They were omitted from the programme of bombing raids which flattened much of the rest of that country. If a place had already been partially destroyed, how could the effects of the new weapon be properly measured and assessed?

But the Japanese were only the present enemy. Just as the hydrogen bomb peeped over the shoulder of the atom bomb, so the next war, as this one drew towards its end, increasingly occupied military and political minds. And in that war it was clear who the enemy would be: the Russians, whose twenty million dead in the Allied cause had alone made possible the defeat of Germany. For General Groves, there was never from about two weeks after he took charge of the Manhattan Project any illusion but that Russia was the enemy. – The project was conducted on that basis, he said. I didn't go along with the attitude of the country as a whole that Russia was a gallant ally.

Many agreed with him. For John von Neumann, as for Dr T., the Russians had always, from childhood, been the enemy. The present situation could be no more than a temporary accident. As von Neumann saw it, this was unequivocally a three-way war. He said: At that moment two of the enemies had to all advantage got into a fight of their own. It was perfectly proper to exploit this. As far as developing the atomic bomb was concerned, what all of us had in mind in 1943 and 1944 was this.

All? Not quite all. Niels Bohr, who arrived at Los Alamos in December 1943, thought the Russians should be invited to Los Alamos: after all, the British were there. That was an

94

extreme position: not even Oppenheimer, who revered Bohr, would go quite so far as that. But many found it hard to view Russia as the enemy at this time. One of the few scientists who liked General Groves (his views on the necessities of security and the undesirability of free exchange of information were anathema to most of them) was Sir James Chadwick, discoverer of the neutron, who was head of the British contingent. Groves often called by the Chadwicks' for a meal and some relaxed conversation. Also present on these occasions was Joe Rotblat, a young Polish scientist who had come over with Chadwick and was living in his house while awaiting the completion of some bachelor accommodation. One evening in March 1944, Groves came to dinner. – Of course, he said, what all this is really for is to keep the Soviets in their place.

Rotblat was appalled. He thought he was working to prevent a Nazi victory, and now he was told that the weapon they were preparing was intended for use against the Russians, millions of whom were dying in the same struggle. Rotblat had no illusions about Stalin – had not the Nazi-Soviet pact hastened the invasion of Poland? But he felt deeply that they were betraying an ally. He immediately decided he must leave the project.

Departure, at that juncture, was not easy. Too much was at stake. The first person Rotblat told of his decision was Chadwick. But when Chadwick mentioned it to security, he was shown a thick and incriminating dossier implying that Rotblat was a spy. His plan, they said, was to return to England, and then to be parachuted into Poland in order to transmit atom secrets to the Soviets. This had been arranged with a contact in Santa Fe.

Rotblat had indeed been visiting Santa Fe, although not for this purpose. He was saved by the agents' excessive zeal: in their desire to provide solid evidence against this suspicious character they had fabricated dates and conversations which could be refuted. They had to apologise, and promised to destroy their files. – I was lucky, he said. I could get away.

He was forbidden to disclose the real reason for his departure. What would happen to the project if everyone was infected with an attack of contagious conscience? The story (suggested by Chadwick) was that he was worried about his wife and family in Poland and wanted to try and find them. This was true enough in itself. So he left; and stopped off in Washington to visit the Chadwicks, who happened then to be there. He had with him a box full of his research notes and correspondence. Chadwick personally helped him put this box on to the New York train. But when the train arrived a few hours later, it had disappeared, never to be heard of again. General Groves was taking no chances.

Was Zigi's experience like this? He would never describe it. – I don't like to think about that time, he said. I can only try to undo some of the harm we did. All he would talk about was the black hole into which he was immediately plunged. Because of course, once you had left the Project you weren't allowed to discuss it with anybody. The last year and a half of your life, as far as the rest of the world was concerned, was a blank.

Nor was it possible to find out what was going on. *Would it work?* Many who shared Rotblat's and Zigi's reservations could nevertheless not tear themselves away before they knew the answer to the great question. Their hope was that, before the end, some fatal flaw might appear. Had it yet emerged? What was happening? The escapees did not know; they could not ask. They were in purdah. More to the point, they were almost certainly being followed. General Groves was not a man to leave such details to chance. Does this account for Zigi's failure to contact Bettina and Marianne? Does *anything*?

I have never previously given much thought to this episode, but now that I begin to do so, it puzzles me. It is all too out of tune with Zigi's character, as I know it and as Bettina has described it. Rotblat is a comparatively self-effacing man. It's easy to imagine him racked by conscience. But Zigi? Self-effacement was never a Martian characteristic. The Hungarians of my acquaintance were not discreet. They did not keep their opinions quiet. Zigi certainly didn't. The whole of the second half of his life was predicated upon his not doing so. He wore his social conscience blaringly on his sleeve. His style was marked by a total lack of faith in other people's ability or desire to implement whatever steps he saw as being immediately necessary. He did not like to let matters take their own course. This desire for control – not just of people, but policy, scientific and political – marks all the Martians. Perhaps it is a consequence of having lost all control over their own lives during the fatal decade of the 1930s. Never again. From then on, they were going to be the ones directing events. The Minta boys had got the bomb going, and they were not about to relinquish their grip upon the world it would create.

Does a covert departure, hushed-up and disguised, chime with this? Was this the way to affect great affairs?

Another thing. Joe Rotblat says he had to fight with himself before he could let himself be persuaded to go to Los Alamos. But it does not seem from Bettina's account that this was Zigi's position. On the contrary: according to her he was totally wrapped up in his work. Fascinated by it to the exclusion of all inconvenient considerations, such as family life. So what caused the sudden change of heart, the irresistible access of remorse?

And if Rotblat was perceived as a security risk, if even he found such difficulty in leaving Los Alamos before the end, how did flamboyant, indiscreet Zigi ever slip that leash?

The only possible answer to these questions would seem to be that, while he was at Los Alamos, he underwent a sudden metamorphosis, becoming all the things he had not been before and would not be afterwards. Can I believe this?

Surely, somewhere, he must have described what happened? His collected words are all around me. Books, magazines, newspaper articles. I have looked through them all. Nothing.

Who would have known the truth? His colleagues? It seems unlikely. The cover story, whatever that was, is the one they would have bought. Rotblat's worries about his family are still cited by colleagues in their memoirs as the main reason why he quit the project. I could ask them, of course. They're getting old now, but a lot of them are still around.

And, Los Alamos being American rather than British, there

is someone else I can ask. The horse's mouth. The people whose job it was to collect dossiers on Joe Rotblat and everyone else, for use in time of need. The agencies themselves.

Time to write some letters.

III

I have a neurotic inability to believe in any process I cannot actually see or otherwise experience for myself. When the girls were little, I tended to discount reported headaches or tummyaches because *I* didn't hurt. (This may, of course, be put down to a mere excess of maternal empathy. But I have never been burdened by any other such manifestation.) Likewise, I find it hard to believe that what I send out will be received. What possible connection exists between my dropping the letter into that little box and its reception in another town or another continent? I feel that I am broadcasting to the void, sending messages to the far galaxies. They may, in a million years, be received. I am often pleasantly surprised, but no amount of prompt replies can allay my fundamental distrust.

In the case of the American Freedom of Information Act, this attitude is merely realistic. The FOIA requires American government agencies to release copies of documents on request, subject only to certain specific exemptions. It also requires each agency to notify the requester within ten working days whether or not it will comply with a request. Agencies are permitted to take an extra ten days 'in unusual circumstances'. In practice, things are not always so simple. The CIA and FBI in particular, which receive many such requests and are congenitally unwilling to comply, tend to use delaying tactics. If they postpone their reply long enough, perhaps the requester will get discouraged, or even die. You are therefore advised to keep on hustling them.

Since my requests are directed to the FBI and to the Army

security department, it is with even less expectation than usual that I toss my pieces of paper into the postbox. I ask to see the files on Dr Zsygmond von Fischer and also (as an afterthought) on his wife, Bettina. I also send letters to various emeritus professors, mostly scattered around America. None of Zigi's London friends were connected with this period of his life.

The emeritus professors all reply surprisingly fast. They seem glad that a biography is being undertaken, and are happy to help in any way they can. Yes, of course they remember Zigi at Los Alamos. He worked in the Theoretical Division: a man of ideas rather than an experimentalist. He left towards the end of 1944, because he had been taken ill and prolonged hospitalisation was necessary. There was no secret about this: but perhaps he did not think it interesting enough to discuss. None of them seems to know the exact nature of Zigi's illness. One or two hope politely that there was no recurrence. The general assumption is that this illness was not entirely unwelcome. Given his subsequent career, it can perhaps be viewed as a convenient excuse for departure.

Recurrence? Not so far as I am aware. Apart from the asthma and hay-fever which beset him from time to time, Zigi always seemed to me exceptionally healthy. He was not one to make light of discomfort. On the contrary. He made the most of every cold or attack of flu, always took pains to ensure that any room where he was expected to spend time should not be too hot, too cold, too draughty, too airless; was a fastidious eater and an often unaccommodating guest. No serious illness, let alone a recurring one, could have passed unremarked. But of a mysterious ailment necessitating his departure from the bomb project there was never any mention. It was lost in the general fog which obscured Zigi's war years.

What was this illness? Was it genuine, or merely a front to mask the real reason for his departure – *pour ne pas décourager les autres*? Perhaps the security documents will throw some light on the business. If, that is, they ever arrive.

A month passes: nothing happens. Of course, the post between Britain and the United States can be erratic. Allow a week in each direction. I wait two weeks more. Still nothing. I write again, enclosing a copy of my former letter. Summer is passing. Susanna has broken off with one boyfriend and acquired another. Rose returns from Poland, where she has been spending part of her vacation with a Pole she met at university, passes through on a clothes-washing mission and sets off again almost instantly. Tony seems to assume I have abandoned the contentious biography. He doesn't mention it, perhaps for fear that this will set the whole process going again. Nobody mentions it. Fania has settled into a subdued routine. Her lodger has left, and she can't face trying to find another one. Too much trouble, she declares. We try to encourage her to think again: a lodger means company and some income. But also, she retorts, certain adjustments she can no longer be bothered to make. From time to time signs of her old combative verve flare out, but then the flame flickers and gutters. Is it age? Or the lack of someone to fight with? I could offer myself. Perhaps indignation would lift her back to life. But I haven't the heart, or maybe the courage.

Time for direct action. I have a list of all the FOIA legal and administrative contacts at the various agencies, their names and phone numbers.

They deny all knowledge of my letters. I fax through copies of the originals and all the reminders. Aren't they supposed to respond within twenty days? More than twenty days have passed.

Many people request such information. My requests will have to wait their turn.

How long will this take? Can they give me an approximate time when I might expect this information?

Perhaps two or three months.

Thank you. I'll call in a month just to see how things are going.

You're welcome, Ma'am.

In a month I call. Yes, I am remembered. When may I expect . . . ?

Two or three months.

But that's what you said a month ago. Surely the list must move?

Let me just check that.

Six weeks.

I'll call in a month.

I don't really believe in these documents. I don't think they're going to arrive, always assuming that they exist at all. But I am wrong. Just before the day marked in my diary to renew the assault, a large brown envelope drops on to the doormat. Luckily, Tony has already left. I make a mental note to make sure I get to the post in the morning before he does. Where the Pentagon leads, can the FBI be far behind?

IV

I had anticipated some difficulties (other than mere delay) in obtaining these documents. In Britain, even the thirty-year rule which eventually reveals some of the workings of government to the public gaze does not apply to the files of the security services. The doubtless bulky dossier compiled by our domestic spooks on my Uncle Zigi is closed to me. But here on my desk is a picture of his life as seen through the eyes of various American security agents, fifty years ago. I don't know if bits have been omitted. If so, it hardly matters: there's enough to be going on with.

The FBI, of course, picked up all the Martians when they arrived Stateside. Technically, they were enemy aliens; they had families back in Hungary which might have rendered them liable to blackmail; and they were engaged in top-secret research, not to say meddling (or trying to meddle) in politics. No matter that Zigi did not actually join in the expedition to see Einstein: he would have gone, if pneumonia hadn't intervened. (So was it another bout of pneumonia, this illness he contracted at Los Alamos?)

It's an odd feeling, reading these papers. A sort of peep-show. The biographer as Peeping Tom, peering at people's lives through periscopes. I've imagined enough amateur detectives in my time. There's a certain professional satisfaction in ascertaining that they really must feel as ambivalent, as furtive, as I had supposed.

The surveillance begins in 1939, just after the business with the Einstein letter, when the Uranium Project was getting slowly under way. Marked by a complete lack of urgency on one side and intense frustration on the other.

Subject is 6'2", about 30 years old. Well built, fair hair. Looks Aryan but mixes mainly with people of Jewish extraction. That is to say, mixes mostly with physicists. *Wife small, dark, 25–30. One small child. They have an apartment on 113th Street. Subject spends little time with family. Leaves apartment approx. 9.00 most mornings. Goes straight to restaurant on 113th and Broadway. Orders coffee, doughnut. Likes to chat with waitress, a tall, dark girl.* The classic situation. Man with child-bound wife seeks child-free sex. Not that Zigi needed an excuse – it wasn't as though he ever had to live with a small child again, and he philandered on none the less. I watch him as he lurks around the restaurant, waiting for his waitress to come off duty; as they take the bus together to her apartment. I see him emerge. He makes his way back to 113th Street. Kept late at the office again.

Otherwise, *Subject meets few people outside his work. Sometimes addresses a colleague in a foreign language.* Probably Szilard. He was working with Fermi at this time. They disliked each other heartily, but intellectually each could find no substitute for the other. They were working on the chain reaction. Very likely Szilard used the Martian code to give vent, more or less discreetly, to his personal feelings. He, too, of course, was being followed at this time: his predilection for interfering in politics made him a particular bugbear of the security forces. First of all he nagged to get the bomb under way; then, when it was achieved, he devoted himself to preventing its ever being used; and *that* having failed, to its internationalisation. What a pain in the butt! They faithfully noted his roly-poly Jewish appearance, his preference for breakfasting in delicatessens and other such relevant details. But it is Zigi, not Szilard, whose life lies before me on the table at this moment.

And not just Zigi. My instinct was right: Bettina, too, had an agent assigned her.

10.30: Subject leaves apartment with child in perambulator. Walks downtown to Metropolitan Museum. Meets woman, 25–30. Fine morning. They sit on seat outside museum. Speaking in German. 11.30, into museum. 12.00, into Park. Buy sandwiches. Friend identified as Minna Siegel. Musician, ex-girlfriend of known Party member. Together to Siegel's apartment, W.90th Street. Together there till 3.25. Subject leaves apartment building with child, takes subway uptown. Buys can of paint. Back to apartment.

This, of course, was a period of acute unemployment. How else can the multiplicity of agents be accounted for? One for each foreign scientist, one for his wife . . . Maybe this was a special case? Maybe Bettina's communist past was not so secret as she thought?

Bettina is learning her way around New York. I admire her bravery: a big city is a frightening place to confront on your own. And Bettina is almost always on her own (except, of course, for the child), or would be if she did not make determined efforts to find friends. I follow her odyssey in these clumsily typed documents. She is not without contacts. The group they met through their old friend Oppenheimer. The fellow refugees, acquaintances from Budapest who now become friends, in whose homes she spends the evenings when Zigi works late at the office. Abe Kustow. I follow her to his law offices. The agent notes that Kustow is one of a group working to bring in and find jobs for Jewish refugees. No doubt he has his own agent assigned to him. No doubt his dossier would be supplied to me, on request.

It seems for a while as though Bettina is of more interest to the agency than Zigi. They note her increasing involvement with known Party members, the probability that she herself is a member. Her secret: secret only from Zigi, who, unlike the FBI, is not party to his wife's telephone conversations. Bettina starts her kindergarten. Her meetings with Abe Kustow become more frequent. Then the reports tail off.

Towards the end of 1942, however, they begin again with

new urgency. For now America is in the war, and the scientists are in the front line of her war effort. Zigi, along with his fellow Martians, is in the front line of that front line. The seed sown by the Einstein letter has finally begun its delayed but violent germination. It's a new scenario, and nobody is quite sure how to deal with it. As the imperturbable Johnny von Neumann put it: We were all little children with respect to the situation which had developed, namely, that we suddenly were dealing with something with which one could blow up the world. This was a very peculiar situation.

For the first time, the American Army had to concern itself with security. This came no more naturally to the Army than to the scientists it was trying to control. – It was the first time that the Army really knew that there was such a thing, if you want to be perfectly frank about it, said Groves. The scientists were not in sympathy with compartmentalisation. They were not in sympathy with the security requirements. Groves did not hold this against them. He quite soon resigned himself to the inevitable fact that the Manhattan Project would never be a truly military organisation.

Naturally, as far as possible, no personnel were taken on who were not approved by security. There was a difficulty here, however. The assiduity of the FBI uncovered many contacts that, to a security-conscious eye, were highly dubious. But if all these dubious figures were excluded, who would remain to make the bomb? The FBI would begin by excluding Dr J. Robert Oppenheimer himself: the Director of the laboratory, the kingpin of the project. – The recommendations of the security organisation were adverse to Dr Oppenheimer, recalled John Lansdale, who was in overall charge of security for the Project. They recommended against clearance. But General Groves was adamant. His view was that Dr Oppenheimer was essential and we would clear him for this work whatever the reports said. There were also other dubious employees. Why? – My only answer, said Lansdale, is that we continually had to exercise judgement as between obvious all-out security and the necessities of the project.

It comes as little surprise to learn that Zigi was one of these 'dubious employees'. The correspondence he occasioned lies before me now. Lansdale advises strongly against his hiring. – We don't like his background, he writes. His wife is an active Party member. Is he really essential? Oppenheimer insists that he is. – There are not many top-class scientists, he replies. Von Fischer is one of the best. I have known him for years. I can personally vouch for him.

So he came: but the suspicions of those who were paid to have their suspicions did not abate. Oppenheimer vouched for him, but what kind of assurance was that? In 1943, the FBI's worst forebodings about the Project Director appeared to be confirmed.

During the winter of 1942–3, while he was still working at Berkeley, Oppenheimer was visited at his house by an old friend, Haakon Chevalier, who, like Oppenheimer, was a radical with many communist acquaintances. If not red, then pink.

Chevalier told Oppy that he had been approached by a man called George Eltenton, an Englishman then living in California. Eltenton had a means of transmitting technical information to Soviet scientists. How, he didn't say.

But that's terrible, said Oppy. That's treason.

Chevalier agreed.

That was the end of it, Oppy said later. It was a very brief conversation.

But that was not the end of it. For some months, Oppenheimer said nothing about this conversation. Then, in August 1943, he mentioned it to a Lieutenant Johnson, a security officer at Berkeley. He was prompted to do this because Lansdale, visiting Los Alamos, had mentioned that there were worries about security at Berkeley. – You should keep an eye on Eltenton, Oppenheimer said.

Why? asked Johnson.

At this point, Oppenheimer invented what he later called 'a cock-and-bull story'. He said Eltenton had approached three different people, through intermediaries. Oppenheimer would not name these people. – I was an idiot, he said. I was reluctant to mention Chevalier. No doubt somewhat reluctant to mention myself.

Having saddled himself with this story, he had to stick to it. He did so through two more interviews. Eventually, in a conversation with Groves, the truth came out. – We must know the names, said Groves, and, finally, Oppy gave them. By that time, however, the damage was done.

I think the only person that needed watching or that should have been watched was Eltenton, said Oppenheimer. But as I concocted the story that did not emerge. Instead, he himself was watched, more closely than ever; and his enemies bided their time.

So that Oppenheimer's recommendation, in security terms, was not much of a recommendation.

You did have certain employees, did you not, that the project had at Los Alamos who were kept on the basis of what might be called a calculated risk? Lansdale was asked during the hearings which, in 1954, and as a result of this 'cock-and-bull story', finally brought Oppenheimer down. – Why did the project employ some people of that character?

Lansdale replied: It must be remembered that the Germans were far ahead of us in the development of an atomic bomb.

By the end of 1944, however, that myth had been exploded. Everyone knew the main enemy had changed. In the eyes of the security boys, fellow travellers were even less of an asset, even more of a liability, than before. Up to this time, employing a communist might well have been necessary to ensure the Allies got the bomb before Germany. Now the risk was no longer worth taking. But getting rid of such people was not so simple, given what they already knew. – It was just as difficult to get rid of a Cabinet officer in Washington that the country is behind, because you had all of the political play in there, said Groves.

Each case presented its own difficulties, imposed its own delays. First, suspicion must be built up into a convincing case. Then some way of getting rid of the suspect must be devised. And it must always be remembered that they were not dealing with soldiers here, but with articulate, insubordinate scientists.

As for Zigi, the truth of what they did with him lies before me on the table.

Zigi's departure from Los Alamos was not voluntary.

No, he did not want to leave. The knowledge that the German threat was lifted did not deter him, the awareness that the Russians, our brave allies, were now the real target of the Manhattan Project's masters did not surprise him. The Martians had had early lessons in political realism. Above all he was, as Bettina had thought, fascinated by the work. He, no less than Teller, revelled in it. The incomparable company, the dazzling intellects, the unlimited possibilities! How could he leave?

The answer is simple. He was thrown out, kicking and screaming.

Am I surprised by this? In a sense, of course, I am. My whole view of Zigi – the view which he always presented to the world, myself included – is founded upon this one highly moral gesture. The rest flows logically from it. Others have repented – after the event. Zigi and Rotblat alone acted upon their principles at the time.

But in another way I have known this, or something like it, ever since I met Bettina. The final confirmation of an infidelity rarely comes as a surprise. You shut your eyes for as long as you can, but once they are prised open, the news is no news. People are consistent. And this particular act of principle was inconsistent with Bettina's Zsygmond.

By 1944, Bettina was no longer living in 113th Street. She had moved in with Abe Kustow, who lived – as befits a successful lawyer – on Central Park West, near the Museum of Natural History. This move, I see, occasioned a good deal of flurry in security circles. Kustow was something of a devil figure to them, as he was to remain throughout his life. The notion that a central figure on the Manhattan Project, a scientist privy to its inmost secrets, should be connected – however involuntarily – to such a person, appalled them. Of course, it could be argued – as Oppenheimer argued, not wishing to be deprived of one of his key men – that Bettina's move detached her from Zigi, rather than allying him with her doubtful circles. But there was the child, their daughter Marianne. It was hardly likely that he would wish to detach himself from her definitively. She would always present possibilities for blackmail.

So – what was to be done?

A plan was evolved. Its originator was Lansdale. Some discussion went on between Lansdale and Groves as to the best line to take regarding Zigi. He could not be conveniently shipped into some fighting unit overseas, as had been done with some other young men who had worried them. For one thing, he was already thirty-six – not young, in fighting terms. Nor was he very fit, though New Mexico seemed to be doing his asthma good. More importantly, he was too well connected, too well known in scientific circles: no one would wear it.

Then Lansdale had his brilliant idea. Could they not make use of Zigi's ill-health, such as it was? Might they not engineer a medical check and X-ray? And might that X-ray not show up a suspicious patch on a lung? He had, after all, had that bout of pneumonia in New York. Such a finding would call for a prolonged course of treatment – bed-rest in a sanatorium. Lansdale knew of several excellent sanatoria in the vicinity, where Zigi could conveniently be kept an eye on. New Mexico, with its dry mountain climate, was full of such places.

This correspondence took place between May and September, 1944. Groves was enthusiastic. They wasted no time in putting their plan into effect. By October, Zigi was safely ensconced in his sanatorium. He remained there, presumably, for the remainder of the war. Regular medical reports were returned to Lansdale. The patch on his lung started to shrink as the spring of 1945 turned to summer. It disappeared, as if by magic, in August 1945

VI

I try to picture the sanatorium. I hadn't realised, reading Zigi's description of these blank incommunicado months, that he was describing his surroundings, not just his mind. The picture he gives is of a bleak internal landscape racked by doubt; a questioning of the whole nature of science. Its uses, its misuses, the chance that leads in one direction rather than another. Anguish of mind that can only have been heightened by the hearty, health-obsessed atmosphere of a TB sanatorium. Lots of open windows, bed-rest, bossy nurses. Lots of boring invalids eager to talk about their symptoms, the war, their real, pre-TB lives. An entire culture, wiped out by the discovery of streptomycin. Which, luckily for Lansdale and Groves, did not happen until four years later, 1948. Or they'd have had to think up some other story.

I turn the pages of Zigi's account of his departure, which has since become so famous. It's not long – a mere pamphlet, really: it began life as a speech addressed to one of CND's Hyde Park rallies, and was expanded later by popular request, published and distributed by a small press turned from poetry to politics, whose finances it secured for that year. But in the light of what I know now, I find it worrying. It reads differently. Factitious, self-justifying. All those fine words, the rallying-cry of Zigi our champion, the scientist for peace. We all responded to it – hundreds of thousands of us. It struck the chord we wanted to hear.

But what connection can there be between those words and his real feelings during that time? Frustration is what he chiefly must have felt. Fury and frustration. Was that the source of his new moral stance? It looks like it. If you can't join 'em, beat 'em. Revenge: what can compare with it as motivation? Especially to a character like Zigi, so arrogant, so possessive of a grudge. He sees Bettina as the source of his present troubles: he cuts her out of his life. As for Los Alamos, if they don't want him – he will do his best to bring them down. When the time comes.

How much did Zigi know? How much did he suspect? Did he guess he had been set up? He must have wondered – the other patients, the nurses, must have wondered – why he didn't have that tubercular cough, that intermittent fever.

Presumably there were other patients? He hadn't done anything criminal, after all. Ten months' solitary confinement would have been a cruel punishment for his wife's having run away with a left-wing lawyer. As it was, the whole thing must have been unbearable enough. A fit and healthy man, full of intellectual exhilaration, in the midst of the world's most fascinating project, is suddenly snatched away and set down, for no good reason, in an isolated TB hospital. Nothing to break the monotony of the days. No contact with colleagues. No visits. As far as they were concerned, he left for some unknown destination. Their letters are vague on the subject. He became ill. Was taken ill. Had to leave. It was very sudden. No doubt there was discussion, for a while. Then, as it always does, life closed once more over their heads. Present urgencies overcame past curiosities.

And what better prison, what more secure confinement, than a sanatorium? What you must do is rest and get better. For after the war, when life begins again. Letters out, letters received – all at the mercy of the nursing staff. No un-authorised exit: and if there were, what would you find? Mountains, canyons, more mountains. Somewhere – maybe not too far off – he knows everything's still going on. The excited discussions, urgent calculations, hypotheses, experiments. The enthralling world of physics – his world – from which he has been exiled. Why? For what?

How ceaselessly he must have asked himself that question; how belaboured his brain. Did he connect his exile with Bettina? A few letters, she said. Then they stopped. Why? If nothing else, his child was still his child. But if he made the connection, that might explain it. Sitting there, day after day, overwhelmed by boredom and frustration, what had he to do but select a target for his anger? Zigi was not an even-tempered man. Not one to resign himself. His rage, his fury, are barely to be imagined. And never let us underestimate the wound to his masculine pride. *Bettina* had left *him*. If she had done what a wife should – what all the other wives had done – come with him to the Hill – then all this might have been avoided. She would have been on the spot; no awkward questions would arise. But no. Instead – this. Why had he married her? Why brought her with him to America? He had given her a new life. And in return – this. This! Perhaps he saw the cessation of all contact as the only alternative to murder.

What were they doing there at Los Alamos? Had they overcome the problems? Was there, after all, some fatal, unconquerable flaw? Would he ever know?

He had to wait until 6 August 1945

That day, he knew. That day, everybody knew.

CHAPTER 6   6 AUGUST 1945

I

As 1945 drew towards summer, everyone, knowingly or unknowingly, waited for the world to be changed.

I picture Zigi sitting, lying, pacing, in that unknown place, his comfortable, healthy prison, waiting for – it. The unmentionable, that might not even take place. I shall have to try and locate it, this sanatorium; but its whereabouts hardly matters. Wherever it was, the facts are the same. The war grinding on towards its end. The race going on in that place of which he was no longer part. Would they make it in time, the awful, fascinating thing? And would it work?

In Los Alamos, towards mid-July, tensions rose. The weather turned thundery. Half the population – the wives, the technical workers – were not in on the secret. They knew, of course, that *something* was being built, but they did not know what it was. Everyone, however, knew that some sort of climax was approaching.

The test code-named Trinity was scheduled for the night of 15–16 July. The place selected for it was called Alamogordo, about two hundred miles from the mesa. Preparations had been going on for weeks. About fifty scientists and a journalist from the *New York Times* were to be present (but on the night the darkness rustled with unauthorised watchers). – Next week, Ed McMillan told his wife Elsie, we will quietly and separately leave the mesa, the cars to reconvene at the test site. In all probability the zero hour will be very early the next morning. If all goes well, I will be home sometime in the early evening of that day. Be sure to look out of the baby's window toward Alamogordo. You may see the flash.

But the hours passed, and nothing happened. The weather, which had been forecast good, had broken. Would it clear in time? The wives watched from their windows.

Suddenly there was a flash, said Elsie McMillan, and the whole sky lit up. The time was 5.30 a.m. The baby didn't notice.

Did Zigi see that flash? Even if he was near enough, he would not have known where to look, nor when. I expect he was asleep.

They gave out dark glasses, said Richard Feynman. Dark glasses! Twenty miles away you couldn't see a thing through dark glasses. So I figured the only thing that could really hurt your eyes – bright light can never hurt your eyes – is ultraviolet light. I got behind a truck windshield, because the ultraviolet can't go through glass.

Time comes, and this *tremendous* flash out there is so bright that I duck, and I see this purple splotch on the floor of the truck. I said: 'That ain't it. That's an after-image.' So I look up, and I see this white light changing into yellow and then into orange. The clouds form and then they disappear again; the compression and the expansion forms and makes clouds disappear. Then finally a big ball of orange, the centre that was so bright, becomes a ball of orange that starts to rise and billow a little bit and get a little black around the edges, and then you see it's a big ball of smoke with flashes on the inside of the fire going out, the heat.

All this took about one minute . . . Finally, after about a minute and a half, there's suddenly a tremendous noise – BANG, and then a rumble like thunder – and that's what convinced me.

The man standing next to me said: 'What's that?'

I said: 'That was the bomb.'

After the thing went off, said Feynman, there was tremendous excitement at Los Alamos. Everyone had parties, we all ran around. I sat on the end of a jeep and beat drums and so on. But one man I remember, Bob Wilson, was just sitting there moping.

I said: 'What are you moping about?'

He said: 'It's a terrible thing we made.'

I said: 'But you started it. You got us into it.'

You see, what happened to me – what happened to the rest of us – is we *started* for a good reason, then you're working very hard to accomplish something and it's a pleasure, it's excitement. And you stop thinking, you know; you just *stop*. So Bob Wilson was the only one who was still thinking about it, at that moment.

But even for those who did not stop thinking, it was hard, at that supremely complex moment, to sort out what was to be celebrated, what was to be mourned. For Oppenheimer, life had been synonymous with the bomb. – For the last four years I have had only classified thoughts, he told Wolfgang Pauli. How could the intellectual and technical triumph, the culmination of so much effort, fail to elate him? – After Alamogordo, his walk was like *High Noon*, said I. I. Rabi, who had refused to work on the bomb but had agreed to come and hold Oppy's hand at this culminating moment. – I think it's the best I could describe it – this kind of strut. And after Hiroshima, standing on the stage of the auditorium, pumping his clasped hands above his head, he told the whistling, cheering, stamping scientists that it was too early to determine what the results of the bombing might have been, but he was sure that the Japanese didn't like it. His only regret was that they hadn't developed the bomb in time to have used it against the Germans.

But five days later, when the war ended, the elation had fallen away. He was on the train to Chicago with Robert Bacher. Bacher produced a bottle of whisky. They drank a token toast from paper cups, and went to bed. The elation was finished for ever.

Thirty-six hours after the test explosion Fermi, Bethe and Victor Weisskopf drove to a point near the epicentre. They saw a flat area about four hundred metres in diameter in which the sand of the desert was glazed into a solid reflecting surface. The sand had melted in the tremendous heat, and then solidified. The tower from which the bomb had been

suspended, and some nearby huts, were not just destroyed –
they had vanished. They had vaporised into gas.

Science provided the most fearsome weapon of the previous
war: poison gas. But poison gas was of little intrinsic scientific
interest. The atomic bomb was a different matter. It was so
fundamental, so difficult, that it was irresistible. What
physicist would not be tempted to release the power that fuels
the sun? When (in 1951) Dr T. and his colleagues finally hit
upon the fix that made the Super a practical possibility, even
Oppenheimer, who was against the Super, recognised that it
was 'technically sweet'. And recognised the allure contained in
that little phrase.

Mephisto hides amid the arcana, and beckons.

II

The events of that summer can be seen as a stately and
enigmatic minuet of death. The air was full of secrets,
decisions, arguments.

On 12 April, Roosevelt drafted his last cable to Churchill. –
I would minimise the general Soviet problem, he said. A few
hours later he complained of a terrific headache and collapsed.
He died later the same day.

Harry Truman took his place in a state of almost total
ignorance about foreign policy. He had met with Roosevelt
just twice since the election. – I am new at this thing, he said on
4 May. And a few weeks later: You don't know how difficult
the thing has been for me. Everybody around here that should
know anything about foreign affairs is out.

Whatever he knew or did not know, he was not a man to
minimise the Soviet problem. As June ran into July, and it
became clear that the Japanese were ready to surrender, he
juggled two conflicting objectives. The first was to end the war
before the Russians entered the Far Eastern theatre, which
they were eager to do in order to extend their sphere of
influence in that part of the world. The second was to wait

until he could, if possible, use the atomic bomb, thus demonstrating once for all the immense superiority of American force. The news of Trinity was flashed to him on 16 July, the eve of the Potsdam conference between himself, Stalin and Churchill. It took another five days for the full report to reach him, and it excited him so much that Churchill, baffled, enquired what had come over the President. Churchill got his own reading of the report next day.

On 24 July, Truman recorded that he 'casually mentioned to Stalin that we had a new weapon of unusually destructive force'. Stalin appeared unmoved. 'All he said was that he was glad to hear it and hoped we would make good use of it against the Japanese.' It was assumed this indifference was due to his ignorance. But this was not the case. Klaus Fuchs had been passing back regular reports. And the Russians had their own uranium bomb programme led by Igor Kurchatov, although it was less advanced than the Americans'. After receiving Truman's apparently casual message, Stalin called his foreign minister Molotov aside. – They simply want to raise the price, he said. We've got to work on Kurchatov and hurry things up.

Of course, Stalin had no more idea than anybody else – being a man of limited imagination and no science, probably rather less – what the use of this new weapon might entail. Who could imagine a thing whose like had never been seen on earth before? Only the words and descriptions of God in his various forms seemed to approach the awe and terror of $E = mc^2$. President Truman wrote: We have discovered the most terrible weapon in the history of the world. It may be the fire destruction prophesied in the Euphrates valley era, after Noah and his fabulous ark. Churchill observed: The atomic bomb is the Second Coming – in Wrath. Oppenheimer famously quoted the Bhagavad Gita: I am become Death, the Shatterer of Worlds.

Oppy's friend Rabi, himself a Nobel laureate, thought that this tendency to mysticism was the reason he made no great discoveries, despite his tremendous gifts as a physicist. Rabi talked of Oppy's 'feeling for the mystery of the universe that surrounded him almost like a fog . . . At the border [of what was known in physics] he tended to feel that there was much more of the mysterious and the novel than there actually was . . . Some may call it lack of faith, but in my opinion it was more a turning away from the hard, crude methods of theoretical physics into a mystical realm of broad intuition.' But such a realm is for most people both more graspable and more acceptable, in relation to such terror, than the stony abstraction of a book of equations. So the bomb was immediately endowed with superhuman dimensions, deflecting responsibility from the puny shoulders of scientists and politicians on to Holy Writ and impersonal fate.

The Martians had been instrumental in releasing the genie from the bottle. Could they stuff it back in again? Szilard had been the catalyst for the Manhattan Project. Now, once again, he foresaw what might be in store. On 25 March 1945, he got Einstein to write a second letter to Roosevelt. His intention was to try and dissuade the President from using the bomb as a weapon of war. – Before the end of the war we shall use atomic bombs against Japan, he wrote. The first bomb that is detonated over Japan will be spectacular enough to start a race in atomic armaments between us and other nations . . . The greatest danger arising out of a competition between the US and Russia which would lead to a rapid accumulation of vast quantities of atomic bombs in both countries, consists in the possibility of the outbreak of a preventive war.

An appointment was arranged for 8 May. But by then Roosevelt was dead. Szilard therefore approached James Byrnes, who was to be Truman's Secretary of State. – Well, said Byrnes, you come from Hungary – you would not want Russia to stay in Hungary indefinitely.

Szilard, in despair, got up a petition against the use of the bomb which he circulated among the atomic scientists. He sent a copy to Edward Teller, who discussed it with Oppenheimer. Oppy disagreed with Szilard. – This is a weapon which has no military significance, he said. It will make a bang – a very big bang – but it is not a weapon which is useful in war.

Oppenheimer thought the Russians should be informed

about the bomb, and that it should then be demonstrated in Japan. For him, there was never any question of not using it once it was ready. Only maximum effect would be sufficiently terrifying. His last-minute instructions were all concerned with achieving the greatest possible destruction. – Don't let them bomb through clouds or through an overcast. Got to see the target. No radar bombing; it must be dropped visually. If they drop it at night there should be a moon; that would be best. Of course, they must not drop it in rain or fog. Don't let them detonate it too high. The figure fixed on is just right. Don't let it go up or the target won't get as much damage.

Destroying a city was not in itself the point. The point was to terrify war out of the world.

He assured me, said Teller, that the right decisions would be made by the leaders in Washington, who were wise people and understood the psychology of the Japanese. My predominant feeling following our conversation was relief – I did not have to take any action on a matter as difficult as deciding how the bomb should be employed. Teller did not sign Szilard's petition.

None of this was of any interest to Truman or Byrnes. Useless or not, on 6 August the first atom bomb was dropped on Hiroshima. Processions of charred, hairless ghosts wandered through a waste of corpses and ashes. Japan surrendered, but not before a second bomb had been dropped. It was announced that the two bombs had saved 500,000 American lives. Russia, racing east, managed to claim the Kurile Islands as booty before the war finally ended. And the great secret, the only real secret, was out: the bomb was possible.

6 August 1945. The day I was born.

III

The German atom scientists were among those who had not known what they were waiting for. They were doing their waiting at Farm Hall, a sprawling Georgian mansion near

Cambridge, to which they had been whisked by British Intelligence, away from a transit camp in Belgium where (it was rumoured) the plan had been to shoot them. Unaware of this detail, they had mixed feelings about the move to England. They thought (wrongly) that, being near Cambridge, they would see their British colleagues, but on the other hand they were much further from their homes and families.

On 6 August, they had been at Farm Hall just over six weeks. – I wonder whether there are microphones installed here? mused one. Heisenberg laughed this off. – Microphones installed? Oh no, they're not as cute as all that. I don't think they know the real Gestapo methods; they're a bit old-fashioned that way.

He was wrong. All the rooms at Farm Hall were wired for sound. Every exchange was transcribed and translated. The horror and astonishment of that August evening are recorded forever in blotchy carbon copies. Mine are only the latest of many fingers to turn the dog-eared pages.

The first to hear the news was Otto Hahn, who in 1938 had discovered the fissionability of uranium. He was informed by Major Rittner, the British officer in charge of the scientists, that an atomic bomb had been dropped. – He was completely shattered by the news, Rittner reported.

Hahn had contemplated suicide when, in 1938, he became aware of the terrible potentialities of his discovery. He felt that now these had been realised he was to blame. He needed several drinks before he felt calm enough to go down to dinner, where he announced the news to his fellow detainees.

Hahn said: They can only have done it if they have uranium isotope separation. If the Americans have a uranium bomb then you're all second-raters. Poor old Heisenberg.

Heisenberg could not believe that the report was really accurate. – Did they use the word uranium in connection with this atomic bomb? he asked.

No.

Then it's got nothing to do with atoms, Heisenberg declared. He added: But the equivalent of 20,000 tons of high explosive is terrific . . . All I can suggest is that some dilettante in America who knows very little about it has bluffed them.

Nobody, however, could really be satisfied with this easy dismissal. As the evening went on, the consensus was that this really was an atomic bomb. The transcripts of their conversations over that evening and the following days and nights show them trying to reconcile violently conflicting emotions. Chagrin that the Americans had succeeded where the Germans had not alternated with relief that they had been spared this terrible responsibility. National pride fought with a certain self-congratulation at having held back; incredulity vied with pique.

Walther Gerlach, who had been co-ordinator of the German bomb project, guessed (correctly): They have got '93' [plutonium] and have been separating it for two years.

Karl Wirtz, one of Heisenberg's students, said: I'm glad we didn't have it.

Paul Harteck, a chemist, said: Who is to blame?

A voice said: Hahn is to blame.

Carl-Friedrich von Weizsäcker said: I think it's dreadful of the Americans to have done it. I think it is madness on their part.

Heisenberg retorted: One could equally say, That's the quickest way to end the war.

Hahn said: That's what consoles me . . . Once I wanted to suggest that all uranium should be sunk to the bottom of the ocean. I always thought that one could only make a bomb of such a size that a whole province would be blown up.

Heisenberg was annoyed to have been taken by surprise, after working so many years in the same field. He said: There is a great difference between discoveries and inventions. With discoveries one can always be sceptical and many surprises can take place. In the case of inventions, surprises can really only occur for people who have not had anything to do with it. It's a bit odd after we have been working on it for five years. He added: I would say that I was absolutely convinced by the possibility of making a uranium engine [an atomic pile] but I never thought that we would make a bomb, and at the bottom of my heart I was really glad that it was to be an engine and not a bomb. I must admit that.

Weizsäcker said: I believe the reason we didn't do it was because all the physicists didn't want to do it on principle. If we had all wanted Germany to win the war we would have succeeded.

But Erich Bagge, who had been a pupil and devoted acolyte of Heisenberg, could not feel so sanguine. He said: I think it is absurd for Weizsäcker to say he did not want the thing to succeed. That may be so in his case, but not for all of us. Weizsäcker was not the right man to have done it. He added: It is quite obvious that Heisenberg was not the right man for it.

The discussion raged back and forth. How had the Americans purified the necessary uranium? What resources had they devoted to the bomb? The Germans guessed that $500,000 must have been devoted to the project. (The actual figure was four thousand times that.) As for manpower, 120,000 slaves had been devoted to the building of the V1 and V2. Would these resources have been diverted if they had requested them? Probably not, Heisenberg thought. – We wouldn't have had the moral courage to recommend to the government in the spring of 1942 that they should employ 120,000 men just for building the thing up.

I sit and turn the greasy pages. I follow the scientists as they disperse, as they get drunk *à deux* in their bedrooms, as Hahn weeps. Once again there is that curious, ambivalent biographer's feeling: a mix of godlike omniscience and eavesdropper's guilt.

IV

I notice that Fania's house has become, if that were possible, even dustier than before. Who can blame her? She doesn't care, and Zigi, who did, has abandoned her. I offer to pay for someone to come in and clean every week. She doesn't want to accept.

Why not? I have someone. Housework's only bearable if it's a job you're paid to do. You'll feel better.

Darling, at my age you only feel worse.

She sits in her kitchen, tiny in the old armchair. She is evanescing, day by day. If things go on like this she will vanish in a puff of dust, indistinguishable from all the other layers already spread around us. Perhaps that's why she doesn't want the place tidying. She feels more related to the dust than to anything else.

Grey July rain beats on the window. July the third. Tomorrow is Fania's birthday. I know the date because she always complained it was the same day as American independence day. Everyone had always been invited to another party already. Fania was always keen on parties. Pretty clothes, music and dancing. The pleasures of the flesh.

I want to buy you a birthday present. Let's go to Liberty's and find something nice. You always enjoy the sales.

Too many people.

Come on, it'll do you good. We'll get a taxi. All part of the present.

So rich all of a sudden? But she allows herself to be persuaded.

At my age, she says, sitting in the taxi, birthdays represent a certain achievement. As a cause for celebration, I'm not so sure.

What were you doing on my birthday, Fan? Do you remember?

Your birthday? Your last birthday?

No, my real birthday. The day the bomb dropped. You know, people are supposed to remember what they were doing when they heard Kennedy was dead. That sort of thing. When you heard the news.

Oh, *that* day. She gives me a sideways glance that can only be described as coy. Yes, I remember.

Well, then?

I was in bed with Zigi, she says. We hadn't known each other long, and that was where we preferred to spend our time. I knew your mother was in labour. I was hoping we might – But it didn't happen.

Why not? Did you ever try and find out?

I miscarried. Several times. And then it was too late.

The taxi is marooned in a traffic-jam. I should be over-flowing with impatience, kicking myself for not taking the tube like a normal human being. But for once, the longer we stand still, the happier I shall be. Let us try and sort all this out. I say, as casually as I can manage: When did you meet, then? You and Zigi?

That summer. I don't remember exactly. We'd known each other two or three months, by then.

What were you doing?

I was nursing. I met Zigi in the hospital. It was a teaching hospital, he became very interested in some of their tech-niques. That was when he first got involved in immunology. He was there for observation or something of that sort – he was never very clear about it. It was a difficult time for him, of course. He made friends with some of the doctors. He knew one of them from Budapest – an old friend of his who'd come over here as a student to get qualified. Sandor and I were seeing each other from time to time – he was very attractive and his wife was somewhere else. I don't know where she was. It was the war, you took what was there and didn't ask too many questions. And then Zigi came along and we fell in love. He never seemed very ill to me. Perhaps meeting me helped cure him, she observes briskly as the taxi moves off. Whatever he had, it wasn't infectious. I can tell you that.

Did you just put the radio on and hear?

Yes. We'd – we were having a cigarette. I remember that. And I turned on the news. It didn't mean much to me, of course, then. What was more important was the end of the war.

But Zigi must have realised.

· Of course.

Did he try and explain?

No. She pauses, thinking back to that day, perhaps. The smell of sex, sweat, cigarettes. The hours that have passed like minutes. The irrelevance of everything that is not that bed in that room. Casually, the radio is turned on. One of those old bakelite wireless sets, that warmed up with a slight whistle, with a round dial around which are set wavelengths and mysterious names of towns: Daventry, Droitwich, Hilversum. Here is the news.

He didn't say anything. I remember he sat up very suddenly, as if he had been hit or something. He was shaking all over. I touched him but he didn't notice. He got up and got dressed and left the room. Without a word. I saw him the next day. He said he was sorry, that he'd explain another time.

You didn't know before, that he was involved – ?

Of course not. That was a condition. They allowed him to leave on condition he didn't speak to anyone about it. What he'd been doing.

We arrive at Liberty's. Fania was right: there are too many people. We plunge in among the scarves. I urge her on. She selects a fabulous Italian silk and cashmere number that sets me back the best part of £100. I don't begrudge a penny of it. I am walking on air.

Writing a biography is like collecting. The elation of filling in the gaps; finding the missing piece. I can't wait to get home and gloat over my new acquisition.

I never could really believe the scenario of the sanatorium-as-prison. It smacked too much of the later excesses of the Soviet Union. Psychiatric hospitals full of dissidents? That wasn't Groves and Lansdale's style. This was America, after all, the Land of the Free. More likely, they would have talked it through. – Dr von Fischer, we have a problem. We're not happy about your politics. Okay, your wife's politics. I'm sorry, sir, but you will appreciate, we can't take any risks here. Now we don't want any scandal, and we must have security. We must be sure that nothing is said or passed on. If you will co-operate with us, I'm sure something can be worked out . . . If not, well, we should be obliged . . . But it's not what we want. No, sir.

What was worked out? What agreed? The cover story. The sanatorium – one of those listed by Lansdale, no doubt. And, after a discreet interval, a passage to Europe. Perhaps he could specify his destination – the hospital where his old friend worked. The Martians kept in touch, they knew about far-flung friends and cousins.

So long as we know where you are. And don't try anything foolish. Not that you would, sir.

So Zigi met Fania through the good offices of US Army Security. And all the rest followed.

I

SOME PEOPLE STICK their photographs into albums. I have never managed to acquire this habit. Mine remain in their wallets, heaped up in drawers, spilling from bureaux. It was easier for my parents: there were fewer photographs then. The pictorial record of their lifetimes fits into two not particularly large boxes.

How many times have I pored over their contents? The sepia tints of my father as a curled, befrocked baby. My paternal grandmother (whom I never knew), monumental in her long Edwardian gown. My mother on girls' outings from the office, Thirties bobs and brave, lipsticked smiles, arms linked on the seafront at Brighton. On her way to school and, later, work, she used to pass a billboard advertising Courage's Ales. Take Courage, it said. She read this as a special exhortation to herself, and tried to live up to it.

Family weddings where a face stirs the occasional flicker of recognition. Is that tailcoated wag my sedate Uncle Harry? that coy, décolletée stunner, leaning on a pillar, hands clasped beneath her cheek in traditional dirty postcard pose, my Aunty Bessie?

Here is Fania in profile, aged about twenty. What a beauty! The high, pure forehead, the firm, straight nose. They are still there; the eye still flashes, on occasion. But the thick black hair has thinned and whitened, the roundness of the lips and chin, the white pillar of neck – withered. Like one of those dried flowers everyone's taken to arranging these days. No scent, no colour. But the skeleton remains. Cheekbones survive the ageing process.

About a third of the way through the box, I make my appearance. A family group in the back garden of my grandparents' semi. On the reverse in my father's writing: August 1946. My father sits on the grass: I perch on his thigh, round cheeks, wispy one-year-old hair, staring intently at his breast pocket while he points at the camera in a vain effort to make me face towards it. My mother sits beside us, hugging her knees. Towering over us, a row of aunts and uncles. My white-bearded grandfather, small and neat, my pretty, plump, worn-looking grandmother. Zigi and Fania are directly behind me and my father. Zigi looks enormous beside diminutive Fania. His arm is around her shoulder; his hand dangles proprietorially over her breast. She leans blissfully against him: the newly-wed. The pair of them burn out of the picture like plums amid suet. Fania's vivid beauty, as always, makes all the other women look like puddings. And Zigi's impatient intelligence, that quality he always had of a bomb about to explode, sets him apart from the other men, as it always did. You can sense it even in this dog-eared family group. It was part of the secret of his immense, unfailing charm. The mere act of his taking time to devote attention to you made you feel flattered. Of course, this also ensured that he was greatly resented. But all he had to do was turn the beam of his charm upon the slighted one, and lo! a convert was born.

They were by then legally married: in Liberty's, having a cup of tea after we'd bought the shawl, Fania volunteered that the scene she'd been describing in the taxi took place not long before that event. – Not that we cared, she said. What importance have those things? And my experience of marriage had not been so good. (And what of his? Did he never mention it? Were there no old friends, no relatives, to make awkward comments? What of Sandor, the Budapester, Fania's erstwhile boyfriend? Perhaps he had left Hungary before Zigi married Bettina.) But it was easier for him to stay in the country that way, said Fania. So that's what we did. One mustn't be rigid.

Fania is absorbed in Zigi. But the reverse is not true. As in that other photo, his wife is not his main concern. He appears vaguely discontented. His gaze is turned inward: his thoughts are elsewhere.

Where? Perhaps it is himself he is trying to make out. Who is it standing here in this back garden in Hendon? Is this the old Zigi, the one Bettina knew, ready – eager, even – to abandon his wife and baby daughter to the irresistible call of the bomb? Or is it the new model, the one I shall grow up with, leading the fight to get the thing wiped off the face of the earth?

My picture of him seems to grow less and less definite the more I find out about him. That is to say, the picture I used to have is dissolving, and the one I am building up is far from complete.

Where does my old Zigi begin – the one I used to know, the one before I started to find things out?

Insofar as these things can be dated, I suppose the answer is: about the time this picture was taken. Here they are in London, Zigi and Fan. Fania presents her new husband to her family. What do they know of him?

They know he is from Budapest, and that he no longer has any immediate family there: that his parents died in concentration camps, that he has no brothers or sisters.

They know he is a physicist and very clever, and that he was one of the team that worked on the atom bomb.

They know he left the bomb project before the end, and that he doesn't like to talk about this.

They know that he has turned his back on nuclear physics and has taken up microbiology. He is at present engaged in immunological research for the Medical Research Council. He has no wish to work on any more ways of killing people. Curing is his line now.

Hold it a minute: I have a piece of evidence here. Among the package of FOIA papers sent me by the US Army were a couple I haven't yet mentioned because we hadn't yet arrived at the point where they were relevant. But we are there now. They are dated December 1945 and January 1946, copies of a correspondence between Col. Lansdale, who was instrumental in getting Zigi sent to the sanatorium, and Sir John Cockcroft, who was just then in process of setting up the British Atomic Research Station at Harwell. It appears that Zigi has applied for a job there. Perhaps Cockcroft has written to Groves asking for a reference, or maybe Lansdale has otherwise got wind of Zigi's application. On 14 December 1945, Lansdale writes to Cockcroft advising against this appointment on the grounds of Zigi's strong left-wing connections. – His ex-wife is a communist, writes Lansdale, and has recently remarried to a notorious Red. Fischer's young daughter is living with them. In view of the adverse security possibilities inherent in this situation, you may feel this appointment is inadvisable. A brief note from Cockcroft acknowledges receipt of this information.

There is nothing to tell us about Cockcroft's final decision. But it is unlikely he ignored Lansdale's advice. The British were anxious to retain American co-operation in atomic matters, and must have been aware that this was by no means a foregone conclusion. In 1948 Admiral Lewis Strauss, a member of the Atomic Energy Commission in charge of America's policy in this field, recorded his opposition to continuing technical co-operation with Britain. He felt Britain was 'far to our left' and might pass 'the secret' to the communists, 'some of whom actually sit in Parliament'. His was an extreme position, but not unique. The British wanted to defuse such suspicions where they could. The fact that Zigi moved to London rather than Harwell indicates that he was not offered the post. Perhaps this was why.

I've tried to locate the other side of this correspondence, together with any material Harwell may have relating to Zigi. I've asked both at Harwell itself and at the Public Record Office. I need hardly say that my efforts have been in vain. This is the kind of stuff that, in Britain, is routinely weeded from such files as are reluctantly allowed out into the open. But one thing is proved. Nuclear physics – and, more to the point, bomb-making, which is what went on at Harwell – still attracted him, even after the war. That is what he would have done if he could. Immunology was definitely the second choice. Did Fania know about this? Did she know he planned to drag her to a bleak Berkshire hilltop, removed from all civilised amenities? Certainly neither she nor Zigi ever mentioned it. I imagine he didn't dare confess his plan while the outcome was still uncertain. Had he gone there, I can't imagine Fania would have stayed with him. She would have loathed the place, both socially and politically.

Presumably he would not have been told the reason for his rejection: simply that he was not to be offered the post. At any rate, the long tentacles of McCarthyite paranoia stretched no further. His career subsequently progressed unhindered – flourished, indeed, in spite of opinions and actions that would quickly have propelled him on to the American blacklist.

So it was by no means the case that the new Zigi emerged fully formed, phoenix-like from the ashes of the old, forged in the crucible of isolation during those months at the sanatorium. On the contrary: he was a creature of circumstance. A role creeps up on you, and suddenly it has taken you over. You are what you have become, and if the past must be rearranged to fit – then so be it.

Zigi always said it was Eddie Angell who introduced him to immunology. That, at least, is easily confirmed. Eddie is still around, so I rang him to check. Yes: during the war he was working in the medical school attached to Liverpool University. Being a Quaker he was a conscientious objector, but this presented no problem since he was in a reserved occupation. He, too, met Zigi through Sandor, who was a colleague in the medical school.

Is Sandor still alive? I ask. Did they keep in touch?

We used to meet from time to time, says Eddie. He died quite recently, as a matter of fact.

In 1946 Eddie moved to London, to work at the Medical Research Council's laboratories at Holly Hill in Hampstead. Zigi, who of course knew by then that he would not be able to go to Harwell, had just declared his intention to make microbiology and not nuclear physics his new field of interest. Through Eddie's good offices he was offered a job at the MRC. He happily accepted.

I'm sure Eddie was instrumental in the formation of this new Zigi. *He* would never have had to contemplate such self-invention, because he never had a moment's doubt about who he was. Such self-confidence, combined with such sweetness, is rare and makes a strong impression. Zigi always remained somewhat in awe of Eddie Angell. Would Eddie have been shocked had he known the rickety basis of Zigi's fine new principles? I doubt it. Present acts interest him, not past waverings.

Zigi and Fan bought the West Hampstead house in 1946. It was near the Finchley Road with its congenial Hungarian restaurants, and not too far from the MRC, but not as expensive as Hampstead proper. They had very little money. Perhaps my Uncle Harry made them a loan. The top floor was let to lodgers. Every morning the two of them would set out on their bicycles, up the hill to Hampstead. Fania had a job at a bookshop in Rosslyn Hill. She enjoyed that a lot: she earned a little money, and the time was pleasantly filled. Perhaps it was a distraction from the babies which kept failing to materialise. She had not yet developed her interest in painting. At lunchtime they would meet in a pub for a drink and a sandwich, and in the evening they would cycle back down the hill again, bags of provisions dangling from their handlebars. They were both very happy. Zigi was becoming fascinated by immunology, and was beginning to think about the work on antibody selection for which he later became celebrated. They had lots of friends, Zigi's Hungarians, the literary crowd around the bookshop, the left-wing scientists Eddie Angell frequented. And they were in love. Fania in particular liked to talk about that time: it was the best time of her life.

It seems clear why the relationship with Fania lasted while that with Bettina did not. Bettina said she was not at first in love with him, and that he was attracted to her because she could take him or leave him, which was probably quite true. But this state of affairs did not last long. From the moment she arrived in Copenhagen Bettina was dependent on Zigi, both materially and psychologically, and this was the undoing of their marriage. His relationship with his imploring, adoring mother had set the pattern for his dealings with dependent women. But Fania's relationship with Zigi was never like that. This was partly a function of circumstance. In Copenhagen, Bettina *was* dependent upon Zigi: he was the reason she was there at all. In England, at first, it was the other way about. It was Fania who was at home, she who offered Zigi security by marrying him. Later, of course, character came into it. It is clear to anyone meeting her that Bettina, for all her intelligence, is a sweet, soft thing. But Fania is steely. Not that she isn't warm and generous – I of all people know that – but she is firmly self-regarding: quite as self-regarding as Zigi ever was. In that way, they were perfectly matched.

Zigi liked to talk about his impressions of English life. Before he arrived, he had a very detailed picture of what it would be like. He was acquainted with its literature and outward appearance from the Hungary of his youth, where Britain was a sort of ideal culture-model. Unsurprisingly, he found that the model had not prepared him for the reality. A particularly great shock for one reared up in the necessity of breeding geniuses, was the British attitude to intellectual competitiveness. He was nonplussed by the quintessentially British notion that it was possible to be 'too clever by half', and that such a phrase was a term of abuse. When he was a child, intellectual virtuosity was lovingly fostered as a necessary tool for eventual survival: now here were parents concerned only that their children should not be caught 'showing off'. After he had been here a few years, of course, he discovered that this abhorrence of obvious effort was merely a pose, a national style, beneath which all the usual tooth-and-claw competitive passions raged. This discovery occasioned him not a little relief. He used to argue fiercely with my parents about all this. They were firmly against 'showing off' (to which I was fatally inclined). – I believe this pose is not without a certain importance in national life, he said. It gives people who are really quite stupid a self-confidence to which they are not entitled, and allows them to rise to positions of disproportionate power. (In his thick Martian accent, with its rolled r's and deep vowels, such phrases sounded truly terrifying.) It is merely a question of what is to be the dominant problem in national life. Where I grew up, the national vices were generally corruption and laziness. Here, the problem is the rejection of intellect and the active welcome of idiots. Which is worse? I find it hard to decide.

Did anyone ever ask him why, given these deep national flaws, he picked England rather than America (where uninhibited competition undoubtedly reigned) to live in? Probably not. There were so many possible answers. Fania was English. England was a good place for medical research. His political inclinations fitted in better here. He allowed all this to ride. He was simply himself, the postwar, post-bomb Zigi who had landed fully formed amongst us.

So, in this summer of 1946, he finds himself once more in a new country. Powerless again. But quiet acceptance is not Zigi's mode. All the Martians are programmed to strive for power, to achieve control. Now, released from the political impossibilities of the 1930s, each of them will make his own way towards that goal. Why did Zigi leave one communist wife only to marry another? It is hard to believe this was a thought-out strategy. But subconsciously, did Fania's beliefs add to her attraction for him? The Americans had shown how far they trusted him. He couldn't know why his application for the Harwell job had been rejected, but he may well have guessed. There were not so many physicists of his calibre and experience knocking around that his services could be so blithely dispensed with. Perhaps this, too, was part of the route to the new Zigi. To hell with them. He would be what they suspected him of being. They had deprived him of his access to power, so he would deprive them – and in particular his luckier classmates – of theirs. As far as in him lay. That would be *his* route to the golden goal. Vengeance is mine, saith the Lord. Elias Canetti said: How easy to say: Find yourself. How scary when it really happens.

In 1946, America is still the only nuclear power. But nobody is relaxing. For if one war has ended, another seems certain to begin. When? No one can be sure. But soon. Not long after Hiroshima and Nagasaki brought World War Two to an end, Zigi wrote an article which was published some time later in the *Bulletin of the Atomic Scientists*. – We are drifting towards a war between the United States and Russia, he wrote, and we are moving towards this war with incredible speed. When the imminence of such a catastrophe first becomes apparent it is usually declared to be 'unthinkable', just as the last war was declared to be 'unthinkable' around 1934. The threatening conflict has passed beyond that stage and everyone is thinking about it.

Indeed: and the behaviour of those in the know is hardly reassuring to the general population. The US Secretary of the Navy, James Forrestal, will shortly commit suicide – throw himself out of a window – 'because the Russians are coming'.

How long will it be before the Russians have their own bomb? In the view of most scientists, about five years. General Groves thinks, not less than twenty. Some think, never. For them, atomic power is America's great secret which, if closely enough guarded, can surely never be stolen away.

The Minta boys have few illusions on this score. They know that Russia has scientists perfectly capable of making an atom bomb. They are preparing for the coming war. Theodore von Karman has been asked to define the future of aerial warfare. His study – *Where We Stand* – predicts such futuristic fantasies as supersonic combat aircraft and guided missiles. These are the delivery systems. The payloads are the province of – who else? – Edward T.

In 1946 as in 1942, 43, 44, 45, Teller is obsessed by the superbomb. But he is in despair. Most scientists do not share his sense of urgency. They have little stomach for continuing work on nuclear weapons. They are drifting away, back to their old laboratories. Oppenheimer, much distressed after the bombing of Hiroshima and Nagasaki, will not stay at Los

Alamos. – Touch me, he says, meeting Teller. I just resigned as director.

For a while, the future of the lab is uncertain. Then the decision is taken to continue it. Will Teller remain?

Only under one of two conditions. Either they must institute a vigorous programme for refining fission weapons, including at least twelve tests a year, or they must concentrate on the hydrogen bomb.

The new director explains that, taking political realities into account, neither of these alternatives is possible.

Dr T. therefore decides to return to Chicago.

That same evening, Oppy and he meet at a party. Teller repeats that afternoon's exchange. Oppy says: And don't you feel better now?

No, says Teller.

In September 1949, in line with scientific predictions (but still a bolt from the psychological blue), the Russians explode their first atom bomb.

What is to be done now? Dr T. has not the slightest doubt. Is it not obvious that the Super must be pursued with all possible vigour?

Oppenheimer disagrees. The Super, he feels, should *not* be pursued. If the Russians produce such a weapon, America's large stock of atom bombs will be a comparably effective response. National security requires neither its development nor its possession.

It is a remarkable coincidence, wrote Teller, that with few exceptions, those who favoured a prior warning to Japan later argued for continued development of weapons, whilst those who recommended immediate use of the atomic bomb argued after the war for cessation of all further development.

His argument was that conscience is an irrational and muddled guide. One might pursue the Super while still retaining one's claims to morality.

Argument is a rational exercise. But Teller's attachment to the H-bomb was something more, or less, than rational. Logic and prudence could not quantify it. – He loves those things, said a colleague. It is partly the magic of it – to control nature.

Control – that word again. Mephisto knows his man. What is on offer here, as all those biblical metaphors recognise, is godlike power. But only *one* godlike power: extermination. Creation is not on the menu. Can the power of extermination be rationalised into morality? It's happened once before this century. In fact, it's only just over. Mephisto always dangles the same temptation. – Nothing, he whispers, is inherently evil. In the right hands – *your* hands – it may become a force for good. Only the wrong people will be purged. All the right people will be spared.

How, in the middle of the twentieth century – this century of camps and exterminations, of ideals which so quickly become ideologies – is it possible for an intelligent man, a moral man, to believe these sophistries? Oppy can't. Having seen what they have made – the bomb they produced with such enthusiasm, and its effects which he himself was at such pains to maximise – he rejects them. No man, he feels, can remain uncorrupted by such power.

Mephisto must therefore destroy him.

At this point, it is by no means certain that Teller will be allowed to create his Super. It dangles before him, just out of reach. He is not in a position to ensure it: he is not in control. Oppenheimer once told Teller that scientists had no right to use their prestige to try and influence political decisions. But in this debate, it is Oppenheimer who holds (despite his principles) the official position. He is a member of several influential committees, and chairman of the General Advisory Committee to the Atomic Energy Commission.

Teller has no official position. He has only an increasing number of devoted friends in high places, who have been won over by his enthusiasm and charm and a certain winning diffidence. To these friends, many of whom have suffered the cutting edge of Oppenheimer's contempt, the thought that Oppy still retains his influential position is intolerable.

Oppenheimer's committee advises against the development of the Super.

Teller is appalled and terrified. He bets a friend that if the United States does not proceed immediately with a crash programme on the Super, he will be a prisoner of war of the Russians in the United States. But this disaster is averted after all. In January 1950, President Truman announces his decision. He is going to ignore the committee's advice. The Super is to be pursued.

This decision was made four days after Klaus Fuchs's confession that he passed on secrets to communist agents. Truman asked: Could the Russians produce it? Advised that they could, he decided to go ahead.

Oppenheimer wants to resign after the rejection of his advice, but is persuaded not to do so. His position, however, remains anomalous. The side in the position of greater formal superiority has lost, but it retains its formal position. The side that has won still feels that it is fighting against the odds.

III

The story of Oppenheimer and Teller is a mesmeric tragedy that the greatest master might have been proud to invent. In most of the stories of life at Los Alamos, the hindsighted reader is struck by the mismatch between atmosphere and subject. The tales are all of casual gaiety, making-do, the intense pleasure of the intellectual quest; meanwhile the *raison d'être* of all this lurks, toad-like, in the background.

But in the case of Teller against Oppenheimer, the quarrel, the protagonists, the staging, are all as gigantic as the central plot: whether permission will be granted to destroy the world, should that prove desirable. The surface simplicity, in which Oppy, who stands in the way of the Super, must be destroyed by its champions, chief among them Teller, is matched only by the deviousness by which he will be brought low. In the end, it is Oppy himself who provides the weapon by which he is cut down; while Teller is all but destroyed by his own victory.

The first public hint of what was to happen was the appearance of a strange article in *Fortune* magazine attacking

Oppenheimer. In 1953, on the basis of a denunciation, President Eisenhower ordered an investigation to determine whether or not his clearance should be terminated. The subsequent public hearings became a *cause célèbre*.

By his own account, the first Teller heard of it was in early December 1953. He was waiting to see Lewis Strauss, an old partisan of his, and enemy of Oppenheimer's, who was then Chairman of the Atomic Energy Commission. Strauss was unexpectedly called away. Teller waited. Strauss returned in uncharacteristic agitation and led Teller immediately into his office. – This isn't to go any further, he said. I've just been to the White House. The President wants me to institute official proceedings to review Oppenheimer's security clearance. I feel terrible. I really hope he won't go ahead with this. It'll be a disaster for all of us.

By early 1954 the question hanging over Oppenheimer's clearance has become public knowledge. Teller and Oppy meet at a seminar. Teller says: I'm sorry to hear about your problems.

Do you believe I behaved in a sinister way? Oppy asks.

Certainly not.

Do me a favour, says Oppy. Will you go and talk with my lawyer?

Teller agrees. Oppenheimer is not present at this interview. According to Teller, the lawyer tells him nothing he doesn't already know.

Time passes. He is called to testify at the hearing. The attorney for the Atomic Energy Commission, Roger Robb, asks for a meeting. Robb asks: How are you going to testify – for Oppenheimer or against?

For, says Dr T.

I want to read a part of the testimony to you, says Robb.

Teller sits there: he feels a little uncomfortable, but having been briefed by Oppenheimer's lawyer, can find no grounds to refuse Robb. Robb then reads Oppenheimer's sworn testimony regarding the Chevalier affair.

I will never forget, says Teller, the shock that this portion of the testimony produced in me.

Robb asks again: 'Should Oppenheimer be cleared?'

I don't know, says Teller.

Before Teller testified, he spent several hours with Hans Bethe and his wife Rose, who tried to persuade him not to appear. They failed. A friend, Freeman Dyson, ran into Bethe by chance in a hotel lobby that day. – He was looking grimmer than I had ever seen him, Dyson recalled. I knew he had been testifying at Oppenheimer's trial. 'Are the hearings going badly?' I asked. 'Yes,' said Hans, 'but that is not the worst. I have just now had the most unpleasant conversation of my whole life. With Edward Teller.' He did not say any more, but the implications were clear. Teller had decided to testify against Oppenheimer.

What Teller actually said was: I would personally feel more secure if public matters would rest in other hands.

Both the Security Hearing Board, by a vote of 2 to 1, and the Atomic Energy Commission, by a vote of 4 to 1, decided to withhold security clearance from Oppenheimer. The dissenting opinion of the Security Hearing Board stated that there was not 'the slightest vestige of information' to indicate Oppenheimer's disloyalty, and offered, as the highest possible recommendation: He hates Russia. But despite such well-directed hatred, Oppenheimer was done for.

Much of the evidence during the hearing concerned his opposition to the Super, and whether or not this could be construed as being unpatriotic. But in their final majority opinion, the Security Hearing Board's only real argument against granting him clearance was the stupid story regarding George Eltenton and Haakon Chevalier, events which had taken place in 1942 and which had been known since 1943. They had not been acted upon at the time, but that did not diminish their usefulness. They were a weapon to be kept in reserve and used when the time came. The time had come.

FBI papers uncovered under the Freedom of Information Act throw new light on the affair's genesis. They make it clear that the Chevalier affair was only an excuse, a peg on which to hang a prosecution. Oppenheimer was destroyed because he stood in the way of the Super. The papers show that Dr T.

spoke secretly and at length with an FBI agent on two occasions during May, 1952. Harold P. Green, the AEC lawyer who drafted the charges against Oppenheimer, told a meeting of the American Historical Association in 1975 that 'a very substantial portion of the charges, certainly most of them related to the H-bomb, were drawn from the FBI interviews with Teller.' In those interviews, Teller charged Oppenheimer with opposing and working to delay development of the H-bomb. His interviewer said: He would do most anything to see [Oppenheimer] separated from his advisory position.

Why this vehemence? Six days before Teller was due to testify at the hearing, an AEC public information officer who visited him reported to Lewis Strauss: Teller feels deeply that [Oppenheimer's] 'unfrocking' must be done or else – regardless of the outcome of the current hearings – scientists may lose their enthusiasm for the nuclear programme.

Mephisto exacts his price. At a conference soon after the hearing's end, Teller, who so abhorred ostracism, found himself ostracised by those who had until now been his closest friends. He retired to his room and wept bitterly in Mici's arms.

Later, he said: If a person leaves his country, leaves his continent, leaves his relatives, leaves his friends, the only people he knows are his professional colleagues. If more than ninety per cent of these then come around to consider him an enemy, an outcast, it is bound to have an effect. The truth is it had a profound effect. It affected me, it affected Mici, it even affected her health.

His health, too, was undermined: two years later he had his first attack of ulcerative colitis, a disease that dogged him for the rest of his life.

He had made his choice: he was the servant of the bomb. – I am leaving the appeasers to join the fascists, he said. In the new weapons laboratory which was set up for him at Livermore in California, he could pursue the bombs of his dreams with unconstrained vigour. This was henceforth his kingdom; there he was, and would remain, king. King of the Bombs.

His life was devoted to the Super, to its multiplication, its betterment, its propaganda. This devotion led to curious paradoxes. Much of his energy, in the following years, was spent trying to persuade people that H-bombs and their tests were not, after all, so very dangerous. He could even contemplate nuclear war with some equanimity. With proper civil defence, he thought such a war could be survived. He had to believe these things. How else could he have undertaken the work which now occupied his life?

One of Teller's colleagues, his fellow Martian Eugene Wigner, said: He is the most imaginative person I have ever met, and that means a great deal when you consider that I knew Einstein. But another, I. I. Rabi (like Wigner a Nobel laureate), said: He is a danger to all that is important. I do really feel it would have been a better world without Teller. I think he is an enemy of humanity.

In 1960, during the first great wave of revulsion against the bomb, Zigi wrote an article about all this. In it, he considered the irony that the most powerful destructive force in history had been liberated by the traditionally powerless: the Jews of central Europe. – What is its attraction for us? he wondered. Is it so that we can say: You spurned me, and now see what happens? The Germans have assumed the traditional Jewish role – of moral outcasts. If they are to become the new Jews, are we to become the new Germans – international destroyers?

From this fate Zigi – by then so thoroughly established in his new persona – was busily trying to exempt himself. But he was nothing if not clear-eyed. Zigi of all men knew that contingency, only contingency, decides that one man shall become King of Destruction and another the White Champion opposing him.

IV

1954. That summer I was nine. Nearly nine: July 1954, my father has written on the back of the photo. I am standing in the garden of our house. My friend Bella stands beside me. We squint into the sun, heads slightly bent, wearing artless little-girl smiles and short, faded cotton dresses, smocked. My hair, cut short with a fringe, looks doubly dark beside Bella's long, flaxen locks. She is much taller than me, solider, longer-legged. I have known her for two years, since we both started at the same school, aged seven. You could not imagine, looking at our good-girl faces, the complications of our relationship. I can still remember my pleasure and surprise that she should have chosen me for her friend. Little girls need best friends: most of the anguish in their lives comes as the result of a best friend's betrayal. Not that Bella betrays me *very* often. When we are instructed to find a partner – we are always being told to find a partner – my heart does not automatically sink. I know Bella will probably be there, turning towards me. It is only occasionally – just often enough to make it plain who calls the shots here – that she looks elsewhere, leaving me standing unwanted, my eyes pricking, my heart full of vengeance. This vengeance is never enacted. How gladly I welcome her when she turns back to me! She is popular, good at games, a natural member of every club and clique. Why did she pick me? Perhaps because I offered no real competition – she was always, indisputably, cleverer and prettier – yet was not shamingly unacceptable. A fine balance.

Bella's father was a Labour MP. He was on the fringes of the Cabinet, but had still not quite made it when Labour were defeated in 1951. However, he managed to hold his seat, which of course lessened the blow. We used often to visit each other's houses. It was at Bella's that I was first introduced to the joys of Marmite, a delicacy unknown to my mother. She lived in one of those streets which climb up to Hampstead from the Finchley Road, not far from Zigi and Fania. It turned out that Fania was a friend of Bella's mother: she had recently begun painting in some earnest, and belonged to a local group which Mrs Brockenhurst also attended. They visited each other's studios. That was how Zigi first got to know Hugh Brockenhurst. Everyone, therefore, was delighted when Bella and I became friends.

Bella used to visit my house more often than I visited hers. I lived near our school while she had to travel three quarters of an hour each way, so it was easier for her to come to tea with me than for me to go to her. Also, her mother went out more than mine and was always grateful for somewhere to park one or both of her daughters. But we didn't usually want young Sarah hanging around. She spoiled our games. I don't remember what happened to her. Perhaps she, too, had a convenient friend nearby. Mrs Brockenhurst would come and pick Bella up in her car. My mother never learned to drive.

When Mrs Brockenhurst descended to collect Bella she was always charming and polite, but never lingered longer than the necessary minimum. – So kind of you, Mrs Sievers. I'd better not keep you. And my mother would say, quite sincerely: It's been a pleasure, Mrs Brockenhurst. The two mothers never made it to first-name terms. If the Brockenhursts hadn't known Zigi and Fania, I should probably never have found out what their first names were. Life was courtlier then. Rose and Susanna's friends never called me anything but Miriam.

My mother had a particularly soft spot for Bella, who, she used to say, didn't get much of a home life. She sometimes referred to her as poor little Bella, which I found inexplicable and annoying. I couldn't see anything poor about her. Undeterred by scorn, my mother would always make something *nourishing* for tea on days when Bella came. Smoked haddock with poached eggs, home-made cakes, of which she always had a large selection: those lemon curd fingers, those chocolate sponges of my youth ... But for me the Brockenhursts' home life represented the pinnacle of desirability. Life at our house was so predictable and unexciting: there was nothing remotely raffish about it. The Brockenhursts were definitely raffish. They occupied the lower half of one of those enormous Edwardian houses which sprawl, unglamorously but comfortably, over much of north-west London. Mr Brockenhurst was almost always absent, at the House or at his surgery or at a meeting. The mantelpiece of their big sitting-room, which had non-matching, faded armchairs and an enormous sofa from which it was impossible to rise once you were seated, was always filled with invitations. Bella and Sarah and I didn't go into the sitting-room much. We spent most of our time in the kitchen, which was a semi-basement, with french windows onto the back garden. Mrs Brockenhurst gardened. Her garden was a romantic tangle of grey leaves and old roses. My mother thought little of it. She, too, liked gardening, but her preference was for flowers, lots of them, in bright colours.

My father was in coats. He wasn't particularly interested in coats, but coats was where there had been an opening when the time came for him to earn a living. What could be safer than coats? Everybody needs them; they wear out at regular intervals and have to be replaced. He might as well be the one to replace them. Now he was in charge of the business. I loved visiting the factory, all those bolts of cloth, those busy people engaged in mysterious tasks, the offcuts to make beds or clothes for my dolls, the wonderful trimmings and buttons. But in the Brockenhursts' world this mysterious glamour fell away. The Brockenhursts and their friends were interesting people. That was what one aspired to be – an interesting person – and it was soon clear to me that interesting people were rarely in coats. Nor were they to be found in our unfashionable suburb at the end of the tube line.

Where would I have been, socially, without the fortunate chance of being related to Zigi and Fan? They were certainly interesting – much more interesting than Mr and Mrs Brockenhurst, or so it might have seemed to an unbiased eye: that of my parents, for example. My father, a hard man to please where politicians were concerned, was particularly scornful of Hugh Brockenhurst. I remember one particular occasion when he figured in some newspaper article and drew down torrents of ridicule over the tea and toast. – An MP! scoffed my father. One of our rulers.

Why shouldn't he be an MP? I demanded furiously. This kind of talk made me uncomfortable. It seemed disloyal.

Because he's an ox, said my father. He looks like an ox and he is an ox. An ox's brain in an ox's body.

Nat, be quiet, said my mother. Bella's Miriam's friend.

I'm not talking about Bella, said my father. Bella's another matter. She'd be an excellent MP. I'd vote for her any day. If I ever saw a natural politician, it's Bella.

It was true that the elder Brockenhursts were not impressive to meet. They always seemed devoid of definition, in a peculiarly British way. It had been bleached out of them. They both had hair which had once been fair but was now losing its colour (and in Mr Brockenhurst's case, its substance). They were tall and somewhat stooping, and tended to dress in shades of fawn and pale grey. Mr Brockenhurst, on the rare occasions we saw him, always looked very tired, with double bags under his eyes, while Mrs Brockenhurst's habitual expression was one of sadness. Perhaps this was because she saw her husband so rarely that the occasions when he was present could never live up to her expectations. In the presence of little, dark, darting Fania and tall, elegantly bearded Zigi, with his thick accent and worldly-wise, intelligent eyes, they might have been cardboard cutouts.

A frequent topic of conversation between my parents was the mystery of the friendship between the Brockenhursts and the von Fischers. They were clearly cynical as to its well-springs, although much of what they said was incomprehensible to me.

I remember one of these conversations particularly clearly.

I was sitting behind the sofa at the time, a favourite spot of mine. There was a small space into which I liked to creep, smelling deliciously of carpet and curtain, between the sofa's straight back and the curve of the bay window. Of course my parents would not have talked so freely had they been aware of my presence. I knew this, and therefore listened with special concentration.

I'm only saying they're human, said my father. In human relationships, there has to be give and take. It's like business. Everyone has to think they're getting something out of it. The Brockenhursts know the right people, Zigi sees a way into politics. All right. So what do Zigi and Fan offer? The pleasure of their company?

Why not? They're very interesting.

Interesting! A man like Brockenhurst doesn't have time for

people just because they're interesting. Everyone has to count. There has to be a reason. If you ask me it's not him, it's her. Have you seen the way she looks at Zigi? When we were round there last Saturday morning she just *happened* to drop by. I don't know how Fania stands it.

Poor woman, said my mother darkly. I wondered why she thought Fania was poor, but it soon became clear that she was referring to Mrs Brockenhurst. – He's a brute, you know. The other day when she came here to pick up poor little Bella, she was wearing dark glasses though it wasn't at all a bright day. I wouldn't be surprised if she was hiding something.

A black eye, is that what you mean? said my father, sounding horrified. Brockenhurst? There was a pause while he took this in. Then he said contemptuously: Well, what can you expect of a pig but a grunt, I suppose. My father was a gentle, honest man, and loathed and despised violence and underhand dealing. It was taken for granted that all politicians are underhand: Hugh Brockenhurst therefore exemplified the worst of all worlds. This view of things meant that my father lived in an almost perpetual state of indignation, which he sublimated into the deepest cynicism I have ever encountered. By comparison, my own view of life remains mild and trusting.

Yes, I understand he can be very violent, said my mother seriously. Fania was telling me. She doesn't like him at all. Doesn't trust him. But of course he's been very good to Zigi.

Not as good to him as his wife's being.

Fania knew what she was taking on, said my mother. I could hear the shrug in her voice. – She wasn't exactly an inexperienced girl. She loves him, and that's that. They have their own way of doing things, that's all. It's no good trying to understand other people's marriages.

I, too, had noticed Mrs Brockenhurst's dark glasses. I had regarded them as merely another example of her extreme sophistication. I couldn't really make out what my parents were talking about, though I understood enough to be vaguely disturbed. The notion of family discord – of violence, even – was so remote from my own experience that, although I heard the words, I didn't associate them with solid reality. But they were worrying enough to remain memorable. I'd noticed that Bella didn't talk much about her father. But then again, why would she? We had other, more interesting topics to discuss.

I thought about Saturday morning. There was a watchmaker in Child's Hill, not far from Zigi and Fania's house, who had an interesting sideline in complicated glass animals which I coveted and adored. The previous Saturday my father had taken me there to buy a wonderful crocodile, all wafer-thin green frills and tiny teeth, which I had been loving from afar for months. Afterwards, we had gone to Fania's to display the acquisition. I was just unwrapping it when Mrs Brockenhurst arrived. She said she just happened to be passing. – Zigi, you said you'd show me . . . or something like that, and he said: Oh, yes, and they left the room. Soon afterwards, Zigi stuck his head round the door and said he and Joan were just off for a minute, there were some papers of Hugh's she wanted to discuss with him. Then we heard the front door shut behind them. We just went on admiring my crocodile throughout all this, or so it seemed to me, but obviously my father's attention had been elsewhere.

Fania was quite unperturbed, and we soon found out why. Mrs B. was not the only visitor that morning. We were stowing the crocodile gently back in its tissue-padded box when Fania announced that she was just off, she was going out to lunch. She hurried us along rather obviously, presumably not wishing too much of her and Zigi's private affairs to be displayed before the gaze of the family. But she was too late (or he was too early). The doorbell rang to reveal George Frenkl, smiling broadly, a bunch of flowers in his hand. He was a very attractive man, of medium height, expansive, well-padded, with the air of one who welcomes all life's little pleasures, and as many of its larger ones as may be permitted. He seemed surprised to see us there, but greeted us cheerfully. – We were just off, said my father. Nice to see you again. – Always a pleasure, said George.

It was after this interesting encounter that the exchange between my parents regarding Zigi's and Fania's friends took place.

Was Zigi's friendship with the Brockenhursts really as cynically founded as my parents obviously supposed? Did he pursue it only because he could see his future role opening out before him? It seems improbable. How many people really plan their lives? Side-turnings open where we least expect them; apparent diversions turn out to have been the main road after all. But maybe inklings of a possible route were beginning to suggest themselves. And in 1964, when Labour was finally re-elected, the Brockenhurst connection came into its own. Zigi by this time had become famous in scientific circles for his work on antibody receptor mechanisms, though he was never to achieve the Nobel Prize that some so confidently predicted for him. He made a welcome addition to Harold Wilson's scientific team, and was soon being talked of as the next Chief Scientist.

Zigi might have given up bombs for microbiology, but he retained his Martian nose for power, actual and potential. The quiet suburban streets of my childhood must have seemed far removed from the melodrama then being played out between his erstwhile colleague Oppenheimer and his old classmate Teller in Washington. But Zigi had not retired from the fray. He was just biding his time.

CHAPTER 8   WE ALL SIT DOWN

I

UP TO THIS point, Zigi and I have not been important features of each other's existence. For me, he has simply been part of the family: a given, like the kitchen table or the house we live in. As for him, either I did not yet exist, or else I was a child, which for Zigi was tantamount to not existing. People, for him, were only really born around the age of eighteen.

All this, however, is about to change. The French use the word *formation* – a training-up, an induction course. For the next several years Zigi is to be an essential part of my *formation*: he will profoundly shape my life. His story becomes, for a while, inseparable from my own. And the pretence which I have up till now maintained, that it is possible to separate author and subject, must be definitively dropped. Isn't Miriam's Zigi as much a part of Miriam as her own younger self? The biographer's aim is to inhabit the subject, to get inside his head. But whose head are we talking about? If the biographer becomes the subject, then who is that subject but an aspect of the biographer? They are intellectually inter-twined, thrown together by the exigencies of the project just as Zigi and I were thrown together by circumstance.

Is the inside view the most revealing? Inevitably, it's skewed. The gloss changes, the emphases are historically unreliable. Miriam's Zigi is not necessarily the world's Zigi. Other people's lives can be scrutinised, discussed, their recurring patterns analysed. But one can't do the same job on oneself. From the inside, life seems an arbitrary, patternless muddle. As for the possibility that others might be viewing,

analysing, gossiping, that oneself might be an object of study –
who could imagine it? Why would anyone bother? On the odd
occasion when it becomes clear they *do* bother, the effect is
almost shocking. When Derry accepted my first book he said:
Funny, isn't it. You know, we often used to wonder what was
going to happen to you, Miriam. You and Bella.

We? I said. Who was *we*? And why should anything happen
to us?

Tony and me, of course, he said. Well, it was clear
something would. And it has, hasn't it?

My mind was filled with this new picture of the two of them
discussing *us*. Of course, we discussed *them* often enough.
What did he . . . ? And what did you . . . ? On and on we
went, into the night. It was the inexhaustible topic. But the
notion of oneself as object never fails to disconcert.

So Zigi, at this point, becomes less an object, more an
ingredient. Naturally, my view of him changed and developed
with the years. To begin with, he was quite simply a hero. My
hero, and my generation's.

II

Early March, 1961. It is half-past five: a bright, raw evening.
Bella and I are waiting for the tube at Golders Green station.
We are still best friends, uneasy allies. I haven't yet learned to
play power-games. Bella is capricious, but I am always,
boringly, available. And now that we are approaching the
cut-throat world of sex, I know that she is likelier than ever to
betray me. Solidarity has no place here. Wouldn't I betray
her? Judging by present form, I shan't have the opportunity,
so the dilemma will not arise.

We have shed our school uniform and are clad in our other
uniform: duffel coats over black. Black sweaters, black tight
skirts, black fishnet stockings, black platform shoes. Black-
rimmed eyes are the focal point in our pale-lipped faces. It is
the Juliette Greco look. It's fine on Parisian nightclub singers,

and not at all bad on tall, blonde Bella, but it does little for round, dark Miriam. Still, there can be no arguing with fashion. My hair, which I am growing, is tied up on top of my head in a short bouncy tail. Taken in conjunction with my artful fringe, I hope this makes me look like a French tart out of one of those Impressionist paintings. I have not confided this hope to my father, who has taken to making tasteless wisecracks about my excursions into fashion. For the first time in my life I agree with my mother that not everything is a joking matter.

We are bound for our Mecca of the moment, the Partisan coffee-bar in Carlisle Street, Soho. The Partisan is a focus of left-wing activism, and we are left-wing activists. Well, we have to be something, don't we? Fifteen years old: a person needs her niche in the world. We don't feel easy with rock-and-roll, however much we may wish we did. As far as we are concerned, Elvis might as well be a visitor from Venus. And, whatever our aspirations, the likes of Greco and Piaf can only be distant goddesses to wholesome virgins like us.

So how are we to fill our spare time and *meet boys*? At tennis clubs? We are not sporting. Being Girl Guides? We may be wholesome, but not *that* wholesome. Pursuing film-stars and theatrical idols? There's little real satisfaction to be got from lusting after a picture on the wall of one's room.

Politics, however, are a different matter. They are part of our culture. They bind us together. At home – Bella's, obviously, but also mine – they are daily, urgently, contentiously discussed. Their complexion is never in question. Even my mother has not yet progressed very far in her journey rightwards. We still subscribe to the *New Statesman*, though (my mother now insists) more for its literary pages than for its political view. That's her story.

The nature of our social life is therefore settled. The schools of London are filled with people like us – the offspring of liberal intellectuals. And we all meet weekly at the Partisan, to listen to a speaker and discuss the questions of the moment.

These questions – inevitably, for are we not the children of the Bomb? – revolve largely around nuclear matters. For these are the years of Kennedy and Khrushchev, marked by a series of terrifying excursions to the brink. Last year, the Bay of Pigs. This year, the Berlin Wall. Next year, the Cuba crisis. Each time, we wonder as we go to bed whether the world will still be here tomorrow. No wonder the Campaign for Nuclear Disarmament gathers strength daily.

We are not without hope: for between those bouts of stomach-churning belligerence President Kennedy, terrified perhaps by his own brinksmanship, is trying to control the genie. If it can't be forced back into the bottle, it can perhaps be cut down to size. The President has set up an Arms Control and Disarmament Agency and a moratorium on nuclear testing has been in force for the past two years. It is hoped (though not by Dr T., who fiercely argues its evils before a succession of Senate committees) that there will soon be a treaty to ban such testing altogether. The British government is with Dr T. on this. The British government is an irrelevance in this matter, but that of course is precisely the battle it is fighting.

This evening, we are to discuss The Arms Race. And who is the speaker? None other than my Uncle Zigi. He is becoming something of a public figure. His work on antibodies has made headlines in the scientific press, and he is in demand, as a literate scientist, for programmes such as *The Brains Trust* and *Any Questions*. Also, through his friendship with Hugh Brockenhurst, he has become involved in Labour Party politics. Zigi sits on a science policy advisory committee, an educational commission of inquiry. He is one of the many central Europeans who are now influential in British cultural and educational circles. They alone, in these cynical times, seem to have before them an ideal Britain towards which they strive: the Britain to which they fled before the war, the Britain about which they learned in the authoritarian lands of their childhood. Such visions are no longer available to the native-born.

On the question of nuclear disarmament, which has notoriously split the Labour Party down the middle, Zigi speaks frequently, and with the authority of personal experience and proven moral rectitude. He reiterates that unless something is done, it is clear that civilisation will end in our lifetime. He will get that something done if he humanly can. In other words, he has re-entered the game. Did he think, when he turned to microbiology, that he had left the nuclear arena for ever? He has found a new role for an old rivalry. Once again, he stalks his erstwhile classmate. He has assumed the persona which is to be his for the next thirty years: Mr Clean, the Man who Renounced the Bomb. This reality is far more substantial than the one it has superseded, grounded as *that* was in nothing but shadowy facts. Does even Zigi believe in those facts any more? Insofar as they are recalled at all (and if he forgets them, who else is there to remember?) they perhaps assume the blurred outlines of a dream, or nightmare. He, almost alone, left the bomb project: *that* is the fact upon which we must focus. Zigi the White Champion is donning his armour.

On the other side, the black side, Dr T. fights what he, too, takes to be the good fight. Without tests, how can he develop better, more modern bombs? And without these bombs, how is the Free World to survive? Dr T. is desperate. It is not simply that he sees his life's work threatened: he is perpetually terrified that his worst fears are being realised, that the Soviet Union is pulling ahead in the great nuclear game. In 1957, the Russians launched Sputnik, and cold panic lodged in the hearts of the West's weaponeers. For the first time, America, hitherto safe from all attack, might be threatened. Dr T. fills the President's ear with siren whispers of neutron bombs and anti-missile missiles. Why isn't he rearming? Why is he tying the experimenters' hands behind their backs?

We, meanwhile, are caught powerless between ideologies. All we can do is inform ourselves, and shout as loud as we can. That's what we're on our way to do. We leave Tottenham Court Road station and thread our way towards Soho Square, with its dinky little toy house in the middle. Despite all the dire events we are about to ponder, I am filled with nervous delight. Coming here always excites me. We are taking possession of our bit of London; truly in the middle of things at last. The nearer we get to the Partisan, the more excited I become. As we go inside, anticipation fills me to the exclusion of almost everything else. Anticipation of what? Who knows? Of something. *Something!*

The ground floor, where we come in, is a café, firmly intellectual, with blond wood and chess-boards and newspapers on sticks. Downstairs is a jazz cellar, where the other day some man said he would like to paint me. – I can see you, he said, in black and white stripes. (He never did commit his stripes to canvas, however.) Downstairs is for frivolity. There is even a small space where, from time to time, couples expertly jive. But we are not yet old enough to be frivolous (and we haven't really learned to jive). We are bound upstairs. Upstairs is a long room where our meetings are held. Where the serious business takes place.

Upstairs is already crowded. In front sits John, the secretary, whose job it is to concoct a programme of speakers and who was so grateful when, swelling with pride, I offered to try and get Zigi along to address us. I knew he would be happy to come. I alone in the family approve of his new incarnation. Fania, who might have been expected to do so, is disgruntled, the more so because she knows that, politically speaking, she should support him. And, politically, she does support him. Her disgruntlement is purely personal – a fact which only increases it. The fact is that, these days, she hardly sees Zigi. His new role as saviour of the world has seduced him more completely than any mistress (though no doubt Fania has her dark suspicions in that direction as well). Zigi is out almost every night, speaking and politicking. His days are spent at the laboratory. And what is left of their life together? Fania's time is not occupied with children. She and Zigi used to eat out a lot, go to concerts, theatres, dinner-parties. It's not much fun doing these things by oneself. – Saving the world, she snorts darkly. What does he think he's saving it *for*?

Fania, at fifty, has lost none of her vivacity and flirtatiousness. She is not one to moulder at home, rebellious but faithful (and would Zigi want her to?) Nor does she do so. If he is not going to be around, she will arrange her own life accordingly. There are family mutterings. Blame is discussed, apportioned, reapportioned.

Why doesn't she join more fully in his political life? She has always been a political activist. But she is uncomfortable among the aggressively intellectual ladies of the CND front line. She is not educated; not, despite the painting, a professional in her own right. She does not interest them as he does. In those circles, she is a purely secondary figure: Mrs Zigi. – I can't stand them, she grumbles, dreadful self-satisfied snobs. Who do they think they are? Their cause, disreputably but inevitably, becomes inseparable from this personal dislike. When I visit the house in West Hampstead these days, I am uneasily aware of a background of simmering fury. No wonder Zigi prefers to spend his evenings elsewhere. At places like the Partisan he can be sure of his meed of admiration. He is becoming a public figure, and he enjoys it. He can't get enough of it.

As soon as we enter the room, Bella is engulfed by friends and admirers. She will ignore me for the rest of the evening, until the time comes for us to catch the last tube home. (Now, having been through it all myself, I can appreciate my parents' heroic self-restraint. Now I know that, although they were always in bed, lights out, by the time I got back, this did not mean they were asleep. Only the shutting of the front door behind me released them into unconsciousness.)

I look around for the haven of a known face. I locate one: the brother of another schoolfriend. He is short – scarcely taller than I am – and a trifle spotty, but I am ready, painfully, humiliatingly ready, to forgive him these defects. He is a boy, I know him, and there is a spare seat beside him. I slip into it. On my other side is a large, shambly boy with sandy hair who is having trouble arranging his arms and legs. It is obvious that he has recently acquired several inches to which he is not yet accustomed. As the less than enraptured possessor of copious new breasts, I can only sympathise.

At this moment there is a buzz from the front of the room. Zigi enters, accompanied by this term's chairman, a bustling, self-important, plumpish youth. The buzz of conversation drops. All eyes turn towards them. The official part of the meeting is about to begin.

Zigi is an imposing figure. He has shaved off his beard. It disappeared when I was about twelve, and he would have been approaching fifty. I remember my father commenting acidly upon this event. – Beginning to turn grey, he said. Can't have that, can we? Young ladies might get quite the wrong idea. – Really, Nat, said my mother. Why shouldn't he shave off his beard if he wants to? It's a shame he didn't do it before, I think he looks much better without it. It wasn't that she approved of Zigi's vanity, but she always stood up for her family when, as so often, they were criticised by my father.

What did Zigi say that evening? I can't remember. I imagine he pursued his favourite themes – the themes he would continue to pursue for the next twenty-five years. The arbitrariness, the emotional rather than military basis, for Britain's – our – possession of nuclear weapons. (That heavily-accented, central European Britishness!) The necessity of making clear, in the teeth of official obfuscation, exactly what the effects of a nuclear attack would be. The military uselessness of such weapons. The terrifying trigger-happiness of the generals, uncontaminated by imagination. (Field-Marshal Montgomery said, about this time: Personally I would use nuclear weapons first and ask afterwards.) The necessity, if we were to survive, of getting rid of these dreadful weapons which he, Zigi, had helped spawn. He said these things and wrote them, hundreds, thousands, of times. I heard him say them, I read his writings. He introduced me to the politics of protest, as he introduced me to so much else.

It is not that I have no memories of that meeting. I do. But they are exclusively social, or visual. I can feel the stuffiness of the room, over-filled with our eager breath. I can see Zigi, in my mind's eye, addressing us earnest adolescents with that flattering gravity we demanded, and received, from our illustrious speakers. I can see him mouthing, but the movie is silent. I can only imagine the sonorously accented voice; the manner, courteous, worldly-wise, rather tired; the jokes, one eyebrow lifted; the slightly snuffling laugh. I can see the questioners, who always seemed to me so cogent and intellectual. (And who *were*: did we ever again scale such purely intellectual heights, uncorrupted by hidden agendas or *partis pris*?) I can recall the heady pleasure of knowing that I am related to the speaker. The nervous wondering – Can I frame a question so that my intelligence and this relationship will both be revealed to the room at large? The acute consciousness of (albeit imperfect) male presences on either side of me. The sensation of being grown-up – of sitting in this room with my peers gravely thinking about the world's great problems, which were now our problems, and what we could do about them. But of what was said – nothing remains.

Is this because I never had an actual thought while I was young? It sometimes seems so. I sometimes pick up a book which I know I read as a student. Invariably, it is new to me; I have no sense of ever having looked at it before. Yet there is my name and the date on the flyleaf, and the evidence that someone – presumably my then self – has read it, or at any rate left hairs and breadcrumbs between the pages. And, were I in any doubt, I should know, from looking at my own daughters, that my youth cannot have been as thought-free as it now appears. Is theirs? Clearly not. Equally clearly, thinking is not the most important component of their lives – as, these days, it is of mine. What is? Sex. So, when they get to my age, that is what they will remember. QED.

III

Easter 1961: my first Aldermaston march. My parents are not too happy about my going. I suspect that my mother has been listening to aunts. Only fifteen! Four days! What are they going to do *at night*? But they let me go. I caught the tail-end of a telephone conversation. – She's an intelligent girl, my mother was saying. You can't treat them like babies. Besides, all her friends are going.

That is to say, Bella is going. As I point out, this is

something that concerns our generation. Who made the bomb in the first place? Theirs (specifically, Zigi). And who is suffering? Ours. The moratorium on testing has recently ended, and once again the atmosphere is being showered with radionuclides. – What do you think we're all eating for breakfast here? I demand, pointing to our porridge and cornflakes. Milk? Not just milk. Strontium 90 and iodine 131, that's what. They get into your bones and give you cancer. My mother looks stricken. She doesn't really approve of Zigi's rabble-rousing, she's becoming almost as paranoid about Russia and communists as Dr T. himself, but I've got her where it hurts here. What does poison know of politics? – Let's hope you get somewhere, then, darling, she murmurs. The best of luck to you.

We have reached an amicable compromise. I won't go for the full four days. Bella is. But her reasons are not necessarily the same as mine. I am filled with anti-nuclear fervour and other, unspecified excitements. But Bella's motivation is more complex. I have the distinct impression that the consciousness of annoying her father plays no little part in her determination to march. Hugh Brockenhurst is on the pro-nuclear wing of the Labour Party, and is probably regretting the day when he introduced such a troublemaker as Zigi to its bosom. So naturally he's not too pleased to see Bella aligning herself so wholeheartedly with his opponents.

I'm jolly well doing the whole four days, she announces defiantly, and I don't care what he says.

Indeed, which of the Brockenhurst family does support its best-known member on this issue? Looking over some old cuttings, to try and recapture the detail of those days, I notice a photograph: the front of the Aldermaston march setting off. It's dated 1960 – the year before Bella and I began to frequent the Partisan. There are the usual crowd – Michael Foot, Vanessa Redgrave, Bertrand Russell, Canon Collins, A. J. P. Taylor. There – at the end of the line – is Zigi. And who is that beside him? Not Fania. No – blurred but unmistakable – it's Joan Brockenhurst.

Well, now, there's a thing I hadn't remembered, or perhaps

had never registered. I could swear she wasn't on my first march, the next year. Surely she and Zigi weren't still – ? As I recall, the family gossip had died down by then. He'd moved onwards and upwards, or at least elsewhere – that was the assumption.

I could find out easily enough, I suppose. All I have to do is ask her. It's years since I've seen her. Not since Susanna was a baby. But that's hardly surprising. Bella and I lost touch. Life moved on. But I imagine she's still around. How old would she be now? Mid-seventies, perhaps. I wonder if she's still living in the same place?

The phone directory still lists Brockenhurst, J., at the old address. What happened to H., I wonder? No doubt I shall find out. I dial the number, which was once so familiar.

Hello?

Yes, it's her, all right. I'd know that voice anywhere, even after all these years. Slightly challenging, slightly suspicious. You always felt you had to justify yourself.

Mrs Brockenhurst? It's Miriam Oliver here. Miriam Sievers.

Goodness! What can I do for you? How many years is it? Not accusing, hand her that. But hardly welcoming.

Well, the thing is, I'm doing a biography of my Uncle Zigi. I rush on, before she should get the wrong idea. Not probing into their private affairs – perish the thought. – I was looking through some old Aldermaston stuff and there was a picture of you two together. So I suddenly thought you might be able to throw some light on – on the start of his involvement with politics.

D'you really think so?

Could I come and see you, perhaps?

Why not? When did you have in mind?

I don't know. Today? Tomorrow? How are you placed?

I get the impression that, these days, Joan Brockenhurst's time is all too disposable. I am to visit her this very afternoon, around half-past two.

The house is unchanged: perhaps a little more dilapidated around the windowframes. The figure who opens the door however, is not dilapidated in any way. Joan Brockenhurst used to be so distant, hiding behind those dark glasses; a wavy, indefinite figure, blurred around the edges, unwilling to draw too much attention to herself. But now the dark glasses have gone, along with the slight stoop and the apologetic shades of grey. On this sultry August afternoon she's wearing a long, loose dressing-gown affair in old-rose muslin which accentuates her imposing height. Her hair, which I remember as wispy mid-brown, is shiny white. Evidently losing her husband – however that was achieved – has transformed her life.

You're looking very well, I say.

Thank you. She smiles; obviously can't quite bring herself to say the same of me. It can't be denied that I have felt and looked better in my time. The war of attrition with Tony, the worries about Fania, are getting me down. My hair is noticeably greyer, and I'm losing weight. Elegant slenderness, unless care is taken, becomes mid-life scragginess. And these days I don't really take enough care. I can see as much in Joan Brockenhurst's unwavering eyes. My regime will change as from tomorrow. As from this evening. That piercing stare has convinced me. My problems are showing. There's no deceiving Mrs B. She's been through it in her time. She knows the tell-tale signs.

She leads me through the familiar hallway, down to the kitchen and out into the garden, where a white table and a couple of chairs are set under the old, remembered apple tree. – Drink? she says, and without waiting for a reply fetches a jug of lemonade from the fridge, and a couple of glasses. – No good drinking alcohol in this heat, she says. I sit. She sits. She smiles and pours the lemonade. – Well, she says. Miriam. After all these years.

Did Bella tell you? We met at Zigi's memorial service.

Yes, I think she did mention it.

She could have given you a lift, if you'd wanted to go. Or I could. I didn't think of it.

Oh, no, I don't think so. She smiles, dreamily, distantly. I don't think Bella's world and mine much interest her any more. All she wanted, all those years, was to be left alone. And now she has succeeded. The last thing she needs is to revive old complications.

I saw this picture –

So you said.

Well, I was surprised. Because I know your husband was so against CND and all that.

Yes, he was. She takes another sip and leans back in her chair. I disagreed with him, that was all.

What can I say to her? I know what I *want* to say. Were you Zigi's mistress? Did your husband really beat you up? What happened to him? But I can't. We know each other both too well and not well enough for that. There was a moment when we might have become friends, when she was so kind about money for an abortion. But the moment passed, and it's twenty-five years since then. A lifetime. Susanna's lifetime, to be precise. And she was always rather intimidating. *That* hasn't changed.

D'you know how Zigi got involved with CND? I ask tamely. Anything to get the ball rolling. Was he in it from the beginning?

No, she says. I was. I introduced him to it. There was some sort of committee meeting, we were going over lists of possible speakers. We had endless actors and playwrights and novelists and so on, and Alan Taylor was grumbling about how there weren't any nuclear physicists. In America nuclear physicists were leading the campaign, but here I suppose they were all working for the government. They'd probably have been sacked. I said, I think I know someone who might help. So it was agreed that I should put it to him.

Surely he'd thought of it for himself?

Not very obviously. Though of course some of his friends – people like Eddie Angell – were in it from the beginning. She gives me an odd look, quizzical, considering. – I don't know how well you knew your Uncle Zigi.

I'm beginning to think nobody knew him very well.

Possibly not. This would be – what? 1959? It was hardly for me to talk about purity of motive, she says bitterly. I don't know if you realised, but Hugh and I did not get on terribly well. He always said that the only reason I was so hot on CND was because I was trying to destroy his career – he was a Gaitskellite, very much against. That always made me very indignant. But who knows whether he wasn't right, to some extent.

I think about Bella. She had a double motivation, then. Going marching wasn't just a declaration against her father, but an expression of solidarity with her mother.

What did Zigi say?

He wouldn't commit himself at once. That was hardly a surprise. In all the years I knew him, I don't think I ever saw him act impulsively. Certainly not in matters of politics, and hardly ever in other matters, either. She gives me that quizzical look again. Everything had to be weighed up, what would be the advantages of doing this or doing that. And the disadvantages, of course.

Yes, I can see it. The aim, as always: power. Advantages: a platform, more contacts, the possibility of stepping out from behind the scenes and becoming a public figure. Who would be a backroom boffin given the possibility of centre stage? Not Zigi. Disadvantages: Is this the best way to play it? Old habit advises caution. He is British – but only Brit*ish*. Might not too much of the wrong sort of attention destroy rather than enhance a promising political career? But, in the end, the ayes have it. The Labour Party always admires a man of principle. And of course there's the old matter of revenge. Scores to be paid off. He can see how that enforced departure might now be used to some effect, and in a way that'll have Lansdale and Groves gnashing their teeth. How can he resist?

But he gave you a reply in the end.

Oh, yes, it didn't take too long. We catch each other's eyes and giggle: we know our Zigi. He said he was trying not to think about nuclear weapons any more. But he'd do it if I really thought he could be of use. He was in this special position, of course, he'd actually walked out of Los Alamos, and perhaps we could make something of that.

Had he ever mentioned that to you before? Why he left?

She thinks, slowly sipping her lemonade. Why this sudden embargo on alcohol? She's right, of course, wine and spirits don't quench your thirst (and I can't imagine her drinking beer), but it's somehow not what I would have expected. She certainly wasn't teetotal when I knew her. Perhaps she's drying out. That might account for this curious, slowed-down, swimming detachment. Or maybe it's just a reaction to the awful memory of her husband. – No, I think that was the first time. All I knew was that he'd left there before the end.

So that was the moment! The Man of Principle is born. We are not often privileged to witness the birth of a myth.

Of course, once he'd decided, says Mrs Brockenhurst somewhat acidly, he became one of the most active of us all. Nothing could stop him.

I went on the 1961 march, I say. Were you there? I don't remember Bella mentioning it.

No, she says. I became less active after 1960.

Because of Zigi?

Why should Zigi have affected it one way or the other?

Why, indeed? Her eyes meet mine: wide, opaque. She pours some more lemonade. It's clear she isn't going to say any more. I may think what I like, but she's not going to confirm or deny. I could harry her a bit, of course. Quite often, if you can once surprise someone into starting, out it all pours however clamlike their original intentions. It's a tactic I've used before, on the odd journalistic assignment. But I can't bring myself to try it with Joan Brockenhurst. I've known her too long, our relations are – in one way and another – too delicate, too complex. Also, I don't want to upset her. Zigi caused her enough trouble while he was alive. Why should he return from the dead to upset this fragile equilibrium she's finally achieved?

Besides, I can fill in the blanks myself, up to a point. When the Brockenhursts became friendly with the von Fischers, Joan Brockenhurst fell in love with Zigi. That much was always clear. Did they go to bed together? Her remark about his never acting on impulse leads me to believe that perhaps they did not. It was Hugh, not Joan, who was in a position to do Zigi some good. What would have been the point of alienating him? I imagine Joan understood this perfectly well. It's more than possible that Zigi put it to her in so many words. That would certainly have been in character. But by 1959, Zigi was less dependent on Hugh Brockenhurst. He was acquiring his own contacts, getting established in political circles on his own account. So Joan decided to try her luck again. Maybe this time she would persuade him. And maybe she did, in some passing way. She must have been an attractive woman – I can see that now, what her potential might have been, if she'd ever fulfilled it. Very English upper-middle: how could he resist such an anthropological education? But it could never have lasted. Zigi would never have risked compromising himself for Joan Brockenhurst. Miserably married as she was, she would too quickly have become dependent, importunate – a nuisance. Complications, scenes, melodramas, were the last thing he was looking for. Fania, I'm sure, was quite aware of this. She never saw Joan as a threat. On the contrary – they were friends. If Joan really was in love with Zigi, this must have been particularly galling for her.

So it ended – if it ever began. Once Zigi was in politics, far more interesting women than Joan Brockenhurst would have been available. After that, she would have kept out of his way. Why view the painful spectacle?

What happened to your husband? I ask.

He died, she says vaguely. Years ago. Didn't you see the obituaries? Sorry, that's a silly question. Obviously you didn't. She leans back in the chair, stares up into the apple tree. Some of the apples are just beginning to flush and ripen. The sky is a heavy blue-grey. – It's going to storm, she says idly, all engagement – all pretence of engagement –vanished. – How's Fania? Is she helping you with your book?

She's fine, I say. Don't let's risk being the kind of person who actually replies when asked a formal question. Missing Zigi.

Don't we all? says Mrs Brockenhurst. Queenly, vague, she picks up her glass and drifts back into the house as the first thick drops of rain begin to fall.

Bettina, Fania, Joan. Driving back to Islington I think about them. Alone, alone, alone. Obviously, this is not necessarily unwelcome. Joan Brockenhurst is not unhappy, as she certainly used to be. But the price of survival has been disengagement. Otherwise, there's nothing for it but to put a good face on things.

I let myself into the house. The girls are away, Tony's at the office. Nevertheless, my life is still peopled. For how long?

Bettina, Fania, Joan, will not dismiss themselves from my thoughts.

IV

Zigi, of course, was on the 1961 march. He was up in front with the celebs, where he belonged, enjoying the limelight. I kept out of his way. The last person I wanted to run into was a member of the family. Vicarious prestige was quite enough for me on this occasion.

My plan, altogether less ambitious than Bella's, is to take an early train to Reading, join the march there on its second day, spend one night out at Slough, come back home next evening when we reach London, and return for the final day. – If you can still walk, says my father. I pack my rucksack (newly acquired) with a sleeping-bag (also newly acquired – but I shall have to get these things at some point, shan't I?), spare socks and innumerable chicken sandwiches made by my mother. The march is due to assemble at 9.15. By 9.30 I am in Reading, stepping nervously out of the station in search of my peers.

The optimism, the innocence of youth! How did I ever expect to find my friends, just like that, amid the teeming throng? Perhaps I didn't expect to. But I certainly expected *something*. Just like when I approached the Partisan. The same feeling. All nerves at the ready, all receptors quivering. The H-bombs may be the excuse, but the march is the thing. Compared to this, the possibilities it offers, what are H-bombs? An abstraction; a bogeyman; an excuse. Naturally I hate them. What right-minded person wouldn't? I really do object to having my world littered with them. What can I do about it? March. So here I am, marching. Whoopee!

Me – and thousands of others like me. I scan them, wondering what lies in store. At the front is a row of well-known faces. The usual suspects. Ancient Bertrand Russell, tiny and upright. Michael Foot, dishevelled as always. J. B. Priestley, round and bluff, whose article in the *New Statesman* was the original catalyst for CND. I can recognise Vanessa Redgrave, and John Neville, our class's universal pin-up. That's where Zigi will be, though I can't just see him. I'm going to keep well away from them, and him. This is not an autograph-hunting expedition, nor a family outing. It's –

What is it, exactly? Why, it's what you care to make it. Let's put idealism and indignation to one side, take them as read. They are part of the reason everyone's here, but not necessarily the whole story. Zigi has his reasons, Bella has hers. And I have mine.

For me, this is a social and sexual challenge. What interests me is the body – or bodies – of the crowd. The mean age seems to be about seventeen (my partial eye focuses only on what is of interest to it). There are thousands of them, rucksacked, young, trembling (with nerves, with excitement, with desire, and also with cold, for an icy Easter wind is blowing). And there is someone I know. Isn't it? Yes – it is, I'm sure of it. The boy I was sitting next to the day Uncle Zigi came to talk to us at the Partisan. The one with all the arms and legs.

Hello.

He looks at me, puzzled.

Wasn't I sitting next to you at the Partisan the other day? The day Zsygmond von Fischer –

Oh, yes! Recognition gleams in his eye. He has a Scottish accent. We may have sat next to each other, but it's the first time we've spoken. He disappeared rather promptly at the end of that meeting, from the room or perhaps merely from my field of consciousness. I was probably too busy staking a claim to my exalted relative.

He's my uncle, actually.

Oh. Is he? Really?

We exchange necessary details. Names, schools, possible mutual acquaintances. It turns out he is at school with my friend's brother, the one who was sitting on my other side. – Is he here today?

He said he would be, but I haven't seen him.

We look around. We are the only people we recognise, for the moment at least. What luck, to have found each other! (At least, this is what I feel. And Derry, for that is his name, Derry McCulloch, doesn't seem to object to my company.)

At this moment, the march begins to move off. We are just behind a jazz band. They tune up and launch into the Saints, not yet as hackneyed as it is to become – and anyhow, what do we know from hackneyed? We sing along and bop to the music. On our way to Slough.

> *Come, friendly bombs, and fall on Slough!*
> *It isn't fit for humans now.*

It was my first demonstration. I have been on many since. They never fail to move me. What else can we do, we poor fodder, how else make ourselves felt, how else affect events? Numbers are all we have to set against the private paranoias of power. There is a sense of exuberant vindication, of family feeling. Everyone, as far as the eye can see, is an ally. We are so many: who can resist us? We move in a blissful cocoon, staring triumphantly, pityingly, out at the unhappy souls who are merely watching from the sidelines. Join us! Give in, you know you want to! They look so miserable. And we are so joyful, with the intoxicating euphoria of the crowd.

And the knowledge, equally intoxicating, of Derry marching here beside me.

I steal a glance at him. He's tall, perhaps not quite so tall as my Dad, who is six foot, but a good deal broader. Already, and he's only sixteen. His arms are a little too long for his frame, which gives him a slightly shambling gait, but reassuring. There is nothing fierce about him. His thick, sandy hair is cut somewhat jaggedly. He is wearing – need I say it? – jeans and a donkey-jacket. Just like me. Peas in a pod. They all look alike, don't they. Though when you get to know them you can actually tell them apart quite easily.

We march and we march. We go rather slowly. It takes much longer to move ten thousand people than ten. I swap some of my mother's chicken sandwiches for some of Derry's chocolate. I also have a thermos of soup, which we share. (These days, if I go on a march, my thermos is filled with gin and tonic.) Ken Colyer's Jazzmen play on. Finally we reach Slough. Evening is drawing in. The wind is still cold. Efficient ladies allocate us to various overnight havens. By now, Derry and I have spotted some other faces from the Partisan, including Bella, who is with the secretary, John. We are all sent to a church hall somewhere in a back street. We make our way there and park our rucksacks and sleeping-bags. Somewhere, hot food is on offer from a stall. We drift over. The evening drifts by.

I move through it all in a blanket of happiness. This is my first taste of peer-group living, unsupervised by parents or teachers, Brown Owl, group leader or aunt. This is real life at last. Back at the church hall someone is playing a guitar. We sing along. A bottle of whisky passes from hand to hand. I take a small sip. I have never tasted whisky before. It tastes hot and curiously varnishy. Derry takes a rather larger sip, but then he's larger altogether, and Scottish as well. He probably has whisky quite often. We queue up for the toilets, cursorily brush our teeth. We spread out our sleeping-bags. People are beginning to pair off now. Bella and John are kissing. Bella is more advanced in these matters than I am. She is bolder and more attractive, and I have noticed that on our Partisan evenings she tends to disappear with a member of the opposite sex, not to reappear until the last possible moment. Once she vanished altogether: I had to go without her. She turned up at school next day with huge bags under her eyes, and wouldn't say what she'd been doing the night before.

I feel nervous and slightly irritated, excluded, as one does when one's companions retreat behind a wall of sex. Then I feel a hand on my shoulder. It is Derry. Awkwardly, he pulls me towards him. Awkwardly, I respond. We fall back on to the sleeping-bagged floor. He moves his face down towards mine. We start to kiss. At first we keep our mouths shut, but then I feel his tongue trying to force itself between my lips, so I let it in. He tastes of whisky and toothpaste and of some other, undefinable taste, which is his own taste. His hands travel over my body, somewhat uncertainly, though less uncertainly than mine. I can feel a lump in his groin, and a responding heat in mine. (Thank goodness today isn't my period! What on earth would I have said? What could I have *done*?) The lights have been turned out. The darkness around us bumps and rustles. Our kisses become longer, harder, more impassioned. I begin to feel slightly nervous. No one in my class at school, not even Bella, has lost her virginity. We all talk about it incessantly, and I'm sure they haven't; I'm sure I'd know if they had. But apparently it's terribly easy to do, and terribly hard to stop once you . . . And you can't just lead somebody on and then say no. It isn't fair. That's being a tease, and no girl wants to be known as a tease.

Now I feel Derry's fingers fumbling with the fastening of my bra, which I wasn't going to bother to take off tonight. Somehow this isn't a situation in which you undress to go to bed. In fact, I hadn't even got round to taking off my sweater yet. Derry struggles away. It isn't easy. My bra is a stout affair. I feel I should offer to help him, but instead I lie there woodenly until finally he defeats the hooks and eyes. I feel his hands on my breasts, and give thanks for the darkness. If I'm going to keep in control of this (but do I want to?) it seems clear I shouldn't leave things too long. We are both breathing very hard now. His hands are on the waistband of my jeans, unbuttoning, un-zipping. He leads my hand towards his penis, whose detail I have avoided picturing, preferring to remain immersed in the unfamiliar delights of kissing. He begins to unzip his own zip.

Is this where I want to do it, to lose my virginity, that fabled commodity? On a communal floor with someone I hardly know? And what if I should – get pregnant? I'm sure he won't have – And I certainly haven't –

Look, Derry, I mumble, you know I really don't want to – well, you know.

He gives no sign of having heard.

Really. I don't.

I pull away.

Okay, he whispers. Don't worry. I won't.

And he doesn't. My hero.

We retire to our separate sleeping-bags. Eventually I drop off. But before I do, I rehearse – once, twice, twenty times – every detail of every embrace. Derry's kisses will accompany me on buses and trains, in classrooms and in my chaste daughterly bed, for many weeks.

The real thing, however, is not repeated. The next evening we reach London, to spend the night at our respective homes. And in the morning, when I arrive at the rallying-point in Turnham Green, I can't locate him, though I know he must be around somewhere. In fact I can't see anyone I know. So I spend most of the day with a group of Young Socialists from Manchester, who are quite nice but not particularly interesting. And when we reach Hyde Park I slip off home without waiting for the speeches. Even though Uncle Zigi is billed to be one of the speakers. It's cold, and I'm tired, and I can hear him any time.

Next time I went to the Partisan, Derry was not there. He went on not being there. Maybe he never came very regularly. Maybe he'd given up politics. Maybe he'd moved back to Scotland. Maybe he just didn't want to risk running into me again.

V

My early sexual education continued to be associated with Ban the Bomb demonstrations, which meant that after Aldermaston, it went into abeyance for some months. First we had to concentrate on our O-levels, which took place that summer term. And then came the summer holidays, which were spent between the boring bosom of our families and awkward French and German exchanges. My exchange partner was a coquettish and fashion-conscious Parisienne, a member of the haute bourgeoisie, who was much concerned with her social activities at the Racing Club. I, however, had no opportunity to observe these, let alone join in them, as her family spent the summer near Chamonix with a flock of cousins who mostly ignored me. Her ambition was to have three children, a cook, and a car of her own, like her mother; I am sure she has fulfilled it. I felt like a lumpish oaf beside her, and this was how she saw things, too: I later found a letter she had left in our house, written to her by a Parisienne friend whom I met briefly. She's not *that* plain, it read. Her breasts are grotesque, of course. But she has quite a nice nose.

Real life resumes on 17 September, which is the date of a big demonstration in Trafalgar Square, to be followed by a mass sit-down. Permission for the Trafalgar Square meeting has been refused. It is the first time this has ever happened: Trafalgar Square is one of London's traditional venues for such occasions. The Committee of 100, which is organising the demo, has nevertheless gone ahead with its plans. So its leading members have been clapped in jail until after the event. There are many eager volunteers to take their place. We are among them.

Do be careful, darling, says my mother, handing me the usual sandwiches. (How she spoiled me! – Make your own, I would have said to Susanna or Rose. Have said, indeed. – Or don't, suit yourself. Starve. Feel free.) At first I am inclined to refuse them, but common sense prevails over dignity. By the time six o'clock comes I shall be hungry – what's the point of denying it?

Don't worry, Mum. What can happen to me?

Anything, say her eyes. I refuse to meet them. – Don't get arrested, she says. We don't want to have to bail you out of prison. She says this as lightly as she can, but for her it is no joke. I, on the other hand, quite fancy getting arrested. She knows this. My father has washed his hands of the whole affair. He is at a football match.

If I am, Zigi'll be there to look after me. They're sure to arrest him too.

My mother shakes her head. Generations of Ukrainian pogroms have left her with an almost genetic disinclination to tangle with the police. People like us should be grateful to live in peace. We shouldn't tempt fate. Fate-tempting, however, is the nature of sixteen-year-olds.

By four o'clock I am at Golders Green. Bella is waiting as usual. She looks pale and tired. Perhaps she is nervous. I am quite nervous myself. If so, she isn't admitting it, any more than I am. Half an hour later we arrive at Trafalgar Square. The rain has stopped. All the streets are full of people, and the square itself is packed. There is only room for a single line of traffic in front of the National Gallery, and sometimes even this is blocked, despite the vigorous efforts of the police. Because of the ban the demonstration has acquired its own momentum, something quite separate from its original object.

At five o'clock there is a cheer as the members of the Committee walk down the steps of the National Gallery, where they had arranged to gather earlier. Zigi is not among them. He draws the line at law-breaking. Such behaviour does not befit the respectable Englishman of his Budapest imagination. During the hours that follow, I occasionally glimpse his tall, unmistakable figure walking around and conversing with recumbent friends, but he does not join them on the ground. I wave, but he can't see me – mine is just one more waving hand among so many. There's no chance of getting up to him in the mêlée. More and more people pack into the square. The crowd is like a sea. Bella and I are tossed back and forth. It is partly exciting, but partly terrifying. More police arrive. Near St Martin's some people begin to sit down. Bella and I are standing on the steps, which are private property and so no business of the police, and from there we can get a good view of what is going on. We are eating my sandwiches. When they are finished I say: Shall we go and sit down? Bella agrees. We go. The police are arresting sitters all around us and carrying them off to the coaches waiting ready in the Strand. We sit on nervously. – Come on, says a policeman, what's a nice girl like you doing in a place like this? Get up and move on, there's a good girl, or we'll have to arrest you. I do nothing, of course.

Three policemen pick me up by the arms and legs. I go limp, as per our instructions. They cart me towards the Strand. I am terrified that my glasses will fall off, but they don't. I am tossed, none too gently, into a bus, but suffer only a few bruises. Bella has not been so lucky. Only one friendly British bobby arrested her, and he dragged her by the legs. By the time she gets to the bus she is very shaken, bedraggled and crying. I put my arm around her and try to comfort her. After a while her crying is interspersed with nervous giggles.

Well, she says, maybe that'll do it for me. Maybe that's just what I needed.

What on earth are you talking about?

Oh, Miriam, she says, I think I'm pregnant. And she starts to cry again.

Eventually the bus fills up. One man is thrown in so roughly that he hits his head against a step and is stunned for some minutes. Bella has mostly stopped crying, though she still gives an occasional sob. We are driven to Cannon Row police station, where we are kept waiting for a very long time. We sit and sit, feeling nervous and angry, as slowly, very slowly, we are processed. We are not allowed to telephone. Surely this is against the law? I think of my parents sitting at home. My mother will be anxious, my father angry. But if we can push the government into banning the bomb, their sacrifice will not have been in vain. Politicians, of course, scoff at the mere idea that we might affect policy. But hindsight and the release of papers justify us. If the Cuban crisis had happened a year earlier, so that it coincided with the high point of public protest, then our momentum would probably have been irresistible.

We sit and sit. I can think of nothing but Bella's plight. She looks wan, dishevelled, completely miserable. I should like to do something for her, but what? I should like to talk to her – to ask her all about it – but a crowded police station hardly seems the place for intimate enquiries.

Finally it is our turn. Our fingerprints and details are taken. I think of giving a false name, but can't bring one to mind in time. Will we be kept in overnight? What will my parents say?

But it turns out this is not to happen. The cells are full to bursting. There's no more room, nowhere to put us. We are let go, with a caution and the assurance that next time we shall not be so lucky.

Outside it is dark. It is nearly midnight. We make our way to the tube. Free at last to talk of personal matters, I blast in with the question that has been echoing round my head all evening: Whose is it? As soon as this is out I feel ashamed of such low curiosity in the face of crisis.

Bella replies without hesitation or apparent offence taken: Sam Corbett.

Sam Corbett! I digest this. Sam Corbett is a glamorous figure, one of CND's showbiz stars. He is to be seen singing topical songs weekly on television. I look at Bella with a new awe. I try and imagine them together. Sam Corbett is short and swarthy, with thick stubble. The few times I've been anywhere near him he has smelt strongly of beer. Like so many, he is more glamorous on the screen than in the flesh.

Are you in love with him?

I don't know. I thought I was for a time.

What are you going to do? Marry him?

He's married already.

I think about our future lives. We have just entered the sixth form. The next few years are safely mapped out. A-levels, university. Five or six years' grace before we have to face up to real life. And now Bella – I try and picture what it would be like. Having a baby. A baby, for God's sake. Who wants to spend their life looking after a *baby*? And if one has to do it, would one rather do it with or without Sam Corbett? Be an unmarried mother or irretrievably stuck with – well, maybe Bella doesn't see him the same way I do. She can't, or she wouldn't be where she is, would she?

Have you told your mum?

I haven't yet. I was hoping . . .

How long – ?

A couple of months.

What are you going to do? Have it?

Oh, Miriam, I don't know. How can I? But how could I bear to – get rid of it?

I consider this. I am slightly surprised by Bella's indecision. If it was me, there would be no hesitation. Straight to the abortionist's. The only barrier would be the money.

Would he pay?

I haven't told him.

You'd better tell someone. Tell your mum. I bet she'll help. She's awfully nice about that kind of thing.

Bella would never talk about what happened over the next couple of weeks. But she didn't have a baby. Maybe her prayed-for period arrived, and she never was pregnant after all. Maybe the rough handling had the effect she'd hoped. Maybe she told her mother and an abortion was swiftly and discreetly arranged. What I do know is that, before long, she was proudly showing us all her new Dutch cap. Her mother had taken her to a clinic to have her fitted up.

I didn't know whether to envy her or not. I certainly couldn't imagine broaching such a subject with my mother. So for the moment I stuck to my virginity. Better safe than sorry.

That was the high point of my early protesting career. A year later, the Cuba crisis stopped us breathless in our tracks. The politicians had terrified even themselves, almost to death. A year after that, the Partial Test-Ban Treaty was signed. Atmospheric tests were outlawed.

Dr T. campaigned furiously against the Test Ban. He was just getting interested in anti-ballistic missiles, and how could they be tested underground? The notion that (as intelligence indicated) the United States had far more nuclear weapons than the Soviet Union, was anathema to him. He refused to believe it. The Senate, however, chose to put its trust in the CIA and voted against him. After that, people stopped worrying about Strontium 90 and turned their attention to other things, such as Vietnam, and the best way to blow their minds. Even though testing was not banned altogether, enough had been done to take the edge off the issue. CND declined. Just in time, Zigi resumed home life. His marriage revived, though on a new footing. – I was not going to drop all my friends, Fania said, just because he decided the world was safe for a few more years.

She told me this during one of the many intimate conversations we were to have over a cup of coffee or glass of wine in her kitchen over the next few years. For my life, too, was about to change; and one of the consequences of that change was my friendship with Fania, the one I am now endangering.

CHAPTER 9   RELATIONS

I

OCTOBER 1964. BELLA and I have just arrived at Cambridge. Genuine students at last! And still together, sort of, though not at the same college. Bella is at New Hall, reading economics: I'm doing English at Girton. At this point, however, so soon after our arrival, we still seek each other out amid the sea of new faces.

I am looking at a photo taken that October. It is Rag Day. We are draped decoratively around a tree, clutching musical instruments – I have a mandolin, Bella, a guitar. Once again, we are dressed in black – black sweaters, black tights. Perhaps that was the requirement for whatever rag stunt it was we were participating in. Bella has changed very little in the past few years. She was tall and slim at fifteen, she is tall and slim now. Her long face with its regular features is as impenetrable as ever. Her fair hair is done in a French pleat at the back of her head. She is graceful and elegant. I shall never achieve these qualities, but I have improved somewhat since the nadir of my early teens. I have slimmed down a little, and my glasses have been replaced by contact lenses, whose acquisition has enabled me to see my naked face, unblurred, for the first time since I was a child. I look cheerfully impudent. I was ill during the summer holidays, ran a high fever and lost seven pounds, so my shape is uncharacteristically svelte. I do not expect this bonus to last.

We are with a couple of boys. One has sandy hair, large features, and arms too long for his thick-set body. It is, yes, my old friend Derry McCulloch. I ran into him at a meeting of the Labour Club, and we greeted each other with joy. Auld acquaintance (and ours, though not prolonged, was certainly intimate) has a good deal to recommend it when one is trying to gain a foothold on the greasy social pole here. He, too, is reading English. He is at King's. He has fallen in love with Bella, whom he met when he came to tea in my room at Girton two weeks ago. I am not pleased about this, although I can't imagine ever wanting, ever having wanted, to go to bed with him. (He's not the only person I haven't been to bed with, either. I'm still a virgin, at any rate in the strictly technical sense. We are talking about the olden days here, before the Pill – in fact, it has recently appeared, but can only be got on prescription, and most doctors still look askance if you request it and are blatantly unmarried. Bella, safe with her Dutch cap, remains the exception, not the rule.) I probably wouldn't have minded so much if it had been anybody other than Bella. She seems always to be standing in my light. Derry was in some sense mine, and now she has taken him over. I sometimes feel as if I shall never escape her.

Beside Derry stands a tall, blond youth with a pleasant, open face. He looks optimistic, as though life's worries will always bounce off him. To a certain extent this is and will remain true: an attractive and unusual quality when not (as so often) allied to stupidity. Tony Oliver is an anthropologist, also at King's. He went to public school. I haven't encountered any public school boys before. All the boys I knew in London went to day schools. Tony's been at boarding school since he was eight. I try to imagine what this must feel like. Is it what prompted him to study anthropology? Is there any more outlandish tribal habit than the way in which British parents of a certain social and financial standing decline to participate in the upbringing of their children? Tony declares he is in love with me, but I just laugh at him. How can anyone be in love with me? Especially this blond *goy*. It's absurd. Laughter is the only possible reaction.

And yet – I'm drawn to him, and I'm not altogether happy about it. Is this why I laugh, to conceal from myself, as well as from Tony, certain worrying aspects of this attraction? There's something nagging there at the back of my mind. I could probably identify it if I tried – but I don't want to try. I push it away, and concentrate on the here and now.

I can feel it again, that state of mind, as I look at the photograph. But now everything is clearer. Time has passed, and what was then unthinkable can no longer be ignored.

If I like him so much, my blond *goy*, why not just let myself go with the flow, as I did (well, almost) that time with Derry in the school hall at Slough? What's the point of all this soul-searching? Why not just do it and see what happens next?

One reason is that going with the flow has never been my forte. Quite the contrary. I am not by nature a Sixties person, happy to surrender myself to substances and circumstances. My preference is to stay in control at all times: ergo, *not* to let go. But that could be overcome – were it not for that something else lurking there in the background.

Which is? Which is – to do with why I like tall blond men.

Well, doesn't everyone?

Not if you come from my background, baby. A nice Jewish girl does not meet tall blond men. The men she meets are dark. Short and dark, tall and dark, fat, thin, witty, taciturn – but dark. Aren't we all supposed to marry replicas of our fathers? And what n.J.g., I ask you, has a tall, blond father? None, of my acquaintance. For us, tall blond men carry highly negative connotations. They are members of the master-race, or Poles and Ukrainians bent on pogroms. They are not good news. They are alien, they are Other. Even today, this assumption regarding the colouring of my immediate family remains so deeply ingrained that for many years I was slightly surprised to find myself owning a marmalade *cat*.

But let us look a little further. Isn't there a tall blond man right in the centre of the family picture? Not quite my father, but indubitably my hero. Yes –

Tony and Zigi never really got on. They had no time for each other, despite the fact that, on all fundamental issues, they were in agreement. Zigi thought Tony a plodder. He lacked glamour, he lacked brilliance, he lacked speed; he was too solid, not intuitive, needing to build up his arguments from the bottom rather than leaping instinctively to the unexpected but correct conclusion (which was Zigi's speciality). Tony, for his part, thought Zigi a show-off (a concept Zigi despised), untrustworthy, intolerant, unkind. Each of them was correct, though of course only partly.

I remember standing with Tony in Hyde Park, during one of those enormous demonstrations the Peace Movement organised during the early 1980s. Everyone was listening to Zigi, who was orating from the podium. He was still a wonderful speaker in spite of his accent, carrying the weight of his years and his learning, fiery and handsome still as he approached his mid-seventies. I was rapt. All around us, eyes were being furtively dabbed. Tony said, as he could never resist doing on such occasions: Amazing how he gets his effects, isn't it! What an old fraud! What a performance!

I rose to the bait, as I always did: Why must you always be so unpleasant about him? In what way is Zigi a fraud? Name me one way he's a fraud.

I wouldn't even bother to try, said Tony. It's not something you care to see.

Several hundred thousand other people don't care to see it either, or so it seems.

No, that's right, Tony agreed. They don't. But then, they don't know him personally. Why don't we drop the subject?

We dropped it. It was a subject we were forever dropping. Similarly, when Zigi made one of his patronising remarks about Tony, I would tell him to shut up. If that was what he thought I didn't want to know. But my discomfort (not to speak of Fania's and the girls') never deterred either of them for a moment. They were too intent on their game.

This old antagonism is, I'm sure, one of the reasons Tony so hates my undertaking Zigi's biography, though he won't say so. (Exactly the kind of thing Zigi couldn't stand. In such a circumstance, *he* would have said so, without the slightest hesitation.) The old man's finally out of the way, dead at last, and what happens? Risen from the grave, still absorbing my attention. Still the old rivalry. Rivalry? Yes: for it is clear, looking back, that it was I who was at the centre of their mutual dislike, piggy in the middle. Not that any of us (except possibly Zigi, always so detached) would allow ourselves to realise quite what was going on. But now I can see it. Distance finally allows me the grandstand view.

At the time this photo was taken, however, Tony and Zigi had not yet met. The tensions, the difficulties, were still in the future. Despite minor annoyances such as Bella, this was a completely happy time, bliss without reservation. Childhood passed in a state of unconsciousness. Adolescence was filled with striving and uncertainty. And all too soon uncertainty will regain its sway. In a few months my parents will be dead and I shall be entangled in black tentacles of limbo. But for this brief interval – perfection. I am surrounded by friends, reassuring old friends, exciting new friends, friends yet to be made. I am treated as an adult, I am responsible for myself – but not entirely: in the background, there is always the reassurance that, in the midst of this independence, I am still someone's daughter.

How important this is when it comes to keeping the rest anchored down, I shall only realise when it is no longer true.

II

Fania insisted on meeting me off the train when I got back from my holiday in Greece. At first she wanted me to phone her once a week, something my parents would never have done. – But darling, I am very new to being a parent, you'll have to make allowances for me. – Aunty Fan, I said, you've got there without having to go through the childhood bit. What you have here is an adult. – Sort of, she said. We were both half in tears, as usual.

I explained that phoning from God knows where was likely to be no easy feat, and finally she agreed. – So phone when you get back to England, she said. When you get off the boat. I'll meet the train at Victoria.

The tube bumps its slow way towards West Hampstead. – Really, I say, you didn't need to come. – But I wanted to, she says. You know how I hate sitting at home waiting for things to happen. For people to arrive. I can't concentrate on anything. I'd rather spend the time this way. She looks sternly ahead, bolt upright in her scarlet lipstick and emerald-green shirtwaisted dress, disclaiming any intrusive sentiment. Actually, I'm grateful to have her there. Greece was a hiatus. Now life begins anew, and I have no idea what it will be like.

We've got a lot to do, she says briskly. You must decide what you want to do about all the stuff in your house. I thought you might like to put some of it in the flat, to make you feel more at home. Then the rest can go into storage, or you can sell it. And then we must get the house on the market. A house is a responsibility, you don't want to be saddled with that kind of thing. Whereas money's always useful. Your Uncle Harry will help with all that.

I don't need a whole flat. I'll hardly ever be there, you know.

It's not so enormous. A room and a bath. And that way you can come and go when you are around without getting in my way.

So here I am in my own little flat, with my own old bed and my books and my favourite armchair. As Fania said, it's very small. A big bedsitter, tiny bathroom, tinier kitchenette, crammed in under the eaves. Every young woman's dream: a place of my very own. But I don't feel comfortable in it. Shall I ever? Fania doesn't keep a particularly comfortable house, and this is still more hers than mine. Whatever their other responsibilities, most women maintain (albeit resentfully) a constantly running notice-board in some part of their sub-conscious. It is plastered with little notes: Toilet-rolls finished, get more butter, ant-powder, window-cleaner needs paying, what shall we eat tonight? But Fania, early on, made a conscious decision to excise this facility. These things do not interest her, and this lack of interest is not merely intellectual, it is a point of principle. So that where my mother's house was always warm, clean and full of delicious things to eat, domestic life at Fania's is a hit-or-miss affair. Her mind is on other matters. I admire this principle. But it does not make for comfort, and I am still used to being looked after. I have not yet acquired the habit of fending for myself.

Our old house, the last time I saw it, was still filled with my mother. Tins full of home-made biscuits, cupboards full of cans, packets and clean linen. (Someone, a neighbour or an aunt, had cleared out the fridge, the vegetables, the fruit: at least I didn't have to face actual mould.) When we went there to decide what I wanted to keep and what was to be sold or put in store, the sense of normality – of ordinary life, my mother out in her garden, my father merely delayed at the factory – was so strong that it nearly destroyed me. I couldn't bear to leave, but neither could I bear to stay. Fania led me gently away and, that night, gave me the first sleeping-pill of my life. The next day, I came out in boils.

I sit in the silence while London hurries on around me. Out of one window I have a panoramic view of back gardens, some filled with old mattresses, others with flowers; out of another, the dingy street. At home, the silence didn't worry me and the views were so familiar that I no longer saw them as separate from myself. But here, each creak may or may not carry some meaning. What's Fania doing now? Painting? If I go down she'll feel she has to stop and entertain me. She'll feel I'm unhappy, that something is wrong. Which of course I am, and it is. But not on account of her. Sometimes she comes up here to see me, but not too often. She doesn't want to intrude. And what do we have to say to each other, now that we're so much together? We haven't yet evolved a life for ourselves.

The front door slams and I see her walking energetically down the street. This somehow frees me to go downstairs. I look into the studio. Fania does abstracts in oils, rather flat juxtapositions of colour. At their best they sing. What's on the easel at the moment, however, hits a decidedly sombre note. My mother was always her favourite member of the family, and Fania is of a generation most of whose friends are drawn from within the family circle.

I hadn't realised how little she and Zigi see of each other, even when Zigi is not spending most of his time saving the world. Previously, I'd tended to meet them on social occasions requiring the attendance of both partners. These days, Zigi is immersed in a heady mix of science and party politics. The notion that he has become a member of the British establishment delights him. Power! He revels in its scent. He is an addict, and power is his drug.

But Fania has little in common with his scientific colleagues. And she can't stand his political friends. – Darling, why would anyone become a politician? They're parasites. They don't *do* anything. Nothing but a lot of hot air. More she won't specify. This is an area of silence. Like Joan Brockenhurst, she prefers to avert her eyes. Furthermore, as a communist, she finds the pale pink compromises of a Labour government even more distasteful than the out-and-out horrors of the Tories. So she takes refuge in the arts. She frequents a group of painters who meet at the Arts Centre in Arkwright Road. They held an exhibition last year, and Fania, to her enormous satisfaction, sold two canvases. The only interest she and Zigi share these days, as far as I can make out, is music. They're avid concertgoers, and of course there is Zigi's piano. Even so, they seem happy enough. They respect each other, they're used to each other. As my mother said, Who can fathom other people's marriages?

And who, at the age of twenty, is likely to try? What words can convey the complete solipsism of that age, when other people are registered only as and when they impinge on oneself?

Zigi, to the twenty-year-old Miriam, is a glamorous and romantic figure, the more so for being rarely visible. He knows everyone, he affects real events. His opinions become policy. Power is seductive, even – especially? – to the unworldly. Now, when I meet a powerful man, I look at him and wonder what distasteful acts raised him to his present eminence. Then, I was not so cynical.

I like to sit in his room, as I am doing now, because it is redolent of him – literally. He is fond of cigars. Fania doesn't approve of this. – The smell of cigar butts, she says. Feugh! Can you think of anything more disgusting? And so bad for his chest! He waves this away. – I shall take my chance with mortality. I shall die of cigars, maybe. A good death. Don't you think so, Miriam? The house is filled with the mingled smells of cigar smoke and oil paint. I sniff them, and try to feel part of them.

But I don't sit long. I've got to get dressed and go and meet Zigi at Harrods. It is August: my birthday. This evening we are going to Glyndebourne as a birthday treat. They're performing *l'Incoronazione di Poppea*, that exquisite celebration of lust. The house was full, but Zigi got tickets. He can always get tickets for anything. For me, Zigi is associated with treats. It is the unfair privilege of an acquaintance undimmed by the quotidian.

This morning, he and I are buying the picnic. He, unlike Fania, is not indifferent to the niceties of the palate. We wander around Harrods food hall. – A ridiculous idea, he says. Only the British, with their awful weather, would insist on having a picnic and not a good restaurant as part of a great cultural institution. But still, we shall do our best and pray that it doesn't rain.

We do our best. Smoked salmon, cold duck, potato salad, raspberries, meringues, cream. A bottle of champagne which will travel in a plastic bag filled with ice. Having acquired all this we sit down for a light, late lunch.

We sit side by side in one of those stylish, uncomfortable little cafés which are scattered around various corners of Harrods. The walls are mirrored, to make the cramped space seem larger. Every time we lift our heads, we are forced to study ourselves from various angles. A dark, eager girl in a bright pink dress, hair cut in a bob to accentuate high cheekbones; a tall, elegant, middle-aged man, fair hair turning silvery grey, dressed in a blue denim summer suit that makes him look slightly foreign, raffish, exotic. Each of us is highly aware of the other's presence. Being with Zigi, having lunch with Zigi, is not like having lunch with one's uncle. I have known him all my life. But I do not feel relaxed when I am with him. When I was a child he was just another relative. When I was growing up he was a hero, a source of status and prestige. And now?

Now, I feel as nervous as if I were on my first date with a new boyfriend. Stomach tightly clenched, so that I can hardly eat. Conscious of every gesture, every word, every sartorial detail and defect (dress slightly too tight round the hips, a grass stain on one shoe). Conscious of his physical presence, the lift of an eyebrow, his long, elegant hands. Zigi has just bought me a birthday present: a bottle of perfume, Hermès' *Calèche*. – This will suit you, I think. How does he know? Don't let's ask. Accept it and be happy. I have dabbed some behind my ears. Is it too much? The unfamiliar smell drowns out my carrot soup. Not that that matters. At this moment, the food is entirely by the way. The only important thing is that I should measure up to – whatever it is Zigi wants me to measure up to. Not that I ever shall. I shall never be glamorous or sophisticated, never achieve that languid, unsurprised Marlene Dietrich worldweariness which would be my ideal. On the contrary, I am giggly, loud-voiced, easily astonished, easily pleased. No amount of *Calèche* can undo that.

I take a spoonful of soup. In the mirror, I can see Zigi watching me. He looks – concentrated. A drop of soup splashes on to my dress. I blush scarlet and dab at it with the napkin. Why can't I *control* these things? Lucky the colour's not too far off. Perhaps it won't show when it dries.

So, says Zigi. I hardly see you.

This is not true. He sees me every day, almost. What he means is: I've never noticed you before. For the first time, I have become worthy of his undivided attention. I bask in its warmth. I accept it as a compliment to my present self; I choose not to notice its patronising implications. – Tell me about Cambridge, he says. What are you studying?

English.

English! Why?

Why? If I am to be truthful, because I couldn't think what else to study. – An excuse to spend three years reading, I say.

Didn't you think of doing science?

Science? I stare at him.

What use is English in the modern world? he demands, in his thick, un-English accent. Vo-rrrld. – Don't you want to influence affairs? You've got to understand how things work. Where would I have been if I'd studied German literature instead of physics?

Oh, yes, and what did you do? You invented the atom bomb. That influenced affairs, all right.

He looks cross, then resigned. He shrugs. – You're right of course. But we didn't abdicate responsibility. The opposite, rather. It wasn't just a question of changing the world once. We go on trying to change it. Look at my old friend Edward Teller. He also is saving the world, in his own way. Politicians think they shape events. But the real force is science. We have to try and steer them in the right direction. How many scientists, out of all the thousands of scientists, really influence events? Twenty, perhaps even fewer. I am one. Teller is another. He's been pushed underground for now, like his tests. He isn't appropriate to the moment. But he will surface again when the time is right. And then we must be ready to fight him. Zigi looks invigorated by this prospect.

So what do you think I should be doing? (Enough of this philosophising. Let's bring the conversation back to the only really interesting subject.)

Molecular biology, he replies without hesitation. That is where the next revolution will come from.

How can I do molecular biology? I don't know the first thing about it.

If you really wanted to, you could of course. If you had been *my* daughter. If you had been my son, absolutely. But being who you are, it doesn't really interest you. You are a beautiful young girl, and your mind is on other things. I don't know whether that's how it should be, but that's how it is.

He is wearing that *concentrated* look again, and this time it annoys me. What does he think I am? Someone looking for an easy way to spend three years before retreating into marriage and motherhood?

You assume I don't have any ambition at all.

What is your ambition?

Bella and I have discussed this. We have reached the inevitable conclusion. Politics is where we shall make our

mark. There aren't many women MPs, but there are some. –
The only drawback is, says Bella, you have to go to an awful
lot of boring committees and be polite to all the ghastly people
on them. My father's always grumbling about it. Nevertheless, we feel prepared to make this sacrifice.

I thought politics, maybe.

Oh, politics, he says. For politics, I agree, an English degree
would be perfectly sufficient.

How can you say that? You're involved in politics, aren't
you?

Not as a politician, says Zigi. I told you, politicians are
puppets. All they know about is politics. I put words into their
mouths. That is real power. Shall we have some coffee?

III

This was the period of Harold Wilson's first administration,
elected to run on the white heat of technology, and Zigi was
one of its white-hot technocrats. In spite of his scornful words
about politicians, he was becoming more and more immersed
in that world, and less and less a practising scientist. His best
work, the antibody research that won him his FRS, had
mostly been done in the late Fifties. Now he was becoming
more of a figurehead at the lab, setting up projects and letting
younger colleagues run them. Meanwhile he was Science
Adviser to various ministries, and a frequent visitor, along
with his schoolmates, the economists Nicky Kaldor and
Thomas Balogh, to Downing Street. Once again, the Minta
boys were massing.

It was in this guise – as a scientific-political *éminence grise* –
that he came to Cambridge to address the Union. I forget what
the motion was they were debating; something about science
improving life. It was the spring of my third year – early May.
The weather had not yet turned hot – that generally happened
a couple of weeks later, during exams. I, like everyone else I
knew, was revising for my Finals while, at the same time,

undergoing job interviews, which took on a wonderfully unreal quality. At the end of term I was booked to go to the King's May Ball with the boyfriend of the moment. This was not Tony Oliver. He was still around, but in the background. A staunch friend – that thankless role. I had by now accepted that he really was in love with me, but I still felt ambivalent about him. I cried on his shoulder when love affairs crashed, and then plunged once more into the maelstrom. He made half-hearted attempts to get involved with other girls, but nothing seemed to last. He was in the middle of one of these affairs at the moment. He, too, would be at the King's May Ball. So would Derry, with Bella. Derry still lusted after Bella, and sometimes she indulged him. She and I only met, these days, when we happened to run into each other in King's.

Zigi is to speak in the evening. He has sent a note asking if I will have lunch with him: he would enjoy a day in Cambridge.

I wake up with that knot of excitement in my stomach. I told my friends I was having lunch with my uncle. Lunch with uncle! What could be more anodyne? Or more misleading? I don't feel this way about any of the young men I've met at Cambridge. Compared with Zigi, they all seem so – well, young: unformed. He's so brilliant, so elegant, so *distinguished*. It seems inconceivable that any of them will ever turn into anything that can compete. (And they will not.)

Most of the morning is spent deciding what to wear. It's got to look terrific but casual, as though I just flung on the first item that came to hand. I try on every garment in my wardrobe, and return to the one I first thought of. I put on some makeup, take it all off, put it all on again. I look at my watch. God! I should have left ten minutes ago!

There he is, sunk in an armchair in the Garden House foyer, smoking and looking resigned. Marlene Dietrich would saunter up casually. I wave, call, run towards him. When will I ever learn? He grinds out the cigarette, kisses my cheek. Holds me away from him and looks at me smiling. Keeps his hand on my arm.

Do you want to eat here, or shall we drive into the country

somewhere? He indicates his car, a large, shiny Humber, standing in the hotel carpark. He has come a long way since those early bicycling days. I love riding in the Humber. It makes me feel sinful and extravagant, like a kept woman. Fania is always nagging him to get something smaller, less showy, more economical – a Mini, for example – but he won't. Zigi in a Mini – a ludicrous, unthinkable combination. Looking at the Humber, he can be sure that he has really arrived, that he is somebody. Perhaps, too, he likes to watch its effect on girls like me.

Here, why not? I oughtn't to take too long, I say dutifully. I've got an awful lot of work to do.

You'll be better if you don't think about it for a while.

He orders a sumptuous lunch, the best the Garden House can do: probably nothing very wonderful to him, but my only point of comparison is college food. The wine is delicious. Any remaining thoughts of revision slip away. After we have drunk our coffee he says: What shall we do now? Entertain me!

I feel a sense of relief. I, too, don't want our lunch to end just yet. But what can I suggest? My mind goes blank. – A walk by the river?

I am not interested in rivers, declares Zigi, who, as usual, knows exactly what he wants. Show me Girton College. Now *that* will be a new experience.

Well, if you really want to . . .

We drive in state, in that shiny Humber, through the archway under the lopsided tower, into the gloomy courtyard full of drainpipes. On the lawns, just as on the day I heard of my parents' death – two years ago now – people are playing tennis.

What do you want to see?

I want to see where you live, of course. It is the first time I have penetrated into a convent.

It's hardly that!

I have to admit, however, that the look and feel of the place are pretty conventual. Long, brown linoleum corridors, doors opening into little cells, each with its studious inhabitant. All

Girtonians, I have always thought, should be issued with rollerskates. My room is up on the second floor, under the eaves. The ones on the ground floor are cosier, but less private, as people are liable to use your window to climb in after a late party.

I open the door. Mine is a very large room: plenty of space for a grand piano or a substantial sculpture. I have neither, so it feels somewhat cavernous. There is a chaise-longue under the window, a narrow bed against one wall. An armchair, a desk, a rug, a bookcase, a wardrobe, a cupboard for drinks. Zigi shuts the door behind us. I go over to the window, beneath which tennis-players frisk.

All through lunch we have been staring at each other in a sort of trance. Zigi has been telling me inside stories of political life, but I haven't really heard what he was saying. It's like that time at Harrods. My ascent into his field of vision has altered our relationship. After all these years as an uncle, he has suddenly become an insistently physical presence. Instead of listening to his words I find myself staring at his mouth, hypnotised by those moving lips. It's a wide mouth, sensual, expressive, with an ironical curl at the corners. I like mouths. I like Zigi's mouth.

I am kneeling on the chaise-longue, looking out of the window. He comes and stands beside me. – I suppose you have a great many lovers, he says.

What does one say, if one wants to be a woman of the world?

A few.

We remain there, silent, in frozen frame. Outside, the film continues as before: the tennis-balls thud crisply back and forth on the courts beneath the window, there is a constant traffic of bicycles on the drive leading to the front gate. Zigi says: I am obsessed with you, Miriam. I have to tell you this. Since you left the house to come back to Cambridge I have thought only of how I might arrange to see you.

I say nothing. I can think of nothing to say.

You must help me.

How can I do that?

He puts his arm around me, pulls me off the chaise-longue, pulls me towards him. He stares at me for a while, then kisses me very gently. My head is whirling, possibly because of unaccustomed amounts of wine with lunch. What should I do? Well, it's clear what I *should* do. I should detach myself firmly and unequivocally and send him about his business. Tell him he must never do such a thing again. I should be horrified. But I am not, as he knew I would not be. I am curious, and excited, and frightened. And not a little flattered. And, now that the moment has arrived, not at all surprised. What else did I think would happen, once we got up here? What else could possibly happen? I kiss him back, which is what I have been longing to do for the past two hours. What were they but a postponement of this moment? Why did we waste all that time eating? And what follows is inevitable. Zigi is no tentative young man, to be fooled around with, so far and no further. No.

How old is he? Fifty-eight, fifty-nine? How is it possible that I find him so attractive? – An old man like me, he murmurs. And you are so beautiful. But there it is. He is still very handsome – the unfair advantage of the ageing man over the ageing woman. And, of course, he knows what he is doing. He should – he has been doing it for nearly twice as long as I have been alive. His controlled passion is far more exciting than the hungry, callow kisses I am used to. And power. Power is aphrodisiac. Now, I can see that this was probably the point of all those lunchtime stories. Now, I can see that I was probably looking for a father-figure, or some such psychological truism. Then, I was not so detached. When Zigi kissed me, I knew that, more than anything, I wanted this to go on. I wanted it never to stop. Zigi could do anything he liked with me. I knew it, and so did he.

He guides me towards the bed, undresses me, undresses himself. His body has none of the flabbiness of middle age. This tautness is achieved, as I know, by regular exercise: he swims a mile every morning. Fania is always teasing him about it. – Zigi is keeping himself beautiful. I don't ask who for. – I think while I swim, he protests. Some of my best ideas have come while I was swimming. – I know better, she says. And now, so do I.

And so we do what all this time he has been planning we shall do, what this day was designed to lead up to. What am I to say? No, don't, like that time with Derry, like all those other times since? What, for God's sake, is the point of being a virgin? The truth is that, disoriented as I have been for the past two years, I haven't dared to do it for fear that once I started, I should never stop. In my search for intimacy – any intimacy – I might have chosen that constantly dissatisfied promiscuity which I see in so many of my friends. If with one, why not with everybody else? But I didn't. I have been brutally shown that the outside world is beyond my control, so I feel I must at least control my own life. In this way, as in many others, I have held myself back for fear of falling headlong. I have built barriers around myself because I don't know where I'm starting from, so I don't know where I'll finish. And gently, slowly, irresistibly, Zigi is dissolving them. Is that such a bad thing?

Unexpectedly, I find myself almost detached. Well, I think. So this is it. I reflect on how improbable it seems that such an activity should be associated with procreation. No wonder some savage tribes have never twigged the connection. And this isn't just the simple act. This is adultery. This is incest, almost. Will everyone know? I can't imagine that they won't. It will be visible to all, written on my forehead in letters of fire, like in that story by Hans Andersen. I shall cycle through town and everyone will point at me.

Are you sure? he says at one point. And I am. I can't remember ever wanting anything so much. So I nod. Yes, yes.

Is it safe?

Safe? What does he mean by that? Is the door locked, is someone going to walk in and catch us? It is; they're not. Of course it's safe. I can't wait another second. – Yes, yes, I murmur. It's safe. Afterwards, I realised he probably meant something else. If I had other lovers, then it stood to reason we must use something. In that sense, of course, it was not safe. Still, just the once. My very first time. It'll probably be OK. I'd have to be really unlucky.

The fact that I have *not* had other lovers is quickly apparent. Zigi props himself on one elbow and looks severe.
– Tell me the truth. Was that the first time?

I nod. He catches his breath, raises one eyebrow, drops on to his back and clasps his hands behind his head. Whatever his imaginings may have been, it is certain defloration was not one of them. Virgins hold few attractions for Zigi. They have little finesse and are prone to undue emotion. Moreover, he undoubtedly guesses that, despite what I led him to understand, I was unprotected. Still, he says nothing. What, now, would be the point? What's done is done. We must hope for the best.

A little later he says: Miriam, my darling Miriam, you must forgive me. Today I have acted very badly.

What are you talking about?

You know perfectly well what I'm talking about. Such a thing, however delightful, must never be repeated. I shall always be your friend, never forget that. More than a friend. But – not a lover. You must have other lovers, he says firmly, his curiosity satisfied, his obsession slaked.

Then he looks at his watch. Luckily, he has a pressing engagement. Small-talk is hardly in order after what we've just been doing, and neither of us really feels like doing it again. Or, rather, Zigi doesn't (presumably his staying-power isn't what it was; presumably, too, he doesn't like to be reminded of this fact). And I – will go along with him. Don't I always? In any case, it is later than we thought and he must get dressed in order to dine with the President of the Union.

And I must get down to some of the revision from which he has so successfully distracted me. I don't succeed, however. All I can think about is Zigi, and what has just happened.

After he has gone, I lie there, trying to collect myself. What am I to think? What am I to do now? Find other lovers, he said. But it's not so easy. There's only one person I want to go to bed with just now, and that's Zigi. He, however, could not have been more definite. It's not going to happen.

194

Never again. We have had our moment of bliss, and very delightful it was. Each of us needed what the other had to offer. That was it. No more. More would be folly beyond contemplation.

Oh, well. At least I shan't have to worry about my damned virginity any more. It's like getting married. Once you've done it, you can think about other, more important things.

Writing his biography, how (if at all) would I portray this episode? Could it be done objectively, without a pejorative moral stance? Only with difficulty. He was a practised womaniser. I was an inexperienced girl – even more in-experienced than he realised. I suspect that inexperience was new to him – he had probably never met it since Bettina first came to Copenhagen. It was probably that, combined with my proximity and independence, which so aroused him. All this and the salt of quasi-incest. How could he resist?

Does that make him a monster of depravity? Seen objec-tively, of course. But that makes me a victim, deprives me of all volition, which was not the case. I wanted it quite as much as he did. Never did fly enwrap itself more willingly in the spider's web. Who, indeed, was the spider, who the fly? And in one important sense he did me a favour, released me, freed me from myself – although, as was soon to become clear, in another way he materially deprived me of my freedom.

IV

So the month passes. I revise, and take my exams, and whirl away the night at my May Ball, the length of which, and the sight of each other over bacon and eggs in the early hours, effectively finishes that particular romance. I receive my upper second. And my period, about which I have been making urgent calculations, fails to materialise. Not that there is anything to worry about, surely? I only did it just that once. The one and only time. Bad luck of that kind happens to other people, not to me. It's the excitement, I tell myself, and set out on a holiday party to Italy before taking up a job which Zigi has found for me, working as researcher to a Minister. – You said you wanted to go into politics, he says. Perhaps you should have a look at it. Come and have lunch and see if you get on. And we get on fine, the Minister and I, so that is fixed.

As for Zigi, he is noticeably matter-of-fact in his attitude towards me these days. Not unfriendly – certainly not. Didn't he put himself out to fix up this job? And doesn't that prove that he thinks about me? On the other hand, he has definitely reverted to uncle mode, and brisk uncle mode, at that. Clearly (and understandably), he is terrified that our little encounter at Cambridge may have aroused certain expectations in me, which he is determined to smother at birth. In this he is successful. I feel positively guilty when I look at him and recall – all those things I mustn't recall. What chance have I, faced with such an adversary? The moral high ground is Zigi's natural habitat. Only a surreptitious squeeze of the hand when we say goodbye convinces me that the whole thing wasn't just a dream.

It transpires that Bella, too, will be around the House of Commons. We seem fated always to stay within sight of each other. She did some acting at Cambridge, but wasn't good enough to contemplate the professional stage. Her father has got her a job as secretary to a friend of his. So here we are, both of us, circling around the political fringes. Is this the start of those careers we always promised ourselves?

Fate, or nature, is determined that I shall not have such an easy life. In Italy, I miss another period. There can really be no more doubt. My breasts start to ache, I have terrible indigestion, I am unnaturally tired at the end of the day.

I am pregnant.

What am I to do? Who am I to confide in? Bella? When she thought she was, she told me. She'll have useful contacts. Of course, she'll assume I'm getting an abortion. So, of course, will Zigi. How horrified he'll be. He'll blame himself, and therefore me. I shall be a walking reminder of his guilt. Why did you let me? Why did I, indeed? Why? Such a little thing. Such a little moment. And now – the rest of my life. I really can't face telling Zigi. Though if I do, the money won't be a problem. And nor, I suspect, will finding the right person to do the abortion.

But the fact is – I don't want an abortion. I want this baby. Zigi's child. Perhaps he needn't know it's his. Perhaps I had a little orgy to celebrate my disposal of that unwanted virginity, and to round off my time at Cambridge. And perhaps I didn't. He'll know, all right.

Tony Oliver is here with me in Italy (there are six of us, we've borrowed a villa belonging to someone's parents). As usual, I've returned to him in adversity. Should I tell Tony? I'm not sure I can bear to, just yet. Or the others. I can't face the thought of a committee sitting to discuss my future. I feel like a holiday, not a wake. Not that these things can be kept quiet indefinitely. But it doesn't show yet. And one thing it does mean, I can sleep with anyone and not worry about the consequences. They've already happened. So I surprise Tony by giving him a birthday treat (my birthday, my twenty-second). My tall, blond lover! After all these importunate years. Who am I with, who am I really with, as we embrace each other?

Inevitably, actuality doesn't quite measure up to anticipation (not that I anticipated as much as he did). But, he assures me, things will get better with time. Maybe. I comfort myself with the thought that his body is much more beautiful than Zigi's. (But what does beauty matter?)

My predicament, however, cannot be ignored for much longer. And there is, in the end, only one person I can talk to about it. Aunty Fan, who else? But how do I face her? I don't know. I just know that I will. That madness with Zigi exists in its own bubble, quite separate from the normal life she and I conduct. I'll speak to her the minute I get back.

Fan, there's something I've got to tell you.

We are sitting in her kitchen over breakfast. Zigi is out swimming. (And who is he keeping himself beautiful for now?) After that he's got a full day in his laboratory, and this evening there's a committee meeting at Westminster somewhere. I ought to be at Westminster myself, soon. My

Minister's secretary phoned yesterday evening to make arrangements. I went along with them, pro tem.

She looks at me narrowly. – Is it what I think it is?

I'm pregnant.

I thought so.

How could you tell? I look down at my stomach. Still flat.

I just can. What are you going to do about it?

Aunty Fan – the thing is – I want it.

She sighs. – Darling, are you sure? You know what I'm going to say. But it's true. You've got your whole life before you. Don't mess it up now. I can give you the money, and I know someone who knows a good man.

I shake my head. – I've been through all that. Honestly.

A hundred, a thousand times. Because this decision is not in character. I don't like babies. Never have. My real self has not changed since I was sixteen and horrified at the prospect of poor Bella's being landed with some squalling infant and forfeiting the rest of her life. Only circumstances have changed. Now that my parents have died, this baby has made me realise how I miss that irrevocable, unquestioning relationship. I yearn for it. I love Fania, very much, but it's not the same. And the only way to have it again is to make it for myself. It's all their fault. If they hadn't died – well, if they hadn't died, none of this would have happened. But they did, and it has, and although it is inexpressibly inconvenient I'm not about to dispose of it now it's here. We are ruled by needs and compulsions that we can scarcely identify, let alone control. Convenience runs a poor second. I need this baby emotionally as much as I don't need it any other way.

Fania sighs. – Who's the father? Anyone I know?

I shake my head. – It's not someone I want to marry. So I don't want to say who it is, because this is my decision, and I don't want to drag him into it.

He is in it. And he hardly dragged himself.

It's no good asking me. I'm not saying, and that's that.

We sit in silence. I sip my tea. The smell of coffee makes me nauseous these days.

When's it due?

End of February, I think.

And what are you planning to do till then?

Work. Zigi's fixed up this job.

I know, he told me. All right. At least you've got somewhere to live. But what will you live on, once it's arrived? Babies don't come cheap, you know, and once it's there it's there. How can you do a job when you have a baby?

I'll work something out. I'll find a nursery. Don't worry. I shan't ask you to babysit. I know you're not keen on babies. We'll be as invisible as mice.

How do you know what I feel about babies? And this isn't any old baby. This is my first grandchild we're talking about. Why can't I babysit it? I shall probably dote on it!

So then, of course, I burst into tears. She hugs me. Soon we are both chattering away excitedly. And by the time Zigi reappears at about ten o'clock that evening, it's all decided. I am to take up my job as arranged. I am to work like a slave and make myself indispensable. When the baby is very small it will anyway be portable. And after that we shall see what arrangements can be made.

He's surprised to find us so animated. Looking at him, I know I can't face explanations, not now, certainly not in front of Fania. I leave her to break the glad news.

Zigi, I need hardly say, is appalled. Appalled. The next morning he comes up to my flat. He knocks carefully and loudly before he comes in.

Fania says you're pregnant.

Yes.

And you insist on having it.

Zigi, don't do the heavy father on me. Not you.

He sits down grumpily and looks at me. I say nothing. Nothing is said. Nothing is going to be said. No pretences about who else may have been the father. No recriminations. Nothing. Just nothing.

This is your programme, he says. Entirely yours.

Who's arguing?

Why do you insist on destroying your life?

I'm not destroying my life. Why should a baby destroy my

life? There's life after babies. Everything's under control. Fania says she'll help me. We'll work things out. I think she's rather looking forward to it, I add.

This baby is entirely your responsibility, Zigi insists coldly. He intends to make quite sure there will be no misunderstanding here, that everything is clarified while other avenues are still open. Events seem to have slipped their leash. There must be no ambiguities about what may or may not be expected of him. – Fania will help you if that is what she wants, but I don't want her burdened with responsibility for it.

I say nothing. I merely meet his eye. He sighs windily.

And what about your job?

I'll do my job. Then we'll see.

So that is what I do. And because I know what I'm going to need, and we can make our arrangements early, things do more or less work out. I find a nursery and book a place for my bump, which is now distinctly apparent. My employer, who is (as luck will have it, some luck at last!) a woman, is sympathetic and agrees to go along with my plan. I shall drop the baby off every morning; Fania will pick it up when I can't get back in the evening. My friends are horrified and fascinated, in about equal parts. Tony is covered in confusion.

I thought – I thought you meant you were safe. Oh, God, Miriam, I'm so sorry. Why didn't you tell me before?

Because it's not yours. How could it be? February. That was August we were in Italy. Simple arithmetic.

Whose is it, then?

That's nobody's business but mine.

And the baby's.

Possibly, but don't let's worry about that yet.

Tony is wondering whether to become a professional anthropologist. At any rate, he has decided to do a PhD. He is going to study the survival of Buddhism among the Buryats of Siberia. Before going to Buryatia, he must spend a few months at Moscow University. He is due to leave in a month.

I shan't even be here when it's born.

Why should you?

Because – how many times do I need to say it?

Say it again. It makes me feel almost human.

He shakes his head. – You really are crazy.

When the baby is born, she looks so like Zigi that I can't imagine how anyone can miss it. The forehead, the nose, the chin – all his. Is Fania blind? She certainly spends enough time gazing fondly into my daughter's face. Perhaps we only see what we're looking for, and whatever Fania's looking for, it isn't this. Or maybe she does see, but prefers to keep quiet about it – yet another case of being able to ignore what you don't explicitly know.

As for Zigi, now that the baby has arrived, he seems unexpectedly pleased.

What are you going to call her?

Susanna.

Fania approves. – After your mother. (In fact my mother was called Shoshana, always referred to as Shoshy. I am not risking that for my daughter.) Little Susie, chortles Fania, picking her up. What would she be? A granddaughter? No, a great-granddaughter! Think of that, Zigi. Great-grandparents!

Zigi catches my eye, then looks away. He does not comment. Clearly this concept does not please him, any more than would the biologically correct designation. It has been agreed that we shall never refer to the mystery of Susanna's parentage. And we never do. What difference does it make, anyway? Daughter, granddaughter, great-granddaughter, it's all the same to him – women's work. Until she grows up and becomes interesting. And *then* I'll start to worry. No, what am I saying? I keep telling myself that I am not related to Zigi except by marriage. And he'll be past it by then, anyway.

V

So the next year passes, as years with a young baby always pass, in nappies and bottles and constipation and diarrhoea and wind and vomit and indecipherable howls and hastily thumbed manuals and teeth and smiles and a desperate, never-fulfilled yearning for a complete night's sleep. Fania is wonderful – it is she who makes all this possible – but the one unbreakable condition is that nights are my affair. As she points out, the great thing about being a great-grandmother rather than a mother is that, when you've had enough, you aren't stuck with it. You can hand it back. I leave Susanna at the nursery on my way to work, Fania picks her up at the end of the day if I can't get back in time. And in the evenings we are together, Susie and I. Mine, mine, all mine.

All this takes its toll. My work is interesting and demanding, the baby is demanding and, I have to admit, not yet very interesting – though I am scolded for saying so. – She's so *good*, says Fania reproachfully. I've never known such a good baby.

What would I have done with a troublesome one? Become even shorter-tempered? Murdered her, maybe? Even less sleep? Even less time to think?

No; that's not quite accurate. A baby doesn't deprive you of thinking-time – only of *consecutive* thinking-time. It's impossible to complete any single task or project, material or mental. But the constant stream of calls upon the attention never entirely engages the mind. It doesn't preclude the kind of constant, ongoing conversation I conduct with myself throughout that first desperate year. Is this really *my life*? I ask myself every night, as, after Susie is safely bedded down and before I follow her to hoped-for oblivion, I pick up armies of small primary-coloured plastic objects from the floor, hoover up crumbs, run the washing-machine in Fania's kitchen. Can this drudge be *me*, last year's bright and hopeful girl? Nothing seems so endless as babyhood, while it is in progress.

I can't grumble, though, can I? I am the only author of my misfortune. Nobody's fault but your own. Not Susie's, with her terrible dependency, her tender, downy head – that ball filled with future, that box of potential, potential ally, potential enemy, potential genius. Not Fania's. Not, as he has made so very clear, Zigi's

I grow unprecedentedly thin. This, I feel, is a bonus. Zigi agrees. – Motherhood has certainly improved your figure, my dear Miriam, he remarks cheerfully. What can I say? Gee, thanks. But awkward exchanges such as this are rare: *any* exchange is rare. I see little of him. Babies, even when not potential sources of embarrassment – and had he been in any doubt as to Susanna's parentage, he need only look at her face for such doubts to vanish – are not his scene. Moreover, this particular baby presents an unusually taxing problem of etiquette. How is he to behave? If he pays us no attention, he is unfeeling. If he pays us overmuch attention, everyone – the world in general, myself in particular – may draw wrong conclusions. Jocularity might seem crass. Solemnity might infer opprobrium – hardly his to parcel out. Not surprisingly, he takes refuge in absence. That, at least, cannot be misunderstood. To say that he is uninterested in Susie is to understate the case. He is virtually unconscious of her, his indifference is total. Why was I shocked when Bettina told me how he walked out, all those years ago, on her and Marianne? If he could behave like that with us, why not with them? And if with them, then how much more inevitably with us. *They* weren't even an embarrassment, socially speaking at least. As the months pass, it seems less and less believable that he has anything to do with Susanna's presence. The events of that far-off day – which even at the time had appeared so improbably related to procreation – acquire an increasingly dreamlike aura.

Meanwhile, he is much taken up with some genetic experiments he is conducting at Imperial College, where he now holds a chair. And with other unspecified activities. Wasn't that Bella I glimpsed him with the other day, in a Westminster corridor?

So what if it was? It was probably nothing. He knows her. Why shouldn't he say hello, if they happen to meet? I only saw them just that once. One mustn't blow things up out of proportion.

I know now that my instinct, that immediate flush of boiling certainty, was correct. It wasn't nothing: *that* was what he was doing, all those evenings when he wasn't at home. Attending unspecified committees of two. Was I jealous? I certainly did not experience that unmistakable, unconquerable, masochistic urge to find out more – how long they'd been seeing each other, the hours and locations of their trysts – all those unbearable details which are the knots in jealousy's scourge. Nor did I feel jealous in the wifely, possessive sense. How could I? I had never had that sort of claim upon him. Nor, even, were my feelings sexual. I didn't want Zigi back in my own bed. There had been a time when I did, early on, but that had passed. Sex requires energy, and all mine was spoken for. I wasn't thinking about sex at all just then, with Zigi or anyone else. But – I saw him that day with Bella, and *knew* even as I rejected the knowledge. Such awareness, if not actual jealousy, is something closely related. Bella, always Bella. Anyone else – *anyone*. I could happily have killed her.

It was freedom, not Zigi, I coveted. Time was passing and life and fun were passing me by. There's nothing like evenings alone with a wailing baby to make you reflect on the freedom you (but not others) are deprived of. And all the rationalising in the world – the knowledge that this was entirely your own decision, that it was perfectly clear what you were embarking upon, what the terms were to be – can't prevent the reflection that a baby is a two-person production. You know you're in love when all the clichés in the old songs feel literally true – you really are walking on air, there really is a song in your heart. So with this situation. The phrase 'left holding the baby' was in my case merely factual.

Zigi was simply never around. He had never been an assiduous homebird, but this was something different. His life was elsewhere. Fania did not comment, and I did not raise the subject. She, too, was out a lot, but not with Zigi. She was keeping her end up, but it was more a question of principle than of pleasure. She looked suddenly older. Her face showed lines I hadn't previously noticed.

It is only recently, since Bella and I resumed contact, that I have found out what was really happening then. The affair between her and Zigi, which started out as a flirtation of the sort both of them were constantly conducting, quickly became something much more serious. Where Joan had failed to rouse him (and what, if anything, did Bella know of that?), Bella succeeded only too completely. Out of the blue, they found that they had fallen in love with each other. Zigi was horrified. He was, as I have said, a man who liked – who imperatively needed – to be in control of events. But he was not in control of this. It became obsessive, on both sides. They simply could not keep their hands or minds off each other. People started to talk. It became clear that the situation could not continue. Bella urged Zigi to leave Fania and marry her. She wanted his child. Didn't he want a child? she asked. With her, he could have one. – Think, she said to me only the other day, what a wonderful child it might have been.

She told me this over lunch. Since Zigi's memorial service we've taken to meeting every now and then, to see an art exhibition perhaps, or just to have a drink or something to eat. Every couple of months or so we snatch a pocket of time out. There is too much shared history there. Having found it again, why let it slip back into oblivion? Bella is so chic, so blonde, so intelligent, so ambitious. So like Zigi. She didn't know about Susanna, of course. She still doesn't. How furious she would have been (and may yet be). Our friendship was never a comfortable one, we could never genuinely rejoice in each other's successes. Not when they hit too near home. And what could hit nearer home than this? I had the baby Bella wanted. I (or, rather, Susanna) was the spanner in her works.

Poor Bella! It was exactly the wrong line to take. At the mention of the magic word 'child', Zigi lost interest. It was as sudden as that.

Zigi is cured. He resumes home life. The new lines are smoothed away from Fania's face. Another fence in the marital steeplechase has been safely negotiated.

Susie's first few all-consuming months pass. Routine begins to spread its soothing balm. It becomes clear that life will continue, that no more ghastly shocks or revelations are in store, that a *modus vivendi* can be established. The day comes when Zigi and I manage to pass on the stairs without embarrassment. Gingerly, these meetings are extended, until, eventually, we manage something not unlike a civilised conversation. At any rate, it'll do for now. What do I want, effusiveness?

VI

From time to time I receive exotic letters from Tony, who is in the field in Buryatia. He could be said to be enjoying himself, though his idea of enjoyment is not mine. He returns home towards the end of 1968, when Susie is nine months old. He, too, has become very thin. Buryat food did not agree with him, and not much else was on offer. We survey each other. He has never met Susie: he left before she was born.

He picks her up. He is much easier with babies than I am. Comes of having lots of younger siblings, he explains. – Well, he says. Aren't you a charmer. Doesn't look much like you, does she?

No. She looks like her father.

Does she, now? Do you see much of him?

Sometimes.

Tony does not see his future in academe. – I've had plenty of time to think, he says. Maybe I'll write up my thesis some day. But it's all too ingrown for me. I thought I'd try journalism or the BBC. I quite like the idea of radio. I can offer them some first-hand material, at any rate.

Tony is an operator. Before long he has his job in radio. In the evenings, he often comes round to visit. When Susie has gone to bed, we, too, go to bed. – I preferred you plumper, he says.

Did you? I quite like the new me.

I've got a proposition for you, he says one day, and then falls silent.

Propose away, then.

That's it.

What? You mean –

206

I mean I'm asking you to marry me. Why don't we get married? After all these years, here we still are, after all.

And you don't mind Susie?

No, I don't mind Susie. Actually, I think she's quite a plus. Perhaps we could have another to keep her company.

So we get married. Why not? What do married couples do that we don't? Nevertheless, questions bubble up. I push them firmly to the back of my mind. What have I done to deserve a man like Tony? What does he see in me? And what, if we are to be brutal, do I see in him? He, as he's often told me, is a one-woman man. I'm the only girl for him. And I? Were it not for circumstance? Were it not for circumstance, I might be Brigitte Bardot. But circumstance has brought out aspects of Tony – generosity, warmth, gentleness – that are hard to resist. So why should I resist them? He's a good man. I'm very fond of him. I think he's admirable and intrepid. But – I'm not in love with him. Perhaps 'in love' is not a necessary prerequisite for marriage? *Il y a toujours un qui baise, un qui tend la joue.*

I still have the money from my parents' house, which my Uncle Harry invested for me. We use it to buy this house (just in time: property prices are about to begin their ever-upward spiral). It's not too far from Fania on the North London line. And Zigi, don't let's forget him. A child should know its great-grandparents.

Naturally, Bella is told of our plans. We arrange to meet for lunch. Zigi does not figure in our discussions. She's sounding rather shrill these days, drinking rather a lot. Or maybe it's just that I see her with the jaded eyes of one sunk in domesticity. She is working as secretary to a Tory MP. – I think he's rather super, don't you? she confides.

To me he is a standard Tory, receding hair brushed back and cut rather long with that slight upper-class curl on the neck, shiny face, well-fed, well-encased figure. He is perhaps more literate than the average: he recently published a novel, a spy story, and the word is that, even if not great literature, it was exceptionally well-informed. If he isn't a spook himself, he is spookily connected.

He seems very nice, I say noncommittally.

My parents disapprove frightfully, says Bella with pleasure. That old edge between her and her father hasn't diminished with time. On the contrary: the years have only sharpened it.

Well, it's only a job. Isn't it?

Oh yes, of course. But you know what I mean.

Soon afterwards, I find out what she means. She has moved in with her MP. He plans to divorce his wife and marry Bella. Poor old wife, or perhaps not. Poor old Brockenhursts, definitely. I imagine disapproval is hardly the word for the chagrin they must be feeling. Not just a Tory: a paleolithic Tory. And Bella? Is this the culmination of all her plans? Political wifehood? I feel saddened. This marks the end of something. Our childhood. Our friendship. I can feel it in my bones.

In Bella, Zigi finally met his match. She was not one meekly to take whatever he chose to dish out. When he so brutally dropped her, that, as far as Bella was concerned, was not the end. It was just the beginning. If not the beginning she had hoped for, then another. Michael was Bella's definitive adieu to idealism, an instrument, a path to her own ends. Michael was to be, among other things, Bella's long revenge upon Zigi and all his works. Including me.

Whatever the complications of my relationship with Bella, she had until then been one of life's fixtures. There was so much we didn't have to explain to each other, so much we'd done together. And now a curtain descended. She was there no longer. She was hidden from me. I thought it was because of Michael, but it was of course Zigi who had come between us. The great unspoken. She didn't know my secret; I didn't know hers.

Tony and I were not invited to her wedding. Perhaps this wasn't so surprising. Circumstances dictated that it should be quiet – a somewhat hole-in-corner affair, if we're going to be catty. But the party afterwards was large and lavish, and we weren't invited to that, either. I heard about it from Derry, who said he spent half the evening looking out for us. Like me, he professed himself quite unable to understand why Bella had suddenly decided that this was to be her life. I suspect we each knew half the story. Derry, who had always been Bella's confidant as Tony had always been mine, knew about her hopeless passion for Zigi, and knew this was at least partly a rebound. And I knew about the history with her father, whom this marriage seemed equally clearly designed to punish.

While it is all going on, much of this is opaque to me. What is it about me, I ask myself, that Michael so resents (for I can only assume that it is he who is behind this sudden severance)? There is some mystery here.

When the matter comes up in conversation with Zigi, I am startled by the vehemence of his response. – Your friend Bella is a fool, he says. That man is a shit. He brings this out with his habitual pleasure in the colloquial; but there is some other feeling there as well (as the choice of colloquialism would indicate). The possibility of jealousy crosses my mind, but this is out of character. Jealousy presupposes an emotional engagement that is absent from Zigi's affairs. I picture him always as a solitary: that, in the end, was his tragedy – or Fania's. But if not jealousy, then what? The mystery appears insoluble. I file it away in my mind, along with other miscellaneous conundrums. My father always advised me that the most important drawer in the filing cabinet was the one marked F&F: File and Forget.

At my wedding party (to which Bella and Michael are invited, but which they predictably fail to attend), my family's collective sigh of relief is almost tangible. I see aunts whispering in corners, running their eyes critically over my new spouse. I don't need to be told what they're saying to each other, over those peculiar cocktails of cherry brandy and advocaat which they unbelievably favour, a layer of bright red floating on a bed of thick yellow, like some kind of child's jelly. Perhaps they need the reassuring sickliness to reconcile them to the alcoholic content. My aunts are not great drinkers. – She's a lucky girl, Aunty Rivvy is undoubtedly confiding to Aunty Pearl. Not many young men would be so happy to take on someone else's child. A goy, of course, but beggars can't be choosers. It's lucky Nat and Shoshy didn't live to see this. *Oy gevolt!* – I told them, Aunty Pearl tells Aunty Rivvy. When she went to university, I told them. Too much independence, and what happens? Not that the baby isn't a lovely child. She reminds me of someone. Who is it? Miriam? No, she doesn't really look much like Miriam, does she?

So there we are, Bella and I. Forward to the future, one hand safely enclosed in that of a new husband while with the other each of us waves to our Svengali, lurking in the wings over there. We have confounded all hopes, all prophecies. She's got a Tory and I've got a goy.

Thus do children fulfil their parents' dreams.

VII

Looking back – something I have rarely done until now – it is astonishing that our marriage survived a year, let alone – what is it? Almost twenty-five. Our silver wedding looms. Darby and Joan. How have we done it? Against the odds, as Tony's mother no doubt pointed out to him in no uncertain terms. She never approved of me. When we got married, Tony's family and mine did not mingle. They stood together in a corner, a small bulwark of dauntless English yeopersons marooned amid a swirling mass of rootless cosmopolitans. He has an older sister and three younger brothers. At that time they all lived in Shropshire, where Tony's father was a vet. They led the kind of country life, full of animals and orchards, that I had hitherto only read about in novels. We went to visit them, Tony, Susie and I, shortly after the marriage had been decided upon. We drove from London in Tony's car, one of those sage-green beetle-shaped Morris Minors that district nurses used to use.

It's a long drive from London to Ludlow, especially with a baby. The idea was that we should stay overnight. The weather was cold and bleak – February or March: there were no leaves on the trees, and little pockets of unmelted snow were still lying in the fields. By the time we got to Tony's parents' village, it was getting dark. We'd been telling Susie for the past three hours that we were nearly there. And then we drove over the brow of the hill and there it was, down in the hollow. –That's the house, said Tony. Standing just back from the road there.

It was one of those black-and-white half-timbered houses you find in that part of the country. A little bit of Old England. A fine place, had I been in the mood to appreciate it. Inside, there were lots of dogs and stone-flagged floors and riding-boots in muddy heaps. Susanna, who had never seen a dog close to, at once started to howl, and would not be consoled. She would not smile and pretend to be a model baby. She spat out Mrs Oliver's boiled eggs and hung on grimly to her filthy corner of greyish blanket.

Tony's father was spared this scene, as he was out with his arm up some cow. Mrs Oliver watched as I struggled with Susanna. There was a grim little twitch at the corner of her mouth which pretended to be a smile. She was a lean, no-nonsense woman, also a vet, a partner in the practice (she dealt with pets), unmade-up, with a good-looking bony face and pepper-and-salt hair. She looked from me, with my streaming, scarlet infant, to Tony, and back again. There was no need for her to say what she was thinking: her eyebrow, raised as she turned away to fetch some warm milk for a bottle (put a plug in it and, please God, we may have a little peace), said it all. Later, I saw her looking at Tony. He was lounging on the dog-haired sofa, joking with his sister and one of his brothers (the other two weren't there: they were both away at school, being made over into proper Englishmen). That look! When I caught it, it almost made me cry. Nobody should be loved that much. Who can bear such a responsibility? Her beautiful, golden boy. The brains of the family, her eldest son. What was he getting himself into? What was he tying himself down to? A bawling brat before anything had even begun. And not even his! Why was he doing it? Choosing me must have seemed like a rejection of all she stood for. Perhaps that's just what it was. I didn't ask; he didn't say.

211

On that first evening, I remember sitting round the dining-table (Mr Oliver had by now returned). I forget what we ate. What I remember is the silence. Nobody spoke, except to request the salt or the water. Were they somehow paralysed by us? Didn't they feel able to speak in our presence? Everyone ate, without let or comment. I had never before encountered such a phenomenon. I dropped a few jocular remarks: they sank like stones in that well of silence. In my family, meals were a continual argument. When all other topics were exhausted, we argued about the food. Here, that would have seemed somehow indecent. Perhaps it was me, making everyone feel awkward? I asked Tony, in bed that night, whether he thought this was so. – No, he said, it's always like that. They've all got their own projects, and that's what they think about. They just want to get back to them.

And these were people to whom I was now (or soon would be) related, if only by marriage! My in-laws! How could they and I possibly be members of the same family? No doubt they felt equally incredulous.

So there we were, Tony and I. A united front against a hostile world. That's how I always picture the ideal marriage: forward with linked arms, in the socialist-realist mode.

An image of beguiling, fundamental simplicity. But of course, our situation was not so simple. There was the great lacuna, the never-mentioned topic which was nevertheless so centrally and unavoidably *there*. Who was Susanna's father?

I had made up my mind from the outset that, on this issue, there would be no compromise. There were only two possibilities: abortion or silence. Anything else, and every-one's lives would be destroyed. There were to be no excep-tions, no reasons why. Never apologise, never explain. – I'm not saying, I said to Tony. Not now, not ever, not to anyone, not even you. That's the way it's got to be.

What about Susanna? he said. People need to know these things. You'll have to tell her, one day.

We'll cross that one when we come to it. If you want us, you'll have to take us as you find us.

And that's what he did. It was my good fortune that Tony

truly – inexplicably, as far as his mother was concerned – loved me. We became a joint venture, the three of us; soon, the four of us.

Naturally, the time did come when Susanna wanted to know. And wasn't she entitled to? Of course: but the same old prohibitions still applied. I told her, as soon as she was old enough to understand, that Tony was not her biological father, but that we had married while she was still a tiny baby and that, in everything that mattered, she was his daughter and he was her daddy. I told her, later and privately, when she asked again, that her real father was someone I loved very much but did not want to marry. When I could, I would tell her who it was; but that wasn't possible yet. – Would I like him? she asked. – Oh, yes, I replied. I think you'd like him very much.

I still haven't told her. The time has still not come. Is that one of my reasons for doing this? From time to time I fancy I catch her eyeing me. Is it my imagination? The projection of my own guilt? There is a distance between us that I don't experience with Rose. Who causes it? Susanna? Me? Zigi. That ubiquitous barrier falls between us.

As for Tony and Fania, what did they suspect? I never asked. And they in their turn remained silent. The truth perhaps lay hidden in some concealed unacknowledged part of their minds. If it had been revealed, it might not have surprised them. Shocked, but not surprised. I don't know if Fania and Zigi discussed it. They must have done: how could they not? I imagine Zigi just shrugged his shoulders. I can hear his voice. – If she does not want to say, who are we to enquire? Perhaps he simply operated his facility, the one my investigations have so amply revealed, for shutting out unwanted facts. Perhaps he was simply able to blot out the knowledge that Susanna was his daughter. I have already described how Fania was slightly constrained with Susanna as she got older, easier with Rose, while there was always a great closeness between Susanna and Zigi. How much all this had to do with unacknowledged consciousnesses, I don't know. As usual, I didn't ask. That's been my motto, the basis of our family life.

If it ain't broke, don't fix it.

CHAPTER 10   BOYS AND THEIR TOYS

I

It is 1982. Susanna is fourteen, Rose, eleven. Tony is now in science journalism. He some years ago discovered an unusual aptitude for explaining arcane scientific technicalities in a compelling and comprehensible way. He is much in demand among scientifically illiterate editors. He is also making a good deal of money ghosting books for famous but unliterary scientists. I, too, do some freelance journalism. It fits in easily around the demands of domestic life – ideal work if you can get it. And I have plenty of contacts. I gave up the Westminster job when Rose arrived, but I still know people there, and then there are Tony's colleagues, and various Cambridge friends. Getting going wasn't so easy, but now I usually manage one or two pieces a month. I also write detective stories from time to time. The confines of genre give me more confidence. I think up outré deaths for my enemies, and then turn them into novels. It affords a certain vicarious satisfaction.

I am engaged on one of these, pondering the next twist in my plot, when the doorbell rings. It is a pair of Jehovah's Witnesses. They are a young couple, a white boy and a black girl. We engage in the usual doorstep to-and-fro. There have been a lot of Witnesses around recently. I am usually fairly brutal with them, but this couple for some reason intrigues me, so I don't shut the door in their faces. When they have reached the end of their spiel, conversation moves on to personal topics. They have just married. I ask idly: are they planning to start a family? They reply gravely: No, not just yet. They've decided they won't have any children until after Armageddon. They are expecting this to happen any moment now.

They are not alone. For the second time in my adult life, the end of the world seems nigh. The Last Days are here again. And this time I am not shielded by solipsism or sexual stirrings or the inability of extreme youth truly to envisage the end of everything. On the contrary, I am naked: I have two children. Once again we are marching against the bomb. Once again, it's Aldermaston for Easter. We had turned our attention to other things, but Mephisto had not disappeared – he was merely resting. Now here he is again, up to his usual tricks. Setting his blindfold over people's eyes, pouring soap-powder into their brain-pans. How else is it that whole populations seem actually to be contemplating nuclear war with resignation, if not actual enthusiasm? How else is it that we are a mere couple of hundred thousand gathered here, and not several million?

As we link arms in the sleet to make a human chain around the bomb factory, I think about the last time I was here. Twenty years since the first time around. What an anniversary! In another twenty, shall I be here yet again? Shall I – or anyone else – be anywhere? It doesn't seem likely. It really doesn't seem likely. Those Jehovah's Witnesses will be free to have their children only too soon.

For it isn't just they who are thinking about day-to-day life in terms of Armageddon. Jehovah's Witnesses can only hope, but the people in control, people who can actually put the thing in motion, are talking in the same terms. The US Secretary of State for the Interior has declared: I do not know how many future generations we can count on before the Lord returns. The Secretary of Defense has read the Book of Revelation and believes the world is going to end. – Every day I think that time is running out, he says. I fear we will not be ready. I think time is running out . . . but I have faith.

Faith! God save us from those who rely upon faith! The President himself, the old man with the coal-black hair and the red, red cheeks, the man with his finger on the button, is another. He recently said: I sometimes believe we're heading very fast for Armageddon right now.

They're all expecting to be raptured. When the moment comes, their souls will leave their bodies and go whizzing in a direct line up to heaven. There are bumper-stickers to that effect displayed on half the cars in the Bible Belt. Tony and I saw them on a trip to Texas and Oklahoma last year. *In the event of Armageddon, this car will be driverless.* What have they got to fear? In their view, nothing. What have we got to fear? Plenty.

How has it happened? The Cold War was just that – cold, an engine for keeping the economy ticking along nicely without actually having to fight. War has its uses, after all. It took a war to end the Depression. A small war here, a small war there. But nobody seriously wanted another big one.

And now here they are, these old men, raring to go. We are not dealing with mere politics here, we are dealing with prophecy, with Fate. All those apocalyptic metaphors have had their effect. They have insinuated themselves into the political thought-process. The bomb has become a force of nature, like hurricanes, only to be mitigated, never controlled or abolished. The bomb is God-given. Trinity's offspring has become the Lord's own weapon. This is nothing less than Holy War, the final confrontation of Good and Evil. President Reagan has said so. – In your discussions of the nuclear freeze proposals, said Reagan, I urge you to beware the temptation of pride – the temptation of blithely declaring yourself above it all and label both sides equally at fault, to ignore the facts of history and the aggressive impulses of an evil Empire, to simply call the arms race a giant misunderstanding and thereby remove yourself from the struggle between right and wrong, good and evil. The grammar's fuzzy, but the sentiment is clear enough.

We are discussing this speech at Fania's birthday dinner. It is a hot July evening, and we are eating in the garden. There is no wind. The air is filled with the scent of honeysuckle. You can see the stars even above the glare of London. The *Bulletin of the Atomic Scientists* has just moved its clock forward six minutes. It stands at four minutes to midnight. Midnight is Armageddon time. I say: I can't bear it. They don't care if they destroy everything. And what can we do?

Zigi says: You are right. I am very frightened at this situation. More than ever before.

We are drinking Montrachet, so much more delicious than champagne. He takes a sip, slowly, as if any sip might be the last of all. He says: It is not as if people do not speak. But nobody listens. They are hypnotised by the missiles. They have to pile up more and more, they don't dare to stop.

Zigi is seventy-four. He is still a striking figure, still tall and upright, his hair still thick and silvery-white. He has become a scientific elder statesman. His researching days are over: now he pronounces. He is an emeritus professor, he chairs Royal Commissions. Four years ago, he received a knighthood: he is Professor Sir Zsygmond, Fania is Lady von Fischer, a handle which both amuses and appals her (but, it has to be said, the pleasure is quite evidently greater than the pain, despite her principles). He carries the prestige of those who have had the ear of power, even though those in power now are no longer interested in what he has to say.

Zigi is sitting beside Fania, across the table from me. For the last fourteen years he has been careful always to maintain a table's width between us. Circumstances have dictated that that far-off Cambridge afternoon and its consequences can never recede into the background of consciousness, as might have been possible had we not been related. We can never escape each other. At every family gathering there we are again – Zigi, Miriam and Susanna. How often do we meet? Once or twice a month at least. He has watched his daughter change from a baby to a thoughtful, rather solemn child – Susanna has never had laughter to spare – and now into a graceful girl. She's escaped those puppy-fat traumas I had to endure. What does he think, how does he feel? I have no inkling. I have no entry into Zigi's inner thoughts. I shall always be your friend, he said. More than a friend. But that's not how things have worked out. Not that he is *un*friendly. Why should he be? His feelings towards us – towards Susie and me – are, I am sure, entirely benign. He wishes us well. But from a distance. He is wary, impersonal, slightly detached. If I were a vain woman I might tell myself that he never dared come closer for fear of falling once more into my irresistible arms. But I have never bothered to deceive myself. That day, I know, was a sort of madness. It wasn't so much that we took leave of our senses as that we succumbed to them entirely. We were possessed by frenzy, in the true dionysiac sense. Had it not been for Susanna, the episode might have brought us closer together in delightful complicity, eventually receding into the misty distance. Had it not been for Susanna.

But Susanna is: at this moment, helping herself to more salmon mayonnaise. Up till now he's more or less ignored her: she has been a child, and therefore negligible except as a catalyst for these unsettling emotional complications. But now she's growing up. Soon she'll become visible and interesting. I wonder how they'll get on then? My gaze rests upon her, admires her long, strong, delicate hands (a legacy from Zigi), and lifts – to see her father engaged in identical contemplation. He catches my eye and turns seamlessly to address Tony about some book they are co-editing. He won't engage with me. He refuses, and it isn't just for reasons of prudence or embarrassment. It's edgier than that. What Zigi feels is resentment. It began the day he realised that, however hard he tried, he wasn't going to browbeat me into having an abortion, and it's never lifted.

This would appear a most unreasonable reaction. In a sense, I was letting him have it all ways. I wasn't proposing to destroy his child, nor to saddle him with her, nor to cut off relations or interfere with his home life. But still he feels insecure: and insecurity is the one thing he can't bear. He has to be in control if he is to feel comfortable with life. And in this situation he is not in control.

Look at it from his point of view. Over the past thirty years he has laboriously carved out a niche for himself in public life. Being a public figure, in the forefront of events, is important to him. And his particular role is dependent upon a certain moral spotlessness. How avidly his enemies would seize upon this scandal! Public life, private life – all down the tubes. No, he's got to be unimpeachable. And Susanna's his Achilles' heel. Nobody must know about her. Unfortunately one other person already does know. Me. And I'm a loose cannon. When I insisted on having the baby I broke free. Who knows what I mightn't do next? Stand up, knock my spoon against my glass, clear my throat and launch forth. Ladies and gentlemen, I have an announcement to make. This may surprise some of you . . . And who, looking at Susanna, would not know that I was telling the truth?

An improbable scenario. Nevertheless, it might happen – it or something like it. And if it did, *he couldn't do anything to stop it.* In that sense, he can never forget that I have him in my power. And he can't forgive me.

There's something else I suspect he can't forgive. It's perverse, but then Zigi is perverse. He hates the thought that I may spill the beans, any time and without his permission. But at the same time he's furious that I've never told Susanna. His daughter – and who's her daddy? Tony, whom she loves, and who loves her. And about whom Zigi feels so extremely equivocal.

None of this, of course, may be admitted, to himself or anyone else.

The balmy, scented evening laps us round. We eat our salmon and sip our wine (tonight, for the first time, Susanna is allowed a small glass) and go on talking about Armageddon and its promoters.

For a long time, during the Seventies, we did not talk very much about politics. Zigi was occupied with education and science, Fania with painting, Tony and I with our careers and our daughters. One of Britain's pleasant peculiarities used to be the way in which politics was segregated from the rest of life. But now all that has changed. Everything is political. Everything is polarised. And people like us, who dislike what is going on, have been allotted a role. Bella's husband was on the television the other night. He appeared to be covered with a thin film of oil. Everything gleamed: hair, cheeks, teeth, tie. He always seemed slightly overfilled, but these days the purple flesh seems on the very point of escape. His mode is orotund, sub-Churchillian. How can Bella bear it? The mere thought of him makes my flesh creep. And she has done more than think about him: they have two children to prove it.

He was talking about a sinister new force in the land: the enemy in our midst. – You may not recognise them. Very possibly they do not recognise themselves, though some most certainly know just what they are doing. But, as surely as any fifth column, they are eating away at the foundations of our state.

Who are these internal enemies? Oysters and champagne, you would think, looking at him. But no: he meant us. All those who dare to disagree with what is going on.

I say: Did you see Bella's Michael the other night, sounding off on the telly?

I heard about it. Do you still see her? Zigi asks.

Not for years. Do you?

Occasionally. I don't know what made her marry such an unpleasant man.

Once again, there is more feeling here than one might have expected. I look at him in surprise. What's he got against Michael, apart from what we all have against Michael? Nobody else seems to have noticed anything strange, however.

Tony says: I've always thought it was a way of expressing how she felt about her father.

She is evidently a masochist, says Zigi. He says this almost affectionately. These days, Bella can be dismissed in a sentence like any other unimportant bit-player. At the time of their liaison, her name was never mentioned. That subterranean part of myself which registered (but never recognised) their involvement has also noted this change of tone. Unlike her husband, who remains, for whatever reason, an object of hatred, Bella is no longer troublesome. She does not insist on occupying more mental and emotional space than is comfortable. Unlike some, she had the tact not to procreate.

Bella has become a political figure, just as she always said she would. She has achieved this indirectly, by establishing a sort of salon. Her husband lost his parliamentary seat not long after they were married, but his political thrillers kept him in the public eye and the political-literary swim, and he regained it in 1979. The books are very popular, and they have made him rich. They are still set chiefly in the closed world of spooks, full of authentic-sounding jargon. It's a world as unreal as fairy-tales. Perhaps that's what they are – fairy-tales for the Cold War.

Bella's invitations are keenly coveted – now that he has been re-elected, more so than ever. Needless to say, they do not drop through my letterbox. The curtain that dropped between us when she married Michael has never lifted. I'm surprised to hear Zigi is on her list. He's a lion, of course, though slightly outdated, and of the wrong complexion. Perhaps Bella thinks he is now a toothless lion.

Does she ask you to her parties? What are they like?

No, no, not the parties. Sometimes I run into her.

How can he just 'run into her'? Where? Why? Not without previous arrangement, given the lives they both lead. The thought crosses my mind: Maybe they're having an affair? (Now that my own feelings are no longer engaged, I may permit myself such speculations without courting a nervous breakdown.) Is that why Zigi hates Michael? But at his age? And the way things are now? That would almost constitute a perversion on Bella's part. I wouldn't put it past her, now that I think about it.

Zigi says: Anyhow, I'm going to give them all a shock. But he refuses to go into any further detail.

Zigi's principal preoccupation at this time is the BBC's annual science lecture. He is this year's lecturer. It is an honorific affair. In some ways the invitation seems surprising, given this government's policies, Mrs Thatcher's loathing of what she sees as the BBC's leftist bias, and Zigi's political history. But the invitation is of course to Sir Zsygmond the scientist, the establishment figure. It is a long time since Zigi was controversial.

He has been at work on his script for weeks. Nobody has been allowed to see it – not even, or so I believe, his producer.

Who is a mere producer to insist that Zigi present his lecture for comment and editing? He has never been easy to bully, and now such a thing would be almost impossible. It is assumed that his speech will be about science education policy, though this is more controversial than you might suppose. Oxford recently refused Mrs Thatcher an honorary degree because of her attitude to education in general and science in particular, and she is humming with rage at the insult.

The event is to be televised live. There is an invited audience. Naturally, we are part of it. We sit in the front row with Fania. She is dressed to kill in scarlet. The girls chatter excitedly. Susanna has been sulking a lot recently in the classic fourteen-year-old way. She refuses to say what's biting her, and my mind, fuelled no doubt by guilt, always homes in on the thorny topic of my continuing refusal to name her natural father. Not that I mention this any more than she does; but it's always there in the background, perhaps more in my mind than hers. Today, however, all sulks are forgotten. We crane round to see who else is here. There are various faces we recognise either because we know them personally or because we've seen their photographs in the papers. If we can't identify the rest, this merely demonstrates our ignorance of who's who.

A hush falls. The lights dim in the body of the hall: the stage glows under the television arcs. Zigi enters, together with the Chairman of the BBC governors, who is to introduce him.

The Chairman is a rotund figure, a wealthy aristocrat who likes to participate in public life, cultured, apolitical. He looks shellshocked. What can have happened? He is supposed to introduce Zigi, surely not a very difficult or contentious affair? But he can hardly bring himself to speak. Zigi, tall and stately, strides calmly to the podium, unruffled as ever, and stands expectantly, waiting to begin. He looks towards the Chairman, who is apparently about to have an apoplectic fit. He opens his mouth, but still no sound comes out. There is an endless silence (about fifteen seconds, I reckon later: an eternity). Finally, he achieves speech. – The BBC, he stutters, is a deeply tolerant organisation, the embodiment of this country's principles of non-censorship. The breadth of these principles is demonstrated by the fact of tonight's lecture. The BBC, while happy (he does not look happy) to welcome Sir Zsygmond von Fischer, dissociates itself from what he has to say. Then he steps down and, with a face like thunder, resisting the evident temptation to walk out then and there, takes his place beside Fania. Clearly he has had a look at Zigi's mysterious script.

Zigi launches into his speech. He speaks, as always, with detachment. His has never been an impassioned style: it tends, almost, to the languid. He has an unrivalled capacity for making those with deeply felt opinions and more emotion than intellect (myself, for example) feel sweaty and stupid. This loftiness adds a particular force to what he now has to say.

He describes his youth, his salvation through science. – As a young man, he says, I had no religion. As far as I could see, religion had done nothing but harm to the world. Science was my religion. The world was gripped by madness, and it seemed to me that only rational thought could save it.

He goes on to describe how, since those bright but far-off days, science has repeatedly disillusioned him. All the early excitement of physics leading to – the atomic bomb. His espousal, as soon as he could disentangle himself from the bomb, of another field which seemed at that time wholly benign – only to find that it, too, led to a moral minefield in the shape of genetic manipulation. – A friend of mine is an astronomer, he says. What can be wrong with that? He studies the structure of the universe. To do so, he has helped develop powerful radio telescopes. His techniques have been adapted to construct radar and sonar systems for guided missile programmes.

Zigi speaks of his growing conviction that science, in many of its applications, is nothing but an indulgence, a luxury that, maybe, the human race can no longer afford. – Nothing gives me greater intellectual pleasure, he says, than to sit down at my work-bench. I used to want nothing more than to have as many young people as possible share this pleasure. Who can resist the allure of knowledge? of finding out how the world works? of perhaps learning how to control it, how to harness the great forces and wonderful designs of nature? But now I am more and more doubtful. I begin to wonder – should we be teaching science at all? should fundamental science be stopped – in some areas now, in others, as they emerge, later? The worst of all worlds is emerging, he says. Knowledge is power, but perhaps we now have too much power. Science is rational, but it is in the grip of irrationalists, of politicians, of madmen, and they are preparing to destroy us all.

What can we do to stop this? he asks, and answers his own rhetorical question. – Everyone must do what he or she can, and scientists can perhaps do more than most. Some forty per cent of engineers, probably more physicists, in this country, are employed devising ways to kill people. It is the same in the United States, probably even more in Russia. Without scientists, there would be no H-bombs or guided missiles. How many of them visualise what they are doing? To them it's an interesting problem. They've never been in a war, they don't know what it's like to be someone's target or to kill somebody. They only know the exhilaration – the exhilaration of destruction from a distance, the exhilaration of having solved a problem. We somehow must work against this detachment, because it is this detachment that is putting the world in danger. Without the scientists, the military are helpless. We are their enablers, and we must stop. We must have a scientific strike against war.

But of course, he adds as an afterthought, it is not *just* up to scientists. All of us must do what we can. We must all protest in every way possible against this grotesque misuse of knowledge. I urge you not to sit back and let life slide out of your hands. We must make ourselves felt, we must demonstrate in every way we know how. Do not wait for tomorrow. Tomorrow may not come.

He stops speaking. I remember an argument I once had with Zigi about whether great scientists are necessarily any good at other aspects of human life. I thought not: he disagreed. A truly great scientist, he said, is probably a truly great man. People recognise this. It isn't just mindless glamorisation. This evening, I can see what he meant. Zigi is generally recognised as a great scientist. This evening, for the first time, I feel that he may be a great man.

The audience look stunned. This is not what they had been expecting. There is a sprinkling of applause. Tony, Fania and I clap heartily. Susanna and Rose are in paroxysms of enthusiasm. The Chairman, on Fania's other side, sits stonily on his hands. He is probably thinking of his licence fee negotiations, which will not have been helped by Zigi's performance this evening. The Prime Minister, not the same Prime Minister who made him Sir Zsygmond, would probably like to deprive him of that knighthood this very second. But it is too late. Nothing can be done. The horse has left the stable. The BBC's airwaves have been used to urge the public to join the big protest rally against the siting of cruise missiles in Europe which, as everyone knows, is planned for the day after tomorrow. All that remains is to bolt the stable door. The annual scientific lecture will henceforth be abolished.

After Zigi steps down, and the transmission ends, there is a buzz of talk. Gloomy BBC executives huddle together. Zigi is surrounded by enthusiasts: in the space of an hour, he has become once again a political figure. Other members of the audience mutter and shake their heads. The irresponsibility! Has he no thought for the miserable BBC? How could such a thing be allowed to happen? To use such an occasion for rank political propaganda!

There was a dinner after the event. It was held in a small dining-room behind the auditorium. There were ten people present. All of them, except Zigi and Fania, were deeply embarrassed. The Chairman was so furious that he could not bring himself to speak. Not a word did he utter. The others made small-talk. Zigi, an opera fan, cheerfully discussed music with the Chairman's wife, who was on the board of Covent Garden. – I felt so proud, Fania said. For some time I had been wondering why I stay with Zigi. He is not an easy man, as you know. But this evening I knew. No, I didn't know what he was going to say. Nobody knew. How could he have done it otherwise? They would never have allowed it. As it is, that can be their excuse. He wouldn't show them. They'll never let it happen again, of course.

And of course they didn't. But it was too late. The deed was done: Saint Zigi was born.

II

So here we are, lined up for (or against) the Final Battle. The Forces of Good versus the Forces of Evil. The Emperor of the Last Days versus Antichrist. As for who is who, who good and who bad, who right and who wrong – that, as usual, is a subjective judgement. Saint Zigi on one side: Saint Edward on the other.

For Dr T., too, has received his apotheosis. On 23 March 1983 President Reagan, on television, introduced SDI, the Strategic Defense Initiative – more generally known as Star Wars. – Let me share with you a vision of the future which offers hope, he said. It is that we embark on a program to counter the awesome Soviet missile threat with measures that are defensive. . . . I call upon the scientific community in our country, those who gave us nuclear weapons, to turn their great talents now to the cause of mankind and world peace, to give us the means of rendering these nuclear weapons impotent and obsolete.

Dr T. was invited to the White House for this occasion. He did not know why. He had no more idea than anyone else what Reagan was going to say. But when he heard it he knew – for the second time in his life – that the President was speaking directly to him.

Ever since the atom bomb had been achieved he felt he had been struggling against the grain, a struggle which took its physical toll in those persistent attacks of ulcerative colitis. He had to fight his fellow scientists for the H-bomb. He had to fight President Eisenhower to avert a test-ban, which under President Kennedy was actually set in place. Later, in the 1970s, things went even further. Treaty after treaty – the ABM treaty, SALT I, the spectre of SALT II – put the free world at the mercy of a Russian signature. And what was that worth? Teller knew: nothing, precisely nothing. – An agreement with the Russians, he said, will be essentially as good as their word, and no better.

Dr T.'s apotheosis, as was only proper in a case of sanctification, occurred by way of a miracle. In 1981, at a conference on nuclear war, he was gloomy. He predicted that the Soviet Union would win. But the West might yet be saved if some miracles occurred. Fortunately, there had already been one – the election of Ronald Reagan.

Dr T. knew that if he could only arrange to see Reagan alone, he could show him the future. Reagan was an old friend: Teller and he first met when Reagan was Governor of California in the 1960s. Then, Reagan's fixation with the Final Battle was just beginning. – For the first time ever, he revealed to a startled dinner companion in 1971, everything is in place for the battle of Armageddon and the second coming of Christ.

But access to the Governor of California is easier to arrange than access to the President of the United States. The President's advisers, aware of his suggestibility in this area, kept Teller from him. Time after time, the tête-à-tête was not arranged. Teller complained of this conspiracy in the course of a television interview watched by the President. And on 4 September 1982, he got the meeting he was waiting for.

Mr President, Teller plunged in as they shook hands. Third generation, third generation. He was speaking of the next generation of nuclear weapons – the anti-missile shield that would guarantee victory when the inevitable time came.

It was what the President wanted to hear. – When the submarine was first proposed, nobody believed it, he remarked at the end of the meeting.

Star Wars was Reagan's own and particular project, a film-star's name for a film-star's dream. Unlike his advisers – including Teller – Reagan was terrified of nuclear weapons. He spoke of Armageddon, but could not really face it. Since becoming President, he had had to participate in doomsday exercises in which he was forced to consider what he would do if he was told that missiles had been launched against the United States. – They were a very unsettling experience for him, his Secretary of Defense, Caspar Weinberger, observed. He had a very deep revulsion to the whole idea of the nuclear weapons. The spectacle of not having any defences, having these things coming in, and what does he do as President? Does he order retaliation or what? How many minutes have we got? Twelve minutes, nine minutes, all that.

From this vision, Dr T. and his anti-missile shield released him.

What will SDI consist of? What will it not consist of! Particle beams, space-based interceptors, pop-up interceptors . . . And, Dr T.'s own prize and particular contribution, the newest, most secret addition to the US armoury: the X-ray laser, whose beams will be a million, possibly a billion times brighter than the nuclear weapon which will merely be its trigger. On 23 May 1983, the President awards Edward Teller the National Medal for Science, America's highest scientific honour, for his 'outstanding contributions', his 'leadership in science and technology'.

The X-ray laser. It is Dr T.'s dream, Uncle Zigi's nightmare. It was originally conceived as a medical tool, but medicine does not have the funding a weapons lab commands. – Until 1980 or so, says its young inventor, I didn't want to have anything to do with nuclear anything. Back in those days I thought there was something fundamentally evil about weapons. Now I see it as an interesting physics problem.

It is beautiful and elegant as a concept. But will it work? Colleagues are sceptical. Says one: Is Edward an engineer? No. Is he a systems designer? No. Is he a military planner? No. He was enthralled with the principle and rightly so. The principle is in fact that beautiful. But he is not the kind of guy who ever got hooked on building things. His first H-bomb was the size of an apartment house. Edward is a physicist with a fantastic creative mind. He understands the beauty of a piece of music. But for God's sake don't ask him to design a trumpet.

Can any system stop 99.9 per cent of incoming missiles? Secretary of State George Shultz asks him on the same evening of 23 March when SDI is first announced. Teller can only reply: No. There can be no guarantee of such protection.

But don't let's worry about that just now. Dr T. is a man of ideas, a salesman of ideas. And he has sold his idea to the only one who matters: the President. This is the President's dream, and the President is essentially a broad-brush man. Details do not concern him. Others will have doubts, but he has none. The voicing of doubts is therefore considered disloyal. They are there, but they are stifled. Meanwhile, the Livermore lab is galvanised. The West's most brilliant young physicists are gathered there. Funds are unlimited. A billion dollars for starters: more to come. There are no computers powerful enough to deal with the new concepts that will be needed, so the Livermore boys set about designing them. This will be Ronald Reagan's gift to humanity.

Dr T. sits in his office on the top floor of Livermore's tallest building. The back wall is covered with documents and pictures, including a number of mushroom clouds. Records of a life's work. To his left, a safe for top-secret documents. On his desk, a pot of African violets and a photograph of Mici. He has achieved the highest recognition, unlimited financing. The defence of the free world is in his hands. And still he is not contented. Still he sees himself as the lone battler against universal blindness. – The fact that a great many American scientists, perhaps the majority, are against it, puzzles me, disturbs me, he says. This is a small fraction of the talent there is in America. And almost necessarily it is much less than the talent the Soviets can deploy in the same field. He is, as he always has been, obsessed by the spectre of Russian technical excellence. – If we had worked during the Second World War in the same way, he says, Hitler would have won. The number of people on our side who could make contributions but who instead exhaust themselves in fabricating objections is legion.

Where will it end? We build anti-missile-missiles. They build new low-level, disguised missiles. We build new, low-level interceptors. And so on for ever? Dr T. sees no alternative. – We are not talking about the kingdom of heaven here, he snaps.

Indeed, we are not.

III

I remember the autumn of 1983 as a bad time. The bomb dominated our thoughts as it dominated the news. The build-up to war seemed relentless, and we could only watch in horror. The papers were full of nuclear deployments, while at the same time it was clear that far more was going on than would ever be disclosed. From time to time fat envelopes full of bloodcurdling military detail stamped TOP SECRET dropped through the letterbox. They came from a journalist friend who spent his life ferreting out items the government did not wish us to know. How much of this stuff was floating around the mails? Was our correspondence being opened? Were our phones being tapped? More than once, people heard replays of telephone conversations they had just finished conducting. There was already a war going on, between us and the government, which seemed hell-bent on blowing us all up for our own good.

I ran into Bella about this time. It was in Peter Jones. Sloane Square's just down the road from her house. I was looking for some china, and caught sight of her at the other side of the department. Her back was turned, but there was no mistaking that elegant blonde head. She still wore her hair in a French pleat. My heart jumped and stopped, as if it was an old lover I'd spotted. I rushed over before she had a chance to see me and slide off.

Bella! I said.

She turned, almost knocking over a vase she'd been studying, a horrid, cut-glass thing. What can her place be like if she puts such objects in it? Or maybe it was a present for some unfortunate. She looked at me.

Well, aren't you going to say hello? Am I infectious or

something? Bella, I said, I want to know how you are. How are your children, how old are they, how are your parents, how are you *doing*? This is ridiculous. What did I ever do to you? We've known each other since we were children. Why don't we go and have a coffee?

It was beyond even Bella to avoid me after that. She assented graciously. We went to Peter Jones' restaurant. She looked around anxiously. – Are you worried about being seen with the wrong sort of person? I said nastily. Don't worry, I'm not angling for an invitation. I just thought, two old friends, let's have a coffee and catch up.

She blushed. It's something she's never been able to control, she's always hated it. – Oh, Miriam, she said. Don't. You're looking well.

Actually, I was looking a mess. It was sleeting outside, my nose was shiny scarlet and I was bundled up like a bag-lady. Bella looked exquisite in a fur-lined mac. I said – Oh, what's the point. I felt a fool.

She looked at me, rather helplessly, as if circumstances were just too much for her. – Miriam, she said. I – Look, there's something – She stopped herself. What was she about to say? Why didn't she *say* it?

Something? What something?

Do be careful, Miriam, she said at last. You've always been such an innocent. Things aren't as simple as we thought they were when we were fourteen.

I was going to make some defensive reply. I was going to say, I'd rather gathered that. It was on the tip of my tongue. But then I thought: It's not true. Some things *are* like that. When you're fourteen you see the world in black and white, good and evil. Generally speaking, of course, Bella's right. The world is a complex place and shades of grey abound. But not always. Not in the matters she must have in mind. Those remain obstinately polarised, stuck in simplicity. Black is black, though white is not always snowy white. Dr T. and all his creations are black. All Mephisto's blandishments can't make them anything but evil. They are the forces of darkness. And we? Are we white? Are we God's army, is Zigi the new

Messiah? No. We aren't and he isn't. We're the ones who try and see through that apocalyptic smokescreen, past the hyperbole and war-game meta-speak to the banal simplicities beneath.

I said something like this to Bella.

Oh – She shook her head and got up. She hadn't begun to drink her coffee. – Look out for your associates, she said. People aren't always what you think. And she left. I could only think she was mad.

What were they so scared of, Bella and Michael and the rest of them? Us? Why weren't they scared of what *we* were scared of? Were they living in the same world? Hertfordshire's Emergency Planning Officer informed the Watford Chamber of Commerce that most of Watford would survive a nuclear strike on the NATO command centre at Northwood, four miles distant. Watford would suffer only light or moderate damage. Radioactivity decays fairly rapidly, he said, and if the wind blew it away from Watford, people would not be affected. We reckon it would take an extremely powerful, 20-megaton weapon on Northwood to destroy Watford. That is expensive, and would it be worth it?

No, it was Bella's associates, not mine, that I was worried about. They were the ones with the power. All we had was numbers. We wrote articles, we delivered petitions. We held jumble sales against the bomb. Uncle Zigi barnstormed the country making speeches. The Peace Movement became the largest political movement in Britain, the largest in Europe. It gathered a million protesters into Central Park: the largest in America. Protestant Angst, Assistant Secretary of Defense Richard Perle called it. – It's happening in Protestant Europe and there's no question it's Angst. It's a sense of fear and anxiety – troubled people, troubled governments, troubled coalitions. And it's happened before and it will happen again, and I think it's a phase that they will go through, and we will have to go through it holding their hand. Well, thanks, Mr Perle, as from a Czernowitzer to a Litvak. We Protestants here are staking everything on this life with all its imperfections. It's you Protestants over there, who can't seem to wait for the next one, that give us the Angst.

That Halloween we went down to Greenham Common, the girls and I. Greenham was the base where the cruise missiles were due, little missiles that could be whisked around the country on their mobile launchers. They could sneak under a country's radar defences and take out a target before anyone even knew anything had happened. Just the thing for a nice new war. They were due any day, and we were going to stop them. There were women camping in the mud around the base, pledged to stay until cruise left. On Halloween, two thousand women, us among them, came to Greenham and took down four miles of fence, using wire-cutters. The soldiers inside the fence looked on. They were embarrassed. On 14 November, the first of the missile transporters arrived. On 11 December, fifty thousand women encircled the base. Parts of the fence were pulled down again. There were a lot of arrests. Tony made me promise that I'd keep the girls away from all that, though of course they were dying to be arrested. History repeats itself.

I wish we could stay, Susanna said.

Darling, you've both got school tomorrow, I said. How can we?

That week, it now transpires, was the week it nearly happened. On 2 November 1983, World War Three nearly broke out. Nervousness had been rising for some time. On 31 August, Korean Airlines' KAL 007 was shot down over the Soviet Far East, with the loss of 269 lives. On 25 October, President Reagan personally confronted the might of communism by invading Grenada, a small island in the Caribbean. The Euro-missiles were about to go in. It seemed to Moscow that the Americans were gaining an advantage in the world balance of forces. A nuclear first strike, they concluded, was a serious possibility. And at that moment, on 2 November, Exercise Able Archer began.

Able Archer was designed to test NATO's nuclear attack procedures. As it was first planned, Secretary of Defense Weinberger, the US Joint Chiefs of Staff, the NATO Supreme Commander and President Reagan and Vice-President Bush were all scheduled to take part. They were pulled out at the last moment because of concern over the high state of nervousness in the Kremlin.

Nevertheless, Able Archer remained terrifyingly realistic. Jittery Russian listening-posts picked it up and flashed their alarm along the airwaves. Was it masking a real attack? Western listening-posts noted an exceptionally high level of Warsaw Pact traffic. Nuclear-capable fighters stationed in Poland and East Germany were placed on high alert. KGB intelligence units told Moscow that NATO was moving troops in preparation for an attack. Had the countdown to nuclear war already begun? On the night of 8–9 November (as we sat in our centrally-heated kitchen and wondered how the women camping at Greenham were getting on in the rain, and whether the missiles were in yet) Moscow sent flash telegrams to its KGB stations in Western Europe. They were instructed to gather all possible information, highest priority, on US preparations for a surprise missile attack on the Soviet Union.

Reagan, after reading the CIA's report on that week's events, said: Do you suppose they could possibly believe that? I don't see how they could believe that – but it's something to think about. In a meeting with his senior advisers the same day his conversation, perhaps reflecting what was on his mind, turned once more to Armageddon.

IV

It is the end of October 1984, half-term, when Susanna announces she wants to go to Greenham. Ever since Zigi's BBC lecture, she has been devoted to the Peace Movement. It seems to have filled a space in her emotional life. She hardly sulks any more. – I feel I'm doing something, she says. It makes me feel better. But it's more personalised than that. It's Zigi she's fixated on. Her friends collect pictures of pop-stars and actors. Susie cuts out all Zigi's articles and photos, with which the press, these days, is liberally scattered. She sticks them in a big album she bought. I feel, as may be imagined, ambivalent about this sudden passion, despite the improvement it's brought about in Susie.

Fine, darling, can you get down by yourself or shall Rose and I come too?

Mum, I don't think you understand. I'm going down to stay. You'll have to take me because I'm going to need quite a lot of stuff.

Does my face convey my feelings? What are my feelings, come to that? I say: You're staying there? How long for?

How do I know? I'm sixteen now. It's perfectly legal. I'm allowed to leave school. I want to get things clear to myself. I want to get away from all this – stuff – here. She waves a hand dismissively, writing off the kitchen table, the crockery, the saucepans, the dishwasher, Rose's sweater on the back of a chair, somebody's trainers in the corner. – I thought you supported Greenham. You ought to be proud.

And I am proud. I am. But I'm also terrified, anxious – in short, a parent. Ought I to go there with her? But if I do, who will look after Rose? Tony is away half the time, and she has just started at a new school. She really needs me. And Susie really doesn't. Or at any rate, doesn't want me. I know she'd far rather go to Greenham without me. Objectively, I know this is her first step into independence. Subjectively I feel – that she is rejecting me for Zigi. I feel that her subconscious is telling her what's been hanging between us all her life, and that she's decided to punish me. Such feelings are so disreputable that I can barely admit them to myself.

She looks so like her father, as she stands by the kitchen table twisting her tawny-brown hair into a rubber band. (Isn't she like her Dad? people remark, noticing that she is tall and fair, and so is Tony. And I can only agree.) She's quite a lot taller than I am, and radiates such self-assurance. At sixteen? Surely that must be a false impression? But Susanna has always been dauntingly composed. She seems much more serious than I was at her age. At her age (not that I wasn't also interested in politics) I thought the Aldermaston march was a great, sexy adventure. One thing she definitely isn't going to Greenham for is to meet boys, that dominating motif of my own youth.

At least pregnancy is one contingency I don't have to worry about. Is the opposite sex part of what she wants to get away from? Is this part of my worry? I slap the unworthy thought down. At her age, I was still an awkward child. At her age, my grandmother had her first baby.

What about your education?

What about it? It's got to be more educational than school.

I thought you wanted to be a cellist. You can hardly take a cello to Greenham. They're always being evicted. A cello wouldn't be very practical, it would be the first thing somebody would step on.

I'll take my viola, then I can practise. There's sure to be a lot of time for that. Anyway, what does all that matter compared to getting nuked?

Tony takes it in his stride and goes off to Africa. He is co-writing a book on the Lake Turkana hominids, and is due to confer with his co-author – the scientist whose name will feature on the book's cover. These days, we each have a convenient preoccupation behind which we can retreat, which takes up our time, which is unarguably virtuous. His is his work: mine is the peace movement. Not that Tony isn't concerned with that, but it is only one part of his life. Someone has to earn a living, don't they? But my life *is* the peace movement. What with organising, collecting, demonstrating, consciousness-raising, it is all I can do to keep the household running. My every spare moment is accounted for. As I so often remark, I don't even have time to think these days. What would I do with it, if suddenly some should come my way?

I notify the school. I make sure that further education is not precluded. Susanna stamps with impatience. She can't wait to go.

We all set off on a Saturday morning. It's like taking her off to boarding-school or university. We pack the car with a rucksack full of sweaters and waterproofs, and a tent and groundsheet and sleeping-bag and radio, and the viola, and I press home-made goodies into a corner in a way that reminds me, as things so often remind me these days, of my own mother. In the trailer is a pile of wooden pallets, always in demand at Greenham, protections against the mud now that winter is coming on. In we get: Rose and Susie and me at the wheel. It is a beautiful day, sunny and blue and crisp. Susanna doesn't seem the slightest bit nervous. I am terrified. As we approach Newbury, I can feel my stomach clench.

We arrive at the Common. It's a bitty, scrubby place, tussocky grass, small trees. In the middle looms a high wire fence topped with barbs and razors, behind which squat the humps of the missile silos. On this shining morning there's a surreal beauty about the place. But it's very muddy, even now. Sometimes, when we've been here, the mud has been deeper than our wellington boots.

Some women are sitting around a smouldering fire by a large structure of plastic draped over branches. We approach. They look mildly interested. Susanna explains her plan. They advise us to go to Orange Gate, where the women will be glad of another recruit. The gates have been named for the colours of the rainbow: part of the symbolism of life with which the women are trying to face down the engines of death. The Greenham camp is about symbolism – what else can it be about? It's about opposing force with something that is not force. But, deeply though I'm against the force, I'm not in sympathy with the symbolism. All that mystical feminism, webs and witches and exorcisms – I don't like it. It makes me uncomfortable. I hope Susanna won't turn into a web-making witch.

We unload the car. We set up Susanna's tent, although the women advise that it may be removed in one of the evictions which frequently occur. Many of them live in benders made with plastic sheeting and branches. Susanna, knowing this, has also brought some plastic, just in case. She moves over to the group of women around the fire. She looks edgy. I can guess how she is feeling: looking for someone to whom she can relate. The highest ideals don't change the basics of human relations. They seem friendly enough: an older woman with a Welsh accent, four or five in their twenties or early thirties, one or two very butch with cropped heads, a few layered hippies. They look tired, but not unwelcoming. Nevertheless,

I feel constrained and defensive with them: their gesture, their defiance, is also a comment on the rest of us, however little they intend it as such.

Rose and I stay for a while, but we feel awkward. It's clear that Susie can't really find herself until we leave.

I do think she's brave, says Rose as we start the car. Don't you think she's brave?

I do. I think she's very brave. Life at Greenham is not easy. Quite apart from the usual hardships of living rough, they face constant harassment from the base, from the council, from outraged citizens. But I'm sure she'll be able to withstand all that. If others can, why not Susie? And presumably she has also considered, what I should find more difficult than anything, the question of living communally. The constant committees, the incessant democracy. How will she bear it? I couldn't. That is the thing I principally couldn't bear.

Well, either she will bear it or she won't. Either she'll stay, or she won't. What I'm more afraid of, as we drive towards London and Rose chatters on about school, is that she'll grow away from me. That this is a parting of the ways. That the bit of her life to do with me has ended, and now she's moving on – to Zigi's bit. I'm jealous. What has he ever done for her? What does he care? He's got her anyway.

That winter of 1984–5 was particularly long and hard. Snow fell and fell. Temperatures plummeted at night to unheard-of depths. I lay awake, imagining I could hear the frost crack, worrying about Susanna. I bought her one of those improbable silver sleeping-bags which were one of NASA's by-products, supposed to repel all cold. Moon-booted, anoraked, she looked like Michelin Woman. She seemed to be enjoying herself a lot. She regaled us with tales of climbing the wire, wriggling under the wire, cutting the wire. She danced on the silos to welcome in the New Year. She helped lure a sentry at one of the gates out of his box, which the women then took over, gleefully answering his phone whenever it rang: Women's Peace Camp. – Gee, said the phone, I didn't know you-all had a phone out there.

Another time, after she climbed a petrol-pump, a soldier

stamped on her fingers as she was getting down, then kicked her in the head. The military hated the women. They weren't just embarrassing, they were actively obstructive. Sitting across the gates, weaving their woolly webs, refusing to move, they prevented construction workers from getting in and made the military feel insecure. A politician suggested that a very high brick wall be built, to deprive the women of the pleasures of playing with the wire, along which (when they weren't cutting it) they strung their webs, to which we all, on our visits, attached our children's teddy-bears, photos, baby clothes. But the idea was rejected: the idea, he was loftily told, is not to make the place feel even more like a concentration camp than it does already.

Lying one night in her tent, a loud voice outside said: If I had my way, I'd torch the whole goddam bunch!

The bailiffs confiscated their tents and cut off their water. They were summonsed for breach of the peace. Susanna spent ten days in prison. She refused to work (the prisoners were making plastic toys with little guns), and insisted on explaining at length why not. She was not asked to work again. – I love it, she said. And soon it'll be spring. You should come, Mum. For once, we can really act out our ideals.

I couldn't of course. There was Rose. Women's work: keeping the family going. But more than that, as Susanna probably guessed, I didn't want to. Susanna has an edge of toughness, of principle, that I lack. I support, but in the last analysis I don't act. I donate sleeping-bags, but don't stay to use them. I civilly disobey, but find I have to leave just before the police get really rough. Was this what worried me – that she would find this out, that I would be shown up? She was very charitable. She accepted my excuses. She didn't comment. She just stayed out there at Greenham.

My friendship with Bella is not the only long-standing relationship soured by the political climate, so polarised and poisoned by enthusiasm (in the religio-fanatical sense of the word). My family, too, is split down the middle. There are Zigi, Fania and us – and then there are the rest. Half my aunts, uncles and cousins won't speak to me any more. I found out by chance that the daughter of one of my cousins had got married and had a baby without my being informed of either event, something that would have been unthinkable a few years ago. We met at a barmitzvah which was taking place on neutral ground, and she showed me her new daughter. Her mother, my cousin Evelyn, who has never much liked me, came up to us and said: Was that Susanna we saw on television last week?

I agreed that it probably was. There are often television crews down at Greenham.

She's finished her education then, has she? said Evelyn.

I explained about the viola practice, though with the weather there's been this winter, I don't see how she can have taken her gloves off long enough to do very much of it.

People like Susanna, said Evelyn tightly, should realise what they're doing when they act like this. I suppose you wouldn't know about our efforts to get refuseniks out of Russia? Perhaps you've read about it in the paper. Every week, we hold a vigil outside the Russian embassy. But they're your friends, of course, you wouldn't worry about things like that. Perhaps you didn't know that we still have quite a lot of relatives inside Russia? They rely on us to keep up the pressure. Who knows what's happening to them? And then people like Zigi and Susanna come along and pretend that only our side can do anything wrong. You make me sick! And watched by her mortified daughter, she turned on her heel and left us.

That's what it's like these days. No more fudging the issue with stupid old tolerance. Armageddon looms, and you have to know which side you're on.

V

Susanna spent just under a year at Greenham. She would have stayed longer, but she got ill and had to go to hospital. It was a silly thing, her illness: having survived that frigid winter, she

240

caught pneumonia in September. Got soaked through in a thunderstorm, didn't get properly dry, developed bronchitis, which turned to pneumonia, and suddenly there was a phonecall from the hospital at Newbury. When she got better she came home to convalesce. She was very thin and tired, and the doctors had forbidden her to go back until she was quite better.

It's strange having her in the house again. Rose is overjoyed. They spend a lot of time together. As I feared, however, between Susie and myself things are not easy. There's always a constraint. It's probably my fault. I feel I have been tested and found wanting, and I resent feeling like that. I sit down to the work on hand – a piece on some singer I've interviewed, a chapter of my latest book – and I feel that the world doesn't need it. It's trivial, irrelevant. I resent that, as well.

Slowly, Susanna gets better. She begins to put a little weight back on. The question arises: what is she to do now? Tony and I hope she won't go back to Greenham – not now that winter's on its way again – but we don't feel we can pressure her. It isn't as though things have got any less edgy on the nuclear front. But no, she feels she's done that. She'd like to take up her music again, but she's very out of practice. Slowly, painfully, she starts up, arranges to see her old teachers. Her instruments are at home, so that's where she does her practising. Otherwise, she is out.

Where is she? says Tony. He is home a lot just now, rewriting a manuscript. He, too, is edgy. It's some while since we've spent so much time together. Like Susanna, we are out of practice. And anyway this is a new situation for us. All our years together have been spent, so to speak, over the heads of the children. They have been the basis for our marriage. We have never known each other as adults, only as parents, quite a different matter. Now even Rose is growing up, and here we are, alone together, for the first time in – how many years?

Seventeen. Seventeen years. Last year, Tony's mother died. At the funeral, I realised that I at last feel connected to his family. Time and familiarity have done their work. Which is ironic, because Tony and I are moving further apart. We sit after dinner, and we have little to say to each other now that there is time for some conversation.

Across the room sits a tall, open-faced man, thinning slightly on top. Still good-looking; thickening around the waist, but what's wrong with a little self-indulgence? He hasn't changed very much. Nor, I believe, have I. But I don't feel easy with him these days. I no longer feel that my concerns, now that I have concerns other than the children, are automatically of interest to him. I am opaque to him, and he to me. We have become each other's furniture. Chairs don't have feelings. What does he do, what does he think, all the time I don't see him? Where is he engaged? Not with me. We are sustained by habit. Will that be enough to hold us together, once the girls have gone?

I snap, because I, too, am worried; I, too, find it hard (even after the year at Greenham) to let go. – How should I know? She's eighteen. She doesn't have to ask permission to go out.

Somewhat to my surprise, I find that she is spending a lot of time with Zigi and Fania. Or rather: with Zigi. It's turned out just as Joan Brockenhurst told me it would, all those years ago. Now that she's grown up, he's become interested in her. He is deluged with anti-nuclear correspondence, and he has asked Susanna if she will give him some secretarial help. She is laboriously teaching herself to touch-type. She goes there most afternoons.

Guess who I saw coming out of Zigi and Fan's? she says one day.

No idea.

That man who's married to your old school friend. The one who rants on the box. Michael Overy.

Michael Overy? Coming out of Zigi's? Are you sure?

We passed each other. I was on my way in, he was on his way out. I'm absolutely sure.

What was he doing there?

Zigi wasn't saying. He sort of shrugged and said, Business. He looked like thunder, though.

Tony and I spend some time trying to puzzle this one out. Michael Overy and Zigi hate each other. They regard each other as irredeemable scum. So what are they doing having cosy chats? Is Michael gathering background for a new novel? Is he a secret convert? Is he a latterday Deep Throat, covertly letting our side in on his side's manoeuvres? Sitting at my desk, plotting a novel, I find myself considering this episode in detective-story mode. The trick with genre fiction – detective stories, spy stories – is not so much deception as misdirection. The clues are there all along: they just aren't recognised. The context is unexpected, they seem unimportant, they point in the other direction . . .

It's common knowledge that Michael is, or was, employed by MI6. The phrase generally used is that he has 'strong connections with the intelligence services'. Is his 'real' life, whatever that may comprise, so far removed from the one he describes in those novels of his? If a Zigi were to meet a Michael in a Michael Overy novel, Zigi would be as likely a double agent as Michael. He's got all the qualifications, including improbability (he, after all, is the man of integrity, while the thought of an honest spook – an honest *politician* spook at that – is merely laughable). In which case Michael might be his control, his point of contact with the other side.

A ridiculous notion. I dismiss it from my mind. But these are ridiculous days.

The episode remains mysterious. Zigi won't talk about it. What's one more mystery among so many?

Susanna and Zigi have evolved a routine. They work for two or three hours, dealing with letters and telephone calls, drafting articles, working out itineraries. And when their work is finished, they like to play music together, cello and piano. Zigi was always a good pianist – like so many mathematicians, like Dr T., he could as easily have been a professional musician. With his encouragement, Susanna is recovering her enthusiasm for the cello. She has a place at the Royal Academy, and she'll probably take it up.

And what else? What else is he telling her? – Susanna, my dear, there is something I have to tell you. Your mother and I –

No; I can't believe he'll really do it. Easier to leave things as they are, play the benign grandfather. Pleasure without responsibility. She hints that he is thinking about his memoirs. Did they ever reach some more material state? I suppose I shall never know: Fania will have burned those first of all.

Ever since that first conversation, Fania has never asked me about Susanna's father. She simply got on with being a grandmother. But the older Susanna gets, the more like Zigi she becomes. Not just in appearance – the hair, the eyes, the set of the head – but in style, in gesture; a sardonic turn of phrase, a hurried little laugh. I've noticed that, as the years have passed, Fania's preference for Rose has become more marked. Perhaps it's unconscious, but it's a fact. Rose is her favourite. They go to exhibitions together. They're both more visual than musical. Rose plans to be an architect. Sometimes, Fania takes her to the theatre – a special treat for them both. Rose enjoys the company of the strange, glamorous figure that Fania still cuts. A theatrical setting suits her. She is exaggerated; she and Zigi are both exaggerated. I imagine that's what drew them together in the first place. The first time either of them had met a member of the opposite sex they didn't instantly drown out.

Fania's aged into a tough, sinewy old bird, the kind of fowl her sister, my grandmother, used to boil all day for soup. But she still paints away up there in her studio, puts on her big hat and her high boots and steps out with her friends to exhibitions, films, theatres. The friends, more often than not, are Zigi's Hungarian cronies. They always liked her style. When I was up in the flat and Zigi was out, they would call round and – who knows? I never thought about it at the time, always too wrapped up in myself. It was only later that I remembered the old family gossip. I assume now that they were her lovers. They have remained friends. I hope I have as many good friends, at her age.

Perhaps I should start to collect a few lovers, before it's too late? There's always Derry, of course. He publishes my detective stories these days. We meet from time to time over a boozy lunch or dinner. We had a phase of going to bed – it couldn't really be called an affair: more a pleasant way to end the evening. I enjoyed the protective warmth of Derry's furry chest and long arms. It was really a question of finishing off what we'd begun all those years ago in the school hall at Slough. Neither of us likes unanswered questions. He's not married at the moment, though he has been. There's always some lady in the background or the foreground. Perhaps I shall end up with Derry. He and I have more to say to each other than Tony and I seem to these days. Like Fania and her friends. They're more use to her than Zigi is. She was always a culture-vulture, and Zigi was always an unreliable escort. He always had – always has – something more important to do. Then, he was in the lab, or politicking; now, he is in the train en route to another meeting, another rally.

Zigi and Dr T. From being little boys together in an obscure Central European classroom they have become distinguished old men, on opposite sides of the world, glaring at each other across the political fence. But they are still more alike than not. Each of them thinks, as all the Martians thought, that it is his right, his duty, his fate, to shape the future of the world. And each of them is still possessed by the bomb, the irresistible power to which they sold their souls forty, fifty years ago. Look inside their hearts and you will find a mushroom cloud. One is promoting it, the other opposing it. One has to see it succeed in order that civilisation may be saved; the other has to see it fail for the same reason. But neither of them ever really thinks of anything else.

CHAPTER 11　POTLATCH

I

ALL THIS TIME, I have been aware that there is something I have to do. Something I am shirking. Something which fills me with curiosity but from which I shy away. I have been putting it off, but it can't be postponed indefinitely.

I have to get in touch with Marianne.

I have her address and telephone number. Bettina gave them to me. I assume she'll have told Marianne about my visit. They keep in touch, and Bettina must have mentioned it. She'll probably be wondering why I haven't contacted her. There is no good reason. Simply, I have been trying to get used to the fact of her existence – this woman whom I have never met, and with whom I am so closely connected.

I open my address book. I noted her under M. Marianne Kustow Weinsfeld. Zigi has been obliterated, which is only fair. Was she – is she – aware of his existence? Of the fact that he is her father? There's only one way to find out.

She lives in Maryland. Works in Washington, Bettina told me: she's a lawyer, the universal profession of the District of Columbia. I have two numbers for her, one at work, the other at home. She won't welcome a call at work, but the time difference means that it's only really convenient to call Americans at home first thing in the morning. Which she might welcome even less. This isn't necessarily the kind of call you want to receive over the cereal, or just as you're about to drive off to an urgent appointment.

After all these years of journalism, you'd think I'd be over this kind of nervousness, but it's always the same. Qualms and calculations. I hate making the first phonecall to someone unknown, even when there are no emotional overtones. Of course, I could write. But that would merely be to postpone the moment, and, now that I have nerved myself up, more waiting would be unbearable.

Press the buttons. In an office building three thousand miles away, the phone rings. A bored voice recites: Weinsfeld, Weinsfeld and Schlumberger.

May I speak to Mrs Marianne Weinsfeld, please?

May I ask who this is speaking, please?

My name is Miriam Oliver.

Is she expecting your call?

No, I don't think so.

There is a pause while Mrs Weinsfeld decides whether she is available. A receiver is picked up. – Hello, says a brusque voice. In a hurry, in the middle of important business. This is Marianne Weinsfeld. Who is this, please?

Quickly into my opening spiel. The words tumble over each other, so anxious am I to get them out before she puts the phone down. –Mrs Weinsfeld, I don't know if your mother mentioned me. My name is Miriam Oliver. I'm working on a biography of my uncle. Zsygmond von Fischer. I went to see your mother in San Diego. She gave me your number.

A pause. – Yes, I believe my mother did mention something about this. She's cool, impersonal.

I'd very much like to see you. To talk with you. I wondered if we might fix a meeting?

You're English, aren't you? Are you in England now?

Yes.

You mean you want to come all the way over here just to see me? I really don't think there's anything I could tell you that would be worth a visit. There is a note of finality. She is about to put the receiver down.

No, I say hastily. I'd really like to.

This is something I have given some thought to. The sensible, economical thing would be to do the whole thing by phone. To fix a time when I could speak to her at leisure. But it won't be the same. I've done enough interviews to know that.

Face to face, opportunities arise that can be noticed, acted upon. And then, as always with this book, there is my own personal agenda. I was, in a sense, Zigi's adopted daughter; my own daughter is this woman's half-sister. Now that I know she exists, I have to meet her, see her, speak with her face to face. Now that I hear her voice, now that she is no longer a mere possibility, this need has become urgent.

All right, she says. When did you have in mind? I must warn you, I'm extremely busy.

I look at the blank pages of my diary. – I'm pretty flexible. When would suit you? Perhaps some weekend? I could come to your home, maybe?

I hear the sound of pages turning on a far-off desk. – Well, she says doubtfully. I suppose so. I could see you – how about the week after next? Saturday tenth? I could spare you a couple of hours in the morning. If you're sure you really want to.

I note down the directions to where she lives and give her my number. I'm in the middle of booking a plane ticket when Rose wanders in. Her architecture course is finished. Now she is looking for a job, and living in the flat meanwhile. Rose is small and dark, like me, and easygoing. Susanna makes me feel defensive and vaguely guilty. But life with Rose is devoid of dark undertones.

Going to Washington? she says, when I put the phone down. What for?

Work. Someone I've got to see, I explain evasively. Rose, like everyone except Derry, sides with Tony in this controversy. She disapproves of exhuming people's lives against their will. Also she feels protective towards Fania, her old ally.

Who is it? Anyone I'd know?

Weinsfeld, I say. Mean anything to you? It sort of rings a bell, but I can't just pin it down.

We wander down to the kitchen to make a cup of coffee while we think. I love having Rose around. I know she'll move out when she finds a job, but that's easier said than done these days, and she can't afford rent or mortgage on the odd bits and pieces of work she's getting at the moment. Meanwhile, her loss is my gain. Quite apart from the pleasure of her company,

Tony and I will be definitively on our own when she goes. Susanna's moved out. She's got a boyfriend, a recording engineer, a charming young man. They've bought a little house in Chiswick, near where he works, and well away from the family.

Yes, everyone's leaving. I think Tony's got someone else as well. It's a feeling I've had for some time. I know his work involves a certain amount of travel, but surely not as much as he's been doing recently? I've never kept tabs on him. If he doesn't want to tell me, I don't want to know. That's the way we've always run our lives. Perhaps I feel he's entitled to a few secrets of his own – it corrects the balance. But I've caught sight of him on one or two occasions recently when he was supposed to be out of the country, or at least out of town.

I was surprised by the jolt those glimpses gave me. Tony's never affected me in that way before. I don't associate him with that kind of thumping emotion. That's Zigi's department, Bella's, even. Tony has always been like a river, a dependable flow of calm reassurance. And love: I always took that for granted. But of course there comes a point beyond which love may not be taken for granted any more. I had recognised that, or so I thought. But I see now that I hadn't taken it in, not really, not with all its implications. It took someone else to do that for me.

Someone else. As I spoon the coffee into the cafetière, my mind probes around this novel and unwelcome development. How can he have someone else? How can there be anybody else but me? What's she like, what does she do, where do they meet? Is she married, attached, on the prowl? I have to know these things.

But how can I find out? (And what will I do then?)

I could ask Tony, I suppose. No doubt he'd tell me. He might even welcome the opportunity. But I don't really want to. As Fania always insisted, what isn't said may be ignored. Once it's out in the open, there on the table, a subject for debate and discussion, it acquires solidity and momentum. Before you knew it, we'd be talking about what should happen next, shall he stay or shall he go, arrangements . . . So I say nothing, and here he still is. For the moment. On the other side of the bed, passing the marmalade at breakfast. Suddenly these things acquire a value I didn't know they had. They are the fabric of my life. They are precious to me, and so is Tony. Yes: it's that scenario Zigi predicted all those years ago, the one he held in such scorn. Domestic happiness. What he never achieved. What I realise – now that it is threatened – I want, more than anything else, to hang on to.

I can't really bring myself to say it – I've never been able to – out loud, I still can't: when would be the moment? I thought he must have realised. But perhaps not. And perhaps now he's tired of waiting. It's been obscured behind the silences and distances that have grown up around us. Nevertheless, I love him. It began as affection, but it long ago became something more than that. It's like the way you regard an arm or a leg. He is part of me. Why is it only now that I see it must be expressed more directly? The further apart we move, the more I realise that I shall be lost without him; without *us*. Could I face joining Bettina, Fania, Joan, in the legion of lone women? I don't know whether I would survive it. Being me – just me – is not what I want. The closer it seems to loom, the more certainly I know this. The threat of separation, whether or not imaginary, has concentrated my mind.

Maybe I'm just indulging a claim to emotional property: you can't have him, he's mine, he's always been mine, he belongs to me. But I don't think so. Simply, after all these years, our balance of dependence has tipped the other way. There was a saying in the old Yiddish theatre: When he wants to, she doesn't. When she wants to, he doesn't. When they both want to, the curtain comes down. We have arrived at stage two. It's taken long enough, God knows. At this rate, we shall be in our dotage by the time we arrive at stage three. If we ever get there.

I watch the post for suspicious letters. I walk in un-expectedly on phone conversations. Nothing. He's never left his correspondence lying about: the only difference, to my over-watchful eye, is that now he leaves even less of it than before. As for the phone, I'm out often enough: why would he talk to her when I was home? He's away from time to time, nights, weeks, weekends, but then he always was. There's always some good reason. I throw out one or two tentative questions: the responses tell me nothing. I don't really have anything to go on, just those glimpses and a sense that something has changed. My only certainty is the certainty of long intimacy. I know. I just know.

I sense that I am becoming plaintive. I try sternly to control this. Nothing is less attractive than self-pity. Why actively repel?

What is to be done? I don't know. For the moment, nothing.

When Rose goes, will that be the moment? Will he leave then? Will that be the end of our story?

If I publish this book, he will certainly leave.

So should I abandon it?

Out of the question. It's too late now. It would still hang there between us. I can't leave it half-finished. Zigi or Tony – the old conflict. *La lotta continua.*

It's a beautiful day in late September. Rose and I open the kitchen door and take our coffee out into the sun. When the phase of swings, slides and grazed knees was finally over we gave up the struggle to grow grass in our small, grimy London garden. It's brick-paved now, with tubs and raised beds round the edges. Rose and I sit on the old bench, coffee-cups set on the seat between us. We have the kind of relationship I never had a chance to establish with my mother: two adults, easy friends. How will she react to the story I have to tell? Will it spoil our friendship?

I am recalled to reality by Rose's voice.

Weinsfeld, she says. Wait a minute. Wasn't one of Reagan's people called that? Does that mean anything to you?

Weinsfeld. That's it, of course. He was one of those hawks around the Pentagon. A member of the Committee on the Present Danger, a *Commentary* neo-conservative. Not just a hawk, a hawk's hawk.

Zigi's daughter, Abe Kustow's adopted daughter, married to Dick Weinsfeld? That seems hard to believe.

Is that who you're going to see? Dick Weinsfeld?

No, no. It's a Mrs Weinsfeld. She could be married to him, I suppose.

I've often wondered what they could be like, those people, says Rose.

II

Well, I'm about to find out. I phoned Marianne's Washington office again, and they confirmed that Mr Weinsfeld, the senior partner, certainly was the Mr Dick Weinsfeld who had been Assistant Secretary of Defense during the Reagan administration. I call up my friend in the BBC. I'm trying to get some background on Dick Weinsfeld, I tell her. Going to see him in a couple of weeks. Can she borrow the cuttings file from the library? And could I come over to her office to look at it?

Reading the old news stories I am transported back to those mad days – or rather, those non-MAD days, when the old assumption of Mutual Assured Destruction which had hitherto governed nuclear questions was abandoned for the notion of nuclear war-fighting; of survivability. We were no longer staring into the black pit of the inconceivable. What had until now been unthinkable was the basis of policy. And Weinsfeld was one of the architects of this policy.

His line – the strategists' line – was disdain: the disdain of the professional for the amateur, the rationalist for the sentimentalist. – It is certainly a more popular argument, Weinsfeld remarked in an interview, to say there's no way you can win a nuclear war, that it is too horrible to think about. That appeals to human emotions, and really precludes serious and rational thinking about it.

What a madman! What a lunatic! Zigi's son-in-law, yet. His face looks up at me from a pile of news-clippings. Rather good-looking, in a way: thick dark hair, dark eyes under bushy eyebrows, a cheerful-looking fellow. A trifle thickset, even then. No doubt the hair, these days, is not so dark, not so thick; no doubt the waistband has expanded. And here we still are, no thanks to him. For him, coexistence was not an option. The destruction of the Soviet Union was a prize worth a mere twenty million American dead. That was the professional view. The title of an article in *Foreign Policy* magazine said it all: 'Victory is Possible.' When the Wall came down, when the Iron Curtain dissolved, Weinsfeld's reaction was simple. – We won, he cried. We won! He was quoted to this effect in the *New York Times*. Weinsfeld. Who would have believed it?

The house is quite a way outside Washington. Perhaps they have an apartment in town. They can't commute this distance every day, not if they want to stay sane and awake. It's way out near Frederick, in rolling countryside, with a view to the Blue Ridge on the horizon. I arrived yesterday. Tonight I'm booked back to London. What is there to keep me? (And anyway, I keep thinking that perhaps Tony is taking the opportunity to entertain his friend in the marital home. A shoddy thought, but it won't be dismissed.)

All week, I was waiting to hear her voice on the phone. Expecting it, almost. – Sorry, I'll have to cancel. Too busy. I know she doesn't want to see me, she just couldn't think how to put me off at that moment. I took her by surprise. But no, the call didn't come. I should have called her, to confirm, but I didn't, just in case she discovered a sudden urgent appointment, stretching into the foreseeable future. So here I am.

In early October, Maryland is still warm. A pleasant English summer's day. My rented car purrs along leafy back roads, old clapboard towns surrounded by new tract housing. I stop to look at the map. Maple Lane. Should be the next on the left. And it is! I have no sense of direction. Successful arrival never fails to surprise me.

The Weinsfeld house is a substantial affair. Clapboard, with a big pillared deck in front, set in a large, wooded lot. All immaculately mowed and painted. There's certainly money here.

I park the car on a gravel sweep in front of the house, alongside three others. Company. She doesn't want to face me alone, maybe? I climb the steps to the deck, which is scattered with garden furniture. I knock on the door. I hear voices, from somewhere the other side of the house, but evidently nobody hears me. I try the door. Locked, of course. People in these parts do not invite casual callers. I walk round the deck to the other side of the house. It's on a hill: by the time I reach the back, there's an extra storey beneath me. Here's another door, and people inside the room. I knock. They look up.

I have arrived at what is evidently the family room. It stretches along the width of the house, the kitchen part to my right, eating and sitting to my left. There has been a considerable amount of remodelling going on within this old frame. Two big windows look out towards the Blue Ridge. A man and woman in their fifties are sitting round a table with a young woman and two little boys. The man is Dick Weinsfeld, who looks more like his old photos than I had expected. The older woman is presumably Marianne. She rises to open the door. She does not look welcoming. – Yes? She sounds testy. Perhaps she forgot I was coming. Perhaps she didn't want to remember.

Mrs Weinsfeld? It's Miriam Oliver. I rang you from London. We made an appointment to come and see you here.

Oh, yeah. The woman that's writing the book about Zsygmond von Fischer, right? Well, you're sure lucky to find me here. We were just going to leave.

But you said ten-thirty.

I assumed you'd call to confirm, I guess. She says this accusingly, as though I was in the wrong, not her. She reminds me irresistibly of Zigi – and of Susanna. This is one of their tricks. Looking at you indignantly from their full height when you catch them out in some low manoeuvre. Like Zigi, like Susie, Marianne is tall, though her hair, unlike theirs, is dark. She wears it swept severely back into a knot at the nape of her neck. She has her mother's lively dark eyes. An eyebrow lifts in annoyance. She knew perfectly well I was coming, but had hoped to make her escape before I arrived. A certain lawyerly punctiliousness made her delay her departure until the specified hour had passed, and now she's regretting it. How fortunate that I did not, as is my wont, get hopelessly lost on the way. I can picture the scene. The arrival at the deserted house. The puzzlement. The disbelief. The fury. The unproductive phonecalls. The long wait. What would I have done? Postponed my flight, I suppose. Cancellation charges. Another night in a hotel. A full schedule into which I could not be fitted. It's as well I didn't call to confirm. I can see that I could not have been fitted into today's schedule, either. – Well, she says. Now you're here, I guess you guys'll have to go on without me.

Everyone gets up from the table. Weinsfeld says: Okay, we'll say you'll be along later. So long, Mrs Oliver. Nice to meet you.

I nod. Is it nice to meet him? Not the word I would choose. It isn't that he is unpleasant. On the contrary: he seems charming, open, perfectly civil. It's simply that for the eight years of the Reagan administration I, and millions like me, found it hard to think of Dick Weinsfeld as a human being, a fellow member of our species. We were all, it seemed, to be sacrificed in the cause of his personal hangups. I read a profile of him once which recounted how his parents had fled from some Baltic state when he was an infant, so that his attitude to Soviet Russia was one of bitter personal grievance. Why do we for a moment imagine that politics is in any way rational or objective? Weinsfeld was, is, no isolated exception. The most successful politicians – the most ruthless, the least easily deflected – are those with some wrong to avenge, some hatred to fulfil, some psychopathology to play out. Dr T.'s grandmother with her Russian bogeymen is responsible for more than she realised. And look at Zigi. The same story; merely, chance landed him on the opposite side. What propelled him? Ideals? You must be joking. Thwarted fury, the determination to reassert control over his life and events, to reclaim power. That's more like it.

Now, of course, Weinsfeld can congratulate himself that he has won. A simple view, but that is how he sees it. The Baltic states are free. The USSR is no more. The Cold War is over. The central question is no longer whether the world will get nuked in the name of our best interests or his personal history.

Different madmen control the headlines. Has he therefore resumed – assumed? – human status? This is a question which, fortunately, I do not have to answer. He, the young woman and the little boys – a daughter and grandchildren, it looks like – noisily leave the room. I hear a car start up and drive away. I was only just in time.

Lucky I caught you.

Sure. At least there is to be no stand-off: she accepts defeat gracefully. – Coffee? Or would you like something stronger?

We sit at the table, which is cluttered with cups and plates. – I hope I'm not keeping you from anything important.

It's just a barbecue. At this time of year, you don't know how many more there'll be.

She lights a cigarette, and looks at me over the top of it. It's the only thing I've ever envied smokers: that instant screen they can create. I hide behind my coffee. We study each other.

Zsygmond von Fischer, she says. Not someone I care to think about a whole lot.

I've rather gathered that.

So what got you so interested in him? Did you say you were his niece? I didn't know he had family.

His second wife is my aunt.

She puffs some more, considering this. I drink my coffee.

Okay, she says. You came here to ask. So ask. I don't know quite what I can tell you.

You knew he was your father?

Sure. That was no secret. My parents – that is, Abe and my Mom – they didn't believe in family secrets.

Did they talk about him much?

Not a lot. But occasionally his name would come up. He was active politically, and they approved of what he was doing. Abe always used to say: You don't have to like a man to share his politics.

He didn't like him, then?

Hardly knew him. But he didn't behave very admirably towards his wife and child, as you no doubt know. I guess that coloured Abe's opinions. Zsygmond von Fischer was not a frequent topic of conversation in our home.

Weren't you ever curious to meet him?

Not really.

Your stepfather's dead now?

Who, Abe? Yep. A few years ago. He and Mom just moved down to California. To be near my brother. He's at the University of Southern California. Abe wasn't well, and Mom couldn't cope by herself in New York. So Karl – he's my half-brother, actually – he found them this place. You've seen it, I guess. But Abe didn't last very long there. He was a New Yorker – what was he doing in some joint full of wannabee stiffs in southern California?

Why did they go there, then?

Oh – I don't know. She looks annoyed. How have we got sidetracked on to the evidently vexed question of what to do with aged parents? – People get old. They let themselves be persuaded.

I don't wish to open this can of worms. I have enough worms of my own to contend with. – Zigi never contacted you, is that right?

Nope. Not a word. And not a cent, which I guess is more to the point.

Were you hard up?

She laughs. – No, I guess not. I can't say we were. Haven't you heard of Abe? Abe Kustow. The great liberal lawyer. If he liked you and liked your case, he'd represent you for what you could afford. If you could afford plenty, that's just what he charged.

I say: Wasn't your husband one of Reagan's people?

Sure was. We both were. She stubs out her cigarette impatiently. – Okay, go on, say it. How could a nice girl raised like I was end up working for Reagan? Do you know what my brother's called? Karl. Karl Frederick Kustow. There were no two ways about the way we were raised.

And is he a conservative now too?

No, as a matter of fact he isn't. The only remaining liberal in southern California. She laughs. Our Mom's pride and joy. She and I don't get along too well, but then we don't need to, we don't see a whole lot of each other. More coffee?

No thanks.

She lights another cigarette, and says defiantly: I don't smoke at the office, so I guess I make up at weekends.

Doesn't worry me. Why is she so defensive? Annoyance at having been caught out, probably. I don't expect she much enjoys opening the family closet to poke around the skeletons. Of which Zigi is one she had hoped to erase altogether: a quite supernumerary embarrassment, given her present political orientation. *That* shouldn't have surprised me: this particular evolution was the commonplace of the Seventies and Eighties. Old liberals, faithful Democrats, blamed for Vietnam by the campus radicals, moved in self-justification towards belligerent nationalism. They were practised polemicists: they laid their ventriloquial skills at the service of the Presidential dummy. They directed their fury, their feelings of betrayal, against those Reds by association, the proponents of détente. A similar group clustered around Margaret Thatcher. It was always the one-time left who ended up furthest right. Who is more contemptible than the current adherent of a line painfully and laboriously left behind? Who more blind than one who has not yet seen the light?

Tell me about your life in New York. Did your mother ever talk about Zigi? About their life in Europe?

Zigi? Is that what you call him? She looks at her watch, but I am not to be put off. I nod and lean forward, counteractive body language. As far as I am concerned, our meeting has only just begun.

No, she never did. She talked about Budapest, of course, about what life was like there. Not that often, but when we asked her. She didn't like talking about it much. It depressed her. There were so many people dead, so much lost. She preferred to draw a line. Her life was in New York with us. It was a pretty good life, so why look back? We had this big apartment on Central Park West, always full of people. There were a lot of us, for starters. Abe and Bettina, me and Karl, and then we had two stepbrothers, Abe's two kids by his first wife, David and Irving. His first wife died, I never knew just how. I believe she was a dancer, she wasn't very strong, she found coping with kids difficult. I guess she just checked out. And then there were always other people around. People knew they could come and talk to Abe and he'd do his best for them and they'd meet other people who agreed with them. Yeah, it was a good life. Why should my mother want to think about Zsygmond von Fischer? He did his worst and she survived. I guess she just wanted to put him out of her mind.

She seemed happy to talk about him when I met her.

She shrugs. – Things change. You get old, you're happy to have company while you do your remembering.

But you knew about him.

Oh, sure. I always knew he was my father, and that he'd walked out when I was a baby, and that he was a great scientist but not a nice man. So I guess that's what Mom told me. I just don't recall any one particular occasion when she said all that, okay? These were things I just knew. It didn't affect my life any. Abe was my real daddy for as far back as I can remember. He was just a lovely man.

But you didn't agree with his politics.

Times change.

Didn't you ever feel any curiosity about Zigi? Didn't you ever want to meet him, just to know what he was like?

I guess I resented him too much. How would you describe him? Would you say he was a nice fellow? She sounds aggressive now. For her, I suppose, I am Zigi's representative.

No. The most charming man I ever met, but not nice.

You liked him, though.

Oh, I loved him. When I was young he was a kind of magic figure. And then when I got older – we were too connected to be detached.

In what way, exactly?

When my parents died I went to live with him and my Aunt Fania, I reply with perfect truth. I was nineteen. They were good to me, they helped me through. And he had a lot of glamour. Knew everybody, was very brilliant, very handsome. When you're that age, those things count disproportionately. You'd probably have felt the same.

I doubt it. She clearly thinks little of my discriminatory

powers. Maybe she's right, at that. She says: Why should we think about him? He never thought about us, right? He never mentioned us? Bettina said that the first you knew of her was when you went to Budapest.

Yes, that's right.

I guess that was some shock.

Yes, it was. I can't resist teasing her with the truth. – You're very like him in some ways.

She looks up: I've got her on the raw. – Should I thank you?

Thank him, I should say.

For the first time the atmosphere lightens. She laughs, briefly. Looks at her watch again. Here I am. What more can I ask? Yet I feel this can't be all. Somewhere, there's something that hasn't been said. And she's not going to help me say it. If we stop now, as she is clearly preparing to do, I shall have lost my chance. To keep things going, for something to say, I blurt out: So you never met him? Never felt you wanted to see him?

Oh, sure, she says. I saw him. We spoke.

Where? When?

Reykjavik, she says. In 1986. You want me to tell you about it?

Later, she told me that she made a bargain with herself. She was not going to prompt me. But if I reached this point unaided, then she would tell me. The right button hit the jackpot. If not, off to the barbecue.

The jackpot it was.

III

During the Reagan administration, when her husband was Assistant Secretary of Defense, Marianne Weinsfeld also held an important post. She was on the team of the Arms Control and Disarmament Agency. On the face of it, this was a peculiar choice, though no more peculiar than many other such appointments. Marianne was a hawk; but the new head of ACDA, Eugene Rostow, was also a hawk. He, too, was a

260

devotee of the school of nuclear war-fighting. – Depending upon certain assumptions, he said, some estimates predict that there would be ten million casualties on one side and one hundred million on another. But that is not the whole of the population.

Reagan's private thoughts on nuclear weapons did not reflect the chilling stance of his supporters. Nukes terrified him. His views were no secret: it was just that they seemed not to affect what was actually done by his administration. They also sat strangely with the rest of his political stance. Hating commies, which he undoubtedly did, went with *loving* nukes. This had been true since the days of Joe McCarthy. But thought-through positions were not his forte. Had he been a rational man, the giant potlatch at Reykjavik in October 1986 could never have happened. Potlatch: an American Indian ceremony in which two tribes compete as to which can throw away the most valuable objects. The more precious your discard, the more merit and honour accrue. In the Reykjavik potlatch it seemed, for a breathtaking moment, as though the two leaders, Reagan and Gorbachev, were about to bargain away all their nuclear weapons. And where would that have left the ACDA?

Reykjavik occurred because the Russians were as aware as anyone that Reagan was an actor. He needed a script. Weinsfeld and the rest were there to supply that script and to ensure that he did not deviate from it (as, on heartstopping occasions, he was wont to do). Gorbachev's aim was to ensure that Reykjavik would not be scripted. The real, irrational, unrealistic Reagan would be let loose, and with any luck things would go too far to be reversed by some panic-stricken damage-limitation exercise. Gorbachev had met both Reagans – the one with cue-cards and the one without – and he knew which he preferred.

The role in which Reagan most often pictured himself was one he had played thirty years before, in the 1950s: President of the Screen Actors' Guild. *That* President, affronting the wicked world by the side of Senator Joe McCarthy, said: The communism fight is never won. It always leaves behind a little

Trojan Horse. Hollywood, *that* President felt, was in the front line of the fight. He said: The Russians sent their first team, their ace string, here to take us over. We were up against hard-core organisers.

He beat them in Hollywood: now he would beat them in Russia.

But Reagan also pictured himself in other roles, and one of these gave rise to his enthusiasm for SDI: that of the man who would banish nuclear weapons from a grateful world. SDI would be his means to this end. He loved it because it would enable him to abandon nukes while maintaining American security against the communist threat.

Nobody else saw it this way. The administration ideologues saw it as a means of upping the ante, of forcing the Soviets to compete with technology and expenditures they could never match. The Russians saw it as a terrifying and ruinous escalation of the arms race. Dr T. saw it as a licence to explore ever more ingenious explosive frontiers. Allies saw it as an infringement of the existing Anti-Ballistic Missiles treaty. Strategists saw it as a probably impractical diversion from the serious business of nuclear war. But all this was irrelevant to Reagan's dream of saving the world.

The Reykjavik events occurred because this all-powerful political simpleton encountered a true political rarity: a genuine disarmer. In October 1986, Mikhail Gorbachev had been in power for eighteen months. All his plans depended upon bringing the arms race to an end. But his hopes of getting arms reduction talks quickly under way were foundering amid suspicions and entrenched attitudes. So, in proposing the Reykjavik meeting – officially intended merely to clear the ground for a formal summit – he declined to reveal his agenda beforehand. That way, Reagan's rebuffs could not be scripted in advance.

The Icelandic prime minister had only two weeks' warning that Reykjavik was to host the meeting. It was held at Hofdi House, a plain, two-storey house by the sea that had once been the British ambassador's residence. The talks began at 10.30 in the morning of Saturday, 11 October. They were due to end at noon the next day. The two leaders and their interpreters sat around the Hofdi House dining-table. Their teams (the American team including both Weinsfelds) met more informally upstairs. And the potlatch began.

Gorbachev started it: he proposed fifty per cent cuts across the board in all categories of strategic arms. Reagan was not prepared for anything so sweeping: he had no counter-proposals ready for the afternoon. That evening the two arms control teams met. They worked all night until 6.30 the next morning, with a break from 1.45 until 3.00 to consult their superiors. Great progress was made, but the obstacle was the Euromissiles. Next morning, meeting once more with Gorbachev, Reagan offered to eliminate them. – Literally a miracle is taking place, said Reagan. But then (Reagan used a term from his days as a radio sports announcer) Gorbachev threw the curve.

No cutbacks on offensive arms could occur without agreement on defensive weapons: SDI. It was to be all or nothing. No more forms of words: they were nothing but *kasha* – porridge. – *Kasha* forever, grunted Gorbachev.

The conference was supposed to be ending at noon. Eduard Shevardnadze, the Russian foreign minister, said to the American team leaders, Max Kampelman and Paul Nitze: You are creative – can't you think of something? You are so experienced – can't you think of something?

The Americans thought. They proposed a ten-year period during which permitted research, development and testing would continue on SDI: at the end of that time, all ballistic missiles would be eliminated.

That afternoon, Reagan and Gorbachev met again. The meeting began at 3.25. Gorbachev would have no procrastination: no forms of words to be decided at Geneva sometime. Everything was on offer: but everything must be decided now. They recessed for an hour.

Hell, said Reagan. He doesn't want to set up a summit. He wants to have a summit. Right here.

Gorbachev was very excited. He could not keep still. He sat down, leaped up, went to a window, sat down again. – Everything could be decided now, now, he said.

At 5.30, the two reconvened. There were big practical differences in the offers prepared by their two teams.

Maybe we can sort this out, said Gorbachev.

Yes, said Reagan, we can sort it out. He said: It would be fine with me if we eliminated all nuclear weapons.

Gorbachev said: We can do that. Let's eliminate them. We can eliminate them.

What a potlatch! George Shultz, the American Secretary of State, who was looking on, said nothing. Later, officials wanted to know why he had not acted. How had he been able to sit there and see Reagan throw away the entire US nuclear arsenal? – I really felt that he's the President, said Shultz. He got elected twice. He has made no secret of his views on nuclear weapons. So who am I to stop him from saying what he believes and what he's campaigned on?

I thought the world would have greeted it with great joy, said Reagan.

But SDI rode to the rescue of the US nuclear arsenal. Reagan could not have both his dreams. Gorbachev insisted that, in accordance with the existing Anti-Ballistic Missile Treaty, research, development and testing of Star Wars be confined to the laboratory. – I cannot do without the word, laboratory, he said. He was not to be sidetracked. Reagan offered to share SDI: they would both be protected by it. But Gorbachev was not interested.

I have promised the American people I will not give up SDI, said Reagan. You're asking me to give up SDI. We have an agreement we can be very proud of, and now I'm asking you for just this one thing.

Gorbachev said: It's not a trivial thing – it is everything. Do I understand this is your final position – you will not confine work to the laboratory?

Yes, said Reagan. I cannot give in.

Is this your last word?

Yes.

Gorbachev said: If this is not possible, then we can say goodbye and forget everything we have discussed. You're using one word to frustrate a meeting that promised to be historic.

Reagan said: If you believe the United States wants some military advantage, you should not worry.

I can't do it, said Gorbachev.

Finally Gorbachev said that he would like to move everywhere he could. He had tried to do so. His conscience was clear before the President and his people. What had depended on him, he had done. – I don't know what else I could have done, he said.

I do, said Reagan. You could have said yes.

Mephisto had had a narrow escape. So nearly confounded! But he had been wise enough to insinuate himself into dreams, not practicalities. Weapons are weapons, but dreams are what you choose to make them. Dr T. had his dream; the President had his. They were not really the same. But because neither had assumed the anticlimactic form of reality, neither had substance enough to be bargained away. A dream must be given a chance, even at the expense of another dream.

IV

Outside the Hofdi House, waiting to hear what was going to happen, sit two thousand members of the world's press.

Among them, Uncle Zigi. The events of the past few years have brought him notoriety, and a Sunday newspaper has had the bright idea of accrediting him as a correspondent. First they sent him to Washington, to report on the preparations for this event, and now they have sent him here. He is delighted. – For the first time I am a journalist, he tells me. It is not often that one gets to try out a new career at my age. I have written articles, of course, but this is the first time as a reporter.

I think you're out of your mind, I reply. We are sitting in my kitchen drinking lemon tea. Zigi despises tea with milk.

He looks annoyed. – Why? Can you think of anyone better qualified to report on such a meeting?

No, but –

But. You think I'm too old. An old man, maybe he'll

collapse, maybe it'll all be too much for him. (He is now seventy-eight years old.) It is not a running race, he says. I shall not need to fight for quotes. Everyone knows what is said. I shall hold conversations and comment. And if I fall down dead, it will be only appropriate.

So off he goes to Iceland, to hold the kind of conversations he has always been used to – conversations with those in power, those by whom the decisions are made. Except now he can't affect the decisions: only report them and comment upon them. I have one of the pieces he wrote in front of me now:

This evening, in this small fishing town, the world was nearly saved. President Reagan and Secretary Gorbachev agreed to eliminate all nuclear weapons. The NATO allies were hurriedly telephoned to inform them of the impending deal. They were horrified. All that trouble, all that political pain, to install cruise missiles. And now in five minutes they are to be whisked away! Mrs Thatcher's fury can only be imagined. But she did not need to worry. The danger was averted.

The general feeling here on the American side is not really of disappointment, but of relief, at a peril narrowly escaped. This reaction seems so bizarre that I have been trying to explain it to myself – and to get those who feel this way to rationalise it, if they are able.

One explanation has to do with the extraordinary hold that nuclear weapons exert over anyone who has to deal with them. I am very conscious of this myself, being one of those who was, so to speak, in at the birth. The fascination is, of course, with power. Nuclear weapons confer a sensation of power – extraordinary, godlike power over world events. Such power is addictive. Who would not be God?

More down to earth, though not completely separate, is an attachment to a particular specialism. Whole institutes, hundreds of people, in Washington and elsewhere, are devoted to war games and simulations. Different styles and sizes of nuclear attack are played through on computers.

Different strategies are tested. Some are found wanting; some seem to succeed, if it makes sense to talk of success in such a context.

Will these strategists be able to resist the temptation to see what will happen – to see if a nuclear war can really, as they assure us, be controlled? If something is described often enough, simulated often enough, the temptation to try it out for real becomes overwhelming. One strategist has already declared that 'The United States may have no practical alternative to waging a nuclear war.'

Nuclear weapons cannot just be wished away, say the realists. The last two days have shown that this could happen. It is the other vision, the nuclear vision, which is unreal, nothing but a bad dream from which we can awake if only we try hard enough.

V

I remember him going to Reykjavik, I say as Marianne refills my coffee cup. What were you doing there?

I was part of the team, she says. In ACDA. It was an extraordinary time. The best time of my life, I guess.

She pours herself a cup, and sits down across the table. The atmosphere has changed. She is no longer chafing to get away from me and over to her barbecue. She is back in that vanished world we all inhabited not so very long ago – a world so much more exciting than one dominated by grandchildren, barbecues, and the mundanities of a lawyer's practice. Life had an edge then that it lacks now. Personally, I don't miss it. Zigi did. He was always a man for the edge.

You have to picture it, she says. The Hofdi House. Just an ordinary house overlooking the sea. It's supposed to be haunted, you know. I guess there are a few more ghosts now. There we all were, both the teams, Americans and Russians, packed in there, just talking, like ordinary people. It was the first time that had ever happened. Before, there was always a set of programmed responses, like robots with buttons. But here we all were, with these wild conversations going on everywhere. And no space. When our side needed a new draft, urgently, there just wasn't a room free. All we could find was a bathroom. So we put a board across the bathtub and made ourselves a desk that way. We wrote out the draft on a yellow pad and down it went, to where the bargaining was going on. It really looked as if it was going to happen. Deep cuts. Maybe even the end of nukes. Unbelievable.

Were you pleased?

I guess I was in shock, she says. We all were. At the end, the President was so disappointed, he made us feel disappointed with him. Before that, I guess we thought it had all gone rather well. Far enough, but not too far. Possibilities had been established, but nobody had done anything rash.

So then we got talking with the press, and this old fellow comes over to me. He's really imposing, very tall and straight with a lot of white hair, and he has this thick accent, and I guess I'm somehow intrigued. We all felt, you must realise this, quite spacey by this time. For thirty-six hours we'd been talking and talking, without a break. No sleep. You get on to a kind of high. Anyhow, this old guy comes over. A woman, he says. What's a woman doing here? Nuclear weapons is man's stuff. These are toys for the boys, don't you think? Or perhaps you, too, are a journalist.

No, I say. I'm not a journalist. I'm a member of the team. I'm an arms controller. And I remember I began to laugh, the whole thing suddenly seemed surreal. My job just nearly disappeared, I said. Saved by the bell. So then he asks me my name, and I ask him his. And of course, as soon as he says it I feel – I don't know. How can I describe it? As though someone just hit me hard in the stomach. As though I'd seen a ghost. Which of course was just about the truth. I must have looked as though I was going to faint or something. – Are you all right? he says, and takes me by the arm and sits me down in the nearest chair.

So then I start to think. Am I going to tell him who I am? You are my father. I am your long-lost daughter. And I think, hell, no, I won't. This is the man who walked out of my life when I was two years old. This is someone who is one of my bitterest political opponents. This is not a man I wish to know personally. I just don't want anything to do with him personally. As a journalist I'll talk to him, but that's *it*. But of course all this time I can't take my eyes off him. I can't believe this. You know, I keep looking at him and – I don't know – looking for parts of me there.

So then he says: You really don't look well. Why don't we go and find a quiet place and have a drink? And you can tell me all about your job. I should be fascinated to know about it. I want to know how you feel about it. I am very interested in that. So we go and find a place, a bar somewhere, at the hotel where he's staying, and we talk about my job, and he talks about what Europeans think is going on, and I pretend his name means nothing to me.

Then he says: Perhaps you know my old friend, Dr Edward Teller. And I say, I've met him once or twice. I admire him, he's a fine man. One of the saviours of our country, in my opinion. And suddenly he loses his cool. I'd been wondering when that might happen. He starts in on this – tirade. About how Teller is mad, how he's become obsessed with death, how he likes to imagine himself holding the fate of the Russians in his hand. How the only thing that keeps him going is imagining more and more destruction. How he kids himself that he's not really going to destroy the world – just the Russians. – But he will, says my father, leaning across the table. He's waving his drink in my face. He will. Can't you see it? I sometimes wonder – are you all insane? At this point – you see, I remember every second of it – he puts down his drink and takes my hand. Very courtly and old-world. He says: How can you do it? You seem like a normal enough person, Mrs Weinsfeld. And yet you play these games and pretend that the danger of killing us all is just a risk that's got to be taken. Who are you, Mrs Weinsfeld, if I may ask you, who are you to make these decisions on behalf of the world's population?

So I say: Okay, I'll tell you exactly who I am. I'm your daughter.

Well, he drops my hand like a hot poker. And he stares and stares, just like I've been doing. Now I know what I must have looked like. He says: Marianne. Of course. Now that you say, it's so obvious. What an extraordinary thing. Why didn't you tell me this before? And he goes on staring and staring. As though he wants to eat me up with his eyes.

So what happened then?

Did we fall into each other's arms, you mean? The great reunion? She shakes her head. We did not. We just sat there, staring. I couldn't think what to say, and I guess neither could he. What do you say? I mean, let's get real about this. Fifty-odd years ago this guy stuck his penis into my mother, and here I am. But I haven't ever seen him, not consciously. You don't get related to someone that way. It's you that's related to him, Miriam, not me. I don't know him. He hasn't taken the trouble to keep in touch. I have a perfectly good father who raised me. *He* says *I've* got problems. I guess I'm not the only one with problems. Otherwise, why all this silence?

What happened then?

She shakes her head. – I still can't believe it.

I remain silent. After a while, Marianne goes on: He said. He had the nerve to say. – My daughter. Working with that crew. Those were his words. After the way he behaved. In 1942 he walked out of our lives. I have not seen or heard from him since. And he thinks he has a right to judge me?

She is shaking with anger still, at the memory of it. – I couldn't speak. Imagine it. No sleep. All that emotion and excitement. And now – this. It was too much. I knew if I opened my mouth I'd do something I'd regret. Either I'd have to express all that anger I felt or I'd just cry and cry. And I didn't want to do that. He didn't deserve it. Anger or tears, they're about involvement, and what had he done to deserve that I should feel involved with him? So I put down my drink and got up and left. He didn't follow me. I went back to Hofdi House and met up with the rest of the guys. They were wondering what had happened to me. And we got our stuff together and boarded the plane and came back here.

270

You never got in touch after that? He never tried to contact you?

Nope.

Did you tell your husband?

Nope. Didn't tell anybody. Not Dickie, not my mother, not my brother. I'm not in therapy, so I couldn't even tell my therapist. You're the first one. She looks at her watch. Time for a drink, I guess. I could use one. You?

We sit sipping Bloody Marys, oddly companionable. Outside, prosperous Maryland suburbia. Inside our heads, other landscapes. Marianne has fallen silent. Perhaps she's back in Iceland, drink in hand, and Zigi is sitting where I am now. I am trying to remember what happened when he returned from Reykjavik. Did anything happen? Did we remark on anything? Was there any difference to notice?

He certainly seemed tired, I remember, and thoughtful. I went to meet him at the airport; Fania had flu, or so she said – at any rate she didn't feel like making the journey. I didn't enquire too deeply. She often develops flu when she doesn't want to do something. He was unusually silent on the drive back from Heathrow. And that, too, wasn't surprising. He was an old man. It had been an exhausting assignment, and an emotional one. Dr T. had won again; his camp would be cheering while ours mourned. – Did you have a good time? I said. – No, he replied. I wouldn't describe it as a good time. Thought-provoking, rather.

Thought-provoking: typical. To find a daughter – after so long, and in such circumstances! Marianne: the only daughter he could be certain of. Susanna was never a certainty. A probability, maybe, but that's not the same thing. I was only a surrogate. He must have realised that Marianne's political alignment was no mere coincidence. That, like Bella's marriage to Michael Overy, it was perhaps not unconnected with himself. And then – having found her – simply to be walked out on in his turn. Thought-provoking indeed. I'm surprised, now, that he could manage to converse at all. But he was giving nothing away. He never mentioned it. Never said a word. Perhaps he tried to put it out of his mind. If so, I doubt whether he succeeded. He was an old man, and more used to inflicting pain than suffering it.

I'm not sure how I feel about this ease between me and Marianne. It's almost a family feeling. I have to keep reminding myself that, only four or five years ago, she (or her husband – for of course I didn't then know of her existence) seemed to me wicked beyond description. They were part of my fourteen-year-old's political world, in which there were goodies and there were baddies, and you were one or the other. I had a list of people that, in the event of a fatal illness being diagnosed, I would make it my business to assassinate (having nothing more to lose). Top of the list was our very own Mrs Thatcher; but Dick Weinsfeld's name was not far below. The notion that one might some day hold a conversation with any of these persons was not tenable. Conversations imply some iota of common feeling. There could be none here.

What has changed? Only circumstances. – Would you still like to kill Thatcher? I asked Tony the other day. She was mouthing away about something on the television, nauseating as ever. – No, he said. It's too late.

Can the persons, then, be separated from the policies? Does the evil end with the circumstance? If the two can be separated, I suppose that is where the bomb-throwing anarchists (with whom I so readily identify) went wrong. True, only hateful people would choose to embody such policies, even temporarily. But one can't go around doing away with people just because they are hateful. It's the policies that must be the target. Democracy: politics as assassination by other means. Otherwise the slaughter would be wholesale.

Is Marianne – supreme irony! – a more peaceable person than I am? Does assassination perhaps not figure in her list of fantasies?

After you met Zigi, I say, how did you feel? What did you think about?

I thought about killing the bastard, she says. Just like I always had. It's an old fantasy of mine.

Blood of my blood.

CHAPTER 12   I'LL SHOW YOU IF YOU SHOW ME

I

THE MOMENT HAS come. I've been putting it off, but finally I must face it. This could go on indefinitely. No doubt there is more to be found – isn't there always? – but not by me. I have enough already. After a certain point you realise that to continue is merely to postpone.

It is heaped up all around me, in tapes, notebooks, cuttings, xeroxed pages. And in my memory. Uncle Zigi: our life and times. The full and true story. Now it is I who must face the questions. Why have I done it? And *what am I going to do with it?*

I think back to that day when Derry put the proposition to me. The day of Zigi's memorial service. It didn't take long to dispose of that token resistance I put up, Fania or no Fania. I don't want to make her unhappy, but this was *my* project. The money, the notion that 'somebody ought to do it and you're the obvious one' – all that was beside the point. I had my own good and sufficient reasons for wanting to find out about Zigi.

So that's what I have done. And having done so – am I going to publish it?

Last night, Tony and I quarrelled about this question. It was just one more stage in our long retreat from each other. But the book has precipitated things. Sometimes it has receded, when I've kept quiet or been doing other work, or when he's been away. Sometimes it has loured over us, when I've been preparing for one of my trips, or when I've just returned. But it's never been far off. It has named the distance that has grown up between us, a fatal naming.

It's nearly a month since my visit to Marianne. For a month, that visit has darkened the air between us. – Don't tell me about it, Tony said, as he always says. I don't want to know.

But I want to tell you about it. It's part of my life. How can you just expect me to blot out part of my life for your benefit?

I don't expect you'd find it very difficult. Isn't that what you've always done, all the time we've been married?

I say: I don't know what you're talking about. As though I didn't know! I can feel my heart thumping violently. Here it is at last, the moment I've dreaded. It had to happen sometime, I've always known that. I raise my head, square my shoulders, brace myself. The inevitable words drop from our mouths like lumps of lead.

Isn't it obvious what I'm talking about? Your big secret. The thing you're never free to tell any of us.

You mean, Susanna's father?

What else? Well, I've done my bit. I've never asked. I've never pried. I've never stuck my nose where it's not wanted. And now you can do your bit. Now the boot's on the other foot. You want to tell, but I don't want to know. So you can just shut up. Keep it to yourself. See what it feels like to stay buttoned up. Though I suspect the two things are not unconnected, he says, with the sudden ferocity of revelation. What d'you think I am, blind?

We sit staring at each other across the table, over the cheese plate. Some dried-out Cheddar, the remains of some chalky Stilton, and the blue stain which was the Roquefort. Only its memory remains, wafting from our cheesy fingers. We are alone in the house. Rose has found a job and moved out into a place of her own. That's it: now there's just us.

We face each other, marooned. Since the girls have been away, so, quite often, has he. But just now he is at home writing. He's unusually bad-tempered. Snaps my head off every time he opens his mouth. It isn't like him: he's never been irritable. Quite the reverse: *his* excessive calm has

274

frequently driven *me* crazy. Perhaps that affair I suspected has come to an end. I suppose I can hardly enquire. If so, it hasn't helped. It's merely eliminated distractions – other people. Daily, we meet. For meals, over a cup of coffee. There is no more ducking certain issues, on the avoidance of which, it increasingly appears, our marriage has been founded. Now, having time to converse, we too often find that we have nothing to say, or perhaps that we had better not say it. You wouldn't believe the things we don't discuss these days! They loom beside us, unacknowledged and insistent. What's the point? Why keep on ducking and weaving? What are we trying to preserve? Let's have the truth even if it kills us.

You're right, of course, I say. When did you guess?

I don't know. The first time I looked at her? Whenever I saw the three of you together? I couldn't be sure, of course.

D'you think Fania guesses?

I have no idea. We've never discussed it.

You hated Zigi, didn't you? I realise the full truth, the truth I'd always minimised to myself (they didn't get on, they didn't really understand each other, they just weren't compatible), as I speak it. As so often happens. (As has just happened with Tony? Did he really guess, until this moment? Is this, too, simply a case of things suddenly falling into place?) – Was that why?

Partly, I suppose. I think I just felt I could never compete.

He's right. Zigi was the love of my life. The way Susanna resembles him has always delighted me. I've had my love-affairs since, but the *coup de foudre* never struck again. What chance did Tony stand with Zigi peering over his shoulder?

He was a bastard. I know that. I always knew it. It makes no difference. Wouldn't life be easy if passion were founded on worth? Look at Tony. Charming, reliable, honest, cultured. A good man, who truly loved me. Didn't he deserve as much in return? Whereas Zigi was devious, cynical, brilliant and irresistible. Just like his damned bomb. What a trail of destruction! Bettina, Fania, Joan, Bella, me – and who knows how many more? (A detail I have no interest in unearthing.)

How do you become the devil? By chance, it seems. Zigi

was (let us be kind) the most amoral man I have known. His actions were predicated upon personal gain: intellectual, sensual, worldly. Whereas Dr T. is, according to all accounts, a man of charm and sensitivity. A learned man, a loving paterfamilias. Yet what did Dr T. offer? Oblivion. And Zigi? Not Paradise, certainly. But a continuation of life on earth, which is the nearest most of us will ever get to that enchanted place.

What are we going to do? I say.

It's more a question of what are you going to do, isn't it? he replies. Back to sweet reason. Zigi was never reasonable. – If you really intend to publish this book, then that's it. I really don't see how we could stay together after that.

I wait for him to make some dramatic gesture to match these words. For instance, he could get up and leave the room. Some appropriate punctuation. But that's not Tony's style. Instead he fiddles with the stem of his wineglass, until I have to restrain myself from snatching it from his hand and throwing it at his head. Someone had better leave the room before it is too late, and, *faute de mieux*, it'll have to be me.

Sitting in my study, I think about what he has just said. Here we are. Finally at the point. Life without Tony. On my own. Would it really be so bad? Increasingly, I've been enjoying his absences and dreading his returns. Is this simply the result of a bad conscience, or do I actually – contrary to everything I've been telling myself – prefer life without him? Is it just habit I'm clinging to, nothing more than that? Does he feel the same? I shan't ask him. I might receive the answer Yes.

He assumes that I'm going to publish. But why should I? It wouldn't be in character. I've never been one for getting things out in the open. Civilised life is founded upon the will to keep uncomfortable secrets. You have to live with the consequences of your decisions, not offload them on to everyone else. That's what I've tried to do. And not just me. That's how we've all lived our lives, Fania, Zigi, Tony and I. Until now. Now, apparently, it's bean-spilling time. Why, all of a sudden? No wonder Fania seemed shaken when I (I!)

put this proposition to her. No wonder Tony supported her. Why break the habits of a lifetime?

Perhaps the answer would be to write the book and leave it to be published when we're all dead, should anyone still be interested. The coward's way out. Would that satisfy Tony?

Perhaps. But is that what I want to do? Satisfy Tony? Keep us together till death us do part? The truth game has done its stuff. It sucks. I always thought it did, and now I know. Things can never again be what they were.

Well, perhaps they'd had their day. Perhaps the real act of cowardice would be to pretend otherwise. Perhaps that was why I wanted the excuse Derry gave me.

We sit on sadly, I in my study, Tony in the kitchen (I suppose: I haven't heard him move), contemplating the end. Of what? Not of our lives, certainly, nor even, necessarily, of the best part of them. But of our joint adventure, everything represented by our daughters (yes, ours! Isn't one penis much like another? What's one moment set against years of life together?) and by this house. What will happen? Will the house be sold? I like it here. I don't want to move. Neither, I imagine, does Tony. But what's the alternative?

The alternative is to say nothing, do nothing, let things slide. Shall I do that? I go back down to the kitchen. I stack the dishwasher. Tony reads the paper. Life goes on, apparently.

II

Since Zigi's death, Fania has been diminishing. All my efforts and those of the Hungarian mafia have not been able to prevent it. At first I assumed this was all my fault, that the extra worry induced by my request was weighing upon her. Tony encouraged this view. But now I reject it. She said no, and assumed I accepted that. Why not? It isn't as if I tried to persuade her. I've never talked to her about it since. We are all so self-centred: it's so easy to project our own guilt on to others. It's what I do with Susanna all the time, the source of the uneasiness I feel with her. But of course Fania has her own problems, the chief one being Zigi's disappearance. You can't live with someone like that for forty-eight years and then not miss them when they die. – I have put a lot of effort into my life, she said to me the other day. Living with Zigi required effort, and I did it because he was worth it. I'm not sure how much longer I can be bothered to go on making an effort.

I was passing by, and had dropped in on her as I try to do whenever I can. It was cold: she was sitting in her kitchen, not doing anything much. – Not like you, I said. That was her explanation, and I can see her point. She is not physically or mentally disabled, but she is old in years. While Zigi was alive, she held old age off by main force. That was all part of the effort. The vivacity, the clothes, the presentation. Now she has relaxed, and all pretences, all defences, are down.

Today is the anniversary of Zigi's death – his *yahrzeit*. Fania will burn a candle in his memory. She shouldn't be left alone today. I pick up the phone and call her number. Nobody answers. Perhaps she's out shopping, or up at the top of the house. An hour later I call again. Still no reply.

Now I'm getting worried. It's probably quite unreasonable. She may have gone out. She may just not feel like answering the phone. These things are permissible. Nevertheless, I worry. After lunch I phone again, with the same result, or lack of one. I can't stand it any longer. I get in the car and drive over to Fania's.

The house looks as it always did: tall, red-brick, graceless. No clues from the outside. I ring the bell. I can hear it echoing down the hall. No reply. Ring again. Still no reply. I peer through the letterbox: all I can see is emptiness, closed doors. What now?

I still have a key to this house. Zigi and Fan urged me to keep it. When they went away, I could keep an eye on the place. I haven't used it for years, but I don't expect the locks have changed.

They haven't.

In I go. – Fan, I call. Fania, where are you? Are you there? No reply.

I walk down the hall. It is paved with polychrome tiles, laid in an elaborate geometric pattern. The white door at the end leads to the kitchen. On the left, Zigi's study, his grand piano still standing open, and Fania's bedroom, with its bathroom opening off. (Tony and I organised and paid for this bathroom after Zigi died, when she decided to move downstairs into what had been the dining-room. She said: What use is a dining-room to me? I don't think I shall be giving dinner-parties.) Her studio is upstairs, together with all those other rooms, now unused, where no one ever goes. There are no more lodgers. Dust is everywhere, though of course that's nothing new. Only Zigi's room was regularly vacuumed, on account of his asthma. He refused to perform this task himself, alleging – perhaps correctly – that this in itself was liable to bring on an attack. So Fania did it, grumbling, once a week. – What I do for Zigi. He's used to servants. It's how he was brought up. Now she is released from this drudgery. There are no more exceptions to the house rule.

I look into her bedroom. The bed is made: there is no one there. Neither is she in the bathroom. Zigi's room: uninhabited. The kitchen door is closed. I open it. The *yahrzeit* candle stands on the windowsill in its glass. It is lit. The central heating boiler is going: only the ground floor is heated these days.

The kitchen is a pleasant room, with a window and a glazed door on to the little paved back garden. It is painted white, with some of Fania's pictures on the walls. There is one of the garden, blues and reds and greens, less abstract than usual, that I have always particularly liked. Beside the garden door is an armchair where she likes to sit. She is sitting there now, two library books on the table at her right, facing towards the candle. – Fania, I say. Aunty Fan. She does not reply. I run over to her. She is sitting, just sitting, as so often these days she just sits. I touch her shoulder. She doesn't move. I touch her face. It is cool, though the room is warm. She doesn't respond to my touch. I put my ear to her breast, but I know I shall hear nothing. No movement. I take her hand: cold, cold. I am not surprised. This is what I was half expecting as I drove over, and it's what she would have wanted: dignified, no trouble, no pain, or not of a physical kind. I pull up a chair and sit opposite her, and burst into tears. There is none of that guilty sense of freedom I felt alongside the grief when my parents died. There is only sadness. She was my best friend. Now she has gone.

After a while I blow my nose, wipe my eyes and move towards the telephone. First the doctor, whose number is on a list sellotaped to the wall, alongside mine and Uncle Harry's. She will be along in about an hour: I promise to wait. Then Tony. He was there when I left – I hope he hasn't decided to go out. No: he answers the phone. – It's me, I say. I'm at Fania's. She's dead.

I'll be over, he says. Tony is at his best in situations like this.

Tony arrives first. – Was she ill? he says. I didn't know anything was wrong.

I explain what happened.

The doctor arrives. Yes, Fania is dead. Her heart just stopped. She doesn't need to bother any more. There will have to be an inquest, since no one was here when she died, but it will be a formality. Can we cope with the arrangements? I remind her that it is only a year since we made these same arrangements for Fania's husband.

The undertakers arrive: the body is taken away. I telephone Uncle Harry. He is at his office: despite his age, he still goes in every day. (What else should he do? Play canasta with Aunty Rivvy? That would be enough to drive anyone to instant senility.) – Poor Fan, he says, after a silence. She was lonely, I suppose. There is another silence. Perhaps he's wondering how he'll cope when Rivvy goes. Or vice-versa. They're well into their seventies. With an almost audible grinding of gears he pulls himself back into business mode, when things at once become easier to cope with. – Made the arrangements? he says. That's right. I've got her will here. If you want to come over, we can read it.

Shouldn't her executors be there?

I'm her executor. Come over, it'll give you something to do. You sound upset.

I found her.

That's what I mean.

We drive over to Harry's office in Portland Place. He hasn't changed in thirty years: he is small, compact, rosy, well-upholstered. We are ushered in by his comfortable, middle-aged secretary. He shakes us both by the hand, wishes us long life, and waves us to a couple of chairs. The will, in its envelope, is already on his desk. He opens it. It is not complicated. Zigi's piano goes to Susanna. (Where will she put it? It will fill her entire house.) A few pictures go to different friends. Rose gets five thousand pounds. Everything else goes to me – My dear great-niece Miriam Oliver, who has been like a daughter to me.

Harry says: House-prices have fallen, so you shouldn't have any trouble with death-duties. I know someone who'll give you a nice low valuation for probate.

III

I let myself into the house in West Hampstead. My house. Fania, an ally even in death, has done me a last good turn: given me financial independence, so that Tony and I may decide our future uninfluenced by such sordid considerations as money.

My house. It's a strange feeling. Unconvincing. What am I going to do with it? Keep it? Sell it? Live in it? Let it? Decisions can wait, but not for too long. Until they are made, it's nothing but a burden, liable to break-ins, burst pipes, leaky roofs – all that catalogue of housing horrors.

I don't think I shall live in it. It's not a house I ever much liked in itself. Its only attraction was its inhabitants. What remains is their shell, and what am I going to do with that? All those thousands of dusty books, all those canvases?

First things first. First, everything must be gone through. In a funny way, I quite relish the thought of this. It's a routine job which must be done methodically, which fills the time, which is not too demanding. With added snooper's interest, of course. In all our long years of apparently close acquaintance, how well did I ever know Zigi and Fania? Not very well, if I am to judge by the past year's labours. If I want to know them better, this is my chance.

Where am I to begin? Going through the books will be a lifetime's work in itself. I must get organised. Decide what I'm looking for and why I'm looking for it.

Well, that's not too difficult. I'm looking for Zigi's papers, of course. The ones Fania told me she'd burnt. I bet she hadn't. She just said that to shut me up, so there could be no argument.

Unbelievable, how much paper is accumulated in the course of a lifetime. I'm a thrower-away, myself, and even I have drawers full of the stuff, cupboards bursting with it. Tony keeps everything: he is surrounded by walls of box-files. We could insulate the house with them. I suggested putting them up in the roofspace for that very purpose, but apparently the joists wouldn't take the weight.

I begin in Zigi's room. He had a big partner's desk: its drawers are firmly locked. Haven't been opened since he died, I imagine. There is a key in a little pot on the desktop. I try it: it fits. Stationery. Envelopes, more envelopes. Rubber bands, paperclips, balls of string. He evidently didn't keep his letters in his desk. Where, then? In trays, in files? There are a couple of wire baskets – both empty. A typewriter. Nothing else on or in the desk.

The walls are entirely lined with bookshelves, full to overflowing. One of these shelves used to be devoted to files – don't I remember noticing that row of cardboard boxes? No longer, however. There is a space there – the only space in the room. Everywhere else I'm faced by unbroken ranks of books, political, philosophical, scientific, in German, English, a few Hungarian. There is a filing cabinet in one corner. I try it: it is not locked. The drawers, however, are empty.

For the rest of the afternoon I search for those papers. I take books off their shelves to peer behind them, open fat volumes to see if anything is concealed in their pages, leaf through the music piled on the piano. I *know* he had lots of stuff. Didn't Susanna have to come and help him deal with it three times a week? So where's it all gone?

It's getting dark. I'll come back tomorrow.

Tomorrow and tomorrow and tomorrow . . .

The papers are nowhere to be found. I'm beginning to believe that Fania wasn't joking. Uncle Harry has assured me that everything is contained in the house. There are no safe deposit boxes or other stashes for possible valuables. There is a bank account, containing £150, and a building society account, with £900. Zigi's pension died with him. What was she planning to live on when the building society money was gone? I suppose she'd have had to sell some books or furniture. What an effort, picking, packing. Easier to sell the house and have done with it. We discussed this possibility from time to time. The last occasion was just after Rose moved out. I said: You could have the flat at our place. You'd be self-contained. – Maybe one day, she said. When it gets too much, I'll let you know. But I knew she never would. The whole of her life was in that house. Maybe that's why she finally decided to give up. No more money and Zigi's *yahrzeit*. A terminal combination.

She burned them. She really did. Or threw them out for the dustman. Did Zigi tell her to do it, or was it her own idea? Had she done it when I spoke to her, or did she hurry afterwards to make good her word? Or didn't she get round to it until last week, when she felt she might be going soon? Did I ever notice that space on Zigi's bookshelves before? When did I last see her? Less than a week before she died. Four or five days. She had dinner at our place, and I brought her back in the car afterwards. She opened the front door, then turned and waved to me. – Goodbye, darling, she said. – I'll see you soon, I said. Did she shrug, slightly? She went on waving until I drove away.

Anyway, they're not here.

What now?

I suppose the only practical thing will be to select what I want to keep and then get a house-clearer in. I've offered the girls such furniture as they want, but on condition they make their selection within the next two weeks. Susanna has already decided to sell the piano and buy a good upright with some of the proceeds. She should get a fair bit for that Steinway. Every time I see her I think: Now I must tell her. Today will be the day. But it never is.

Up the stairs. At the very top are the rooms Susie and I used to live in. They're furnished pretty starkly now – we took all our stuff when we left to go to the house in Islington. No memories here. Everything can go. It's amazing to think we fitted into such a tiny space. Now, eight rooms will barely contain the straining possessions of Tony and myself – and we aren't even talking about the girls' flat.

Down a floor. The big front room here was Fania's studio. I open the door. Everything is covered with dust. It's very cold. There's been no heating in this room for months. A smell of oil-paint. Canvases are stacked against the wall. There's still something on the easel: Fania made a half-hearted attempt to keep up her painting after Zigi died, but not for long.

As with all the rooms in this house, the walls are barely visible. Elsewhere, they are covered with books; here, it's a layer of pictures. Fania's favourites, her own and others'. I walk around, studying them. One or two are rather good: I take them down. They can come home with me today.

There's also a big dresser, the shelves cluttered with painters' objects, the cupboards and drawers always locked. I haven't looked in there yet: that dresser's been locked ever since I've known it, and why should Zigi keep his stuff here, in Fania's room, when he had all the rest of the house to choose from? But I've always been curious about it, always wanted to look inside. Now is my chance, if I can find the key. It's a big if. I doubt if those drawers and cupboards have been opened in the last twenty years, and that's plenty of time for a key to disappear in a clutter like this.

I rootle among the paint-encrusted cups, plates, brushes, boxes, squeezed-out tubes which litter the shelves. A key might disappear here within half a minute. Now you see it, now you don't. I work my way along the shelves. There are four of them, the topmost reaching almost to the ceiling.

I shall need a ladder to get to the top shelves. I suppose Zigi and Fan must have had one somewhere, but I don't know where. There's a sort of library steps in this room that Fania used to reach the top of her larger canvases, but they won't get me to the top shelf.

The first two shelves yield nothing. I clamber on to the dresser base and fumble along the third. Clutter, clutter. I sift it all: no key. I can't see what's on the top, from here, but if I stretch up, I can just reach it. I extend a groping hand and feel along, trying not to bring too much dust and old paint down on my head. I feel a plate with various metal objects on it. I try to lift it down, but succeed only in dislodging it. It falls past my head to the floor, where it shatters.

I jump down to examine the debris. Some brushes, some old pens, lie amongst the shards. And – further over, just by the leg of the easel – a rusty key. My heart leaps (so engaged have I become in this probably fruitless and almost certainly anti-climactic search). I try it on one of the drawers. It fits.

The drawers are full of papers: old bills, packets of letters, a few photographs. The key fits them all. Will it fit the cupboards, too? Probably: dressers are not high-security installations. Yes, it does. The cupboards, too, are full: not with loose papers, but with boxes and folders. More letters, and lots of photographs. Is this the stuff Fania said she'd burnt? At a cursory glance, it doesn't seem like it. This is Fania's archive. Zigi is only here insofar as he relates to her. Or that's what it looks like. Only closer examination will tell.

I don't feel like settling down for hours in this cold, comfortless room. Laboriously I transport the papers down to the kitchen, where they can be laid out on the table. The gas is still connected (I must have it cut off: one of the tasks on my list). Fania's cupboards are still full – it's only three weeks since she died. I make myself a pot of tea, find a lemon and a packet of biscuits, turn up the heating. And begin.

Old bills, old CP papers. A file of cuttings relating to Fania's first husband, Joe, who was evidently quite a figure in the prewar labour movement. Boxes of photographs, quite a few featuring the exquisite young Fania with a tough-looking dark young man – presumably this same Joe. Dates and places are scrawled on the backs: Clacton 1933, Hackney Marshes 1934. Some family pictures.

I open a slim album, fake-leather, with a snap fastening. Interest quickens. The photographs here are of Fania with Zigi. Taken when they first met, by the looks of them: they are both in their thirties, certainly not yet forty. The same age as in that family photo I know so well. These all seem to have been taken on a single occasion: Fania is wearing a printed silk dress and a small, brimmed hat, set on one side of her head Forties style; Zigi looks unnaturally chic and slightly caddish in a light suit and polished two-tone shoes. There's a commercial photographer's stamp at the bottom of the pictures. A Liverpool address.

Of course! This must have been their wedding!

I search through the pictures to see if any feature the family. They do not. It must have been a quiet affair, witnesses in a register office. Sandor, perhaps. I could go to Liverpool and find out, but I don't suppose I shall.

Under the photographs there are letters and a few press cuttings. The cuttings are from different papers: wedding announcements. The letters are mostly from the family. Congratulations on getting married. Mazeltov. Lechayim.

There are some from people I don't know, friends of Fania's. Girlfriends, mostly. So glad you've met someone else. Is he really as good-looking as the photo? Lucky you. Where are you planning to live? Come and see us soon.

There's also another letter. It is dated May 1945. Dear Fania, I understand an old friend of mine will be in your part of the world soon. Keep an eye on him: he's worth knowing. I've given him your address (if this is still your address). Best wishes, B.

The address is Central Park West. The letterhead: Mrs Abe Kustow.

I pour myself another cup of tea, and sip it while I try to work out what this can mean. On one level, of course, the meaning is perfectly clear. Zigi and Fania met because Bettina introduced them.

But how could she? By this time she and Zigi were irretrievably estranged. Out of contact. Divorced. How did she put it? Out of the room and out of our lives. It had been as final as that. So how did she know where he was headed, what his plans were? He was newly out of purdah, just released from the sanatorium. On the way to Britain, to join his friend Sandor in Liverpool. *How did she know?*

She knew Fania. That was something she didn't tell me. Not that I asked her; any more than I asked Fania whether she knew Bettina (at first because I didn't know about Bettina, later because I wasn't supposed to know about her).

I cast my mind back to those days I spent with Bettina. This sheds a new light upon her: I look back with new respect. No scatty old aunty she – though the front was impenetrable. It wasn't that she avoided mention of Fania. On the contrary, she wanted to know all about Zigi's new family, how we were related, what Fania was like, whether they had any children. I could have sworn she didn't know any of this, that it wasn't the repetition of old news. And she didn't bat an eyelid when she heard Fania's name. Didn't say: Fania! That's an unusual name! Would she have been a Fania Gold?

Old habit dies hard. The first lesson she had learned when she joined the Party was discretion. A secret is and remains a secret. The things she did tell me were no secret: they were merely things I didn't know before. What else is she guarding there in San Diego, amid the palms and the lush lawns? Has she written these things down, or will she, too, carry them with her to her grave? I shall ring her tonight.

I could ring her now. The phone here's still connected. What time is it? Four o'clock. Eight in the morning in San Diego. I've got her number in my address book. Did Fania have it too? Did they keep in touch? Did she ever call Bettina, sitting where I'm sitting now? Did Bettina call her, after I'd left? Did Fania know what I was up to, all this time? Was she wondering how long I could keep up the pretence, waiting for me to confess?

As I punch in the digits, I'm trying to work out what I'm going to say to her. Bettina? Mrs Kustow? My Aunty Fania's died, and guess what I've found. Had you forgotten?

I hear the ringing, there on the other side of the world. Bettina explained to me how the phone system works at the condo. The calls all go through the caretaker's office: it's a sort of PBX system. Some residents also have their own separate lines, but this way, if anyone's worried about some aged parent not answering, it's possible to check that everything's all right.

I ask for Mrs Kustow. – I'm sorry, says the caretaker. Mrs Kustow passed away.

When was this? I saw her daughter in October, and she didn't mention . . .

No, that's right. It was last week. It was very peaceful. I'm sorry if this has been a shock to you.

He's right, it is a shock. Partly, it's the frustration. There was so much I needed to ask Bettina, and no chance now that I shall ever know any of it. But there's more to it than that. Bettina's death doesn't hit me in a profound, personal way, as Fania's did. Obviously, ours was hardly a deep friendship, though I liked her a lot. But with every death of this kind – the casual, natural cutting-down of a person to whom you were speaking yesterday, last week, last month – the harder it is to avoid the consciousness of mortality. Accidents are accidents – they can strike anyone, anytime. But old age and death happen to other people. Until they start to happen to your friends.

Start from the other end then. *How* could they have met, Fania and Bettina? How could they have known each other?

There was only one possibility. It must have been during the early part of the war, when Fania went to America as an escort to some children who were being sent abroad for the duration. It was the only time she ever got over there. The boat docked at New York, and after she had handed over the children she spent two or three weeks in the city before travelling back with a convoy. She told me about it once. – I had a nice time there, she said. Lots of friends. I was given some introductions. But I couldn't stay, not with what was going on back home.

She never went back. With her politics, getting a visa was out of the question after the war.

Whom would she have known? Communists, presumably. Fania was very active in the Party at that time. Abe Kustow's place would have been a natural port of call. And Bettina was a close friend of his for some time before they married.

All right: so Fania met Abe and Bettina. But how could Bettina introduce Zigi? Still no answer to that one.

I sit there thinking. The tea cools; dusk begins to fall. I munch through the biscuits. The note lies there in front of me, cryptic. There is nothing else in the album to throw any light on the mystery.

I clear away the cup and plate, wander around the house, start to look through the bookshelves. In Zigi's room, face to face with Deutscher's three-volume life of Trotsky, a possible solution occurs to me.

If Zigi, too, was a communist – ?

What Bettina emphasised was the secrecy. In prewar Europe, you did not go round discussing whether or not you were about to join the Party. Suppose Zigi, too, was a member? Bettina might – must – have known, but Bettina wouldn't tell. Much the safest cover, for him, would have been to seem uninterested in such things. Another apolitical scientist.

Let us suppose that this was the case. Suppose that the FBI were right to suspect him, that he wanted to throw them off the track. What would be the best – the obvious – thing to do?

One thing – when his wife became involved with such a notorious figure as Abe Kustow – would be to cut off contact. To make an ostentatious gesture. To walk out of her life. And if that meant abandoning his baby daughter – my guess, knowing Zigi, is that he would not have seen this as an unendurable sacrifice. He was not an unfeeling man, but those feelings were not aroused by small children, even his own. I can vouch for this. It would seem, however, that links were not entirely severed. Some contact – clandestine contact – was maintained, at least for a while.

But why?

Perhaps the reality of Zigi at Los Alamos was neither the story he put about after the war – that he left of his own accord when the German danger was past – nor the one that I have lately taken to be the truth – that he was paranoiacally hounded out of the place, and that the rest of his political life was a sort of revenge for this unfair treatment. There was a third possibility. This was that security suspicions were well founded. That Zigi was a communist and might well pass on secrets; was doing so, even.

One of the puzzling aspects of that apparent job application to Harwell, the one which occasioned the correspondence between Sir John Cockcroft and Colonel Lansdale of US Army Intelligence, was that I couldn't see why he wanted to work there. The reasons he gave for switching to microbiology were so convincing. Quite apart from the morals of the thing, the big problem in nuclear physics had been solved. The rest was embellishment. Microbiology was the new field, where the exciting new discoveries were going to be made. It was the place to be. So why apply to Harwell?

As far as I had been able to see, there were two possibilities. One, that this was his clearest path to a job, the field where his qualifications lay. The other, that bombs retained his allegiance, as they retained Dr T.'s, and that this was a last, vain attempt to follow his heart before being corralled, *faute de mieux*, into pastures new. Neither of these really convinced me. But if Lansdale was right – if Zigi really was passing on secrets – then it made perfect sense. He had no more access to American secrets, so he would have to make do with British. And the British secrets would be at Harwell.

If he had been passing on stuff from Los Alamos, he would have needed a conduit. What more reliable conduit than Bettina, whom he knew and could absolutely trust? And from whom, as far as the world was concerned, he was now totally estranged? It's a possibility: a definite possibility. As to their arrangements – how the stuff was passed – I have no idea. That it could have been done, I'm quite sure. Even in a police state something can always be arranged, and America during the war was no police state.

What did Zigi say about Klaus Fuchs? Dismissed him as having been of little strategic importance. That, of course, is a matter of opinion. Some said he was, some said he wasn't.

But one thing Fuchs undoubtedly did was add fuel to the fires of the Red Scare. And what was the basis of the Red Scare? That even though they had uncovered Fuchs and Nunn May and Pontecorvo and the rest, nobody could ever be sure that all the spies had been caught. Any Red might be a commie spy! Alger Hiss might be a commie spy! Oppy himself might be a commie spy! And in the next wave of spy fever, when Burgess and Maclean defected and it transpired that Maclean had been passing on military secrets, the neurosis was the same. Who was the third man? The fourth, the fifth? The Keeper of the Queen's Pictures – guilty. The head of MI5 – guilty? The security services put it about that the entire Labour government of the 1960s, from Harold Wilson down, was a nest of commie spies, actual or potential. Their rumour-mongering helped hound Wilson from office. Anyone might be a spy. The Prime Minister? That was always too much to swallow. But Zigi had access to government, was part of that government. He belonged to the inner clique, the kitchen Cabinet. His name appears in memoirs and diaries: Went round to No. 10, found Harold with Marcia and Zigi. Yes: a likely suspect. My mother's darkest suspicions confirmed.

Spies, spies. The old childhood game: I'll show you mine if you show me yours. What do spies reveal? The whereabouts of other spies. How it takes you back, back to that other world, that forgotten world we all inhabited so recently. The Atomic Age. Now that it's over, who can believe how terrifying, how all-consuming, how obliteratingly real it was?

If I were to write this book, who would it be about? Zigi the vengeful opportunist? Zigi the idealist? Zigi the mole? Doubtless the truth was never so simple, so neatly divided. Once the idealist imposed himself upon the opportunist, didn't the opportunist become an idealist?

I lock up the house, and pack my loot into the car. A couple of paintings; the photographs; the slim album, with all its contents. I must show Tony. It'll be quite safe. He won't have a notion what he's got in front of him.

IV

Bella's husband hit the headlines the other day. MINISTER: I AM NOT RESIGNING. Another sex-scandal. None of them ever get caught for the real crimes, the daily lies and deceptions and backhanders to friends. They don't even sleep with anybody very intriguing, not like that war minister, Profumo, who was indiscreet enough to share a mistress with the chap from the KGB. That, at least, was a true *faux pas*. This is nothing but the pleasure of catching the mealy-mouthed with their pants down. Who has he been screwing? His secretary, of course. Banality repeats itself. It would hardly be headline news were it not for the fact that the government of which Bella's Michael is an ornament has recently been making personal morality one of its policy planks. Always a risky venture, liable to be undermined by such inconvenient facts as that Michael's secretary recently gave birth to his daughter.

The girl, if the newspaper photographs are anything to go by, is quite a beauty. Surely she could have found someone a bit more glamorous than old fat, balding Michael? I know – none better – that power is an aphrodisiac. But even so – Michael? He was never up to much, even twenty years ago. There is also a picture of Bella, looking expressionless. She is standing by him, actually and figuratively. Yesterday they attended a meeting of his constituency association together.

Poor old Bella, says Tony. We are having breakfast; the paper is spread over the table between us. Fania's death seems to have brought on one of our periodic lulls: the bones of contention are buried once more. Pro tem. Who's going to be the one to dig them out again? – The first Mrs Michael must be feeling smug. Where are you off to?

I'm going to phone her.

I expect her phone's off the hook.

In fact it's attached to an answering-machine. I leave a message, and don't expect to hear from her. But a couple of days later, she calls.

Bella! How are you doing?

Pretty so-so.

The years fall away. Bella's deep voice hasn't changed since we were ten.

Why don't you come round?

We sit in my kitchen over Marks and Spencer sole goujons. Why bother to cook when the blessed St Michael does it so efficiently? Tony is out: we have the house to ourselves. Bella and Miriam, the old firm, still together after all these years. Two hopeful little girls full of potential and ambition. We were going to be famous statespersons. Where did it all go wrong? Miriam at nine was capable of anything. I don't feel so very different from her. Why haven't I done whatever it should have been? Why aren't I famous?

No, says Bella firmly. I am not the person I was when I was nine.

We survey our marriages. Like our vodkas, on the rocks. Shall we stay or shall we go? We marvel at the potency of inertia when faced with the awful upheavals inherent in divorce. The thought of all that unravelling, the terrible effort of getting to know a new person! How did we arrive here? What made us choose one person rather than another? If choose is the word. My own life has always felt inevitable rather than optional. Things and people have happened to me: I've followed breathlessly in their wake. Is this general? Has it been the pattern of Bella's life?

No, she says again. I wouldn't say that.

I say: You know Fania died?

Fania, says Bella. I was so jealous of her at one time. I really couldn't stand seeing her with Zigi. The thought of them together quite made my blood curdle.

Did I ever feel like that, at the height of my infatuation? I don't think I did. Does that mean I loved him less than Bella? I wasn't obsessed. No. But then, she was always more obsessive than I.

I was terribly in love with him, Bella goes on. The great hero figure of our youth. I'd never met anyone like him. I was crazy about him, I would have done anything. I was thinking about it on my way here. All that stuff about choice. You know who made my life what it is? My father. I hated him so much that almost everything I did was a sort of expression of what I felt about him. One of Zigi's great attractions was knowing how furious my father would be. It wasn't just the politics, Dad being pro-nuke and Zigi being anti, it was because of my mother. Did you know they had an affair, her and Zigi? Dad was furious. Not that he was in a position to talk. I simply couldn't resist, not that I wanted to. And then of course Michael. He was nothing but a glorified V-sign, really, at my father and Zigi both. Just one reaction after another. I don't think Michael ever really understood what was at the bottom of it all. He's not a bad man really, poor sod. Just crass. He's only made the usual mistake, getting found out. I don't really feel angry with him. Well, I do, but it won't last. Maybe this time he's found love, she concludes with a twirl of her glass. Can I have another of these?

I've been finding out all sorts of stuff about Zigi.

Oh, really? What sort of thing?

Oh – I temporise, sip my drink. Who is Bella, these days? One of them or one of us? What should I tell her? Should I tell her anything? Will it be taken down and used in evidence against me?

You can tell me, she says. Don't worry, I'll shut up.

Well, for example. He was married before. Fania knew, and she never said anything about it. And –

Yes?

He was suspected of spying in the war. For Russia. They thought he might be passing on atom secrets.

Oh, that, says Bella. Yes, I knew that.

Did you?

She says: It was fairly common knowledge, in certain circles.

There's an effect in television where the screen blurs, and we emerge to a different view of the same scene, a looking-glass world. Perhaps fortunately, it doesn't often happen in reality. Everything slips slightly out of focus as, for the first time, I get a glimpse of our lives as seen by Bella.

Since we re-established contact at the memorial service, Bella and I have met from time to time and she's told me about her affair with Zigi. But now she begins at the beginning. Her story confirms all my mother's suspicions. Hugh Brockenhurst was indeed the dark secret of Bella's childhood.

It's the usual story, commonplace and sad. He seemed such a mild man; unfortunately, he drank, and when he was drunk he became violent. His family were terrified of him. His absences, to which I could testify – I must have visited that house a hundred times, and he was hardly ever present – could not be long enough or frequent enough for them. The more he was at the Commons, the constituency, attending some trade union function, the happier they were. Anything might set him off. And one of the triggers, perhaps not surprisingly, was his wife's involvement with Zigi. Once firm friends, the two men became bitter enemies, personally and politically. Brockenhurst faded out, while Zigi went from strength to strength. What could have been more intolerable? Hearing all this I quite felt for Hugh Brockenhurst, a man I'd never much liked. He died comparatively young, while he was still in his sixties. After a long illness, the obituaries said. I looked them up after I visited Joan Brockenhurst. Of drink, says Bella now.

If Zigi's relationship with me had a strange edge, so did the one with Bella. He had, after all, been her mother's lover. Perhaps it was this spice of illegality that drew him to us. His was a jaded palate. Bella was torn between not wanting to hurt her mother, which meant keeping quiet, and very much wanting to hurt her father, which she could only do by telling all. The precipitate end to the affair tipped the balance in favour of silence. When Zigi dropped her so unceremoniously – forbidding her his office, not returning her calls – after she began to talk about having a baby, she felt so humiliated that she could not bear anyone to know about it. He was, of course, terrified – perhaps only I could have told her quite how terrified. He probably thought that the deed had preceded the word, that she'd already got herself pregnant. I'm sure he always thought it had been my intention to get pregnant by him, that Susanna was the result of a deliberate trick. He must have visualised a London strewn with his by-blows, little time-bombs growing ever bigger, just waiting to blow up in his face at some inopportune moment.

Bella, unaware of this previous history, was stunned by her abrupt dismissal. She was suicidal. She felt that her life had come to an end. She couldn't decide whether she loved Zigi or hated him: she was being destroyed by a corrosive mixture of the two. It was at this point that Michael came along. She had just started to work for him. They were both very unhappy – he and his wife were quarrelling bitterly. He took her out to dinner, and they both poured out their troubles. When Bella got to the end of her recital, Michael said: Zsygmond von Fischer! That old scoundrel!

Bella at once, in the illogical way of these things, sprang to Zigi's defence. And Michael said: But he's a spy!

A spy?

A traitor, Michael declared. He's been passing secrets to the Russkies. I should know. I was assigned to his case.

Michael was younger than Zigi, but still considerably older than Bella. At this time, in 1968, he was in his early forties. He came from an army family, and had shown an aptitude for languages at university. When the time came to look for a job he was told that 'a branch of the Foreign Office' was interested in him. He was interviewed at Carlton House Terrace: everything about the job they were discussing was at once oblique and perfectly clear. He accepted it.

It was when he became a spook that he ran across Zigi. As Bella told the story, Michael had become extraordinarily preoccupied with Zigi during his years with MI6. His unmasking was Michael's personal mission, and remained so even when he had long left the service. The trouble was, that although Michael and his friends were quite sure Zigi was guilty, that he had passed on all sorts of stuff to the Russians and was continuing to do so, they simply could not nail him down. Everything – the people he chose to associate with, the kind of information their Moscow agents in that Chinese-box secret world told them was getting through – pointed in his direction, but there was no proof. No doubt they knew all about his attempt to get a job at Harwell. How they must have wished he'd been taken on! Then they might have caught him red-handed. They tailed him, tapped his phone, opened his mail – all in vain. Their only hope was to make him confess. – You know, said Bella, that was how they got Fuchs. They thought it was him, they knew it must be him, but if he hadn't told them, they'd never have got him. They made him feel so terrible that, in the end, he had to get it off his chest. It was the same with Zigi. Michael was determined that he would be the one who would make Zigi confess.

But suppose Michael was wrong? Suppose there wasn't anything to confess? You said yourself there was no proof.

No, but they all knew. It was just a question of finding the one thing that would tip him over the edge. Make him tell all.

Does Bella really believe this stuff? Do I? When I first started out on this hypothesis it all seemed so clear, but with every word she utters the waters get muddier. She says 'they all' knew. But there was no hint, veiled or open, in all those enormous obituaries. Surely there would have been, had the thing been at all credible? This sort of common knowledge has a way of insinuating itself into such documents. No, I think that for 'all' we may here read 'Michael and his friends'. Bella herself said that Zigi was an obsession of his. And everyone really does know about Michael. He's a byword: on questions of this sort, quite simply unbalanced. He thinks all Labour MPs are probably traitors. Should a Labour government be elected, he'd see its undermining as no more than his patriotic duty, just as he and his cronies did last time around.

And Bella is not an impartial observer of these manoeuvres. When she decided to ally herself with Michael, it was more than just a rebound. It was a conscious act of vengeance. Zigi destroyed her, in a very particular way. Life with her father left her with a distrust of all men, a total cynicism in that direction. For a few brief weeks, her blind passion for Zigi lifted her out of that pit. When he dropped her, she returned to it. She had glimpsed a certain hope – a sort of innocence, almost – and knew she would never experience anything like it again. Perhaps something similar happened with Sam Corbett. But now she was older and more on her guard. She had let herself take the chance, just once more, and what had she got in return? A kick in the teeth. What Michael offered was the opportunity to get her own back. It was her turn now.

I assumed at the time that Bella's behaviour after her marriage – specifically, her reluctance to have anything to do with me – could be put down to wifely loyalty. This passivity didn't seem to chime with the strong-willed Bella I knew, but marriage can have strange effects. I knew she was ambitious, and if her ambition was now all channelled through her husband, then her conduct was perhaps understandable. But in fact there was nothing remotely passive about it. She was determined to avenge herself upon Zigi, and Michael was the instrument by which she would do so. Under those circumstances, how could she and I be buddies? She urged him on. She wanted to see him tear out Zigi's horns, shackle his hoofs, set his tail on fire.

It was Bella who encouraged Michael to go on dogging Zigi when, left to himself, he might have tired of the game. He wasn't getting anywhere. The day Susanna saw him, he had presumably registered yet another failure. By that time Michael was getting desperate, aware that death was only too likely to beat him to the quarry. His chances had always been slight, but they were rapidly becoming nonexistent. What was he appealing to, a gentleman's conscience? Zigi was no gentleman. On the contrary. He was a cad, a bounder of the worst sort. As the years passed, Michael had to watch while his status and influence grew. He bounded on. He was never going to confess. He would die first.

And he did.

A month ago I would have ascribed all these suspicions to paranoia, to the lunatic conspiracy-theories of security services everywhere, enclosed in their own mad world, endlessly chasing their tails. But now, how can I be sure? Who knows what Zigi was or wasn't? The only thing I can be sure of is that whatever he appeared to be – he was not.

Some old KGB chiefs have recently published memoirs describing how they had a direct line to Los Alamos all the time the bomb was being built. What need had they of Fuchs? Bohr and Oppenheimer, if they are to be believed, were constantly passing information to the Russians.

We read these words in the 1990s: in the early 1940s the world was a very different place – a fact easily ignored, as Oppenheimer found to his cost. But at that time, not just Bohr and Oppenheimer but a great many scientists, including Edward Teller, thought that at the level of fundamental scientific principle, there could and should be no secrets.

After the Iron Curtain fell, it is inconceivable that either Bohr or Oppenheimer sought to pass secrets across it. Could the same be said of Zigi? What turns a man into a spy? Principles or cash. But Zigi was not an idealist. Thinking over the possibilities, I can't see him acting, as Fuchs did, for political conviction. His contempt for all political systems – including communism – was, I am sure, perfectly genuine. And he was uninterested in money.

He had his weaknesses, though. Martian weaknesses. He was arrogant and he couldn't resist power. And he would do anything in the cause of science. Science was his religion.

After the war ended, when the world was arranging itself into two armed camps with the bomb at the centre, the Martians tried in various ways to retain their grip on affairs. Szilard worked to neutralise the bomb by internationalising it. Teller did what he could to make sure the Americans would always be one nuclear step ahead of the Russians.

And Zigi? He knew a lot of the Russian scientists from before the war – from Germany, from Copenhagen, from Kiev. They shared his religion, they were fellow citizens of his only country. Afterwards, he met them from time to time, at conferences of various sorts. It would not surprise me if he was indiscreet on these occasions. I can't imagine Zigi feeling himself bound by the politicians he so despised. On the contrary: the fact of prohibition would only have increased his determination to act as he thought best. His capacity for self-justification was boundless. Didn't he, while holding these self-same views, become involved in politics himself? If he wanted to pass on information some might consider secret, I'm quite sure he did. As for danger – he would never have considered the possibility. He took care, he was not a fool. What danger could idiots such as Michael Overy ever pose to a man like Zigi?

I am not going to confide any of this to Bella. Why should I give her that satisfaction? It may seem, as we sit here, that we are back on the same side again, as much as we ever were. The old uneasy yet familiar standoff. But we both know that isn't so. We've moved – or rather, Bella's moved: it seems to me that all I've done is stay in the same place. Maybe that's true of her, too? Maybe she, too, was never what she seemed? One could never be certain, with Bella: now, less than ever.

So I shrug. I say: Well, he suspected all of us, didn't he, poor old Michael? I bet that was him, tapping my phone and opening my mail. Anyhow, he can relax now.

Bella makes no comment. She probably still thinks we were all as guilty as hell, though of what, who knows? Now, however, it is perhaps clear even to her that I didn't know what Zigi was up to (whatever that was). And anyhow, Zigi is dead. The Cold War is over. So I can be readmitted to the fold, up to a point. I can't do Bella any harm any more. She has her plans. She's very well-connected, these days. She's thinking of standing in the next election, as a Tory, of course. She's been promised a safe seat. They're desperate for good women candidates. It seems doubtful whether Michael will be re-selected. We shall hear any day now that he's thinking of retiring at the end of this Parliament. She can afford to be magnanimous. It can only do her good with the voters.

V

And I? What am I going to do?

I think about Zigi's life, which for the past year has been my life. What was it about? Power. The pursuit of power. He couldn't get enough of it. None of them could. Those clever, clever boys, those brilliant, dispossessed young men – how they grabbed it as soon as it came within their grasp! They had to be the ones who would press the world's buttons.

And now *I've* got him in *my* power, pinned down like a butterfly on a board. He's dead, but no matter: I can make him or break him. It's only fair. He did the same with me, didn't he?

What will happen if I decide to publish what I know? Derry and I will make a lot of money, that's one certainty. There's nothing like a real-life spy story, a fourth or fifth or sixth man, to catch the public interest. Secrets, secrets. What secrets are they supposed to have passed on, all these chaps? Blueprints? What of? What use would British blueprints be to rusting Russian industry? News of other spies? What a merry-go-round. The madness of a previous age. The Atomic Age is closed. Ancient history. But still good for a headline and a scandal.

So another symbol will be destroyed, another giant's clay feet revealed. Zigi's private life was a mess, his public persona was founded upon a lie. One lie? A whole series of lies. He skated with such style and aplomb that the ice never cracked during his lifetime. He relied upon nobody guessing, nobody enquiring. And nobody did. (Except Fania? But if she knew, it was because she'd always known, not because she guessed. I still can't make up my mind whose decision it was to ban this enterprise upon which I am engaged.)

Does this diminish the value of that symbol? If I publish, of course. The Michaels will be shown to have been right all the time: we shall all be shamed by association.

And if I don't? Don't they all deserve to know the truth, all those people for whom Zigi was a spokesman, a rallying-point, the epitome of conscience, the champion of us all?

No. What they deserve is *not* to know the truth. All that is required of the White Champion is that he be shiny, effective, and *there*. What's unseen doesn't count: it has no more importance than Satan's perfect bourgeois marriage. If war did not break out, if the Atomic Age is over, that is no thanks to the Weinsfelds and Tellers, the Reagans and Thatchers. Why give them this last satisfaction?

No: this inquiry was conducted for my benefit, not theirs. I had to know the truth. – Would I like him, my father? Susanna asked me, all those years ago. – Yes, I told her. But I knew I was only guessing. I didn't really know him.

Do I know him better now? Zigi's inner life is still a mystery to me. There are too many layers to the parcel: however often we pass it round we never seem to tear through the wrapping to the nugget in the middle. But the externals are finally assembled. To that extent I can introduce them: father and daughter. It wouldn't have been possible before. I couldn't have done it while Fania was alive, both for her sake and because, until she died, I couldn't be sure I'd found out what there was to find. As indeed I had not.

I shall write up my notes, make something coherent of them. Then I'll hand them over to Susanna. My last cowardice. Avoiding the face-to-face encounter to the very end. I wonder what she'll feel. Pleased? Shocked? Surprised? Perhaps not so very surprised. Perhaps this will be yet another of those occasions which are both shocking and at the same time merely confirm things known but not acknowledged.

And then perhaps Tony and I can put this behind us and try to get reacquainted in time for the millennium. Searching for Zigi, I have discovered myself. The real Miriam. She's more ruthless, less compliant, than I'd realised. Not to be diverted by other people's convenience. Willing to take risks – and perhaps now she'll have to pay the price. What will Tony make of her? How do I know? I don't really know what to make of her myself. We haven't known each other long enough.

If I were to publish, he wouldn't bother to make her acquaintance. That would definitely be it. Finish, kaput. But I shan't. No. That's decided.

Shall we therefore continue? It's I who must do the asking now. Is there enough left to hold us together? Shall we still be there, arm-in-arm against the world, when the curtain falls? I should like to think so. Zigi is finally disposed of, his ghost is laid. Now, at last, we can be alone together.

In the meantime, if anyone wants to write Zigi's biography, I can tell them here and now not to bother. The papers have disappeared, and those with the secrets aren't talking.

VI

Ever since I sent that package off to Susanna, my mouth has dried and my stomach churned every time the telephone rang. I don't know which I dread more – confrontation or its absence. What can we say to each other? And yet – if she doesn't respond – what can we ever say to each other again?

But one day I lift the receiver and it's Susie. She says: Mum? Just the familiar monosyllable with that rising, challenging inflection. The direct line to the vitals.

I think we'd better meet, says Susie.

The meeting is to take place in the two up, two down, white-painted cottage she shares with her boyfriend. Her territory. We shall be alone: he's out at work and Susanna has a day free of rehearsals. It's late May already. Those notes took quite some collating. A brilliant, pale-blue morning, a morning to lift the spirits were mine not wholly occupied with apprehension. Susie, when she sees me, bursts out laughing. – Sorry, she says. I couldn't help it. You look terrified. What did you think, I'd eat you?

You might. How do I know?

So the first minutes pass amid brittle laughter and the ritual displacement of coffee-making. But that can't last for ever. Soon, soon, the coffee is made and we must face each other over the steam. The old incubus crouches between us. Now, however, visible to both parties.

Oh, enough of this! Away with him!

So now you know, I say. Were you surprised?

Yes. Well, yes and no. Not entirely. You know how it is.

She looks at me attentively, curiously. Trying, perhaps, to picture the momentous occasion of her conception. Hard to imagine? Impossible. It's hard enough to think of your parents engaged in sex, let alone imagining your mother in bed with someone you only ever knew as an old man. As a grandpa. What did he call her? His 'honorary grand-daughter'. I couldn't help laughing when I first read that one.

I'm glad you told me, Susanna says. We were close before he died. I'm really glad about that now. She sips her coffee: obviously she has more to say, but can't perhaps think how to say it?

Does – Dad – know?

Yes. I told him.

What did he say?

Oh – it wasn't that important. The who of it, I mean. Not after all this time. The important thing was that I hadn't told him. But I couldn't. You do see that, don't you? It wasn't just me. You do understand?

She says slowly: Yes, I suppose so. Some time later she adds: There's something I've got to show you.

She leaves the room. I hear her climb the stairs. When she comes down she is holding a letter. She says: George Frenkl gave me this when Zigi died. I wondered at first why he hadn't left it with Fania.

The envelope is addressed in Zigi's elaborate scrawl: Miss Susanna Oliver. By hand.

May I read it?

Susie nods. – Not now. Take it home. You can give it back next time we meet.

The subject is closed. More may be said, but not today. We move on to mundanities: Susanna's new bathroom. We walk by the river, lunch in a pub. The air is clear between us for the first time in our lives. I feel relieved – more than relieved: light-headed. I knew my secret was a burden: only its shedding revealed its leaden weight. Susie, too, seems elated. Yes, it's a good moment. But not prolonged. I can't wait to be on my own. I can feel that letter burning through my bag.

I quell the temptation to stop at the nearest possible parking-place. This is not something to be skimmed over while the traffic hoots and jars six inches from my head. I force myself to drive home. Let myself into the still-empty house. Rush upstairs, shut myself into my study.

Only the envelope was hand-written. For the rest, Zigi has typed even this most personal of communications. A stickler for clarity to the end.

My dear Susanna. When you receive this I shall be dead. During the past few years we have seen each other a great deal, and I did not want to die without telling you of the great happiness this friendship has brought me. This has been a pleasure in itself – but also for a particular reason.

There has always been a great unanswered question in your life – that is, who is your real father? This is something your mother has not felt able to disclose. Perhaps you will understand why not when I tell you that this mysterious person is myself. I assure you that this is the truth. If you have any doubts, look for a minute in the mirror. So now you know, and you must decide what, if anything, to do with this knowledge. I can only say: Be kind. I say this knowing that I offer no example in this matter.

I hope you will not blame your mother for her silence. What else could she do? The only other possibility would have deprived us of the pleasure of your company.

I must be honest and tell you that I did not welcome the prospect of your birth. This was not just because of possible social awkwardness. Strong emotion is something I have always found it hard to deal with, and what is more emotional than the parental tie? I explain this, or excuse it, by saying that in my life intellect was always a certain source of strength, and feeling, a potential weakness. When I was young, life was insecure. I did not expose myself un-necessarily. By the time I got older, I suppose this had become a habit. So tenderness was never part of my life. I substituted passion, intellectual, erotic and political. But of course that is not the same thing.

You may wonder how I could go through life in this cold-blooded way? To this there are two answers. The first is that my life has not felt cold-blooded. On the contrary it has been filled with excitements. And, secondly, one does not stand back in judgement from one's own life. There is always too much to do – or perhaps I have always been careful to make sure of this.

But our afternoons together introduced me to something I had not hitherto experienced. With you I have felt, for the first time in my life, peace and contentment and a true nearness of spirit. When we were talking, when we were playing our music, I felt at last something that until now I had only heard others describe. To say it was unexpected is to understate the case. How could one expect something one had not previously believed to exist? In my eighties, thanks to you, I became open to feeling.

My dear Susanna, I have felt very close to you, and this has made me happy. Perhaps I have not deserved it. But I wanted you to know this.

With love from Zigi.

Also available in Vintage

Julia Blackburn

THE BOOK OF
COLOUR

'A brilliant fantasy of bizarre and magical imagination'
Mary Wesley, Books of the Year, *Daily Mail*

'Wandering through dreams and nightmares from Praslin
Islands to Mauritius and finally to England, the author
unfolds the troubled lives of her forbears, cursed by racial
prejudice, sexual inhibition and recurrent mental illness.
This first novel is a powerfully and cleverly written expurga-
tion of personal feelings, drawing the reader into a landscape like that of a Dali painting'
Eileen Cowey, *Scotland on Sunday*

'Her narrative vibrates with symbolism and portent. Every
event, every encounter, every object shimmers with talis-
manic power'
Michiko Kakutani, *New York Times*

'If you are going to read this book, read it twice. It is well
worth it'
Natasha Walter, *Guardian*

VINTAGE

Also available in Vintage

Marina Warner

INDIGO

OR,
MAPPING THE WATERS

Inspired by *The Tempest*, *Indigo* traces the scars of colonialism across continents, family blood-lines and three centuries. Rich, sensual and magical in its use of myths and fairy tales *Indigo* explores the intertwined histories of the Everard family and the imaginary Caribbean island where Ariel, Caliban, and his mother, the healer and dyer of indigo, Sycorax once lived.

'*Indigo* explores the nature of power, the human cost of Empire and the theme of dislocation...Vivid, gripping, intelligent'
Independent on Sunday

'Her prose has never been so lyrical, as she yokes Shakespeare references, colonial history and her own sensual experience of the Caribbean with a powerful feminine myth-making'
Independent

'An extraordinary imaginative achievement'
Times Literary Supplement

VINTAGE

Also available in Vintage

Susan Sontag

THE VOLCANO LOVER

A ROMANCE

Based on the lives of Sir William Hamilton, his celebrated wife Emma, and Lord Nelson, *The Volcano Lover* is about revolution, the fate of nature, the condition of women, operatic emotions and stories from *Don Giovanni* to *Tosca*, art and the collector's obsessions, and above all, love.

'*The Volcano Lover* is a slippery, intelligent, provocative and gripping book, and a very good one'
A.S.Byatt

'This is a banquet of a book...The ideas flow like lava from Vesuvius, luminous, fiery and remorseless in their eloquence and curiosity'
Observer

'She has freed her novel from the tyrannical and melodramatic grooves of a history that has already been written, produced something lovely and substantial, and shown us how we might free ourselves'
Guardian

VINTAGE

A SELECTED LIST OF CONTEMPORARY FICTION
ALSO AVAILABLE IN VINTAGE

☐ THE FERMATA	Nicholson Baker	£5.99
☐ CRASH	J G Ballard	£5.99
☐ THE BOOK OF COLOUR	Julia Blackburn	£5.99
☐ PROFANE FRIENDSHIP	Harold Brodkey	£5.99
☐ POSSESSION	A S Byatt	£6.99
☐ NIGHTS AT THE CIRCUS	Angela Carter	£5.99
☐ THE LONGEST MEMORY	Fred D'Aguiar	£5.99
☐ BIRDSONG	Sebastian Faulks	£5.99
☐ GHOSTS OF MANILA	James Hamilton-Paterson	£5.99
☐ OBLIVION	Josephine Hart	£5.99
☐ THE FOLDING STAR	Alan Hollinghurst	£5.99
☐ SCAR TISSUE	Michael Ignatieff	£5.99
☐ SUNRISE WITH SEA MONSTER	Neil Jordan	£5.99
☐ SO I AM GLAD	A L Kennedy	£5.99
☐ THE UNLOVED	Deborah Levy	£5.99
☐ REMEMBERING BABYLON	David Malouf	£5.99
☐ OPERATION SHYLOCK	Philip Roth	£5.99
☐ THE MOOR'S LAST SIGH	Salman Rushdie	£6.99
☐ RADON DAUGHTERS	Iain Sinclair	£5.99
☐ THE VOLCANO LOVER	Susan Sontag	£5.99
☐ INDIGO	Marina Warner	£5.99
☐ THE ACID HOUSE	Irvine Welsh	£5.99
☐ ART & LIES	Jeanette Winterson	£5.99

- All Vintage books are available through mail order or from your local bookshop.

- Please send cheque/eurocheque/postal order (sterling only), Access, Visa or Mastercard:

☐☐☐☐☐☐☐☐☐☐☐☐☐☐☐☐

Expiry Date:_____Signature:_____

Please allow 75 pence per book for post and packing U.K.
Overseas customers please allow £1.00 per copy for post and packing.

ALL ORDERS TO:
Vintage Books, Book Service by Post, P.O.Box 29, Douglas, Isle of Man, IM99 1BQ.
Tel: 01624 675137 • Fax: 01624 670923

NAME:_____

ADDRESS:_____

_____

_____

Please allow 28 days for delivery. Please tick box if you do not
wish to receive any additional information ☐
Prices and availability subject to change without notice.